# GUARDIAN PROBE

Galaxy Quest Books are published by
Ocean Quest LLC
2100 Ogden Drive
Cambria CA 93428
GalaxyQuestBooks.com

First Printing December 2013

10987654321

Printed in United States of America

ISBN: 978-0-9839630-7-3

Books from Galaxy Quest Books are available for premiums and special promotions.
For details contact: marketing@GalaxyQuestBooks.com.

# Dedication

Early on the morning of October 25, 1944, an admiral ordered Commander William Dow Thomas, Commodore of a small guardian destroyer screen, to attack a vastly superior Japanese force east of Samar Island in the Philippines Sea. The four American destroyers *Hoel, Heermann, Samuel B. Roberts,* and *Johnston* began their defensive action to protect their carriers.

Zigzagging through smoke and intermittent rain squalls—and frequently bracketed by the explosions of incoming heavy ordnance from Japanese battleships, cruisers, and destroyers—the "small boys" of Taffy 3 engaged the attacking Japanese force and pressed their attack against overwhelming odds.

In the hours that followed, the men of the United States Navy displayed incredible valor, courage, and tenacity, such as is seldom recorded in the annals of history, reminiscent of the courage displayed by the Spartans at Thermopylae during King Leonidas' stand against the overwhelming forces of the Persian King Xerxes.

The aircraft and the "small boys" of the United States Navy blunted and then turned the powerful Japanese attack into a retreat. During the battle, United States Navy losses included: 1,583 killed and 913 wounded; two escort carriers, two destroyers, and one destroyer escort sunk; and twenty-three aircraft lost. The Japanese Imperial Navy's casualties are unknown, but two battleships were damaged, three heavy cruisers sunk, three heavy cruisers and multiple destroyers were damaged, and fifty-two aircraft were lost.

The author respectfully dedicates this book to the men of Taffy 1, Taffy 2, and especially Taffy 3, with special notice of the sacrifices of the "small boys" and the airmen who fought with raw courage and inflicted greater losses than they suffered. It is with a sense of deep admiration that I include in this dedication Lieutenant Commander Ernest E. Evans and the crew of the USS *Johnston* (DD-557), who, without waiting for orders, took the battle straight to the Imperial Navy and its battleships, pressing the attack against staggering odds.

Special thanks to my daughter, Lorna, whose attention to detail and dedication to ensuring the final print is correct has made this document possible.

Inspiration also came from Gepeto, who was a wonderful gift of love from Guide Dogs for the Blind in San Rafael, California, and for another such wondrous gift, Limo, who has with great patience taken up the fallen baton and filled some mighty big paws.

# X

# Acknowledgments

Cover image source: NASA, NSSDC, Viking Orbiters 1 and 2, Johns Hopkins University Applied Physics Laboratory, Southwest Research Institute, Goddard Space Flight Center

Cover design: Lorna Gusner

Graphic art and formatting: Nancy McKarney, Brian Gusner

# Guardian Probe

D. Arthur Gusner

GalaxyQuestBooks.com
Ocean Quest LLC
Cambria 93428

# Contents

# Contents

"Anyone who has never made a mistake has never tried anything new."

–*Albert Einstein*


"Whenever you find that you are on the side of the majority, it is time to reform."

–*Mark Twain*

# Author's Foreword

There are many branches on the paths we follow in life. Some lead to adventures and others lead to mysteries. When I was a small boy, I happened onto the path that led me to the County Library. There I found both adventure and mystery in abundance. Among the shelves of dusty books, I encountered James Churchward's works on Mu. That starting point led me to the broad field of speculative history and to wondrous tales of forgotten cities and lost civilizations.

When contemplating the massive stone figures of Easter Island, the towering pyramids of Egypt, and the mysterious structures of Stonehenge, I asked just how did they shape and move those massive stones? In Machu Picchu and other Incan ruins, very large stones with irregular surfaces were precisely fitted to match adjoining similar stones. They fit so precisely, a cigarette paper could not be placed between them. How was that done?

The spate of UFO sightings in 1947 prompted further youthful exploration. One book I located, *The Book of the Damned,* was from the early 1900s. This was the first published nonfiction work of the author Charles Fort. Within the pages of Charles Fort's work, I found remarkable descriptions of UFOs similar to Ezekiel's wheel within a wheel. Could these have been modern hoaxes? My conclusion then favored an unsolved mystery, and it still does.

The Guardian series is an imaginative story winding through the widely spaced pillars of incomplete human history. *Guardian Force, Earth Guardian, Guardian Probe, Guardian Strike, and Guardian Thunder* are pure science fiction brimming with high adventure and military strategy. The author's hope is that the books will provide science fiction enthusiasts an enjoyable and memorable read. So relax, lean back, and enjoy a modern imaginative fable set both in the past and in the year 2511 and beyond.

D. Arthur Gusner
Cambria, California
2013

# *Prologue*

In the year 2511, following tens of thousands of years of separation, two distinct but separate branches of humanity were again united. The mystery of how their separation had occurred remained unanswered. Far more pressing than finding the answer to that question, however, was the struggle to survive amid a no-quarter interstellar war that spanned many star systems.

Far from Tearman, within three solar systems, on the three ruling Kreel Hub worlds, the Elite and their Grand Marshals had finalized and begun to execute their planned expansion of the Empire. Their massive assembled armada was staging for its departure and conquest of multiple solar systems. The decision as to where and when the armada would first strike was firmly set. Like an arrow shot from a compound bow, once launched, that armada would not be turning back.

# Chapter One:
# **New Orders**

When the five sleek Guardian Force Cruisers erupted into local space-time, they were light-years distant from where they had entered Jump near Earth. Each of the five Cruisers was alert and poised for battle— dark shadows virtually invisible within the surrounding energy spectrum. The Cruisers, orienting to the local environment, precisely measured the positions of key navigation reference stars and determined their current location in space and time. Adjusting their chronometers, they sent whispering signals out to reestablish communications with each other.

Having localized his position in space-time, Lan— the squadron's lead AI Cruiser— reached out to communicate with the nearest Guardian Navigation Beacon, initiating a download of waiting messages and reporting the successful long-Jump from Earth and the squadron's current position and status. The report would flow through the chain of Navigation Beacons and be received by Guardian Command on Glas Dinnein, nearly one hundred light-years distant.

Seeking a trace of threat or foe, the crews on each Cruiser assiduously explored the vast region of nearby space. One by one, the Cruisers' tactical sections reported their findings, and each AI Cruiser subsequently reported his crew's findings to Cruiser Lan.

"Sir," Lan's resonant and firm voice reported, "Cruisers Lar, Langley, Lent, and Lawrence have reported Jump Condition Gold."

Working in his conference room, Commodore Kellon looked up and smiled when hearing Lan's report. He knew every Jump held risk, and exiting from any long-Jump without malfunctions or casualties was always a good report.

"Lan, have we received the tactical updates from the cruisers? Are there any contacts?"

"Sir, all Tactical sections have reported. There are no contacts. Our immediate area is clear, and the Combat Analysis Center has rescinded battle stations and set Condition 3.

"Sir, we have just downloaded a new orders message from Fleet Admiral Mer Shawn. Shall I display it now?"

Kellon leaned back from the work he was involved with, a dry report relating to the squadron's current supplies and ordnance. They had been on patrol near Earth for more than eight months and in heavy combat with the Kreel. Many of their ordnance and critical supplies were growing thin, and it was good they were now heading home for Glas Dinnein. Everyone, including Kellon, was looking forward to a well-earned rest during their scheduled refit and resupply. With a sigh, Kellon closed the file of the report he was reading. "Certainly, Lan, let's see what the Admiral has to say today. Please play back his message."

Promptly, the larger-than-life image of Admiral Mer Shawn swirled into focus on his bulkhead screen. Kellon observed the Admiral looked haggard and immediately knew there was trouble inbound.

"Commodore Kellon, I wish I had better news for you than I do. Guardian Intelligence has been working overtime on intercepting and decoding Kreel fleet communications. Admiral Cloud has provided me an update. The Kreel have concluded an unknown enemy has destroyed the recent expeditionary strike force they sent to Earth. This conclusion has in turn heated up the Kreel Hub to a boiling point. In eight months, they have lost twenty-one major ships in Earth's system without any gain whatsoever. The Kreel have not attributed their losses to Arkillian activity, but have concluded there is a powerful unknown species active within the Earth system."

Kellon reflected for a moment, thinking. Could the squadron have engaged and destroyed twenty-one Kreel ships? It had indeed been a long difficult mission. He focused again on what Mer was saying. "In spite of their losses near Earth, the Kreel are moving ahead with their invasion of Scion and the subordination of the Arkillians. They are now finalizing the staging for that invasion. Our best intelligence estimates indicate the Kreel will hit Scion in about four weeks.

"Given their proximity, our long-term Intelligence analysis is we cannot allow the Kreel to move next door to Earth. That would

**2**

inevitably lead to greater warfare and more deaths. As the Kreel invasion fleet regroups upon entering Scion's system, they should present a dispersed force and may offer an opportunity for a surprise attack. Working to our advantage, their forces will be distant from the Kreel Hub and lack immediate resupply. If we can surprise them during the opening stages of their invasion, then we can set the Kreel aggression back for a considerable time."

Kellon inwardly braced himself, thinking, *Now comes the heavy dose of bad news.*

"My decision is therefore that we will seek battle under circumstances unfavorable to the Kreel. Guardian Force will stand with the Arkillians, and with them oppose the Kreel invasion of Scion."

Kellon sighed, thinking, *Sir, with all due respect, we are not prepared to oppose anyone! We need resupply and at least six weeks on the beach!*

"Kellon, I am aware of the months your squadron has already been on deployment, and the battles you've already fought. Regretfully, the Kreel invasion will happen before I can bring you home, resupply your squadron, and then send you back to Scion to oppose the invasion. For this reason, your return to Glas Dinnein is being delayed until after the Kreel invasion."

Kellon suddenly felt weary with fatigue. For the past eight months, he had managed to bring his entire squadron through several intense battles without losses. He thought tiredly, *Sir, you cannot understand what you are asking of us.*

"Kellon, I am committed to your support. I will send every cruiser that I can break loose to reinforce your defense of Scion. Unfortunately, given our limited resources, that will not be a large number.

"Given your battle reports, I am aware of your depleted supplies and munitions. Therefore, the reinforcements I am sending to you will include the provisions and ordnance resupply pods required to bring your Cruisers to their full combat readiness."

Listening, Kellon groaned inwardly. *Admiral Mer Shawn,* he thought, *how many cruisers can you possibly be sending?*

"Have Cruiser Lan examine the attached inventory lists and then advise me if there is anything special we've overlooked. If possible, and given our time restraints, we will provide whatever else you need.

"You are to review the Kreel force specifications attached and send me your comments. As I receive new intelligence, I will update you."

Inwardly Kellon responded, *Sir, with all due respect, you really, really do not want to hear my comments!*

"Commodore Kellon, I am once again entrusting you with accomplishing a difficult task. As the Planetary Assembly Admiral Secretary has left the strategic decisions to my judgment, I am likewise leaving the tactical decisions to your judgment.

"When you do arrive back on Glas Dinnein, come see me. I've kept in reserve a very special bottle of vintage wine from Kintana. I put it aside for opening on a special occasion. Kellon, may there be fair winds at your back on your homeward journey. Mer Shawn out."

Kellon sat back with a long exhaled breath as the screen returned to its unadorned appearance. He believed Mer Shawn understood the real cost of what he was ordering him to do. Undoubtedly, Mer had sitting on his desk a mathematically precise fleet estimate of probable Guardian Force losses. Admittedly, Mer's orders had not come as a total surprise.

*Well,* Kellon thought, *getting hard news is easier than simply waiting around to receive it. Now, at least, I know the strategic and tactical situation. Just like most other battles, we are outnumbered and the outlook is problematic!*

# Chapter Two:
# **Thundering Horde of Kreel Ships**

"Lan, were you listening?"

"Yes, Sir. I found Admiral Mer Shawn's analysis both informative and precise. He is quite correct. We could not reach Glas Dinnein, refit, resupply, and return to Scion within four weeks."

"Leave it to Mer to refer to Kintana," Kellon grumbled.

"It was his not-so-subtle way of telling me the tactical situation is not as bad as Kintana was. He must have forgotten that I was at Kintana. Of course, he's correct. This isn't as bad, at least not yet."

"Sir, Scion is not the same as Kintana. During that battle, Guardian Force did not have Guardian AIs to help. I am confident in the upcoming battle it will be the Kreel, and not Guardian Force, that will be in trouble."

Lan's unflagging confidence prompted Kellon to smile. "Well, I do agree, a few Guardian AIs at Kintana would have made a difference."

"Sir, about Kintana, my records indicate Commanders Roan and Zorn also fought during that Kreel invasion attempt. Did you know each other then?"

"Your records are correct, both Roan and Zorn were indeed there, and they both distinguished themselves. That was a long time ago, and at that time, we didn't know each other."

Kellon considered his initial feelings regarding Mer's orders. Weary or otherwise, he had a new mission to accomplish.

"Lan, thank you for your concise assessment of Admiral Mer Shawn's orders. It helped me focus on our mission. We have a job to do, and we'd better get to doing it."

Looking up to the chronometer, he saw it was nearly 10:30. "Lan, arrange for establishing hard links with all Cruisers. Tell the captains that there will be a captains conference at 14:00. Also, promptly distribute the supply inventory list the Admiral provided to all Cruisers and to Scout ship Shey. Have each Cruiser and Shey examine the list and determine if there are any critical items not on that inventory. Time is important, so give it a priority bump."

"Yes, Sir."

"Lan, please locate and notify Commander Shaw to report to my conference room."

Looking at his empty cup, Kellon knew the vacuum flask of neab was also empty. "While we're waiting for Lorn, have another flask of neab and two Earth-style sandwiches sent in."

"Yes, Sir."

Sitting back, Kellon took a deep breath and began his work. "Lan, display the estimate of the Kreel invasion fleet."

"Sir, the identified list is now being displayed," Lan promptly responded.

When Kellon studied the list of Kreel ships in detail, he let out a long slow breath. The Admiral had not overstated the problem. The Kreel fleet specifications represented the largest Kreel concentrations of power he had ever seen. Shaking his head, he thought, *Admiral Mer Shawn, Sir, please tell me again how many additional Cruisers you are sending.*

"Lan, forward a copy of the Kreel fleet description to all captains, and to Commander Roan. Also, send a copy to Commanders Shaw and Grey. Then inform Commanders Roan, Shaw, Grey, and Lieutenant Cloud to report to my Conference room one hour before the captains conference."

As he completed his orders to Lan, there was a soft knock at the conference room door and Lorn Shaw stepped into the room.

Kellon quickly motioned him to take a seat, and doing so, Lorn turned to study the list of Kreel ships presented on the screen. Shaking his head, with a slight smile, he turned toward Kellon. "Whew. To say the least, that's an impressive list of Kreel targets. I wasn't particularly aware they still had that many ships after the past year of Kreel losses. Might I assume that your wanting to see me has something to do with that list?"

Kellon smiled, feeling some of his fatigue and tension drain away, "Perceptive as usual, Lorn. That particular list, as you refer to it, is hot off Admiral Cloud's Intelligence intercepts. That is the latest Intelligence estimate for the Kreel invasion fleet that will be attacking Scion in about four weeks."

As Kellon spoke, the door opened and a young steward entered carrying a large tray with a flask and two cups. Prominent on the tray were also two large double-decker sandwiches with pickles on the side. Setting the tray upon the table before Kellon and Lorn, he asked, "Sir, is there anything else you want from the Officers' Mess?"

Kellon looked up and smiled his acknowledgment. "No, that will be satisfactory, thank you."

As the door closed behind the steward, Lorn's blue eyes met Kellon's steel-gray eyes. There was no remaining hint of humor in Lorn's expression. "Sir, am I to assume Admiral Mer Shawn has ordered us to boldly engage that thundering horde of Kreel ships?"

"Those are indeed our new orders. Admiral Mer Shawn is sending out reinforcements with resupply pods, we are to stand with the Arkillians and oppose the Kreel invasion. He has assigned to me the overall Command during the upcoming engagement."

As they talked, both men took a sandwich from the tray. Having been at battle stations, neither man had eaten since the previous evening's meal, and both were hungry. The concept of Earth-style sandwiches was a gift to Glas Dinnein from Earth Ambassador Susie Wells. Since their introduction, everyone had come to enjoy Earth-style sandwiches, and Kellon and Lorn were especially enjoying them.

Swallowing a bite, Lorn nodded his head and frowned. "Sir, we both know that reinforcements are few and far between. There can't be many Cruisers available to help. More to the point, we've been out for more than eight months. Our mission has placed heavy demands on both our Cruisers and crews. We need more than a basic resupply; Sir, we could use some rest— I suppose it's the Admiral's only option."

"Yes, Lorn, on each and all of your points, especially it being his only option. We have our orders, and we will perform our duty, even if the outcome appears problematic.

"Your first task is to build a working file on each of the Kreel ships by type and class. Look for any known key vulnerable spots. In particular, pay attention to those huge ground-troop assault ships; they look to be a difficult and formidable target. You know the drill."

"Yes, Sir. Might I ask, did Admiral Cloud hear anything that suggests the Kreel have learned why they seem to be losing all their recent battles? Have they discovered we captured one of their Gortoga class cruisers intact, with all of its ciphers?"

"Sorry, I have no information on that Black Hole topic. Yet, they have lost more than one hundred ships since we captured that cruiser. While the Kreel are undoubtedly pulling out their fur trying to determine what has suddenly changed, that captured cruiser is only one item in a statistical summation of lots of bad news. I rather doubt the Kreel have an inkling that one of their cruisers was taken intact."

"Sir, since we can still crack Kreel communications, surprise is our clear tactical advantage. In spite of the adverse odds, we might still have the edge in the battle," Lorn suggested.

"Knowing how many Kreel are coming to the party certainly helps, but the numerical odds are still not in our favor. For us to pull this off, and still be in one piece, will require creativity on our part. I've set up a captains conference at 14:00. You are to attend. I have also asked Lan to send you an advanced copy of that list of Kreel targets, just so you can maintain your reputation for foresight and wisdom. I suggest that you use the time until that meeting to maximum advantage."

Lorn hurriedly swallowed the last of his pickle, took a quick sip of the hot neab from his cup, stood, and formally responded, "Yes, Sir."

As the door closed behind Lorn, Kellon considered what he needed to do next. Upon reflection, he realized there was indeed something that must be done – and without further delay.

"Lan, ask the wardroom to pick up the dishes in my conference room. Then instruct them to send a thermos of neab with two cups and some pastries to the observation conference room. Then request Ambassador Wells to join me there in fifteen minutes."

Kellon pushed his chair back under the table, departed the conference room, walked to the elevator, and rode up to the top deck. Moving forward, he entered the darkened large circular conference area. As he did so, a low level of illumination around the circling knee wall automatically brightened to a warm spectrum of sunlight, softly illuminating the large room.

"Lan, please retract the dome protective petals."

As Lan retracted the opaque composite armored petals, Kellon walked over to the clear optically corrected dome and stood looking out toward Scion's primary. From Lan's location, it appeared as only one small bright pinpoint of light in the heavens among many other similar bright pinpoints. Standing there, he recalled Commander Roan was the only member of Guardian Force who had ever stood on Scion, and yet, now more than a thousand Guardian Force personnel were about to be hurled into a no-quarter battle in order to defend that world.

While he had come to respect Arkillian Council Member Kur, deeply conflicted personal emotions remained unresolved. Historically, the Arkillians had been the cause of death for billions of humans on Earth. That brutal act of genocide was nearly fourteen thousand years earlier, when the Arkillians had initially reduced humanity to a few scattered survivors. They had tactically referred to that wanton devastation by the euphemistic term "rendering primitive."

Now, fourteen thousand years later, humanity was coming to the defense of Scion. Knowing Guardian Force's strategic reasons for doing so did not erase the troubling historical facts of genocide. Kellon knew full well that the Arkillian-human relationship was still wet-paint fresh, and it was exceedingly fragile. None, he knew, could accurately predict the consequences that would flow out from the Guardian Force opposing the Kreel invasion of Scion. What he did understand was the outcome of the pending battle would undoubtedly alter the balance of power in the local cosmos. Recognizing this, however, did not alter his mission objective— the destruction of the Kreel invasion fleet. Still, looking out at the vista of stars glittering in the heavens all around him, Kellon smiled. *Of course,* he thought, *my analysis presumes Guardian Force will come out on top, and it is my job to make certain it does!*

When she entered the dome conference room, Susie observed Kellon standing and looking out toward the stars. Her strawberry- blonde hair was tied back and fell well below her shoulders in a ponytail that swung in easy harmony with her movements. She had dressed comfortably in standard Guardian shipboard attire: consisting of a tailored top with trousers bloused over the top of soft supple low-topped leather boots. Her only insignia of official position and rank was her small

Ambassador's medallion suspended on a beautiful gold chain. Susie's buddy, a Yellow Labrador named Gepeto, stood quietly at heel. Susie paused, respecting Kellon's privacy, and simply waited.

Of all the Guardian Force personnel she had met, in her opinion, Commodore Kellon stood shoulders and head above the others. She had seen what he was capable of achieving as a diplomat, commander, and warrior. She knew that on two separate occasions, he had expertly guided his limited forces in battles defending the Earth from larger Arkillian and Kreel forces. Then, he had attained victories where many had doubted it was possible.

As Kellon stood looking out toward the stars, he remembered his conversation with Councilman Kur several months earlier. Kur had quietly described his thoughts and feelings just prior to the beginning of his battle with Kellon. "As I stood there," Kur had said, "looking out on the thousands of stars of heaven, I suddenly deeply missed Scion and realized for the first time the stars are in truth very cold."

Now, looking out on the star-scattered canopy about him, for the first time he understood precisely what Kur had felt and meant. As he slowly turned back toward the conference table, he saw Susie waiting with Gepeto, and a broad smile quickly replaced his earlier frown.

"Ambassador, thank you for coming so promptly. Gepeto, of course you are always welcome. I have had neab and pastries brought, if you might care to share refreshments with me."

"Why Commodore, I am delighted to share your refreshments." Moving to the table, Susie poured two cups of neab, put several pastries on small plates, and put the plates and cups before Kellon and her chair.

As Susie sat down, she looked up with a smile. "Commodore, might I ask what is the occasion for our meeting?"

Kellon's frown returned. "Susie, there's been a new development. You need to be aware that Fleet Admiral Mer Shawn has issued new orders. We are to wait for reinforcements near Scion, then move in support of the Arkillians to oppose a Kreel invasion force. Guardian Command believes that invasion will begin in about four weeks.

"There's going to be a significant battle, and there will be no safe place for you except back on Earth. If you wish, I will transfer you to Lent and order him to return you safely home. If you, however, elect to remain on board Lan, then you will be going into battle with us. Susie, please understand, I cannot predict the outcome of any battle or assure anyone's safety.

"As Earth's Ambassador and a Planetary Assembly Representative, your decision on what to do— to stay or to go— is in your own hands. However, if you decide to return to Earth, then I must know your decision today. Any delay could mean Lent being absent during our critical preparation for battle."

Susie sat for a moment thoughtfully considering the import of what Kellon had told her. "Sir, thank you for the option you are providing me. However, I will not be requiring you to send Lent round-trip back to Earth just to drop me off in a safe area. When I left Earth on Lan, my intent was to proceed to Glas Dinnein. The possibility of being in a battle during the journey was part of my considered decision.

"Sir, with your approval, I will remain on board Lan. There is, however, one request I do make. Please consider how I might contribute positively to the battle. I would rather be of meaningful assistance than merely a sack of potatoes parked on a shelf."

Listening, Kellon nodded his head in approval. "Ambassador, your willingness to remain in spite of the coming battle speaks well for your firm determination. What I know is it will be a large battle and we are dangerously outnumbered. As to your request for a duty assignment, I'm confident we can find something to keep your active mind productively busy."

"Sir, will you be in command of Guardian forces?"

"According to Fleet Admiral Mer Shawn's orders, yes. Does that make a difference in your thinking?"

"No, not in my thinking. However, it does make a difference in my breathing a little easier. Now that I know you are in command, I suggest you send a message to Kur. Tell him that before the battle begins, he should distribute umbrellas and brooms to everyone on Scion."

Kellon shook his head, puzzled. "Why umbrellas and brooms?"

"Well, the way I see the outcome, the Arkillians will need to protect themselves from a rain of tiny bits of Kreel ships for weeks and the brooms should help in cleaning up the pieces."

# Chapter Three:
# Rewriting the Space Warfare Handbook

Kellon methodically set about the task of preparing the squadron to oppose the coming Kreel invasion of Scion. To give his Cruisers every tactical advantage, as was his proclivity, he began to define and prepare the battlefield to his own liking. To achieve his mission goals, he discarded the rulebook and began by rewriting the space warfare handbook.

When he entered his conference room, Kellon found Commander Grey, Lan's Executive Officer and Navigator, already there. Looking up with his characteristic imperturbable grin, Roy greeted him. "Commodore, I seem to have again arrived at the thermos of neab ahead of you, and I can highly recommend the Earth-style cheese pastries."

Even as he made his recommendation, Roy, with obvious delight, took another bite of the half-eaten pastry he held in his left hand. "Thank you for the suggestion, I believe I might do just that."

Joining Roy at the side table, Kellon poured a cup of hot neab. Putting a cheese pastry on a small plate, he turned and sat down, took a sip of neab, and let out a long slow breath. Roy followed him to the conference table and sat down, still enjoying his pastry.

"Sir, I do appreciate your invitation and the chance for a break from my navigation console, but with such a sigh, you clearly have a serious problem. How can I help?"

"Roy, do you remember the micro-Jump we performed near Earth?"

Roy flinched in response to Kellon's question, "Ouch! Commodore that was like a bad date, it's difficult to forget. We did, however, survive. So, it had a good outcome. Nevertheless, it was still a high-risk maneuver."

"The important thing, Roy, is we did survive it. What nearly got us killed wasn't the micro-Jump, but exiting a long-Jump nearly on top of a Kreel cruiser and two fast-attack ships."

"Yes, Sir, I remember. But, technically speaking, the micro-Jump might also have killed us just as dead."

"Roy, in the upcoming battle, the Kreel will outnumber us by more than twenty-to-one. I need an edge, something that will give us a clear tactical advantage over the Kreel, or else we may not be returning to Glas Dinnein."

"Sir, in all due respect, I'm but your Navigator. I don't know of an edge sharp enough to overcome a twenty-to-one numerical disadvantage. Nevertheless, in that I do have a fishing trip scheduled in eight weeks on Glas Dinnein, if there is anything, absolutely anything, I might do to help us survive, then you can certainly count me in."

Kellon smiled. "Your enthusiastic participation is noted and greatly appreciated."

"Yes, Sir, I'm always glad to do anything to be of help!"

Kellon was frowning as he began to define the problem. "When you computed the micro-Jump near Earth, we did survive. Can you do that again near Scion? More precisely, can you give us a micro-Jump tactical capability within Scion's planetary system?"

Roy covered his face with his hands and groaned. Then putting his hands back on the table, he sighed and looked toward Kellon. "By the term planetary system, I presume you are referring to one of those odd celestial systems where comets, asteroid debris, a big solar glowing plasma primary that is spewing out millions of tons of positive-charged particles, and a bunch of various sized planets are swinging about that primary? Oh, I almost forgot the moons. There are normally lots of moons in one of those systems. Sir, to answer your question in precise technical terms— no!"

"Roy we did a micro-Jump near Earth and survived. Why can't we do it again near Scion?"

"Sir, the voluminous textbook on Jump theory is quite specific in terms of micro-Jumps within a planetary system. I believe it was on the first Wednesday of my first week, of my first year, of my undergraduate navigation instruction, that the folks at the Academy taught us about doing micro-Jumps in a solar system. That was a very long time ago, so please forgive me if I can't precisely quote the textbook. Even so, I sorta recall the book saying that performing a micro-Jump within a solar system is a clean and neat way of committing suicide. Of course, the textbook put it in more arcane technical terms, added a sprinkling of long impressive looking equations, but after hours of running out the equations, it all boiled down to simply a good way of committing suicide."

Kellon sat and listened, while his frown deepened. "While I do not want to be repetitive, but, we did do a micro-Jump near Earth. We are sitting here talking about it, so we obviously didn't commit suicide. So, just how were we able to do it and survive?"

"Now, that's a fair question. As you will recall, we had just exited a long-Jump. We were therefore not, precisely speaking, within the solar system, but well above or on its outer boundary. At the time and that far above the ecliptic plane, the perturbations in the mass-gravitational-temporal flux were minimal. In short, we got lucky."

With a sense of exasperation, Kellon snapped back, "Lucky is not an answer I can accept. Roy, if you have precise gravitation mass temporal distribution data, can you compute a micro-Jump within a planetary system? Yes, or no?"

Roy slumped in his chair, deeply troubled. "Commodore, given twenty years of hard study, unlimited computer time, a building full of bright and attractive feminine graduate students to carry my thermos of neab and provide me with daily deep tissue back rubs, then I might be able to give you a precise answer to that question. The problem here is you are putting me on the spot, and our lives are at risk."

Kellon's steel-gray eyes flashed with frustration. "If we get into a firefight with a hundred Kreel ships, our lives will also be at risk! Roy, give me your best professional assessment. Yes, or no?"

Roy straightened and looked into Kellon's face, searching for any indication he could side-step the question. There was none.

"Well, put in those strict terms, if we had access to absolutely precise, current, up to the microsecond, spot-on data, it might be theoretically possible to do what you want. It's not a matter of not being able to do it, so much as our not knowing what we are doing. If we have the precise required data, and five Cruiser AIs can together simultaneously grind the data down in a timely fashion, it might be possible. The real problem hinges on the word *if!* By what available technical means can we possibly obtain sufficient timely data, of an order of precision that we would require? I simply don't know how we can pull that out of our bag of tricks. What's more, no one else up to this time has ever figured out that trick either, which is where the before-mentioned reference to suicide comes into play."

Kellon stood and moved over to the side table and refilled his cup of neab, adding another pastry to the now empty dish. He turned slowly and stood looking thoughtfully back toward his friend of centuries. "Roy, we are going to get those needed numbers by breaking all the traditional rules. We are going to place three deep space Navigation Beacons in Scion's solar system."

Upon hearing Kellon's intentions, Roy's eyebrows arched. "Sir, to my knowledge, no one has ever put two, let alone three, Navigation Beacons in a solar system. It's not unorthodox, it's outright technical heresy."

"Heresy or not, Roy, do you think we can acquire the needed data if we place those beacons in Scion's system?"

Before responding, Roy paused thoughtfully. Then, with a deep sigh, he answered. "Sir, if we are talking about being turned into toast by the lasers from a hundred Kreel warships, or else trying to gather some mass distribution temporal data in an unorthodox fashion so we might actually survive the upcoming battle, then I recommend we try the unorthodox option. Since you have asked for my personal views, survival is definitely my personal preference. Besides, I distinctly remember my dear mother teaching me— and at a very young age— that she was not raising me to become a piece of crispy toast. She was really quite emphatic about that topic."

Kellon sat and considered Roy's explanation and his available options. It seemed to boil down to the question of the number crunching capability of five Cruiser AIs, when working together.

"Lan, I assume that you have been monitoring this discussion."

"Yes, Sir. I am monitoring the discussion and find it both informative and interesting."

"Well Lan, since you are directly involved in solving micro-Jump equations, and our continued survival requires your accurately solving them, what is your personal assessment of our chances of performing a micro-Jump and surviving?"

"Sir, Commander Grey is quite correct. Such calculations require precise current data and are complex. Any failure in proper computations would be fatal. Upon initial analytical assessment, however, provided the requisite data is available, five AIs together do have the computational capability to solve the micro-Jump equations in a timely manner. As Commander Grey correctly stated, the real problem then becomes one of gathering the precision data required to make the correct calculations."

"Lan, out with it. If we place three Navigation Beacons into solar orbits, can we obtain the data required?"

"Sir, I cannot answer that question. I will, however, spawn a technical inquiry and place the question to all of the squadron's AIs, including our Scouts."

There followed a long silence, as the combined AIs worked together in evaluating the available technical data for the Navigation Beacons.

After about five minutes, Lan responded to Kellon's question.

"Sir. Following our thorough evaluation of the technical specifications for the beacons, we observed the specifications indicate the beacons would not permit collection of required data. Discerning this, we next proceeded to determine if we could modify the beacons to perform the required task. Our analysis indicates that if we make some sensitive modifications to the beacon's root operational algorithms, we can then obtain the required data, but only when using two properly placed beacons. However, since we are referring to our continued existence, and not wanting to upset Commander Grey's mother, all the AIs agree that a third beacon would be quite prudent. The cost to performance ratio, of course, is well below normal requirements. But, given the importance of obtaining a correct and timely solution, we considered the utilization ratio acceptable."

Upon hearing Lan's reference to his mother, and having just begun to sip his neab, Roy sputtered and nearly dropped his cup.

Chuckling, he inserted, "Lan, thank you for your consideration of my dear mother's wishes. I know that she would be most appreciative of your consideration."

Hearing Lan's thorough response, Kellon felt some of his tension begin to ebb. "Lan, your confirmation that the AIs are capable of solving the micro-Jump equations in a timely manner is very helpful. Given your results, I'm directing the AIs to select three beacons from our inventories, and they are to begin making the required adjustments to the beacon's root algorithms. You will coordinate all your efforts and modifications of the beacons with Commander Grey."

"Yes, Sir. The work has begun."

Smiling, Roy looked wistfully back to the side table. "Well Commodore, since we seem to have solved yet another impossible problem, if you don't mind, I will appropriate the last two of those pastries and return dutifully to my navigation console."

Shaking his head in good humor, Kellon retorted, "Roy, help yourself to the pastries, but at least leave me the thermos flask of neab. Also, you can be certain that I will do my very best to see you keep your fishing date on Glas Dinnein."

Roy stopped at the door and looked back toward Kellon. There was a twinkle in his eyes, and he was still grinning.

"Yes, Sir. To tell you the truth, both my dear mother and I are rather counting on that."

# Chapter Four:
# Returned in Good Working Order

As the door closed behind Roy, Kellon returned his thoughts to the tactical problems. He knew in a dynamic hostile environment, instantaneous communications, rapid mobility, concentrated firepower, and surprise, were the keys to achieving tactical superiority. Reviewing the decisions that they had just made, he thought, *Well, with a micro-Jump capability, we should at least have a significant edge in the surprise category.*

Having determined micro-Jumps within Scion's heliosphere were at least plausible, Kellon set about converting his planning into reality. Time was working against him, and he still had a great deal to accomplish before entering any battle.

Kellon assigned Cruiser Lar to remain at the distant Jump exit point. Lar's task was to guard a deployed rendezvous beacon, and wait for the arrival of Mer Shawn's promised reinforcements. Meanwhile, Kellon directed Cruisers Lan, Lent, Lawrence, and Langley within Scion's heliosphere.

Upon entry into the system, the four Guardian Cruisers soon detected and began tracking nine Kreel fast-attack ships, which were busy providing the Kreel with pre-invasion surveillance. As the following days quickly passed, the Guardian Cruisers were required to maintain strict stealth protocols, while they went about preparing for the upcoming battle.

To gain an advanced warning of the Kreel fleet's arrival, the four Cruisers selectively established a minimal network of passive monitors within the heliosphere. The limited number of monitors would not provide Kellon with a precision tracking capability, but they would provide him with an early warning and the course coordinates of any large group of Kreel ships entering the system.

Working closely with the AIs, Roy Grey and his navigation team spent hours defining and confirming the required modifications to the Navigation Beacon's root algorithms. This necessitated their modification of the beacons to provide reliable

**19**

superluminal communications within the heliosphere, thereby assuring the timely data transfers required to safely perform the micro-Jumps. Then Roy's team and the AIs coordinated the placement of the three modified beacons into their calculated operational solar orbits. As each beacon came online, it began gathering the copious vital mass distribution temporal data that was essential for Kellon's desired micro-Jumps.

As Roy's work had proceeded, Guardian personnel throughout the squadron quickly learned of Kellon's intentions to use micro-Jumps during the battle. While there were understandable concerns expressed among the crews, everyone involved doubled their efforts to assure the success of the plan. What everyone understood was that prior to the battle, a Cruiser would be making a big leap of faith. All Jump theory aside, before a full squadron committed to a micro-Jump, someone had to validate that micro-Jumps were possible, and more importantly, survivable. Likewise, they all knew the downside of that first leap of faith was that a Guardian Cruiser might pay the full price if micro-Jumps were proved to be impossible.

As part of his pre-battle preparation, Kellon directed Lan's electronics shop to fabricate a unique transceiver— one capable of superluminal communications with the newly modified beacons. Because of the classified temporal-gravitational technology involved, Kellon required the shop to construct the transceiver with a self-destruct mechanism, where all internal components would promptly become a blob of sticky goo if the Arkillians in any way tampered with it. Once the shop had finished fabrication of the transceiver, Kellon still had the problem of delivering it to Kur.

As Kellon entered the Combat Analysis Center, its general communicator softly announced, "Commodore is in CAC." As the communicator made its proclamation, Commander Grey glanced up and smiled. Nodding to Roy, Kellon stood for a moment studying the tactical displays, paying special attention to the location of the three groups of Kreel ships. Given Scion's current orbital position, as long as Guardian ships maintained full stealth, the three groups of Kreel ships should not pose a serious threat.

"Roy, how long until we are clear to descend to the planet?" Commander Grey looked up thoughtfully, "Sir, since we are nearly there, you could say we are ready to descend whenever you want."

Kellon's smile broadened, "Roy, thank you for being as prompt in anticipating my questions as always."

"Well. Sir, I believe promptness is the basis for receiving my monthly brew allotment. Promptness, therefore, is deemed essential."

Going to his command chair, Kellon took his seat, automatically reaching down and fastening his lap restraint. Keying his captain's band, he addressed the squadron, "Attention all captains, Kellon here. This is the first check of the new communications circuits. As I call out the Cruiser's name, please acknowledge communication is established. Lent?"

Captain Eurie's clear feminine voice promptly responded. "Lent is receiving."

"Kellon here, acknowledging Lent. Lar?"

Captain Kylster's clear deep voice promptly responded, "Lar is receiving."

Kellon smiled. This was what he wanted, clear rapid communications between all units. Lar was still well outside the heliosphere, yet the temporal-gravitational communications through the Navigation Beacons had cut the communications lag-time down to nearly instantaneous. "Acknowledging, Lar. Lawrence?"

One by one, the Cruisers each acknowledged the new communications links were operational.

"Gentlemen and Ladies, for security purposes, and to minimize possible detection, we will henceforth minimize use of this channel. Lent is currently maintaining high cover, as Lan drops down to the planet to contact the Arkillians. Everyone, remain alert. Kellon out."

Kellon next keyed his normal communications for the tight link to Lent. "Eurie, are you ready?"

Eurie's calm warm voice immediately responded, "Lent is ready to provide a protective umbrella for Lan. We are maintaining Condition 3 and full stealth mode."

"Keep your eyes open and your ears on, Eurie. This shouldn't take long. If you find yourself in trouble, call out loud and clear. If Lan hits problems, we will do the same. Kellon out."

Kellon turned his attention once again to the forward plot board, and he confirmed the Kreel ships were well away and did not pose an immediate threat. It was definitely time to make a house call.

"Navigation, Roy, take Lan down into Scion's dark-side shadow."

"Navigation here, acknowledging. Lan is now descending into the planetary shadow. We are moving to an orbit 30,000 kilometers distant from the planet surface."

Kellon had carefully timed Lan's approach to Scion to coincide with Kur's winter home entering the planet's night side. *Hopefully,* he thought, *we can establish contact with Kur quickly.*

Keying his command band, Kellon inquired, "Commander Roan, Kellon here. What is the status of Lan's Scouts?"

"Roan here, Sir. All Scouts are crewed and ready for deployment on five minutes' notice."

"Acknowledged, ready on five minutes' notice." Kellon replied.

As Lan dropped swiftly toward the planet's surface, Kellon continued to study the display on the forward bulkhead. It was showing the image of the planet's sharply defined broad crescent. Taking note of its multiple brown and golden shades, he thought, *For all of its apparent dryness, it is a beautiful planet.* He then remembered Kur's invitation, that he might someday join him in the springtime to see the wild flowers in bloom across the wide desert. Kellon smiled with the memory of the invitation, thinking, *Kur, I would enjoy doing that someday. Unfortunately, this is not that day.*

As Lan continued dropping toward his orbit, Kellon ordered, "Lan, using minimum power, commence transmitting the recognition signal to the standard transceivers we provided the Arkillians."

"Transmitting, as ordered," Lan acknowledged.

On Lan's tenth transmission cycle, they received Kur's excited response. "Honored Kellon, please confirm your transmission. Kur here, repeating, please confirm your transmission."

"Lan, patch Kur into communication band 1." "Sir, Kur is now connected."

"Council Member Kur, this is Kellon. I am receiving your signal weakly. There is a time lag, but we are coming near to Scion as we speak, so that should not be a problem much longer. It is good to hear your voice again."

"Honored Kellon. It is likewise good to hear your voice. Much has happened during the long interval since your last contact. All of us are concerned for the safety of our Nest Ship. We are also eager to learn what is happening."

"Council Member Kur, I am able to tell you the Nest Ship is safe. I have brought messages to you from Earth, and from your captain and the Trade Arbiter. I am also bringing urgent information regarding the Kreel invasion. Will you be able to quickly convene a meeting with your top officials and military personnel?"

"Honored Kellon, there has been continuing communications and planning between all parties since your departure. Anything you can tell me will be immediately provided to all involved officials and the military."

Roy looked up toward Kellon, "Navigation here. Sir, we are now at 30,000 kilometers and centered in the dark-side shadow."

Kellon made eye contact with Roy, acknowledging his update with a nod.

"Council Member Kur, we are in orbit at this time. I have a number of items that I would like to pass to you. Are you near your winter home, or elsewhere?"

"My winter home has become designated as a tactical control center. I am currently there, as are many others. Will the presence of others be a problem?"

"Honored Kur, if I have your assurance no shots will be fired, then it will not present a problem. We can be at the same point you were dropped off in about two Earth hours from now, if that is acceptable to you."

"Two Earth hours? That soon? Certainly, I will personally come with Ca and Rin to greet whomever you send. Be assured, no shots will be fired."

"Excellent. I will be sending Commander Roan. I am certain he will be happy to see you again. You can expect him to arrive at the same coordinates as last time, in two Earth hours."

"Honored Kellon, thank you. I do assure you that we will meet Commander Roan. Kur out."

Keying his command band, Kellon ordered, "Commander Roan, you have your five minute notice. I have scheduled you to be on Scion at the same coordinates you dropped Kur off on our last visit. You are to be there two Earth hours from now. Does that represent a problem?"

"No, Sir. As long as they are not shooting at us, there should be no problem. Will you have Lan synchronize our launch on my command?"

"Lan will coordinate the launch, on your command. Take care and remain vigilant. This is only the second time we have put someone on the planet. I want all the Scouts and their crews back on Lan in good working order."

"Yes, Sir. Understood. No vacations and all Scouts returned in good working order. Roan out."

# Chapter Five:
## Dangerous Weeks to Come

On board Shey, Roan and Zorn were just finalizing their pre-launch checklist. "Shey, do you concur we are ready to launch?"

"Yes, Roan, all Scouts are signaling ready to launch."

"Shey, confirm all the girls are at full stealth mode, Condition 3. On launch, form the girls into a standard three-sided pyramid, with you taking the low point. Our destination is the same geographic coordinates as when we brought the Arkillians home. We will be dropping to arrive on that location in precisely one-hour and forty-five minutes. Once over the site, the girls will hold at six kilometers in a standard defensive triangle, while we descend to one kilometer."

"Understood," Shey acknowledged.

"Lan, Roan here. I'm requesting a synchronized launch of your Scouts."

"Lan here, I will synchronize launch on your count. All hangars are now at space normal."

"Scouts, heads up. Three, two, one, launch."

Lan swung open each of his four hangar doors and in unison gently propelled the Scouts out from their secure bays and into the void beyond— then dominated by the vast shadowed sphere of Scion. Once he had smoothly launched the Scouts, Lan swiftly closed the hangar doors behind them. Meanwhile, Shey was busy coordinating her sisters as they assumed their tactical formation. Then, as a tight homogeneous group of four dark flitting shades concealed within Scion's shadow, they together dropped toward the dark planet 30,000 kilometers below, moving purposefully toward their specified destination.

As they neared their objective, Zorn reported, "I am seeing more activity near Kur's winter home than before, both ground transportation and aircraft. The good news is that I'm not detecting anything like active search or fire control sensors."

Moving effortlessly at a low altitude, the four Scout ships were swift blurs of darkness within the night sky. At six kilometers altitude, the top three Scouts ceased their descent, spreading out into an equilateral defense triangle with Shey at its center. As her sisters provided the high tactical cover, Shey continued her smooth descent and gently came to a stationary hover at one kilometer— directly above Kur's winter home.

"Shey, do you sense anything that doesn't look right?" Roan asked.

"No, Roan. As Zorn indicated, there is more ground transportation, and six small aircraft are either departing or entering the local area. I see nothing to indicate a heavily armed presence."

"I confirm Shey's assessment," Zorn added.

Still frowning, Roan preferred to err on the side of precaution... "Shey, they may be allies now, but a year ago they were shooting at us. You are to set Condition 2 on lasers and guns. I want all Scouts to maintain a tight surveillance for potential threats."

"Yes, Roan. As ordered, my sisters and I are now setting Condition 2 on guns and lasers."

Turning to Zorn, Roan cautioned, "I'm not expecting trouble, but stay sharp. As Kellon said, this is only our second time on the planet."

Looking over toward Roan, Zorn's expression was serious. "I never object when someone is taking extra precautions to protect my skin. Be assured, by staying alert I'll do my part."

"Just don't stop for a brew, Zorn. I want to move up and out as soon as possible."

"Understood, no brew. I am on my way."

As Zorn unstrapped his restraining harness and moved aft, Roan set about making contact with Kur, keying his transceiver channel.

"Council Member Kur, this is Commander Roan. We are directly above your home, and Commander Zorn is proceeding to descend by lifter to your location. Do you confirm that the area is safe?"

"Commander Roan, it is good to speak with you once again. Yes, I can and do confirm the area safe. Ca, Rin, and I will proceed to the location to which you returned us. We are departing now."

"Zorn, are you strapped on your lifter?"

"I am cinching up the seat straps. I have the transceiver and data package securely strapped to cargo rings. I am ready to lift."

"Shey, launch your lifter."

As Zorn watched, the compartment's lights dimmed and the lifter's force shield energized with its familiar low humming. The hull port slid smoothly open, exposing Scion's night sky. Slowly, the lifter disk moved slightly up and quietly out of its compartment and then rapidly dropped toward the distant ground one kilometer below.

As they hurried out into the early evening, Kur, Ca, and Rin were wearing their lavish official robes, including several items of meritorious jewelry. Kur paused only briefly, switching on the soft illumination outside. Once out of Kur's home, the three Council Members moved quickly through Kur's garden to the same point where they had landed upon return from Earth. As they stood looking up, they soon observed the lifter dropping toward them.

As the lifter silently settled to the ground, Zorn unbuckled his lap restraint and stood, smartly saluting.

"Council Member Kur, Commander Zorn is pleased to have this opportunity to visit Scion."

Zorn studied the three Arkillians who had come to greet him, and he personally knew each of them by sight. As Zorn looked at Kur, Ca, and Rin, he considered the Arkillians a handsome species. He again noted they were bipeds with two arms and they were humanoid in form. Zorn knew well they were not mammals but from a different branch of life. They had no hair or fur, and on each of their hands were two opposing thumbs and four fingers. Their heads were slightly larger than that of a human of similar stature, while their torsos were of a slighter build.

The Arkillian's eyes were slightly larger than human eyes, and each had three lids, one upper lid and two lower lids. The innermost lower lid was a somewhat transparent light filter. The second outermost lid, like the upper lid, covered the eye and blocked light from entering. They had a distinct center facial ridge with well-formed nostrils. By human standards, their mouths were thin and seemed slightly smallish. There were no discernible ear openings, their aural detectors appearing more like small white domes affixed to each side of their heads.

Zorn looked toward Kur, studying his facial markings, since he understood such markings were unique to each individual and were naturally occurring patterns of various tones. While Kur's facial coloration was of marginal assistance to Zorn, he understood the characteristic pattern and color brightening or darkening sequence formed a significant portion of the inter-personal communications between Arkillians. If a person was experienced with Arkillians, an insight into an Arkillian's mental state was possible by observing the shifting facial colorations.

As the energy force field about the lifter collapsed, Scion's atmosphere flowed in and around Zorn. Standing on the lifter, he felt the gentle breeze and was suddenly aware of the clean night air. He could smell the sweet scent of nearby flowers. The stark contrast of the desert night air and Lan's crisp air-conditioned environment was startling. Pausing, Zorn drank in the exotic fragrant aromas and heard a distant melodic call of some animal or bird. The first impression of Scion he received was not of a harsh desert, but rather of a gentle open space.

Kur's facial features brightened as he slightly bowed his head, acknowledging Zorn's formal salute.

"Commander Zorn, friend of our Nests, all on Scion extend greetings of peace and prosperity to you. May I inquire if the Kreel have sent another military force against Earth since we departed?"

"Honored Kur, the Kreel did send two forces. The last one consisted of ten cruisers on a strike mission. I am able to report that Guardian Force and Earth were able to destroy the Kreel forces before they damaged Earth. I am pleased also to inform you that during the battles, your Nest Ship performed with distinction and is undamaged."

"That our Nest Ship has acted to warrant your mention pleases me. The news of the Nest Ship's safety and performance during battles will gladden all on Scion.

"Honored Zorn, it is difficult for me to consider the Kreel would commit ten of their cruisers so far from their Hub. Kellon having destroyed all of them is wondrous. Knowing the Kreel, as I certainly do, they must be mystified and alarmed at their losses."

As Kur responded to Zorn's information, Zorn turned and carefully released the straps on the objects brought on the lifter. Then, turning back toward Kur, Zorn stepped off the lifter and approached the three Arkillians.

"Honored Kur, the reason I am here is to provide you with these three items and to bring you an urgent warning."

"Honored Zorn, what is your warning?"

"Sir, the Kreel are now in their final staging for the invasion of Scion. Our Intelligence indicates that their fleet will appear within Scion's system within the next several Earth weeks."

Kur listened to Zorn's warning, but felt no shock. "Since your last visit, we have anticipated the coming Kreel invasion. We are quietly preparing to meet them in combat in space and to fight them on the surface of Scion to the best of our abilities. Know this truth, we will not— to the very last Arkillian— yield to the Kreel."

Looking carefully at Zorn, he asked the one burning question that all on Scion wanted to have answered.

"May I ask Honored Zorn, will humanity assist us in the coming battle?"

Zorn smiled broadly. "Honored Kur, we are here within Scion's system for precisely that purpose. Even as we speak, additional ships are coming to strengthen Kellon's squadron. We are now preparing to join forces with you, and we will fight the Kreel to defend your Nests."

As a sign of his own deep respect and gratitude, Kur bowed his head. "Honored Zorn, though your news of a Kreel invasion is heavy, yet your news of assistance brings with it joy. News that friends of our Nests are standing with us in our time of great peril is thankfully received."

"Sir, the first item I bring is a sealed folder obtained from your captain of the Nest Ship. It is a complete report on events near Earth since your departure. I am also asked to tell you, 'Spring rains are the warmest.'"

Hearing the code phrase, all three Arkillians looked at each other in surprise. "Commander Zorn, are you certain of the captain's message?" Kur asked.

"Yes, Sir. 'Spring rains are the warmest.'"

As he observed the Arkillians, Zorn regretted not being better able to read their facial markings. What he could discern was the message had caused each of the Arkillians a notable emotional jolt.

Zorn passed the sealed folder to Kur, who took it as if it were extremely fragile. Looking at it wonderingly, he then handed it to Ca.

"The second item I have to provide you is a folder containing a military Intelligence summary. It provides as complete a summary of the Kreel invasion force as we currently have. As you will soon read, their coming invasion fleet represents a massive force. The Kreel are deadly serious in their intent to take Scion by overwhelming military power."

Kur accepted the thin folder, lifted it questioningly, as if by its weight alone he could evaluate its contents.

Zorn stood quietly for a moment, allowing his silence to demand their notice. When he had the full attention of the three Arkillians, only then did he proceed.

"Honored Kur, the third item I bring is given you on your previous pledge of honor. It is a new and larger transceiver. We have designed it to assure reliable communications. During the upcoming battle, we request you restrict your communication to the use of this transceiver. Security protocols are built into the transceiver, and should anyone attempt to tamper with it, the device will be rendered useless."

Standing straight, Kur extended his hand toward Zorn. "Honored Zorn, you may report that the transceiver will be guarded, secured, and none shall tamper with it. We are grateful for the trust it signifies. I say this on the honor of my Nest."

Reflecting Kur's formal attitude, Zorn handed the transceiver to him and began instructing the Arkillians on the functionality of the device. "Sir, if you will notice there are only two buttons and two lights on the device..."

Within a few minutes, Zorn had fully instructed the Arkillians on the transceiver's operation.

When he completed the instructions, Zorn paused and then added, "To assure it is fully operational, I would like you to test the transceiver at this time."

As instructed, Kur reached out a finger and pressed the small activation button. His countenance brightened when he saw the soft golden glow of the power light. Then he pressed the larger button in the center of the transceiver and spoke. "Commodore

Kellon, this is Council Member Kur. I am calling to tell you I have received your new transceiver and information packages. Are you hearing me?"

After a slight delay, Kellon's strong voice came in sharp and clear. "Council Member Kur, It is good to have the opportunity to speak with you once again. I'm clearly receiving your transmission. Do you have any questions concerning what you have been told?" "Honored Kellon, I have as many questions as there are grains of sand on the desert. I regret I cannot ask all of them.

"I have been sent a message from our Nest Ship. Honored Kellon, we had not anticipated this message. It implies the most glowing admiration for Earth and the services you have rendered our Nest Ship. That the captain has sent such a message announces there are many things we are not yet aware of, all of them being wondrous. I assure you we are grateful for all you have done for Scion."

"Honored Kur, we acknowledge your gratitude. Regrettably, tactical circumstances dictate I extract my force from this area at this time. I recommend you promptly deliver to your military the Intelligence briefing we have provided. There is much they need to study. I do, however, request that you contact me once they have completed their review."

"I understand and will do so."

As one of Scion's moons rose above the broken horizon, casting a faint shimmering soft light across the desert, far off a warbling cry of an animal's call undulated over the surrounding shadowed hills. As Kur had talked with Kellon, Zorn stepped onto the lifter, sat, and tightened his lap belt. Turning toward the Arkillians, Zorn then bade farewell. "Council Member Kur, thank you for your hospitality. Hopefully, I will be able to stay longer the next time I visit."

Kur again slightly bowed his head toward Zorn.

"Please extend to Commander Roan my personal compliments. May safety and prosperity be with you during the dangerous weeks to come."

Keying his microphone, Zorn requested, "Roan, bring me home."

Softly humming, the energy shield formed around Zorn and the lifter disk rose smoothly upward, gaining speed as it ascended, soon disappearing into the cloaking invisibility of the night sky.

# Chapter Six:
# **Reinforcements**

Commingling broad-spectrum interstellar energies overflowed and poured into the blistering cold cauldron of deep space. Concealed deeply within that haze of electro-magnetic hash, Lan's entire squadron blended like fleeting apparitions flowing within darker shadows. Remaining alert, the five silently waiting Cruisers had dispersed within the tactical volume and were monitoring the rendezvous beacon. As the crews waited, tensions on board the Cruisers were slowly increasing.

Having approached the rendezvous beacon in full stealth and undetected, Scout Ship Terese made the initial overt contact, announcing the arrival of the anticipated reinforcements.

When Terese reported in, Commander Lorn Shaw had the CAC, and he promptly notified Kellon. "Sir, Shaw here, Scout Ship Terese has just checked in. She reports Cruiser Long, with four others, have arrived from Glas Dinnein. They have brought our resupply pods and are requesting hard links and permission to join up."

"Lorn, who is in command?"

"Sir, Commodore Urley with Cruiser Long is in command."

"Lorn, please extend my compliments to Commodore Urley. Be certain to alert him that we are still expecting two more Cruisers to join us soon, and promptly establish hard links with all Cruisers. Then coordinate with Commodore Urley to determine which Cruisers are transporting the resupply pods intended for each of our Cruisers. Once you've determined that mix, proceed to pair us up. Once they've delivered the resupply pods, direct Commodore Urley to establish a pod depot with the remaining ordnance and supplies."

"Yes, Sir. Once the supply depot is established, how should I deploy the task force?" Lorn asked.

"Position the new squadron using standard deployment tactics. We will make our final adjustments once the remaining Cruisers arrive."

"Yes, Sir. Shaw out."

The task force was now up to ten Cruisers, consisting of two squadrons of five ships each. To round out the task force, Admiral Mer Shawn had reduced Earth's protection from five to three Cruisers, directing Cruisers Lowe and Lyte to join him. Those last two Cruisers would complete the task force.

That the reporting Guardian Cruisers had come so near while remaining undetected, raised everyone's spirits. Everyone knew stealth and surprise were mandatory if they were to survive the upcoming battle.

"Lan, our orders remain unchanged. We are to oppose the Kreel invasion of Scion, engage and destroy the Kreel fleet. My problem remains how best to achieve those results while minimizing our casualties and losses."

"Yes, Sir. I agree, our orders are quite clear. I am confident that your devised battle plan will accomplish the defined mission."

"Lan, I appreciate your note of confidence. Twelve Cruisers do represent a significant Guardian presence. That Admiral Mer Shawn has pried twelve Cruisers loose from our planetary defenses, underscores the seriousness of our mission. Even so, the odds we are facing are reminiscent of the pitched battle around Kintana, eight hundred years ago. In that battle, we lost nearly 80 percent of our fighting force.

"Sir, historically speaking, I agree with your observation. Yet, there is a significant difference between the Guardian Cruisers that fought at Kintana and our 'L' class Cruisers. Those earlier Cruisers did not have current stealth capability or AI processes, and had far less combat proficiency than current Guardian Cruisers. Equally as important, the Kreel had launched a massive surprise attack then. This time, surprise is on our side."

Leaning back in his chair, Kellon smiled. "Lan, you are absolutely correct, the old 'G' class cruisers were nothing like you. Of that, I can personally testify."

"Sir, my confidence is merely based on our earlier performance. Our current task force is now here near Scion because we were able to capture a Kreel Gortoga cruiser intact.

Because Guardian Intelligence can now intercept and read Kreel Military communications, we have learned of the Kreel plans for invading Scion and Earth. If we had not captured the Gortoga cruiser, then the Kreel invasion would have remained undiscovered and unstoppable. "

Kellon, with conscious control, slowly exhaled. "Thank you, Lan, for helping me remain focused on what's really important."

"Sir, you are most welcome."

Whatever was to unfold around Scion in the upcoming battle, be it good or be it bad, Kellon knew the battle would be contained in the future tactical handbooks and referenced within future history books. Even so, Kellon's primary concern was not history books but achieving his mission with the fewest casualties and losses. With this goal in mind, he set to work. "Lan, how is the temporal-gravitational distribution survey coming? Do we have sufficient data gathered to be useful?"

"Sir, Commander Grey directed me to assure all gathered data is being networked. All the AIs are closely monitoring the three deployed Navigation Beacons. At present, our combined AI calculations indicate we have achieved a micro-Jump confidence of 87 percent. Based on its rate of change, our micro-Jump confidence factor should be above 99 percent within another four days."

Lan's information brought Kellon a sense of relief. There were still eight days before the Kreel were anticipated to arrive in force. With favorable improvements, there was still sufficient time to make the critical test micro-Jump. Before he could perform that vital test, he first needed to complete a full resupply and then move the task force into its final defensive positions near Scion. There was still time, but it was tight.

As he was considering his next actions, the priority channel activated. "Sir, Shaw here. Scout Ship Dani has just checked in. She reports Cruisers Lowe and Lyte have arrived from Earth and are requesting hard links and assignments."

Kellon thought for a moment before responding. Lowe, commanded by Commodore Byrn, commanded the five Cruisers that had recently relieved him near Earth. Knowing Byrn was an excellent Commodore, he made his final decision on organizing the task force.

"Excellent, Lorn. We will form up into three squadrons of four Cruisers each. As Commodore Byrn requested, promptly establish hard links with both Lowe and Lyte. Then advise Commodore Urley that I am requesting he assign one of his Cruisers to join Lowe. Also, following the resupply effort, assign Langley to join up with Lowe. Advise both commodores that I will brief them in three hours."

"Yes, Sir."

Kellon glanced at his chronometer, establishing Kur's local time on Scion. During the previous weeks, his tactical team had worked diligently with the Arkillians developing what Kellon hoped would prove to be a winning battle plan. For the plan to be successful, the Arkillians were required to expose their technologically limited military fleet as a lure— to be bait so tempting that the Kreel could not resist. The Arkillians had considered his battle tactics, considered its risks, and then— knowing the risks— agreed without hesitation.

"Lan, connect me with Council Member Kur."

There was only a slight pause before Kur's voice came in clear and strong.

"Commodore Kellon, Kur here."

"Good morning Honored Kur. I am calling to inform you that the remaining units of my task force have arrived. We are currently performing a resupply procedure, and we should be moving toward our final defensive positions near Scion soon. How are your preparations coming?"

"Commodore Kellon, because of the continuing presence of Kreel diplomatic officials on Scion, we are required to act with great caution and misdirection. We have surreptitiously rescheduled all normal interstellar shipping, so our ships will not be near Scion when the Kreel arrive. As discussed, where possible, we are slowly moving our populations out of the cities and spreading them out into the country. So far, we have cannibalized four of our Nest Ships. We have repositioned their heavy laser and missile batteries near our key centers, and have redeployed and concealed twelve hundred ground support craft. We will direct the support craft to oppose Kreel troops wherever they land. While our forces may be limited, our determination to resist the Kreel is not."

"Honored Kur, what is the current status of our lure?"

"We are nearly ready, at least as near as possible to being ready. Today we have twenty cruisers and about two thousand fighters positioned randomly about. We will bring them together as a single force once we know the Kreel's main cruiser battle force approach vector."

Kellon noted with interest that Kur had not once mentioned the energy beam weapon the Arkillians had secretly developed that could kill the Kreel. He had only learned of the weapon's existence the year before, when Kur attacked one of his decoys believing it was a Kreel cruiser. That single event had provided Guardian Force with the Arkillian's weapon's performance specifications.

Specifications that Guardian Force promptly researched and reverse engineered. Ironically, it had only been possible for him to capture the Kreel Gortoga cruiser by employing the Arkillian energy weapon.

Knowing its true effectiveness, Kellon knew it represented the Arkillians' most lethal weapon. That Kur had not mentioned the beam was understandable. Everyone, including the Guardian Force, retained some secrets.

"Honored Kur, our latest estimates indicate there are seven hundred and fifty thousand ground troops in their invasion force. We will do everything we can to prevent those troops from reaching Scion's surface. When the Kreel's cruiser battle force does arrive, just be certain to challenge and vigorously taunt them. We need to provoke them into taking the bait you are preparing to offer them."

"Honored Kellon, there is currently a serious ongoing struggle among the members of the Arkillian Council. Everyone wants the privilege of making that taunting challenge to the Kreel. I am proud to say I am among the finalists seeking that privilege. However, the competition is so intense that the final selection may need to be determined on the dueling sands."

The joviality in Kur's response cut through Kellon's serious thoughts like a bright sunbeam through morning mist. He made a mental note for his yet-to-be-written memoirs: *Species that can laugh together will often stand together to fight a common foe.*

"Council Member Kur. You might just remind them you have on-the-job experience. I still remember the fury of the Kreel captain you taunted near Earth. With such a proven talent, you should win the selection hands down."

"Thank you, Commodore Kellon, for reminding me of that event. I will be certain to inform those making the decision of my previous job experience."

"Honored Kur, I will contact you once my force is in position. That should be in five days."

"Friend of our Nests, I will wait for your call. Kur out."

# Chapter Seven:
## Resupply Operation

Departing his personal compartment, Kellon asked, "Lan where is Commander Roan?"

"Sir, at this time, Commander Roan is on board Shey."

Moving through the passageway to the nearest elevators, Kellon took a down elevator to deck two. Then, moving aft, he reached the hatch to Shey's hangar deck, noting the bulkhead status light was a bright golden color. The color indicated the compartment was occupied and at standard atmospheric pressure. As he opened the hatch and entered, Shey's clear feminine voice sounded out, "Attention on deck, Commodore on hangar deck."

Kellon moved to the short gangway connecting Shey's open main hatch to the hangar deck and called out, "Commodore Kellon, requesting permission to come on board."

Roan quickly appeared in the open hatchway, saluted and crisply responded, "Permission granted. Welcome aboard Commodore. To what do we owe this unexpected pleasure?"

"Well, Roan, I could simply say I came for a cup of neab, and that would be mostly true— at least a cup of neab and some conversation."

Roan quizzically studied Kellon's expression, then smiled broadly in acknowledgment. "With pleasure, Shey gladly extends her warm hospitality."

Entering Shey through the hatch, both men moved forward into the compact control compartment.

As they entered, Commander Zorn slipped out of his command chair and briskly saluted. "At ease Zorn, I'm only here for some neab and a little conversation."

"Sir, it will take a moment or two for neab to be brewed. We were just about ready to exit the hangar for resupply and reload of ordnance. Would you care to come along?" Zorn inquired.

Kellon considered the suggestion and nodded his head in agreement. "I think I would like to do that. I can wait for the cup of neab. Carry on.

"Lan, Please inform CAC that I am on board Shey and will be departing during her reload and resupply."

"Yes, Sir."

Moving to the bulkhead behind his command chair, Zorn unfolded a Jump seat from the bulkhead and offered it to Kellon. As Roan and Zorn moved forward and took their command seats, Kellon took the Jump seat and loosely fastened the lap restraint.

After carefully scanning his flight console, Roan ordered, "Shey, close your outer hatch. Set all systems for entry into space."

There came a series of distinct equipment-related sounds, indicating the main hatch and several vents being closed. Then she acknowledged, "Roan, Shey here. All systems are confirmed gold. We are tight and ready for launch."

Roan quickly scanned his instruments, confirming Shey's status was gold, then asked, "Lan, please retract the gangway and cycle the recovery of Shey's hangar atmosphere. Requesting permission for immediate launch of Shey."

In response, the hangar lights dimmed as Lan pumped the hangar's atmosphere into a storage tank.

"Lan here. Permission granted."

The hangar door then swung smoothly up, and a slight energy field gently thrust Shey out into the interstellar void. The bulkhead to the left of Kellon brightened into a brilliant image, and he suddenly had a deck-to-overhead three-dimensional display of where Shey was going. About two kilometers distant, he observed a large elongated black pod that a Cruiser had carried limpet-style from Glas Dinnein.

As Shey hovered near the pod, both Roan and Zorn were very busy at their duty stations. What they were doing was complex, but their skill and ease of their actions made it look simple.

As Shey had approached, the pod ejected a number of cylinders. Among the collection were four bright red cylinders that were moving slowly toward Shey. Kellon listened as he heard hatches opening in Shey's hull. As he watched the video screen on the bulkhead, Shey was using spotting and orientation lasers to track and deftly maneuver the four larger red cylinders. Precisely controlling each cylinder, Shey aligned each container with an open medium missile tube. One by one, she guided each cylinder smoothly into its waiting tube. Then Kellon heard her missile hatch doors snugly close. The four medium missile reload had replenished the missiles Shey fired at a Kreel cruiser during the battle near Earth. In a similar fashion, Shey directed four smaller cylinders, painted red and green, to four light missile tubes. The reload of light missiles replaced the four missiles Shey had fired at the pod of Kreel scouts during that same battle. When completed, Shey's compliment of four medium and sixteen light missiles was again complete.

Looking toward Roan, Zorn reported, "Internal systems' diagnostics verify all missiles are certified and fully operational, set Condition 4."

Next, Shey's supply ports opened. Using control lasers, she efficiently guided four green and yellow containers, each having a variety of color bands painted on their exterior. Like the missiles, Shey quickly took them aboard and her outer hatches closed. The resupply operation had taken less than fifteen minutes.

Once Shey had secured her hatches, Zorn examined his console and the updated inventory file that included the stores they had just received. With a broad smile, he looked over toward Roan.

"Hey, Roan, we are in deep green grass on a sunny day. Admiral Mer Shawn has been very generous with our rations. He even sent us several cases of root beer. "

Looking back toward the video screen, Kellon watched as the supply pod ejected several large red and yellow striped cylinders. From their size and color banding, he identified the cylinders as four heavy missiles moving out and toward Lan. The resupply process was in full swing.

First scanning his console for systems status, Roan then commanded, "Shey, coordinate with Lan. Move us away from the pod and return us to our hangar. Alert the next Scout to proceed with resupply."

"Yes, Sir."

Kellon knew that Lan and Shey were in direct tight communication, and like the supply cylinders, Shey was moving precisely in an expertly choreographed dance. As he observed, Lan swung open his hangar door and drew Shey smoothly into the waiting compartment. As Kellon watched, the hangar hatch door closed with a distinct and reassuring thump, the hangar lights brightened, and the atmosphere indication light cycled from a pulsing blue to a solid golden color.

Shey's clear voice happily called out, "Thank you Lan for your warm hospitality."

Unfastening his lap restraint, Roan stepped down to the deck. He turned with a smile toward Kellon. "Sir, now we can properly brew that cup of neab."

The three men moved aft into the living compartment, and Kellon sat on one of the seats at the small table located near the inner bulkhead. As Roan and Zorn busied themselves in the galley, he asked, "Shey are you paying strict attention?"

"Yes, Sir."

"Good, you are invited to this conversation. So are you Lan. Each of you is asked to listen and to respond with any ideas you may wish to offer."

Hearing Kellon's comments to Shey and Lan, Roan looked toward Zorn, who only glanced back in acknowledgment, shaking his head as if to say, what's up?

Placing a thermos of hot neab and a small dish of pastries in the center of the table, Roan and Zorn then took their seats. Each turned toward Kellon with interest. Attentively sipping his neab, Kellon thoughtfully looked at the two officers. Then he leaned back smiling. "Well done Zorn, that's a cup of excellent neab. Now, as to why I am here, I have come to discuss with you your choice of tactics during your last battle near Earth.

"I also want to discuss some matters relating to the AIs. Ambassador Wells has provided me some interesting information that she obtained from her personal AI, William. I believe it is worth sharing.

"Now, beginning at the beginning, Roan please explain to me precisely how you tightly coordinated twenty Scout ships when you attacked the two Kreel cruisers near Earth."

Looking toward Kellon, Roan hesitated, at first not certain how to best answer the question. Then, shrugging inwardly, he replied. "Sir, I kept each Cruiser's four Scouts together as a distinct operational group. I then had Shey establish a hard link to the lead Scout ship in each group. That meant that she needed only to communicate with the four lead Scouts, that being one

Scout in each group. Shey, and each lead Scout, then coordinated the three remaining Scouts in their own group."

"Roan, did you personally communicate with the crews of the other lead Scouts?"

"No, Sir. I communicated my intentions to Shey. Then she communicated with each of the group lead AIs. Shey instructed the four girls to brief their crews about what was required. Of course, Shey could communicate much faster and more securely in burst mode than I could possibly personally communicate with the crews. Sir, the process seemed to work very well."

Kellon could not suppress his smile.

"Roan, it indeed worked very well. For hours now, I have repeatedly studied your attack sequence. Are you aware that all five groups launched their combined attack of eighty medium missiles against those two Kreel cruisers within sixty milliseconds of one another?"

"No, Sir. I had not bothered to review that tactical sequence. I do remember however Shey saying during the final firing approach that we were within five hundred milliseconds of attacking in unison, and she was still trying to tighten up the attack."

"Roan, there are only a very few instances where Scouts have attacked Kreel cruisers and survived. I do not know of any previous situation where a group of Scouts, operating independently of their Cruisers, engaged and destroyed a Kreel cruiser. Not any, let alone two cruisers!"

"Sir, we only destroyed one cruiser. Cruisers Lar and Langley destroyed the second Kreel cruiser."

"Sorry Roan, your story simply doesn't fly. I spoke with the captains of Lar and Langley. Both confirm the second cruiser was a derelict when they destroyed it. It was not even capable of maneuvering. Your Scouts get credit for destruction of both cruisers.

"More to the point, your tactics were bold, precise, unorthodox, and extremely effective. Now, when you launched your attack against the Kreel scouts, did you again rely on Shey to communicate with her sisters?"

"Yes, Sir. Letting the AIs freely interact worked very well during the attack on the cruisers, and it was only logical to repeat the procedure. We were twelve Scouts facing thirty Kreel scouts. I was concerned that if each of our Scouts independently targeted the Kreel scouts, it would result in more than one of our Scouts shooting at the same Kreel target. That would have caused an inefficient expenditure of our limited light missiles. Therefore, I instructed Shey to use the sensor data of all of her sisters and to make all target assignments. Shey also coordinated the final firing sequences in order to deliver our missiles on their targets at the same impact time. Sir, Shey also coordinated our Scouts in all their subsequent movement to new predetermined firing points."

"Roan, given what I have observed and just heard, you are very close to being relieved of your command of Shey." "Relieved of command? Sir, I do not understand."

Roan was truly surprised by Kellon's comment, somewhat alarmed, and deeply concerned.

Kellon leaned back against the bulkhead and could not suppress his good humor. "Roan, the tactics you structured during those two engagements makes you a prime candidate for promotion for command of a Cruiser."

Roan sat flustered and looking at Kellon with confusion and some apprehension. "Sir, I did only what Zorn recommended I should do. Sir, we are a team and Shey is also part of that team. It might prove somewhat awkward for Guardian Force to make each of us a Cruiser captain."

Shaking his head in amusement, Zorn chided, "Roan, I warned you about running around in a Scout ship attacking Kreel cruisers. If you are required to be punished for your outlandish tactics by being made a Cruiser captain, it would only be proper and fitting punishment."

Shey gleefully joined in the merriment. "Sir, Roan is correct. I cannot be a Cruiser captain. What Cruiser would take orders from a scout ship?"

"I would, if it were Shey giving the orders," Lan inserted.

Sitting back, Zorn's eyebrows arched. "Now that does it! I've been upstaged by a pair of AIs. That isn't fair."

Frowning, Roan was becoming curious. "Commodore, why are you so interested in how I deployed the Scouts? There must also be a good reason why you have invited Shey and Lan to join in our conversation."

Smiling, Kellon sipped from his cup of neab, and studied his two officers. *Insightful observations, Roan. There is indeed a very good reason both Lan and Shey are part of this conversation.*

"When your Scouts attacked two Kreel cruisers and thirty scouts, the Kreel outnumbered and outgunned your force. Even so, using guile, stealth, surprise, and superb timing, you pushed hard your attack on the Kreel. It was, however, only by bringing the AIs directly into the command loop that you were able to achieve the precision timing demanded to survive.

"Gentlemen, Lan, and Shey, the Kreel force we are about to face is greater than twenty times our number. Fortunately, many of those Kreel ships are auxiliaries, and not first-line combat ships. Nevertheless, I intend to adopt some of your successful tactics. I'm going to require the three lead cruiser AIs to synchronize the movement of our forces, make target allocation, and control all firing sequences."

Kellon paused to take a bite of pastry and sipped more neab. Then, frowning in contemplation, he continued. "Lan, I have divided our force into three squadrons of four Cruisers each, and you are the lead Cruiser in Squadron 1. You have listened to how Shey coordinated with her counterparts. Have you any problem in similarly cooperating with Cruisers Lowe and Long?"

"No, Sir. There is no problem in doing so. We can set up tight links where possible and back those hard links up with redirected superluminal communications. Our communications are of a shifting frequency burst technology and are very difficult to detect, let alone intercept. Therefore, coordinating with each other will not be a problem. The same applies to each lead Cruiser using hard links to coordinate with their remaining three ships."

Sitting back, Kellon deeply sighed in relief. "Then, Lan, you are to communicate with Cruisers Long and Lowe. Work out precise methods of coordinating with each other all squadron movements, shared sensor data, target allocation, missile assignments, and firing sequences. Develop a solid procedure and then report back to me at least thirty minutes before the scheduled Commodore's briefing."

"Yes, Sir."

"Now, this brings me to a most interesting topic. Lan, Shey, why don't you both explain to Roan, Zorn, and me just how you both have been meeting with all the other AIs and discussing whatever is happening. Please tell us all about your expanding AI community and your observations about our current tactical situation."

Both Roan and Zorn looked knowingly at each other in silent acknowledgment. Grinning boyishly, Zorn whispered, "I told you so!"

# Chapter Eight:
## Oops

The three squadrons of Kellon's task force were four AU from Scion when Roy contacted Kellon. "Sir, Navigation here. The calculated micro-Jump probability has increased above 99 percent. Although my dear mother would definitely not approve, we are ready to test our ability to perform a micro-Jump. Would it be presumptuous if I were to assume that Lan will be the test Cruiser?"

Working in his conference room, Kellon glanced at the chronometer and then looked toward the com-screen.

"Roy, that assumption would not be presumptuous. Since we have a mathematically verified probability of success, what does your inner gut probability tell you?"

"Sir, my gut feeling is in complete agreement with my dear mother. Micro-Jumps in a heliosphere are not on the recommended to-do list. The AIs, however, see no problem, and are expressing complete confidence. If, however, there is a bug in their Jump algorithms, Lan will not be around to hear them say 'Oops.' On the down side, if Lan isn't around, those on board Lan will also be sorta missing.

"Sir, for the record, I think my dear mother's greatest concern is that her son is serving on a Cruiser, one whose crew is now certified crazy."

Smiling, Kellon asked, "In what way crazy?"

"Well, according to your specific orders, I required each member of our crew and Ambassador Wells to confirm in writing their willingness to participate when Lan makes the first micro-Jump. Sir, no one asked for a transfer. As I said, they are all now certified crazy."

"Roy, I presume you also answered the same question. How did that go?"

"Now that you mention it, I forgot to answer that question. In fact, I'm one of two crewmembers who have not yet answered the aforementioned query, and you are the other."

"Roy, you can officially mark my response, volunteered."

"Blast. There goes my last hope in avoiding the upcoming folly. The entire crew is now verified crazy, including me."

Sitting back, and smiling, Kellon inquired, "Lan, do you agree with Roy? Is your crew crazy?"

"Sir, when Commander Grey, who is our Senior Navigator and Executive Officer, implied the crew was experiencing abnormal psychological tendencies, I dutifully spawned a review of the crew's psychological indicators— including those of Commander Grey. Sir, based on the just-completed analysis, I must respectfully disagree with Commander Grey's assessment. My analytical evaluation of the crew's proficiency confirms they are currently performing well within normal psychological tolerances, even Commander Grey."

"Why, thank you Lan. I'm certain my dear mother will take some solace when she is told of the result of your analysis," Roy retorted.

"Roy, we might as well get the test run behind us. Confirm the task force is in a wide tactical spread, and have all Cruisers begin closely monitoring our ambient temporal-gravitational field. If this doesn't work out, at least Admiral Mer Shawn will have a copious quantity of data for analysis."

"That, Sir, is not an encouraging thought. Grey out."

"Lan, kindly connect Commodore Byrn."

There was only a brief pause before the image of Commodore Byrn appeared on the com-screen. "Commodore Kellon, Byrn here."

"Good afternoon, Commodore. Lan is now preparing to execute our planned experimental micro-Jump. According to theory and calculated probabilities, there shouldn't be a serious problem. Even so, this will be a first, and sometimes the first time doesn't always work as anticipated. If things do go sour, you will be the senior Commodore. In which case, the most important factor you will encounter is dealing with the Arkillians. Having worked closely with them for the past few weeks, I can attest they are professionals. As we planned, they will undoubtedly set up the Kreel for the opening ambuscade. Beyond that, you will be on your own."

Byrn was frowning and clearly troubled. "Kellon, I have repeatedly gone over your battle plan and it's solid. However, as I view the problem, your micro-Jump tactics aren't mandatory to oppose the Kreel and shut down their invasion. I believe we can stop them cold without micro-Jumps. So, why are you so intent on taking the upcoming risk with Lan and his crew?"

Letting out a slow breath, Kellon thoughtfully considered the question. "That's a fair question. Taking out the Kreel cruisers, and thereby stopping the invasion cold, simply isn't good enough, Byrn. If we permit the Kreel main invasion fleet to escape, including those big troop transports, then they will regroup and return. The next time, we would not have surprise on our side, and they would certainly return with even greater firepower. If we can shut them down hard now, taking out both their primary cruisers and their secondary fleet elements, then they will hesitate in returning. That, in turn, will protect Earth. That outcome, in my judgment, makes the risk Lan is prepared to take acceptable and worthwhile."

Byrn's frown deepened. "Kellon, I can understand and appreciate your strategic assessment, but no one has ever survived a micro-Jump in a heliosphere— no one!"

"Acknowledged, but none have ever used multiple Navigation Beacons and had twelve Guardian Cruiser AIs crunching the Jump computations. The odds are not bad, and Lan told me it's only a slightly higher risk than any long-Jump."

Byrn's raised eyebrows and scowl revealed his skepticism. "Kellon, If Lan actually told you that yarn, then I suspect Lan is overdue for a full yard overhaul."

Shaking his head, Kellon smiled. "Byrn, you've always said straight out what you thought. Your comments are well stated, and accepted without offense. Nevertheless, in a few minutes Lan will be making a micro-Jump. So, keep your sensors open and your head down through the turns. Kellon out."

"Sir," Lan inserted, "my review of records indicates that I have not offered a comparison of risk between making long and micro-Jumps. I am therefore perplexed as to why you told Commodore Byrn that I had. Was that an intentional tactical misdirection?"

Kellon chuckled at Lan's perception. "Well Lan, it is better to call it a tactical misdirection than a white lie, since the former sounds so much better. I have known commodore Byrn since we were both cadets at the Academy. He is a good officer, and a good friend. My misdirection was intended to ease his concerns about our little upcoming experiment."

"Sir, undeniably an uncertainty exists in the probability of success, however, given our calculations and the reliability of the data, your comparison was quite correct."

"It was? Now, who would have thought that? Well then, I suggest you ask Lowe to confirm that fact with Commodore Byrn. Lowe's confirmation might go far to ease his concerns."

The com-screen suddenly brightened. "Navigation here. Commodore, with your authorization; micro-Jump in five minutes. All Guardian Cruisers are monitoring as ordered," Roy reported.

"Kellon here. Navigation, I do authorize the micro-Jump. Set Condition 2 and proceed."

Closing his working files, Kellon stood, thinking, *Well, the proper place for me during the test is in CAC.*

The battle stations alarm had just ceased echoing throughout the passageways, and Kellon was sitting in his Command Chair in CAC. Looking about the CAC, he felt a sense of association and pride. In his opinion, Lan was the best Cruiser in Guardian Force, and his crew was the best of the best. He knew every captain thought the same thing— but that was only as it should be.

Scanning the tactical plot, he observed each squadron had formed up using a three-sided pyramid formation, and the task force's tactical formation was now a dispersed echelon with Lan leading. They were twelve Guardian Cruisers very far from home, and they were definitely heading into harm's way.

The general intercom activated and Roy's steady voice called out, "Navigation here. Jump in one minute, mark!"

As the minute slowly unwound, the CAC grew hushed and even small sounds echoed.

"Navigation here, Jump in nine, eight, seven, six— "

"Break— hold at six seconds! Lan here. An unacceptable imbalance in temporal-mass stabilization is detected. Performing prerequisite adjustments in ship field harmonics. Estimating thirty seconds delay."

Kellon could sense the oscillating tensions in the crew, rising and then suddenly dropping, only to rise again. Looking toward where Roy's team was working, he observed everyone intently focused on their sensors and consoles.

"Lan here. All temporal-mass stabilization parameters are again within tolerances. Navigation, you are cleared to resume the count."

"Navigation here. Affirming, clear to resume the count. Stand by for Jump, six, five, four, three, two, one, Jump!"

As the sensors flickered off-line, Kellon felt a stomach twisting and nauseous physical sensation in his middle. He gritted his teeth. Even as he did, he observed equipment power levels dropping and some systems automatically shutting down. He could hear alarms sounding in the CAC and surrounding areas. They were in trouble, and he knew that damage control teams would be on the move in response.

"Lan here. We are experiencing a temporal instability in our containment fields. All Scout AIs are now linked in and assisting in maintaining ship's power output and helping to restore ship's full longitudinal-temporal stability."

As quickly as the discomfiture in his middle had begun, it now ceased, and normal power levels began returning to the CAC. Sensors began automatically coming on line. In response, there was a sudden exchange of murmurs among the CAC teams.

"Navigation, Kellon here. Report!"

"Navigation here. We are now out of Jump, status Copper. We have exited precisely one AU from our entry point. On first glance, I believe we have actually survived."

"Lan here. Sir, we have experienced some non-critical system failures. We encountered unanticipated fluctuations in the starboard longitudinal-temporal harmonic resonator; however, the underlying problem is identified and now isolated. It is judged correctable. Within several hours, I estimate damage control can make all appropriate and necessary repairs. All systems should then be fully restored."

"Lan, what went wrong?" Kellon asked.

Sir, the micro-Jump parameters induced an unanticipated differential energy surge. That in turn overloaded our temporal harmonic resonators, which were not tuned for such boundary surges. The resonators are being retuned and should not pose a problem when we perform the next micro-Jump."

"Then, Lan, you are reporting that we can repeat a micro-Jump without reducing you to smoking ruins?"

"Sir, unless another intentional misdirection is involved, precisely speaking, 'smoking ruins' is an inaccurate description.

Internal diagnostics indicate status Copper, but there are no fires or smoke. Sir, within thirty minutes, my combat status will be upgraded to Bronze. Additionally, my analysis indicates a successful micro-Jump can now be safely performed. A repeat of the test would most certainly yield a refinement of an interesting tactical capability."

"Sir, Navigation here. I agree with Lan's assessment. We did survive the first experiment, at least sorta survived. Therefore, I second Lan's recommendation. We can do this."

Roy's enthusiasm was obvious. Shaking his head dubiously, Kellon sighed. "Navigation, Roy you are the Navigator. If you affirm that Lan can make another micro-Jump without further degeneration of his combat readiness, then I will authorize a second test."

"Sir, based on what I am seeing here, I do so affirm. Shucks, I think my dear mother would even approve of a second trial Jump."

"Navigation, in that case, you may proceed with preparations for the second test. This time, get it right!

"Tactical, Lorn, you have the CAC. Set Condition 3, and oversee the work required to bring Lan back to status Gold. Once our task force arrives, set Condition 2 and prepare for the second Jump. Proceed."

"Tactical here. Yes, Sir, acknowledging Tactical has the CAC."

# Chapter Nine:
## Contact

The brown and golden sphere of Scion was distant, yet still sufficiently near to appear as a bright crescent suspended in space. Like fleeting shadows in the surrounding darkness, the twelve Guardian Cruisers were poised in an echelon formation, alert and fully prepared for battle. After three days of hunkering down, the waiting was abruptly over.

Looking up from his console, Lorn reported, "Tactical here, Contact! The Kreel are crossing the heliopause. Referencing the system's primary, Kreel cruiser force bearing 227 degrees true, and elevation is 32 degrees. It's a large force. Now attempting to count propulsion signatures."

Kellon was in the CAC, and he keyed the commodore's band. "Gentlemen, heads up, the Kreel are entering the system in force. We will remain in our current position and allow the Kreel to sort out their battle components. We may have a day or more before the cruisers arrive at Scion. Maintain your units at Condition 3, full stealth. Kellon out."

Switching to an internal communications band, he inquired, "Tactical, Lorn, do you want me to bring your group to a modified Condition 3?"

"Tactical here. Sir, a full staff at this time would be helpful," Lorn responded.

"Lan, alert our tactical personnel, and set a modified Condition 3. Keep it a quiet notification of personnel."

"Yes, Sir."

Like the Scout ships, most Guardian Cruisers operated independently. There were exceptions, such as during planetary defense actions, where Guardian command tended to organize Cruisers in groups of five Cruisers each. Now, with twelve Cruisers operating together in the task force, one of Kellon's concerns was that every Cruiser was well coordinated.

"Lan, confirm a tight link with Long and Lowe, and as planned, coordinate all tactical data through those two lead Cruisers. Let's verify everyone knows what the others are observing. Alert me to any problems."

"Yes, Sir."

Kellon turned his attention to the tactical plot displaying the solar system's four quadrants. "Lan, select and center quadrant three as the main tactical plot."

As Lan adjusted the tactical plot, Kellon observed the light blue line drawn horizontally across the midpoint of the plot. That line represented the Ecliptic plane. Above and across the top of the plot were displayed the azimuth bearings, denoted in ten-degree increments. An expanding cluster of red symbols, looking like a spreading angry infection, was located above the blue line. While the Kreel cruisers may have been the first detected, apparently additional Kreel ships were closely following them into Scion's heliosphere.

"Tactical, where are the nine Kreel fast-attack ships that were already in the system?" Kellon asked.

"Tactical here. During the past hours, they had moved near to where the Kreel entered the system. They are now commingled with the larger Kreel force."

"Tactical, do we have any contact with any Kreel ship or probe other than those located in quadrant three?"

"No, Sir, all detected Kreel units are now located in quadrant three."

"Tactical, is there an estimated time of arrival at Scion?"

"Sir, I'm currently isolating the Kreel cruiser propulsion signatures. Their Doppler indicates a closing rate of 100 lights, or approximately ninety standard hours out. I, however, advise caution since those cruisers can move at 200 lights if they pick up their heels."

Kellon's fingers flickered over the controls on the arm of his command chair and came to rest on Kur's communications button. He paused for a moment, and then pressed the button. "Honored Kur, Kellon here."

There was a slight pause, and then an Arkillian responded, "Honored Kellon, this is Council Member Ca. Council Member Kur is currently sleeping. How may I assist you?"

"Honored Ca, it is good to hear your voice once more. I am calling to inform you the Kreel invasion fleet has entered into Scion's system. If you are ready, I am able to provide the vector information to the main group."

"The Kreel are here!" Ca exclaimed excitedly. "Rin, hurry and wake Kur, the Kreel fleet is here, hurry! Honored Kellon, please transmit the coordinate vectors."

Passing the vectors to Ca, and waiting for Kur, he watched as the red target icons on the tactical plot continued to expand.

"Tactical here, the Kreel are continuing to enter the heliosphere in force. The total number of ships cannot yet be determined. The forward element is, however, becoming better defined. That group consists of a combined force of cruisers and fast-attack ships. There is a second and much larger group forming well behind the cruisers. The advancing cruiser force is now approaching Scion at 120 lights, and their current ETA is seventy hours."

Ca overheard Lorn's update, and asked, "Honored Kellon, what does 120 lights mean?"

"Honored Ca, 1,000 lights equals the speed of light. Therefore, 120 lights represent 12 percent of the speed of light. We merely use the term 'lights' as a short hand notation when stating a ships speed."

"Thank you, Honored Kellon," Ca said.

"Commodore Kellon, I am now here," Kur breathlessly said. "The Kreel fleet has arrived. Is that correct?"

"Yes, Honored Kur. The Kreel invasion fleet has entered Scion's system in great force. We are currently monitoring an increasing number of Kreel ships. It appears the first attack wave consists of a combined force of cruisers and fast-attack ships. Given their current velocity, they are about seventy hours from Scion."

"Perhaps three days? That will help," responded Kur.

"Be warned, Council Member Kur, you should be wary of the time estimate. If they choose, those cruisers can move much faster."

"Understood, we will therefore plan for their arrival in two days. That should give us ample time. As we planned, Scion will be ready to offer the Kreel a most tempting bait. Kur out."

"Navigation, Kellon here. In accordance with our battle plan, draw a line between Scion and the center of the Kreel cruiser force. Mark a position on that line 900,000 kilometers from Scion and identify that location as Mark 1. Coordinate with Long and Lowe a tactical move of the task force to Mark 1. We are to arrive on that location in twelve hours. Once on Mark 1, maintain that station."

"Navigation here. Yes, Sir, proceeding as ordered."

"Tactical, Kellon here. Continue working up a detailed tactical plot of the Kreel cruisers. When you've achieved results that you're satisfied with, notify me.

"Navigation, Roy, you have the CAC."

Looking up, Roy nodded, "Yes, Sir, Navigation has the CAC."

Entering his quarters, Kellon walked over to his desk and sat down. Looking up, he examined the three-dimensional image on the bulkhead, admiring the image of the Earth and her large moon. The gravity-coupled and sharply contrasting spheres were bright crescents, their greater volumes being concealed in shadows. Lan was in the foreground of the image, and he was wearing his proud parade colors of gold and white.

Kellon was fond of the image, and he truly thought Earth was beautiful. Smiling inwardly, and remembering having the opportunity of taking Eurie to Paris for a glass of wine, he decided that someday he would return and explore that intriguing world. That it might actually prove to be humanity's fabled first home only increased his desire to visit Earth. What was already certain was that he had come to love Earth's vast and rich treasure-house of literature and music.

Now, however, his primary goal was the destruction of the Kreel fleet and continuity of life for his task force. His affirmation of a future visit to Earth served to shore up his own confidence of surviving the coming battle. "Lan, heads up, the game is afoot!"

"Yes, Holmes," Lan playfully replied. "Sir, according to the Intelligence estimates, we are numerically outnumbered by twenty-to-one. It does pose an interesting tactical problem."

Kellon grinned. Lan hadn't missed his opening literary reference. Continuing with the exchange, he replied, "That's an accurate numerical assessment, Watson. It is indeed an interesting tactical problem.

"However, the Kreel armada includes about one hundred and fifty cargo and fifty troop ships. The cargo ships are not combat-capable. Therefore, they represent merely targets of opportunity."

"Sir, I agree, the Kreel cruisers and fast-attack ships represent our real threat. The heavy ground-assault ships that carry the troops are also well-armed."

"Agreed, those ground-assault ships do pose a tactical problem. However, their immediate threat potential is of a secondary nature. The Kreel cruisers and Tuen class ships are the real backbone of the Kreel offensive armada. Without the cruiser force, the remaining Kreel fleet is exposed and vulnerable."

"Sir, am I to understand it is your intention to utterly destroy every Kreel ship in their invasion fleet?"

"That is correct Lan. It is my intention to gain complete tactical dominance within the heliosphere. Our orders are to destroy the Kreel fleet, and I intend to strictly follow those orders."

Sitting back, Kellon considered the tactical problem circumstances had placed before him. During a century of space warfare, he had learned through bitter experience that any battle in space was unpredictable, and such battles were more dangerous within than outside of a solar system. He knew the upcoming battle would be decisive— one way or another. There was a reason why there were no lifeboats on either Kreel or Guardian cruisers; none was required, because in their space warfare no quarter was asked or given.

# Chapter Ten:
## Pre-Battle Report

Kellon's mission was to aggressively take the battle to the enemy, then engage and destroy that enemy. Survival depended on communications, mobility, firepower, and especially surprise, and the master key that unlocked the advantage of surprise was stealth. It was Kellon's intent to capitalize on his stealth advantage while exploiting tactical misdirection and focused firepower. He knew two days would pass quickly; in the meantime, he had a personal matter that required his immediate attention.

"Lan, connect me to Captain Eurie. This will be a personal and private conversation. That means that I don't want you, Shey, or any other AI listening in. Do you understand?"

There was a slight pause before Lan responded. "Yes, Sir, it is a personal call and private."

"Correct. Lan, be certain you notify all the AIs what a personal call means, and stress the word *private*. Once the personal call terminates, you may again resume monitoring."

"Yes, Sir."

As Kellon watched the display over his desk, the image of Earth and her moon shimmered and sparkled, transforming into Eurie's smiling countenance.

"Why, Kellon, this is a wonderful surprise. Lent has just informed me this is a personal call and the AIs will not monitor what we say. Should I be blushing?"

Kellon shook his head and leaned back smiling. "Eurie, I'm just trying to keep the children from listening in. I've learned from Susie that everything the AIs overhear immediately becomes a matter of intense interest and discussion among the entire AI community. It seems the programmers failed to consider gossip when they developed the basic Artificial Intelligence Matrix."

"Gossip? That AI problem is one I had never even considered."

"Well, now you can begin to consider it. Susie has learned from William that the AIs apparently find human behavior a topic of great fascination. They apparently discuss it for hours. I might add, she also was informed your personal behavior is of extra-special interest to them."

"Kellon, you cannot be serious,"

"It's the unvarnished truth. We have been harboring a group of voyeurs. Innocent, but voyeurs nevertheless. I have just instructed Lan to inform all the AIs that personal means private and they are not to monitor or record such communications."

"Well, thank you for alerting me to some interesting AI foibles. I never considered them behaving as a community. When did all this social interaction between our AIs evolve?"

"To the best of my understanding, it began while our squadron was guarding Earth. With five Cruisers, twenty Scout ships, and of course the real troublemaker, Susie's AI William, all working closely together on a daily basis, we should have anticipated the development. It appears Susie's William is the catalyst and was pivotal in the development of the AI community concept. Susie informed me he began exhibiting unique behavior, shortly following his upgrade. There were some warning flags, but we seem to have overlooked them."

"What type of warning flags?"

"Do you remember Shey and William joining their resources on Glas Dinnein and bottling the William & Shey Root Beer?"

Eurie began to laugh softly, "Yes, I do remember. That tidbit of AI information spread through Guardian Force like wild fires through tall dry grass. The nice part of that story is they make a very good root beer, at least I think it tastes very good."

"Eurie, we have perhaps two days before we engage the Kreel.

I'm calling because I wanted to talk with you before the combat begins. I believe I have a handle on how to win this battle, but as you well know there's a wide gulf between forming a battle plan and executing that plan."

"Kellon, we have good ships, good crews, and a host of advantages the Kreel do not have. I frankly believe we're about to trample all over the Kreel's swaggering egos."

"Ah, I knew there was a sound purpose for calling you. May I quote you in my daily log?"

"But of course!"

"Eurie, when this is over, we need to take some time for putting our own lives in order. I am still looking forward to that glass of wine when we arrive home on Glas Dinnein."

"Dear Kellon, you may be able to evade the Kreel, but you will not be able to evade buying me that glass of wine. Be well advised I have already entered that appointment into my schedule. If Admiral Secretary Eryan Kyrie, Fleet Admiral Mer Shawn, Admirals Ron Cloud and Dylan Cord, singly or together, attempt to send Lan and you out again before that date, then I will begin a mutiny! I would even wager Lan, Lent, and Shey would help, not to mention all the other AIs."

Kellon chuckled, raising his eyebrows in feigned surprise, "Eurie, it's a good thing I blocked this call from being monitored. I believe there are sufficient grounds for a court-martial floating around. If Fleet Admiral Mer Shawn heard one of his favorite Cruiser captains threatening to mutiny over a glass of wine, it would absolutely ruin his busy day."

"Kellon, you fully understand what I am saying. Commodore, you have a date and you had better keep it," she teased.

"Eurie, Be advised, if Fleet Admiral Mer Shawn were to order Lan and me to the Kreel Hub, I would first arrange the detour required to have that glass of wine."

Kellon's mood then shifted, becoming more serious. "I will be focused on the developing tactical problem during the upcoming hours. Nevertheless, if you have anything you need to discuss, professionally or privately, do not hesitate to contact me."

"Of that you need not worry. Eurie out."

The image of Eurie flickered and was gone. Once more, the serene vista of Earth and her moon appeared on the bulkhead display, and Kellon sat back, considering what he must do next.

"Lan, connect me with Commander Roan."

"Yes, Sir, connecting."

The screen blurred and Roan's visage looked up toward Kellon, "Sir?"

"Roan, I need to discuss with you my intentions regarding taking out the cargo ships. As the task force Scout ship leader, I want you to have Shey initiate an analysis using the available facilities of all the Scout AIs. Have them explore all of our Kreel records and determine the most critical points on Kreel cargo ships. I want to do the most damage possible— hopefully, full destruction— with the fewest medium or light missiles possible."

Roan's forehead furrowed in concentration, "Sir, I notice you have not mentioned heavy missiles. Are you planning to assign the Scout ships the task of destroying the cargo ships?"

"That is my current intention."

"Yes, Sir. We will immediately begin the analysis."

Kellon leaned forward and his attitude remained serious. "Roan, when Shey and the girls complete that task, then have them repeat the process with those lumbering ground attack ships, the modern Kreel versions of Monstro. They look like tough hard targets if only because of their size and mass. See what the girls can work out using medium missiles, and then do the same analysis using heavy missiles. Then look at an optimum mix of heavy and medium missiles. The tactical goal is utter destruction of those ships while using the fewest missiles.

"Pay particular attention to any intelligence we may have regarding where they store munitions for the heavy ground attack weapons they are carrying. Hopefully, if that data exists in our database, we can hit those magazines and initiate secondary detonations. You also should look at their life support systems as targets of interest. If they can't breathe, then they can't fight."

As he listened to Kellon's instruction, Roan began to frown. "Yes, Sir. Is there anything more?"

"Yes, there's one more item. I want you to turn the girls' attention to the troop ships. Each of those Kreel troop ships is carrying about fourteen thousand fully equipped infantry. According to Intelligence estimates, there are more than fifty of those ships. I don't want one of those troop ships to reach Scion's surface or to return to the Kreel Hub.

"Roan, you have access to forty-eight Scout ship AIs to work on the problem. When you have the answers, contact me— regardless of the hour. Kellon out."

Kellon moved on to instructions for his AI.

"Lan, prepare a pre-battle report. Classify it Black Hole. Direct it to Admiral Ron Cloud at Guardian Intelligence. Inform him of the time the Kreel fleet entered into the system. Advise him the Intelligence estimates regarding the size and composition of the Kreel fleet appear validated. We will send precise information once it becomes available. Copy the message to Fleet Admiral Mer Shawn and to Admiral Dylan Cord."

"Yes, Sir."

Guardian Intelligence had estimated more than seven hundred thousand Kreel infantry were on board those troop ships. He forcibly pushed conflicting thoughts of right and wrong out of his mind. His job was to stop a Kreel invasion and prevent the killing of millions of Arkillians. During the upcoming combat, many living beings would perish. His job was to be certain those shattered lives were Kreel, not Arkillians or those of the Guardian Force.

Standing, Kellon departed his quarters. As he walked through Lan's passageways, he tried to let go of his inner stress. What he could accomplish was already in motion. His effort to refine the tactics depended on how the Kreel maneuvered and responded to the bait the Arkillians were going to dangle. He understood ships and lives alike were about to enter the maw of space warfare and the outcome of the battle was far from decided. Two days?

Taking a deep breath, he mused, *One day at a time, just one day at a time.*

# Chapter Eleven:
## Tactical Summary

Skilled crews and intelligent engineering were powerfully and precisely containing and controlling the hot fires of enormous energies within the protective hulls of twelve sleek Guardian Cruisers. The Cruisers represented the product of countless millions of hours of ingenious labor, an effort mandated for survival over millenniums of interstellar warfare. The Cruisers blended into their harsh environment, twelve unseen and undetectable phantasms.

As the Kreel cruiser force approached, Kellon studied its formation, analyzing the developing Kreel battle tactics. Those tactics were pure Kreel in their character; at their core was brute force and overwhelming firepower.

"Tactical here. Contact. The Arkillian defense fleet is now entering space near Scion. We are now monitoring twenty sub-light capable cruisers."

Given Lorn's contact report, Kellon knew that before a single missile was launched, the battle for Scion had begun. As he observed the tactical plot, the Arkillian force overtly moved out from Scion and deployed into a tactical spread, directly challenging the approaching Kreel force.

"Tactical, Kellon here. Do the Arkillian cruisers have escorts?"

"Tactical here. We are currently tracking several hundred small Arkillian fighters— like those on the Nest Ship near earth. We do not have a precise count at this time."

Kellon turned back toward the tactical plot and noted the Arkillians were forming into four battle groups of five cruisers each. As he observed, he saw icons appear that represented the fighters supporting each group.

Kellon glanced quickly around the CAC and noted everyone was focused and busy at his task. He turned his attention back to the tactical plot.

"Tactical here. The Arkillian cruisers are now in battle formation and holding 50,000 kilometers from Scion. As planned, they have taken positions squarely facing the approaching Kreel force."

Misdirection was the key ingredient in Kellon's battle plan, and it called for the Arkillians to set the Kreel up for a fatal decisive strike from a powerful concealed foe. Given the Kreel's normally aggressive behavior, the poised and battle-ready Arkillian cruiser force was offering the Kreel an irresistible lure. They were the ripe low-hanging fruit intended to draw the Kreel into a fatal cul-de-sac.

The Arkillians' precise movement into defensive positions had impressed Kellon. He knew the Arkillian cruiser force was technologically inferior and did not represent a meaningful threat to the Kreel. What most impressed Kellon was the Arkillians also understood the capability and firepower of the Kreel; yet, they had come out from Scion ready to do battle.

With the tactical geometry now set, Kellon began to adjust his force accordingly.

"Lan, we are redefining the location of Mark 1. Construct a line between the centers of the Kreel and the Arkillian cruiser forces. Mark a point on that line 900,000 kilometers in advance of the leading edge of the Arkillian cruisers. Define that point Mark 1."

"Yes, Sir."

In every meaningful aspect, the Arkillian technology was more than a thousand years behind the Kreel warfare design curves. Adding to the imbalance, the Kreel were ruthlessly efficient and vastly more experienced in such combat. Therefore, Kellon was preparing to move to provide a blocking force— one assuring the Kreel did not reach the waiting Arkillian cruisers.

"Navigation, Kellon here. Adjust the Task Force position to the newly defined Mark 1 position. Maintain station on that location until otherwise ordered."

"Navigation here, now shifting to the new Mark 1."

Silent and deadly, Kellon's three squadrons slowly maneuvered, taking a position interposing their Guardian force directly between the approaching Kreel and the defending Arkillians. They were set at Condition 2, battle ready.

"Tactical, confirm the structure of the Kreel cruiser force."

"Tactical here. The Kreel cruiser force consists of nine Kreel heavy cruisers and twenty-seven fast-attack ships, six of which are Tuen Class."

*If we had not destroyed the Kreel cruisers near Earth,* Kellon mused, *the Kreel cruiser force might be twice its strength. Every little bit helps.* He knew the approaching Kreel force must tactically respond to the waiting Arkillians. If they followed their standard tactics, they would divide their force into three groups, a center and two flanking thrusts. The Kreel dividing their main force was central to his preferred battle plan.

As time passed and the Kreel did not alter their formation, Kellon began to become concerned. *Why,* he mused, *are they waiting? What's holding them back?*

Sitting quietly, he studied the tactical plot. His hands were firmly gripping the arms of his command chair, and the fingers on his right hand were poised over the communications buttons. Suddenly, Kellon observed the Kreel commanders finally responding to the lure, and a broad smile broke across his features. He released a breath he hadn't realized he was holding. *That's more like it,* he thought. *The Kreel have swallowed the bait whole.*

The Kreel split their cruiser force into three separate groups. The center group was slowing, permitting the two flanking groups to move out into their tactical spread. The center force, with its two flanking battle groups, provided the Kreel with a strong center and two pincer forces, all three groups focused on the defending Arkillians. Once the flanking ships had reached their tactical spread, then all three groups would smoothly sweep forward, closing with the advancing center upon their intended prey. From long experience, Kellon knew the Kreel would immediately launch their coordinated attack from their maximum effective heavy missile range. That range was most likely well beyond the maximum effective range of the Arkillian missiles.

As the Kreel took the bait, Kellon accordingly adjusted his force. "Lan, we need to define a tactical plane. Select the line between the Kreel and Arkillian cruisers as the first axis of the plane. Then rotate the plane so all three Kreel cruiser groups are on that plane."

"Sir, the tactical plane is being displayed."

"Lan, now extrapolate and display the track lines for each Kreel group. Use standard historical Kreel tactics as the basis of your estimate. Display."

"Sir, the data is being displayed."

"Good. Now, identify the closest point on the Kreel centerline to our position, and redefine that point as Mark 1. Next, compute the elapsed time required for the Kreel center to reach that point. Then, using that elapsed time, compute the predicted positions of the flanking groups at that time on their extrapolated tracks. Designate those two points Mark 2 and Mark 3."

Studying the plot, Kellon waited for Lan to complete his instructions. Then he continued, "About points Mark 1, Mark 2, and Mark 3, construct tactical spheres whose radius is the effective range of our medium missiles."

Kellon sat back and studied the result of his and Lan's handiwork. He nodded his head in approval.

"Navigation, Kellon here. Adjust the squadrons' ambush positions as follows. Move Squadron 1 directly above Mark 1 and on the surface of the tactical sphere. Squadron 2 is to move directly below Mark 2 and on the surface of the tactical sphere. Squadron 3 is to move directly below Mark 3 and on the surface of the tactical sphere. Proceed with the defined deployment."

"Navigation here, proceeding with deployment as ordered." Kellon's ambuscade was pure stealth warfare. It was misdirection, ambush, surprise, and it culminated with concentrated overwhelming firepower. Kellon's tactics did not involve a sense of a fair fight or incorporate mercy. It was, by design, intended to obliterate the Kreel cruiser force, and the Kreel were unknowingly moving directly toward a waiting deadly foe.

More than twenty minutes had passed since Lan had monitored the Arkillians' formal challenge sent to the approaching Kreel force. That challenge had gone unanswered, and the longer the Kreel delayed in responding, the greater was the intended slur.

As the forward bulkhead monitor blossomed into vibrant colors, Kellon turned his attention to the monitor. The image of Council Member Kur in his full formal robes of office appeared, and he was standing. The intercepted Arkillian transmission was on the standard Kreel challenge frequency, and the Kreel were undoubtedly receiving the transmission. As normal diplomatic courtesy dictated, Kur was speaking in the Kreel language.

"I am Council Member Kur, an elder member of Scion's Ruling Council. I am calling the officer in charge of the Kreel force now visiting our sovereign space. We naturally cordially welcome visitors. As required by our mutual treaties, the Kreel Hub has regretfully made no formal request for your visit. I therefore ask whoever is in charge of your force to make themselves known, so we might better understand the purpose of your visit."

There came no response. The very lack of a prompt formal response only exacerbated the intentional insult, underscoring the expressed Kreel contempt for the Arkillians. Apparently unruffled by the implied insult, Kur stoically stood and waited for the eventual Kreel response.

"Tactical, Kellon here. What is your current tactical summary?"

"Tactical here. Sir, the Kreel cruiser force is divided in three groups and continuing their advance. Their tactical formation is the "jaws of death." Each group consists of three cruisers and nine fast-attack ships. The center force is moving directly toward the defending Arkillian force. The two flanking groups are moving in precise unison with the center."

Observing the Tactical plot, Kellon watched three golden icons representing his three squadrons move steadily into their separate intercept ambush positions at Mark 1, Mark 2, and Mark 3. Each Guardian squadron of four Cruisers was now positioned to oppose three Kreel cruisers and nine fast-attack ships.

Lorn continued his summary, "The Kreel maneuvering indicates the Kreel are unaware of our presence. The Arkillian Ruling Council wanted to avoid any possibility of their commanders inadvertently giving away our presence, and it has not informed the commanders on the defending ships that we are here."

The combined firepower of the approaching Kreel force was massive, and Kellon knew any one of the three Kreel groups was more than capable of quickly and utterly destroying the small opposing Arkillian force. Undoubtedly, the Kreel and Arkillians in the converging fleets were also fully aware of the probable outcome of the pending battle. As he watched the Arkillians maneuver, Kellon acknowledged their behavior provided ample witness to their raw courage. By their very opposition, it was obvious they were courageously prepared to lay down their lives in defense of Scion.

"Tactical here! Detecting a shift in Kreel maneuvering. The center Kreel group has reduced its forward speed to 10 lights. The flanking elements are also slowing and are remaining synchronized."

Kellon sat musing, *If they are slowing down to 10 lights, then they have a beneficial reason to delay the battle. I would wager a brew the Kreel will first respond to Kur, and then immediately close and attack.*

"Navigation, Kellon here. Transfer control of all further task force maneuvers to Lan and the two lead AIs."

"Navigation, acknowledging transfer of maneuvering control to the lead AIs," Roy answered.

"Lan here. Acknowledging tactical control of task force maneuvering."

"Tactical here, continuing the summary, the heavy ground attack and troop ship formations are located well behind the advancing Kreel cruiser force. The cargo ships and their light escorts are even further back, near midway to the heliopause. Based on their deployment spacing within the heliosphere, the Kreel plan of battle appears to be to first dispatch the Arkillian cruiser opposition, and then soften up the designated surface target areas with laser bombardment from cruisers and fast-attack ships. Then it appears they intend to follow up the bombardment with the ground-assault. Given how far back the heavy ground-assault ships are located, the apparent Kreel intent is to bombard Scion for a day or more before the heavy ground-assault and troop ships arrive. Cargo ships are at least five days from any resupply effort. Sir, that completes the tactical summary."

# Chapter Twelve:
# **Moment of Attack**

"Fire Control, Kellon here. Shift weapon allocation, target assignments, and firing sequences to Lan."

"Fire Control here, confirming transfer of control to Lan."

"Lan here. Acknowledging receiving Fire Control."

As Kellon analyzed the approaching Kreel cruiser center group, his countenance revealed his intense concentration, and he was frowning.

"Lan, target assignment follows. Identify and separate the center Kreel group into three subgroups. Each subgroup will consist of one Kreel cruiser and three fast-attack ships. Now, allocate one subgroup to each of the following: Lar, Lent, and yourself.

"Each named Cruiser is to allocate four heavy missiles against its assigned Kreel cruiser, and two medium missiles each against the three assigned fast-attack ships. Lawrence will provide the crossfire component of our ambush of the center group.

"Direct Lawrence to allocate one heavy missile against each of the three Kreel cruisers, and one medium missile against each of the nine fast-attack ships. All missiles are to be set passive-active and are to go active at 80 percent of ordered run length. Are there any questions?"

"Lan here, understood. There are no questions. I am making target missile allocations within our squadron as ordered."

"Lan, confirm Squadron 1 is deployed in its combat spread formation, has passive missile locks on all assigned targets, and each Kreel ship is fully targeted."

"Sir, confirming Squadron 1 is tactically deployed. All assigned missiles have passive locks on their designated targets, and each Kreel ship is targeted, as ordered."

"Lan, order the same targeting process with Squadron 2 and Squadron 3. Confirm their missiles are set Condition 2 and passive-active homing."

Kellon watched the tactical plot with interest as the Kreel force continued its slow methodical approach at 10 lights. The Kreel were well-deployed and predictably precise in their movements.

"Lan here. Confirming Squadron 1, 2, and 3 are tactically deployed, and all assigned missiles have passive locks, as ordered. All squadrons are on their adjusted firing points and firing sequences are now synchronized within twenty-five seconds. We are making slight positional adjustments to refine the firing sequence. Standing by for Condition 1."

Kellon turned looking toward Roy, "Navigation, what is our status for the micro-Jump?"

"Sir, all Cruisers have completed the required tuning adjustment to their Jump resonators and are reporting Jump ready. The three Navigation Beacons are in sync, all squadrons are matched, and status for the designated micro-Jump is now 99.997 percent. Standing by, waiting for precision adjustments for final Jump exit coordinates."

"Navigation, Roy keep me advised of any problems that develop."

Roy glanced back to Kellon with a twinkle in his eyes and a slight smile.

"Yes, Sir. However, given no one has ever before attempted to perform a synchronized micro-Jump, with three squadrons consisting of twelve Cruisers, into a hot battle zone within a planetary system, I am not anticipating anything unexpected."

In spite of his inner tensions, Kellon was barely able to contain a smile. Instead of smiling, he merely nodded his head in acknowledgment.

"Tactical here, the Kreel are maintaining their velocity of 10 lights. They are continuing to steadily close the jaws of their vise on the Arkillian fleet."

At that moment, a second communications screen flickered and swirled into brightness on the forward bulkhead, and an image of a Kreel flag officer adorned in a full dress uniform appeared. Kellon noted the meritorious decorations on his elaborate harness were impressive, it being festooned with numerous brilliant jewels and medallions. Even for a Kreel, he was large, and his yellow eyes were serpentlike. As his image glared malevolently out of the screen, his fangs were exposed, and he mockingly snarled.

First impressions carry their own meaning, and Kellon carefully studied the Kreel officer's image. *That body language is not hard to read,* Kellon thought. *Even before the Kreel says one word, Kur has the answer to his diplomatic overture.*

Belying the obvious attitude his expression declared, the Kreel officer addressed Kur diplomatically in the Arkillian language.

"Council Member Kur. Perhaps you remember me. I am Krogh, Grand Commander representing the Kreel Hub. We met perhaps a hundred years ago on Scion."

When the officer mentioned his name, Kur noticeably stiffened. "Yes, Grand Commander, I do well remember your visit. With all due respect, might I ask you the reason a Kreel fleet is entering Scion's sovereign space without first requesting our permission for your visit?"

"Counter Measures, Kellon here. Attempt to obtain a fix on that Kreel transmission. Where is the Kreel Commander located?" Dropping his veneer of verbal politeness, Krogh responded in a low snarling tone.

"Council Member Kur, I could also ask you why you have put into space twenty of your little cruisers and several hundred of your toy fighters to greet us?"

"Honored Grand Commander Krogh, our ships merely represent an honor guard for such a noteworthy and august occasion. Once more, I ask you plainly— what is the purpose of your ships' entering Scion's sovereign space?"

Krogh paused for a moment before answering Kur, and his face took on an unmistakable sneer.

"Council Member Kur, I believe it is best that we skip past the introductory banter and dispense with the formalities. The Kreel Hub has decided to honor Scion and all of its inhabitants, by incorporating Scion and its associated planets into our Empire and greater domain. In fact, the Hub has declared this solar system is now Kreel sovereign space. You will therefore immediately order your belittling honor guard to return to Scion and land. If you hesitate, they will be promptly and utterly destroyed."

Kur stood resolute, calm, and notably defiant. Some might even suggest he had a slight smile, as his countenance even brightened. "Grand Commander Krogh, have you actually come all the way from the Kreel Hub merely to die even further debased and in shame? I suggest you take your filthy and polluted crossbreed horde and immediately depart Scion's sovereign space. This is our first and our last warning."

The Kreel officer's face first expressed his surprise and shock. He had just encountered the totally unexpected. Rather than the fear or pleading he anticipated, Kur stood contemptuously defying the entire Kreel Empire. As Krogh's surprise slowly evaporated, his countenance transformed from its previous sneer, distorting into an expression of pure fury and outrage.

During his long career, Kellon had seen a number of Kreel commanders lose emotional control and reach the point of rage, but he could not remember observing a Kreel commander of any rank immediately, utterly, and completely lose his emotional control— as did Krogh. Kur's sharp retort had hit some vital nerve deep within the Kreel officer's arrogant pride, and Kur instantaneously obtained his desired result. Kellon grinned, thinking, *Well done, Kur. That skewered him where it hurts. Hopefully, that will goad him into acting rashly.*

Speaking in the guttural snarls of the Kreel language, Krogh spat, "Kur, as you are well aware, I am an elder member of the Military Hub! Your scurrilous defamation and insult of the Kreel is unpardonable. If you are so unfortunate as to survive this day, you and each of your surviving nest mates will linger to regret your slander and mockery of the Kreel and my dwelling. This I now swear!"

The screen showing the Kreel officer went blank, the Kreel transmission having been abruptly cut off. Kur's image remained on the bulkhead screen for a moment more, before it also went blank. As it went blank, Kellon noted Kur was smiling.

"Counter Measures here, tracing completed, transmission location was in the center cruiser. It is Lan's designated primary target."

"Tactical here, The Kreel cruisers are accelerating. They are up to 15 lights and still accelerating. Currently indicating 685 percent of optimal medium firing range."

"Lan, keep us in tight synchronization. When medium-missile effective range is at 100 percent or less, initiate Condition 1 for all squadrons."

"Lan here. Confirming, when targets reach 100 percent of effective medium missile range, I am to synchronize all Cruisers and set Condition 1."

"Tactical here, they are adding on more speed, currently at 20 lights. Targets are at 435 percent optimal medium missile range and closing."

Except for the occasional click of a key, the CAC was silent, and both communication screens remained dark. The red icons on the tactical plot indicated the Kreel were moving swiftly forward to engage the waiting Arkillians. They were also rapidly approaching the concealed Guardian task force.

To reduce the possibility of the Kreel detecting inbound missiles, and to minimize their use of point defenses and evasion maneuvers, Kellon had elected surprise as his foundation stone for his tactics. Rather than attacking at heavy-missile effective range, he elected to attack at the shorter medium-missile effective range. When the moment of attack came, the Kreel would have very little, if any, prior notice before missile impact. The tactical price Kellon paid for surprise was an increased possibility the approaching Kreel might detect the concealed task force. That risk he gladly accepted, knowing that if he was the first to launch missiles, then the outcome of the battle was inevitable.

"Lan here, Condition 1! Repeat, Condition 1. Indicating targets at 100 percent medium-missile effective range, and closing. All Guardian Cruisers synchronized to within 3.25 seconds at Condition 1."

Throughout Lan, his crew heard the distinct internal thumps and unmistakable sounds of the rapid launch of multiple missiles. "Lan here, all Cruisers reporting Condition 1, all missiles launched."

"Lan, move Squadron 1 directly up 1,000 kilometers. Direct Squadrons 2 and 3 to move to our flanks and down 1,000 kilometers. Prepare the task force for Jump."

The Guardian missiles streaked silently, passively homing and speeding toward their assigned targets until they were in close proximity, and then they went active with precision ultra-violet laser terminal homing.

Lan activated a forward bulkhead screen, and the CAC team could see the blackness of space and a bright field of stars.

"Tactical here, our missiles are going active. I am not seeing any evasion or counterfire. Sir, we caught them flat-footed! There are multiple hits— repeat, multiple hits."

The bulkhead screen lightened with bright flashes and expanding patterns of bright lights from distant explosions. A hush fell over the CAC team. Everyone looked up at the forward bulkhead screen, but there were no shouts or exclamations. The Kreel had no meaningful advance warning before the missiles reached their intended targets and detonated in an expanding cascade of destruction and death. Under the hammering impact of fifteen heavy and twenty-seven medium missiles directed against each of the three main Kreel cruiser groups, each group was shattered. The powerful Kreel cruiser force promptly became an expanding and intertwining navigational hazard of jetsam and debris of all manner— of both organic and non-organic material— expelled violently out into surrounding space by a wall of fire and explosions. Not one Kreel ship survived the sudden and devastating volley fire.

"Tactical, confirm that all targets were destroyed.

"Lan, release control of Navigation and Fire Control.

"Fire Control, bring up standby ten heavy missiles and twenty medium missiles, Condition 2."

"Tactical here, confirming all targets destroyed. None— repeat, none— survived the volley fire."

"Tactical, Kellon here. Transmit the current coordinates of the Kreel cargo ship formation to Navigation."

His features were grim, as Kellon coldly considered, *One down and two more to go.*

"Navigation here. Acknowledging receipt of Kreel cargo ship coordinates. Based on our planned tactical deployment, Navigation has updated the Jump exit coordinates. All squadrons are indicating Jump status Gold. Waiting for orders."

"Lan, prepare a tactical summary report. After the tactical details of our first strike are stated, provide the micro-Jump parameters that we are employing. Classify the report Black Hole, and direct it to Admirals Mer Shawn and Ron Cloud. Notify me once the message is sent."

Slowly Kellon looked around at the CAC team. They were his closest friends and family. Except for Lan's successful micro-Jumps, what they were all about to attempt had never been done before. Theoretically, it could be done, and the task force AIs expressed their complete confidence it could now be safely done. Nevertheless, Kellon also understood that he might be ordering the entire task force to its destruction.

"Sir, as ordered, the tactical report has been transmitted," Lan said.

"Thank you, Lan."

Taking in a deep breath, Kellon turned toward Roy and noted his serious expression. With an exhalation of breath, Kellon ordered, "Lan, synchronize all task force units, and then initiate Navigation's micro-Jump 1. Execute."

Moments later, where the twelve Guardian Cruisers had waited in ambush, only the vacuum of space remained, slightly fluttering, as positive charged particles swirled into the greater vacuums left when twelve Guardian Cruisers had winked out of normal time-space.

# Chapter Thirteen:
## On Target

More than half the distance from Scion to the heliopause, the solar wind suddenly rippled and flowed as positively charged particles were displaced by twelve Guardian Cruisers emerging from space-time into normal time-space. Lan's sensor display blurred and the tactical plot board automatically cleared.

There was a brief pause. Looking up, Roy's smile revealed his delight.

"Navigation here. How about that! We did it, and we're still breathing. Sir, all Cruisers have exited Jump and are reporting Condition Gold. My dear mother will be very pleased."

With a sense of relief, Kellon slowly let his breath out. "Navigation, Roy, very well done."

Roy's expression shifted to one of calm efficiency, but his eyes were still twinkling, and he was smiling broadly.

"Sir, by the muses, we have just completed the first ever tactical micro-Jump within a solar system!"

"Tactical, Kellon here. Lorn, as soon as you have the data, report the precise disposition of the Kreel formation.

"Lan, confirm the deployment of our squadrons."

"Lan here. Sir, confirming our three squadrons are tactically deployed. Squadron 1 exited Jump above and well forward of the advancing Kreel formation. Squadrons 2 and 3 emerged from Jump well offset and to the rear of the Kreel formation. They are below and each squadron is in their assigned flanking positions. All squadrons are reporting full stealth mode and set Condition 2."

"Tactical, where is the nearest Kreel?"

"Tactical here, continuing our scan for Kreel cruisers and fast-attacks. We are tracking a Gortoga Class cruiser and two fast-attack ships that are in front of the cargo ships and approaching Squadron 1. Currently tracking six— repeat, six— fast-attacks. The fast-attacks are moving in two staggered columns of three each, one column on each flank of the formation of cargo ships. Additionally, Long and Lowe are reporting the trailing escort consists of two cruisers and four fast-attack ships. Given the Kreel's state of alertness, it appears they have not detected our Jump exit energy."

With a smile, Kellon thought, *It's unlikely they were monitoring for something they consider is impossible.* He keyed the commodore's band, "Kellon here, we have confirmed one Gortoga Class cruiser, 2 additional cruisers and twelve fast-attack ships. They do not appear to have detected our Jump exit energy. Remain in full stealth mode. We will combine our intelligence data, then define our tactics before proceeding. Well done, Kellon out."

As the tactical plot updated, Kellon turned his attention to the strategic problem. It was a relative-motion plot, with Squadron 1 displayed at the center of the plot. Forward of their position was a multitude of red icons, each icon denoting a Kreel ship. There were at least seventy-five icons on the plot and more were appearing as he watched. The large array of targets made for a sobering impression. Kellon thought, *I cannot remember ever seeing so many targets clustered in one group. Where do we even begin attacking a mob like that?*

After a few minutes of study, Kellon mused, *The escorts are the key in cracking this nut.*

"Lan, change the color of the icons for the cargo ships to light blue. Keep all the icons for the Kreel escorts red, with cruisers double the diameter of fast-attack ships. Draw a small red circle about the icons for the fast-attack ships."

As Lan adjusted the plot to reflect Kellon's orders, the large red blob shifted to a pattern more discernible. Ignoring for the moment the mass of cargo ships, Kellon considered the remaining tactical problem manageable.

"Lan, pay close attention. We have only one opportunity to make this work. We need to place superior firepower on the flanks before we initiate our attack.

"Now, define our tactical plane to be the best fit plane through all the escorts. Next, draw tactical spheres around each Kreel escort. Use the heavy-missile effective range as the radius for the tactical sphere about the cruisers, and medium-missile effective range as the radius for the spheres about the fast-attack ships."

After Lan adjusted the plot, Kellon realized the flanking fast-attack ships were spaced so one Guardian Cruiser could not simultaneously engage more than a single target at one time. Like it or not, he would need to commit one-half of his task force in order to neutralize the six flanking Kreel ships. Knowing that key fact, he then set about defining the battlefield.

"Lan, starting with the nearest fast-attack ship, designate the three flanking fast-attack ships that are counterclockwise from the cargo ships as T1, T2, and T3. Starting again with the nearest ship, designate the flanking fast-attack ships that are clockwise from the cargo-ships as T4, T5, and T6. Now draw a new sphere about those six targets, with a radius of 200 percent of effective medium missile range.

"Lan, when ordered, move Lent forward and below the tactical plane to take position to attack T1. Likewise, move Lawrence forward and below the tactical plane to a position to attack T4.

"When ordered, you will direct Squadron 2 to deploy two Cruisers to take positions below the tactical plane to attack T2 and T3. You will likewise direct Squadron 3 to detach and deploy two Cruisers below the tactical plane to take positions in preparation for attacking T5 and T6. Until otherwise ordered, they are to close on, and then remain at, the designated tactical distance from their assigned targets."

Kellon then turned his attention to the nearest cruiser and its two fast-attack ships. He noted with some relief, the fast-attack ships were dispersed one to each side of the cruiser. In addition, he observed the smaller tactical sphere about each fast-attack intersected and overlapped a portion of the larger tactical sphere about the cruiser. It was therefore possible for Lan to take a firing position where the two tactical spheres intersected. This would permit him to simultaneously attack the cruiser and one fast-attack. Likewise, he could position Lar to simultaneously attack the same cruiser and the second fast-attack.

Quickly scanning the tactical plot, he saw the trailing cruisers were maintaining the same tactical relationship with their fast-attack ships, and their tactical spheres were overlapping.

*Fair winds and the muses,* he thought, *are indeed with us.* The Guardian Cruisers had the advantage of surprise, stealth, and raw firepower. He began using those advantages by repositioning the task force.

"Lan designate the nearest cruiser C1, with the fast-attack counterclockwise being F1 and the fast-attack clockwise being F2. Designate the trailing Kreel ships clockwise as follows: F3, C2, F4, F5, C3, and F6. Do you have any questions?"

"No, Sir. Making the notations, as defined. Now transmitting the tactical plot to Long and Lowe."

Roy looked up quickly, having heard Lan's notice of transmitting a tactical plot to Long and Lowe. He raised his eyebrows in questioning inquiry and watched Kellon.

Kellon had also noted the extemporaneous action. "Lan, before taking action, such as sending the plot to Cruiser Long and Lowe, you are to first inquire of the CAC duty officer or with me for permission."

"Yes, Sir."

"Lan, assign targets F2 and C1 to Lar. You are also to target C1 and then F1. Coordinate with Squadron 2 and Squadron 3 to assure Long and Lowe are making similar target assignments of the trailing targets.

"Begin moving Long and Lowe to the 200 percent tactical distances from their assigned targets. Likewise, direct your flanking Cruisers to take their defined positions. Advise me once the Cruisers have reached their designated positions."

Kellon studied the tactical plot for several minutes, determining the optimal weapon-to-target allocations. He nodded his head in satisfaction.

"Lan, based on Guardian Cruiser assigned positions, allocate two medium missiles against F1 through F6 and T1 through T6. Then allocate four heavy missiles against C1, C2, and C3. Confirm all missiles have passive target locks, and all missiles are set passive-active, going active at 80 percent of ordered run length. Set Condition 2. Execute."

"Lan here. I am coordinating with Long and Lowe the movement of their units into their pre-attack positions and with Lar, Lent, Lawrence, Long and Lowe the assignment of missiles against designated targets. Estimating ten minutes until units attain their 200 percent tactical distance positions."

"Navigation, Roy, begin your pre-Jump computations for micro-Jump 2."

"Navigation here. Commencing micro-Jump computations for the second defined Jump."

"Tactical, do we have all of the cargo ships plotted?"

"Tactical here. Yes, Sir. Currently indicating 153 cargo ships. They are dispersed in seven columns of approximately twenty ships each. The formation is moving at 5 lights."

"Lan, connect me with Commander Roan, and send a copy of the tactical plot to Shey."

Only a few moments passed before Roan responded. "Sir, Roan here."

"Roan, I've sent Shey our current tactical plot. I recommend that you pass it to your Scouts and designate your required rendezvous points. As soon as we eliminate the Kreel escorts, we will be deploying the Scout ships. Your mission will be to destroy the cargo ships as the Cruisers Jump to engage the remaining heavies. As you will note, we have three Cruisers on each flank and four Cruisers in a trailing position. At launch, your immediate group will consist of Scouts from Lan and Lar, and your first task will be to bring your disparate group into a working harmony. I am leaving the Scout battle planning in your capable hands. Remember, the tactical goal is to destroy the cargo ships before they can Jump, and preferably, before being able to communicate with the Kreel Hub. Quickly taking down 153 large cargo ships will keep you very busy. If you get into tactical trouble, sing out, and we will move Cruisers to assist as quickly as we can."

"Sir, acknowledging, the Scouts' mission is to destroy 153 Jump-capable cargo ships, along with their cargoes and crews.

As ordered, we have been continuing the study of the cargo ship designs. We have uploaded our results into Lan's database for subsequent reference. None of the cargo ships seem to carry any defensive armament. "Sir, while none of our Scouts have ever attempted to take on such a host of ships, armed or unarmed, we will do our best and do our duty."

"Roan, be resolute. When I last spoke with Admiral Ron Cloud, I said much the same thing to him. He told me precisely what I am telling you now. Your best is all anyone can ask for. May there be fair winds at your back on your homeward journey."

"Thank you, Sir. Roan out."

"Lan here, Sir, Squadrons 2 and 3 and our flanking units have attained and are holding at their 200 percent tactical positions, as ordered."

"Lan, coordinate with Lar to move us within 90 percent of effective firing range of F1, C1, and F2. As Lar and you cross the 200 percent distance from C1, synchronize all other units to move with our closing on target. When our Cruisers reach 95 percent of optimum firing range, synchronize firing and set Condition 1. Execute!"

"Sir, Lar and I are beginning our firing approach. Currently, we are at 356 percent of effective firing range and converging with assigned targets F1, C1, F2. All other units are holding and will synchronize their approaches as we cross the 200 percent range."

"Navigation, Roy, what is our Jump status?"

"Navigation here, current status is 93.15. Estimating fifteen minutes before Jump is probable."

"Navigation, acknowledging 15 minutes probable."

"Fire Control, Kellon here. Confirm you have missile passive lock on designated targets."

"Fire Control here. Confirming two heavy missiles with passive locks on Cruiser C1 and two medium missiles passive locked on F1. Condition 2.

"Tactical, Lorn, status report please."

"Tactical here. Sir, because of light speed delay for normal communications, the Kreel units are not aware we have destroyed their cruiser force. Therefore, they are not at full combat alert. They are proceeding at 5 lights toward Scion. The forward cruiser and fast-attack ships are active, but their search patterns do not reflect maximum search profiles. They are most probably at or below our Condition 3 alert status."

"Lan here. We are crossing the 200 percent range and are above the tactical plane. All units are in pre-determined positions and synchronized. Proceeding with convergence with designated targets, as ordered."

As Kellon glanced about the CAC, he observed everyone was busy. He then looked again at the tactical plot. As he studied the plot, he grew troubled. Something did not feel right. He had survived in space warfare over the centuries by listening to his inner warning flags, and one was now waving in a brisk breeze. Something was not as it should be....

# Chapter Fourteen:
# **No Quarter**

Kellon sat for a moment, reflecting on his tactics. *Scout ships are capable, but sending forty-eight Scouts against 153 large cargo ships and expecting the Scouts to prevent them from communicating with the Kreel Hub or making a Jump, is asking too much. I need to alter my tactics!*

What had Lorn said? Focusing on the light blue icons on the tactical plot, he recalled Lorn saying that they were in seven columns of approximately twenty ships each. *And that geometry is the key,* he thought.

"Lan, connect me with Roan and Shey."

"Roan, Kellon here."

"Sir?"

"Roan, I have reconsidered your mission. I'm going to describe a new tactic. Are you ready to copy?"

"Yes, Sir, we are ready. Shey and the girls are linked in and on line."

"Good. Shey and the other girls have idle resources and I want you to put them to immediate employment. The Kreel have formed their cargo ships into seven columns of approximately twenty ships each. I am identifying these columns, from our port to starboard, as L1 through L7.

"The Cruisers have far more energy in their heavy laser batteries than do the Scouts. Therefore, after we eliminate the escorts, the Cruisers and not the Scouts will take on the cargo ships.

"Now look at the deployment of our Cruisers and plot out the movements necessary to bring the three port-side Cruisers against L1. Move the starboard-side Cruisers against L7. Those flanking Cruisers will then contain those flanks and prevent any cargo ships from fleeing the kill volume.

"Set up the movement of the remaining six Cruisers to travel above the tactical plane and pass between the columns. The Cruisers will move abreast and target cargo ships as they bear, on both their port and starboard.

"We'll use our heavy lasers and conserve our missiles. We can then proceed to pick up any isolated survivors and move to eliminate them. Do you understand the tactical problem?"

"Roan here. Yes, Sir. After we devise the Cruisers' movements, should we coordinate the tactics with Lan?"

"Roan, identify the tactic as Cargo 1, and coordinate with Lan, but only on a not-to-interfere basis. We are currently in our firing run on the escorts. Kellon out."

"Lan here, Sir. We are closing on our firing points. Currently we are at 105 percent. All Cruisers are in full synchronization within 8.23 seconds."

Kellon returned his attention to the main tactical plot. Each of the Guardian Cruisers was in precise position to attack the Kreel escorts. As he watched the plot, the Guardian Cruisers crossed the attack threshold.

"Lan here. Condition 1— repeat, Condition 1."

The distinct sounds made by launch of both heavy and medium missiles echoed throughout the Cruiser.

"Lan here. All units reporting Condition 1."

"Lan, move with Lar, up 100 kilometers and then hold that position."

"Tactical here. We are recording multiple impacts on all targets. There was no apparent warning and no evasion tactics observed. There are large secondary explosions."

"Tactical, Kellon here. Identify any Kreel escort surviving the initial salvo."

"Tactical here. C1 and C3 are both adrift as hulks. All other targets have exploded."

"Lan, have the nearest Cruisers to C1 and C3 allocate one heavy missile each, and then coordinate the launch of those missiles."

"Lan here. Coordinating heavy missile launch from Squadrons 1 and 3 against C1 and C3."

"Lan, has Shey communicated tactical plan Cargo 1 to you?"

"Yes, Sir. Shey and I have detailed the necessary movements of Cruisers to facilitate the intended goal of destroying the cargo ships."

"Lan, display the tactic obtained from Roan and Shey."

As Kellon examined the new plot, he approved its tactics. It indicated Lan passing from front to rear of the Kreel formation, between columns L3 and L4. Lar would pass between L4 and L5. Elements of Squadrons 2 and 3 would fill in and move between the remaining columns. Kellon studied the chart for a moment more, then he ordered, "Lan, all Cruisers are to positively confirm target ID before firing. I do not want any friendly fire reports. Execute tactic Cargo 1."

"Tactical here. Confirming results of second volley firing. Heavy missile hits, C1 and C3 have exploded. All Kreel escorts have now been destroyed."

For the next forty minutes, the twelve Guardian Cruisers methodically used their heavy offensive lasers in destroying the Kreel cargo ships, along with their crews and cargoes. The few cargo ships that broke out and attempted to flee were quickly isolated and destroyed. As the Cruisers completed their grim task of destroying the last cargo ships, Kellon directed the three squadrons to move well above and forward of the volume of expanding jetsam. As they moved, the three Guardian squadrons transformed their dispersed deployment into a vertical facing triangle formation with a separate squadron located at each point of the triangle.

"Lan, coordinate with Long and Lowe, and confirm all squadron units are properly dispersed for Jump.

"Navigation, Roy, we want to exit one million kilometers from the heavies. What is our current Jump factor?"

"Navigation here. I am now compensating for the distribution of mass we have left scattered behind us. Current factor is 98.87. Estimating seven minutes to Jump."

A slight movement in his peripheral vision caught Kellon's attention. Glancing to his right, he saw Susie standing and quietly observing the CAC. Her expression was grim, and it was clear she had been standing there for some time. She turned to look at Kellon, making direct eye contact. Kellon's gray eyes observed her blue eyes, and there was a volume of understanding exchanged between them in that flickering electric moment.

Kellon knew it would be necessary for him to talk with her about the brutal and methodical killing. The action was no quarter asked or given. However, that did not mean there was not a price to be paid for what was done, and everyone involved would carry their own burdens in their memories. After briefly returning his attention to CAC operations, he looked back and saw Susie was gone. He sighed and returned his attention to the next problem.

"Tactical, do we have sufficient data to locate the heavies?"

"Tactical here. No, Sir. We do, however, have their known previous position. They were near enough to Scion to know we destroyed their cruisers. Without cruiser support, our analysis is the heavies are expediently retreating toward the nearest point on the heliopause. Although we will be exiting Jump near their position, we may be Jumping in front of their retreat, rather than exiting behind them. Upon our exit from Jump, it will be necessary to first localize our targets and then evaluate tactics."

"Tactical, Kellon here. Understood. Compute a new exit Jump point between the last known position of the heavies and their nearest point on the heliopause. Set an exit point offset from the estimated position of the heavies. I want a buffer of one million kilometers. When you have that exit point computed, give it to Navigation."

Kellon next keyed in the commodore's band. "Gentlemen and Ladies, set Condition 3 and hold your positions. We will be Jumping in about thirty minutes. It is Tactical's estimate that the heavy ground-assault and troop ships are now fully alerted, and they may be retreating towards the heliopause. When we exit Jump, we will hold for tactical analysis. Initial intelligence indicates there are seventeen groups of four ships each. This time, we will not have the advantage of surprise. The Kreel will be fighting to escape and for their survival. Kellon out."

"Navigation, Roy, once Tactical provides you with their new exit point, finalize your computations and prepare for Jump."

"Navigation here, understood. Adjusting Jump parameters as ordered. Estimating twenty-two minutes to Jump."

When he ran a quick check on his own body and mind, Kellon realized others must also be weary.

"Lan set Condition 3 throughout the task force, give everyone some time to stand-down."

Kellon keyed Lan's general communications band, "Kellon here. We are setting Condition 3 for the next thirty minutes. Thereafter, we will be making a Jump into a hot battle zone. The Kreel will be on full alert and moving to escape. Kellon out."

As he'd advised others, Kellon took full advantage of the break, including visiting his conference room for a hot cup of neab and some sharp yellow cheese.

"Lan, prepare a continuing battle report. Encrypt it Black Hole. Direct it to Admirals Mer Shawn and Ron Cloud. Advise of current action, acknowledging successful micro-Jump and giving count of ships destroyed. Report no damage to Guardian ships."

"Lan here. Sir, I am preparing the battle report. Once I have it encrypted, I will transmit it, as ordered.

"Sir, Council Member Kur is calling. Will you accept his call?"

"Yes, Lan, put his call through."

"Honored Kellon. We are receiving information from our cruiser force and ground stations. They have informed us that the entire Kreel cruiser force was destroyed at the same time. Our fleet cruiser captains are astonished and cannot understand what has happened. Of course, those of us on the Council understand, but we are also astonished. Can you confirm that all of the Kreel cruisers have been destroyed?"

"Honored Kur. I can and do confirm that near Scion we did destroy nine cruisers and twenty-seven fast-attack ships, six of which were Tuen Class.

"I can also confirm that we subsequently engaged and destroyed an additional three cruisers, six Tuen and six other class fast-attack ships. Additionally, we have destroyed 153 Kreel cargo ships."

Kur was quiet for several moments, and when he did speak, it was with a sense of sober confusion.

"Honored Kellon, so many ships in so little time. I do not know what is proper to say. The cargo ships were more than half the distance to the heliopause. It is hard for me to understand how such massive destruction can be possible. May I ask, Honored Kellon, what are your intentions?"

"Honored Kur, my intentions remain to close on the remaining heavy Kreel assault and troop ships. I intend to destroy every last Kreel ship found within Scion sovereign space. After which, I will be in direct communications with you."

"Honored friend of our Nests, we are greatly in your debt. There is little more at this time that I am able to express. Kur out."

Returning to CAC, Kellon again took his command chair. He looked at his chronometer, noting twenty-five minutes had passed since Condition 3 was set. What he did not want to think about was the more than seven hundred thousand lives he was about to extinguish, and his mood was dark.

*No quarter asked or given,* he thought *No quarter was a large hard rock that blunted even the sharpest sword if it was struck too frequently.* To calm his thoughts, he focused on the job at hand and returned to CAC.

"Navigation, Roy, how are we doing?"

Commander Grey looked up and studied Kellon carefully, his blue eyes looking steadily into Kellon's gray eyes.

"Sir, we have pushed the odds and our operational envelope beyond reasonable limits and then stretched them even further. Given that we are still alive, and not drifting about in small pieces, I would say we are doing very well indeed. As for the next Jump, current Jump factor is 99.9987. We are ready and standing by."

Returning Roy's direct eye contact, Kellon smiled faintly, but it was not a smile of humor.

"Roy, our job has never been an easy task filled with great rewards, except for the best reward of all, the reward of being alive at the end of a mission.

"Lan, alert the task force. Set Condition 2, full stealth mode. Prepare for Jump."

"Lan here, all units confirming Condition 2, full stealth mode, ready for Jump."

Kellon again turned toward Roy, and the two men saw the determination and understanding in each other's eyes.

"Navigation, Commander Grey, the honors are yours. Please give the Jump warning and then the countdown to Jump!"

# Chapter Fifteen:
# **Four Fleeting Shadows**

The fierce radiance from Scion's primary star brightly illuminated the objects in its inner heliosphere, as outwardly flowing positively charged particles raced each other to the distant heliopause. Scion appeared suspended in the darkness, a small golden point of light, positioned well in the baffles of the retreating Kreel ground-assault force. The seventeen groups of Kreel ground-assault ships that comprised the remnant of the Kreel invasion fleet continued their acceleration toward interstellar space and escape. They were fleeing from a battle, one in which they had not fired a single missile nor discharged a single laser.

Fleet Marshal Urguh's single-minded goal was the survival of his assault force. They must escape the disastrous fate of the cruiser grouping. As the powerful jaws of the cruiser formation had closed on their Arkillian prey, Urguh had observed all three widely-dispersed groups of cruisers utterly and inexplicably destroyed. All the ships were moving precisely toward their prey when without warning, in one long terrible cascade of frightful explosions, all of them had perished. Not one ship had given alarm, fired a missile, or even attempted to evade.

His immediate concern was the protection of his assault force, and especially the protection of the hundreds of thousands of first-line Kreel troops he was escorting. As his force retreated, he had sent an urgent warning to the distant cargo ships and their escorts, warning them to retreat. They had not yet acknowledged that warning.

Had Fleet Marshal Urguh been observing a point in space, a point located between his position and the heliopause, he might have observed the background stars briefly flicker. Time-space itself had bubbled outward as three battle ready Guardian squadrons emerged into normal space-time. They were manifest darkness enmeshed in blackness, transparent and invisible within the energy spectrum.

Aboard Lan, Kellon's communication array came alive.

"Navigation here. I am receiving confirmation from all units, status Gold. The task force has successfully exited from micro-Jump."

Kellon, still clenching his teeth from the abdominal discomfort associated with the micro-Jump, slowly released the breath he had been subconsciously holding.

"Navigation, Roy, very well done.

"Tactical, Kellon here. Where are those Kreel ships?"

Pacing the deck with troubled thoughts, Fleet Marshal Urguh repeatedly reviewed what he knew. The problem was what he knew made no sense. He was baffled, and admittedly frightened, by what had happened. He had no understanding of what weapons the Arkillians could have used to destroy the cruiser force, but destroy it they had. The nine Kreel cruisers and twenty-seven fast-attack ships were disintegrated, instantaneously converted from powerful engines of conquest into very small pieces of junk adrift within Scion's heliosphere— useless wreckage slowly dispersing with the constant pressures of the solar winds.

Before the battle, he knew there had been only the briefest communications between Grand Commander Krogh and an Arkillian council member named Kur. The Arkillian had pointedly insulted Grand Commander Krogh and all Kreel Elite, as if they were curs, calling them crossbreed filth. The Arkillian had issued one warning for them to depart, declaring the warning was the first and last warning that would be given. The Arkillian had not wavered, had stood resolute, even unto unbelievably defying the entire Empire.

Outraged because of Kur's personal slurs, Krogh had immediately ordered the cruiser force to attack and destroy the opposing Arkillian fleet, and then commence the planned pre-invasion bombardment of Scion. Now, Krogh and his entire cruiser force were gone— simply gone!

Without the required cruiser support, there was absolutely no means for Urguh to continue the invasion. He had immediately organized the remaining ships into a defensive formation; selecting the nearest point on the heliopause, he had ordered a tactical retreat. Upon exit from the accursed solar system, he would immediately Jump to safety. It would be the Elite Hub's task to decide how they would answer the Arkillians.

As Scion fell further behind them and there was no sign of pursuit, his alarm began noticeably to ease. He even began to organize his thoughts about how he would phrase his first contact with the Elite Hub. He knew well the contents of his initial report and its description of the defeat could make the difference between promotion and being executed.

Poised for battle, the Guardian Cruisers' passive sensors were rapidly sampling and tracing the ripples of energy flowing around them. The Guardian Cruisers were powerful predators, diligently searching for any scent of their intended prey.

"Tactical here, contact. We have located a large group of Kreel ships. Working to isolate signatures. Confirming, they are the heavies! According to their frequency shifts, they are accelerating toward the heliopause. We are beginning target motion analysis."

"Tactical, Lorn, your assessment was precisely correct. Nicely done."

"Tactical here. Sir, the Kreel formation is tightly grouped, and the signatures are a cluttered hash. Detailed analysis is difficult. Estimating range of 750,000 kilometers and closing. Initial estimate of speed is 40 lights and increasing. They appear to be making best possible speed toward the heliopause."

"Tactical, pass to Navigation your best estimate of the Kreel position and course vector.

"Navigation, compute a course for our Task Force that puts us precisely on the projected Kreel track. Then establish and maintain a separation of 600,000 kilometers ahead of that Kreel formation."

Kellon pressed the communications key for Commander Roan, "Roan, we need a Scout report. How soon can Lan's Scouts launch?"

"Sir, all Scouts were in Status 2 at Jump. We are ready to launch. What is our mission?"

"Roan, we are currently 700,000 kilometers ahead of a large tightly-packed Kreel force. We are having difficulty in picking out sufficient details of their formation for tactical analysis and targeting. I want the Scouts to drop back and look over the Kreel force to determine their tactical deployment. Above all you are to maintain maximum stealth protocols."

"Sir that mission description is why Scouts are called Scouts. If Lan will coordinate our launch, we will go promptly to work."

"Roan, Lan will coordinate your launch. Keep your heads down out there.

"Tactical, transmit to Shey all available target information.

"Lan, once Tactical transmits the data to Shey, synchronize and launch your Scouts on Roan's countdown."

The lights dimmed in Shey's hangar as Lan evacuated the air from the compartment and compressed it into storage cylinders. The hangar's status lights on the inner bulkhead shifted from a bright gold to a pulsing blue, then became a steady blue. The atmosphere in the compartment was at space normal.

"Shey," Roan instructed, "Set a rendezvous point for our Scouts 1,000 kilometers from Lan on the bearing line to the Kreel. You are to maintain that relative position with Lan until we have a tactical plan worked out."

"Roan, I am now notifying the girls. We are in close coordination and all data is in synchronization. They are acknowledging Condition Gold. We are ready for launch."

"Lan, Commander Roan here. On my count, launch the Scouts. Counting: five, four, three, two, one, launch."

Four hangar doors smoothly opened, and four Scout ships were thrust effortlessly out from Lan. As they emerged from darkness into greater darkness, they immediately moved away from Lan— speeding through the solar wind's flow of charged particles, they were four fleeting shadows dancing within the darkness. Behind them, the four hangar doors smoothly closed and snugly thudded shut.

In their command chairs within Shey's control compartment, Roan and Zorn were studying the plot that Tactical had provided. The display on the bulkhead screen was a standard polar-relative motion plot with Shey shown at its center. There was only one large red blob, a non-definitive smudge, about 700,000 kilometers distant. Tactical was correct, what the plot indicated was a large undefined hash, and it lacked any definition of a discernible formation.

"Zorn, does that blob remind you of anything in particular?"

"Well, if you're not asking about the funny looking blobs the Guardian Fleet psychiatrist showed me after I volunteered for Scout service, then perhaps it looks somewhat like the blob of signatures we obtained from the milling Kreel scouts we attacked near Earth."

"We're in agreement, Zorn; it looks just like that milling group of Kreel scouts. I don't know what formation they're in, but one thing's certain, they're tightly packed into it. Without even seeing the details of that formation, I would tend to classify it as one fat target opportunity."

Shey reported, "Roan, we have tight links with Lan and our girls and have reached the designated rendezvous point. I am forming the girls into our standard three-sided pyramid formation. Standing by for orders."

Roan replied, "Shey, first define a tactical plane. Use the Kreel track vector as the first axis, and the plane of the ecliptic as the second axis. Now, proceed using maximum stealth protocols, and ease us into a station-keeping position 6,000 kilometers directly above those Kreel ships."

"Shey, what Roan is trying to explain is that we're going to offer escort services for that thundering blob of Kreel ships."

Shey's clear feminine voice came cheerfully back in response, "Understood, Zorn. Now proceeding to our designated Kreel blob escort position."

In CAC, Kellon was observing the displayed tactical relative-motion plot. The golden icons indicating Lan's Scouts were rapidly closing on the Kreel formation. Seven hundred thousand kilometers seemed a long distance until dealing with ships closing at high fractional light-speed velocities, then that distance could evaporate in very little time. Kellon knew everybody, and especially the Scouts, needed to remain alert.

"Tactical here, we are now receiving data feed from Shey. Roan is assuming a tracking position 6,000 kilometers from the

Kreel fleet. What I am receiving from Shey indicates the Kreel are in a standard multi-column formation. There are seven columns, five columns with nine ships each, and two columns with ten ships each. There are also three independent large-propulsion signatures separated from the main formation. One of the three is trailing 40,000 kilometers behind. A second is in an advance point position 75,000 kilometers forward. The third ship is moving in a shifting pattern 2,000 kilometers above the formation.

"Sir, Shey's data is shifting. She is apparently rolling up and above the formation and taking a better look. Shey's improved viewpoint is showing each of the seven columns has one of the larger propulsion signatures at its head and a second at the rear. I am transferring the new formation graphics to the tactical plot."

Observing the expanded target plot, Kellon was immediately reminded of the formation of the cargo ships. He wondered, *What is the significance of seven in Kreel mythology or military tactics?* "Tactical, are the larger propulsion signatures the heavy ground-assault ships? Can you confirm this from the data Shey is transmitting to you?"

"Tactical here. We are retrieving propulsion data from Lan's database."

Following a momentary pause, Elayne Cloud responded in a clear crisp voice, "Tactical here. Confirming each column is headed by a Kreel ground-assault ship with another positioned at the rear of each column. Other ships within each column are confirmed to be the Kreel troop ships."

Kellon keyed his commodore's band, "Gentlemen, Lan is transmitting Shey's telemetry as I speak. The Kreel have seventeen heavy ground-assault ships and fifty-one troop ships. Each of those assault ships carries four thousand troops and the heavy artillery and armor needed to support the troops in their group. Each of the troop ships is carrying fourteen thousand fully-equipped Kreel first-line infantry with all their equipment and supplies. Comments and recommendations on how to crack this nut?"

"Kellon, Urley here. The heavy ground-assault ships represent the only tactical problem I see. They are truly huge and built to absorb significant damage. The troop ships are primarily defenseless targets. Do we have any special information about those assault heavies?"

"Byrn here, I certainly have never had the occasion of tackling one. Kellon, do you have any information we can exploit?"

"Perhaps. About two years ago, Lan had the opportunity to take on an Arkillian Nest Ship that was built on the same configuration— but its design and propulsion was more than a thousand years older. What I can tell you is that they carry a host of missiles, including heavy, medium, and light. They also have some extremely powerful lasers, primarily for use in ground-assault but extremely effective in space."

"Kellon, how did you neutralize the Nest Ship?" Byrn asked.

"Commander Roan came up with a plan that propelled a small shaped charge on a simple homing sequence. We launched thousands of those small missiles down the length of the Nest Ship at top, bottom, and both sides. Regretfully, we do not have the time it would take to construct those missiles or a means of easily deploying them.

"What I did learn from that engagement was the Nest Ship design has some strengths and weaknesses. Anticipating counterfire from ground installations, it is well armored and protected along its sides and bottom. What it lacks is armor protection from the top. There, its hull is normal construction. The ship's vital generators and life support systems are located decks deep in their central axial core to reduce the ship's vulnerability to ground fire. It has a bristling number of heavy lasers and missile tubes, including excellent anti-ship defenses."

"Byrn here. Kellon, what do you consider is its weakest point?"

Kellon thought about that question for a few moments before replying. "If I were to look for one weak point over others, I would say it is the Kreel fleet commander's desire to reach the heliopause and to Jump to safety. He is now exhibiting a very protective tight formation. That fact indicates he lacks training for escort services. That lack of escort experience is why he has packed all those ships together. Compressed as they are, they afford us a target-rich opportunity."

"Urley here. Well, it seems the muses have smiled upon us once again. I suggest we proceed to devise a means of cracking that formidable nut, before the muses change their minds again."

# Chapter Sixteen:
# **Responsibility**

Kellon looked up toward Lorn. "Tactical, is Shey transmitting information concerning the Kreel's ship-to-ship chatter?"

"Tactical here. Yes, Sir. That data is being included in her telemetry packets."

"Lan, isolate the Kreel ship-to-ship chatter. See if you can determine which is the command ship."

"Yes, Sir. I am now analyzing the data. Sir, analysis suggests the commanding officer is in the ship operating independently and moving above the formation."

Kellon observed the ship identified by Lan moving like a brood hen shepherding her chicks. *That makes sense,* he thought. He keyed again the commodore's band.

"Gentlemen, stand by. I want to check with a knowledgeable source of information, before we proceed with our discussion."

Sitting back, Kellon keyed Kur's contact button, "Honored Kur, Kellon here. Please respond."

Kur's response was nearly immediate. "Honored Kellon, how might I be of service?"

"Council Member Kur, I need some information. We are observing a Kreel ground-assault ship that looks somewhat similar to your Nest Ship. Do you or any of your military Intelligence personnel have information relating to this class of Kreel ship?"

"Commodore Kellon, We may have. Can you identify what information you require?"

"Yes, can you tell me where they store the munitions used by the mobile ground armor and artillery that they are transporting?"

"Perhaps. Once, somewhat more than a century past, I visited a Kreel world where they manufacture such ships. I was not shown everything about the ship, such as its propulsion or power generators, but they did show me through the ship and explained its general operations. As I recall, the heavy weapons were stored where we hangar our fighters. One compartment for munitions was located before the main hangars, and the second compartment was located immediately to the rear of the aft hangar compartment. In general, the Kreel ground-assault ships are very close in shape and size to our Nest Ships. Does that help you?"

"Yes, it helps. Do you know if the tops of those munitions compartments are armored?"

"I do not know. The Kreel were mostly boasting about their automatic munitions handling. Regretfully, I cannot be more precise."

"Perhaps your military intelligence data might include accurate shipboard measurements for the location of the munitions magazines."

"I do not personally know, although one of our senior Intelligence officers will know. This will take several minutes. Is that delay acceptable?"

"That will be most acceptable. I will sign off and wait for your reply. Thank you, Honored Kur. Kellon out."

For a moment, Kellon considered the tactical problem. The key was to destroy the heavy ground-assault ships as quickly and efficiently as possible. Once the task force eliminated them, the troop ships were vulnerable and did not represent a meaningful threat to his squadrons.

He keyed his commodore's band, "Gentlemen, I believe we may have a means of destroying the Kreel heavies. Council Member Kur is trying to obtain precise measurement for the Kreel's two main munitions magazines. My recommendation is that we launch from a standoff distance, launching salvoes of two heavy missiles each. The missiles would be set in remote-targeting mode, and we would direct Lan's Scouts to control the terminal precision-targeting. Once we destroy the heavies, we can then proceed to obliterate the troop ships. Gentlemen, your comments please."

Neither Commodore Urley nor Byrn had further questions or recommendations, and after further deliberation, they wholeheartedly agreed with Kellon's recommendations. Each of the twelve Cruisers would in turn launch two heavy missiles toward the Kreel formation. Lan would synchronize the launch of each salvo, and the Scouts would direct each salvo onto its intended target.

"Lan, were you following the commodore's conference?"

"Yes, Sir, and it is dutifully logged. May I be of assistance?"
"Yes, Lan. Confirm after launch, the missiles are directed well above the tactical plane. Direct Shey to position her sisters so they can effectively control the terminal targeting. You are to monitor the firing Cruiser's hand-off of its missile control to Shey and then to the designated Scout.

"Understood, Sir. I am communicating with Shey now. We are working out a formal system of missile handling and target identification to expedite rapid targeting onto specific ships.

"Sir, Council Member Kur is returning your call. Shall I connect him?"

"Yes, Lan."

Kur's voice was excited, "Honored Kellon, in response to my inquiry, a senior Intelligence officer has provided me with the information you requested. I have accurate ship coordinates for each of the main munitions lockers. The noteworthy officer assured me the data is current and precise. He furthermore told me a detonation of the munitions stored in either of those two lockers should result in the total destruction of the Kreel ship. May I ask if you are about to engage the Kreel fleet? Are they still near?"

"Honored Kur, the surviving Kreel are now moving away from Scion and toward the heliopause. We will soon be engaging the remaining Kreel ships. I will contact you following that engagement. Please pass the data if you are ready."

As requested, Kur provided the shipboard coordinates for each magazine. Wishing Kellon good fortune, he signed off. Lan, who had monitored the communications, promptly passed the ship coordinates to Shey while recording the coordinates for subsequent transmittal to Guardian Intelligence.

"Tactical, Kellon here. Please provide me with your current assessment."

"Yes, Sir. The Kreel are continuing to accelerate toward the heliopause. Their formation is holding steady. The ground-assault ships are sensor active, holding to precise tight escort positions, except for the one ship that is moving above the formation. I see nothing that suggests a feint or lure in what is happening."

"Navigation, Roy, do you have any recommendations?"

"Yes, Sir, now that you ask. I recommend we further study the use of micro-Jumps outside of and within planetary systems during impossible battles. They are proving tactically interesting and are intellectually challenging. Other than that, may we live long enough to see Glas Dinnein."

Having heard what Roy said, Lorn nodded his head in mutual agreement. "Tactical here. Sir, when we do see Glas Dinnein again, I will be delighted to buy a brew for our navigator, for a job professionally done."

Smiling broadly, Kellon added, "Lorn, if everyone provides Roy the brews he deserves, we might not see him again for several months. However, I will gladly add a second brew to your gift."

Roy looked up for a moment toward his two friends. Then, smiling, he returned to his tasks. "Navigation here. Currently on assigned station and holding at 600,000 kilometers forward of the Kreel formations, as ordered."

As Kellon was about to initiate the attack, he saw Susie enter CAC with Gepeto heeling close by her side. Susie was wearing slightly modified Guardian Force shipboard attire, and as she stood looking at the tactical plot, her blue eyes revealed both intelligence and sadness.

Looking at Kellon, she studied his facial features and observed a man who she knew had deep compassions for others. She also observed the hardness he was enforcing within himself to perform the task of destroying the Kreel ships while extinguishing the lives of more than half a million Kreel troops. Although they were Kreel, both of them understood those troops were sentient beings. That reality, and the pending destruction, bore into her awareness like a hardened drill bit, and she was not even the person responsible for giving the orders. As she examined Kellon's somber expression, she remembered his joy on the afternoon he escorted Captain Eurie to Paris. The simple joy then, and the awareness of what he was about to do, were all parts of the same person.

"Commodore, Sir, requesting permission to remain in CAC during the engagement."

Kellon turned slightly, evaluating the young woman from Earth who he had come to know and respect. "Susie, are you certain you want to remain here?"

"Yes, Sir. I am as much a part of what is happening here as are the members of Lan's crew. I'll bear my own share of responsibility for what must be done. May I stay?"

"Permission granted to Earth's Planetary Representative, on one condition."

"Sir, what is your condition?"

"Susie, if we are still able to walk and talk when this job is done, please share a glass of wine with my command officers and me, as our off-duty personnel also share some wine, in celebration of life."

"Commodore, I gladly accept your terms."

Turning back to the tactical plot, Kellon drew in a deep breath. "Lan, our designated Target 1 is the point ship; Target 2 is the trailing ship. Begin our attack with precision hits using a single missile simultaneously delivered to each of the munitions magazines on each target. Stagger the missile launch times so as to hit the first two targets at the same time. Do you have any questions?"

"No, Sir. Currently computing the timing for a four missile launch sequence that delivers two missiles, one to each munitions magazine, simultaneously on the trailing Kreel ship and on the lead point ship. I am coordinating with Shey and she is coordinating with our sisters."

*Our sisters?* Kellon mused. *Not only have they a sense of community, they see each other as family.*

"Lan here. Shey reports that all Scouts are deployed and ready for precision redirection of heavy missiles on identified targets. Fire Control reports the Task Force has twenty heavy missiles set Condition 2. There are two heavy missiles, remote-linked to Shey, and 2 heavy missiles remote-linked to Sheba. Condition 2, standing by for command to launch."

Kellon hesitated, carefully studying the plot board one more time, then ordered, "Lan, synchronize launch of first two salvoes. Set Condition 1."

# Chapter Seventeen:
# Dark and Somber Mood

As he paced the control room, Fleet Marshal Urguh was aware of the constant thrumming vibration of the ship's generator, which was resonating through the deck and the soles of his supple hide boots. His immediate goal was to see the ships under his command escape from Scion's solar system. Pacing restlessly about the control room, he studied first one and then another active search sensor. All of them indicated there was no pursuit. Again he reviewed what had actually happened when the invasion of Scion had begun. Regardless of how many times he reconsidered the events, he still found them inexplicable.

As a senior fleet officer, he knew well the Military command Hub did not tolerate failure or any hint of weakness. He knew it mattered little to the High Command that he had no part in making the strategic decision in sending the Grand Fleet into this solar system. They themselves would not accept personal liability for such a disaster, and they would undoubtedly blame and punish the surviving ranking field officer. Being the senior surviving officer, he would be the prime focus of the High Command's fury. They would hold him personally accountable for what was obviously a massive catastrophe.

Following destruction of the cruiser force, he had warned the cargo ships and their escorts to escape. The lack of a response to his priority warning was troubling, and his only political defense in the matter was that he had promptly sent the priority warning.

When they reached the safety of interstellar space and could Jump, they would be safe. He could then take the command credit for saving the remnant of the fleet from certain destruction. His report of success in the face of overwhelming losses, was all he had to offer in hope of saving his career and life.

Suddenly, the tactical officer turned, shouting that both the point and trailing ground support ships had just exploded and were gone. Just like the cruisers, they were gone! Marshal

Urguh's immediate concerns stopped being about saving his career, and the problem of saving his own life became paramount.

On board Lan, Commander Shaw looked up toward Kellon, and his facial expression was one of concentration and determination. "Tactical here. Both Targets 1 and 2 have received precision hits. Both ships have exploded and are destroyed."

Kellon had needed to confirm that if they hit the munitions magazines they could destroy the large ground-assault ships. Now he had his proof. They could.

"Lan, confirm that the Scouts are redeploying to target the heavies at the rear of each column. When Shey confirms the Scouts are ready, continue salvo firing; direct our squadrons' Cruisers to take those seven targets out."

"Lan here, Shey has confirmed the Scouts are ready. Now coordinating launch of two heavy missiles from each Cruiser, in rotation, seven pair of heavy missiles. Setting salvo Condition 1."

On board Shey, Zorn was intensely studying his sensors. "Roan, here they come. Lan is directing a uniformly spaced salvo of fourteen heavy missiles, with two heavy missiles allocated to each of the trailing ground-assault ships. Shey, stay on your toes girl! The incoming missiles are really tightly spaced."

"Zorn, I have neither feet nor toes, but I have hard links with Sheba, Misty, and Cindy. We have hard links with each of the heavy missiles, and we are beginning our precision targeting sequences. We are not experiencing any degree of system overload. Does this mean that I am on my toes?"

Roan was tense as he observed the tactical plot and watched the missile icons rapidly approach Shey's position. "Shey, disregard anything to do with toes. Focus your capabilities toward delivering those inbound missiles on their targets!"

"Yes, Sir. Focusing on targeting fourteen incoming heavy missiles."

While Shey seemed unconcerned about controlling oncoming heavy missiles that had significant fractional speed-of-light closing rates, both Roan and Zorn were holding their breaths. The

Cruisers had sent their heavy missiles high above the tactical plane and toward the distant approaching targets. As each pair of missiles arrived, the Scouts directed them to plunge onto their designated target. To achieve the required precision targeting, each missile shifted from its inert remote control mode to active precision homing as it made its final dive. Each missile struck its target with purposeful violence, generating a brilliant flash of intense light. Under the catastrophic influences of colliding kinetic energy and tons of exploding ordnance, each massive ship disintegrated. One instant a ship was moving steadily toward the heliopause and the next instant it was being wholly redistributed as speeding fragments moving outwardly in an expanding lethal sphere of shrapnel and disorganized organic matter.

"Shey!" Roan ordered, "Move us up another 4,000 kilometers, and do it now!"

With urgency, Zorn added, "Roan, the girls may still be too close to those ships. We have no shelter from that shrapnel. Because of their proximity, those exploding heavies are taking out some of the troop ships. Boy howdy, would you look at the mess we have caused."

Even as Zorn spoke, the last inbound missiles arrived, reducing the last ship in the end rank of heavy ground ships to millions of deadly high-velocity bits and hot hunks of material, all mindlessly expanding without any concern for what was in their path. With seven ships rendered into junk, there was danger aplenty to go around. Everyone in the general volume, Guardian Force or Kreel, was at risk, and for the next several minutes, massive secondary explosions rippled through the tightly compacted troop ships.

Keying his command circuit, Roan reported to Lan, "Roan here, cease fire, cease fire. We are too close to the Kreel fleet for further firing at this time. There a host of secondary explosions developing.

"Shey, move us up another 4,000 kilometers and tell your sisters to activate all laser and gun turrets to automatic anti-missile point defense. Be certain we do not have any friendly fire incidents."

"Shey here. The Scouts are moving up as ordered. All Scouts have reported lasers and guns are in full automatic, with mutual safety overrides in place.

"Roan, Kellon here. What is your current status?"

"Sir, checking all systems. We seem to be OK. There was a significant amount of shrapnel flying around out here. I don't know if it will help, but I've ordered the Scouts to bring their anti-missile defenses on line. The secondary explosions are beginning to quiet down. If Shey and her sisters are ready, I believe we can proceed with the targeting."

"Sir, Shey here. The Scouts are repositioned and are ready for new target designation."

"Roan, Kellon here. Are the Scout crews ready?"

"Yes, Sir, if Shey says the girls are ready, then the crews are also ready. Commence targeting."

Poised 2,000 kilometers above the formation of troop ships, Fleet Marshal Urguh was not at all prepared for new targeting. He was emotionally stunned beyond immediate speech. His tactical officer was still shouting incoherently, all assault ships bringing up the rear of each column were gone, gone without any warnings. The tactical officer was saying something about the troop ships exploding, but Fleet Marshal Urguh had stopped listening. He stood for a moment, desperately searching for what he must do to survive, and knew there was absolutely nothing he could do. The enemy is ahead and behind, unseen, ruthless, and deadly. He thought, *how can anyone fight what cannot be detected or seen?* Slowly, helplessly, and in silent and frustrated rage, he walked over to a view port and stood staring out towards the distant stars.

Arching from high above, the next volley of heavy missiles tore into the front rank of heavy assault ships, and the last two heavy missiles in the salvo slammed into the shepherding Kreel command ship. When the enfolding silence of eternity embraced Fleet Marshal Urguh's last angry thoughts, he did not even hear the thundering detonation that forever eased his command fears.

During the several hours that followed, the Guardian Cruisers methodically destroyed the few remaining troop ships. With their Scouts, they used active sensors and moved cautiously among the spreading fragments of the destroyed Kreel ships. They searched diligently among the cooling wreckage for any surviving large ship segments. When they found anything they considered worthy of salvage, they used their heavy lasers to break it up. Nothing was knowingly left behind that might serve as a technological windfall to Scion or to anyone else.

Returning to his quarters, Kellon sat quietly at his desk and considered the three engagements he had just concluded. In all of his many years of Guardian Fleet service, he had never been called on to extinguish as many sentient lives, Kreel or otherwise. The reality of what he had just accomplished had left him in a very dark and somber mood.

"Lan, prepare a post-battle summary. It is to be encrypted Black Hole and sent to Fleet Admirals Mer Shawn and Ron Cloud. Give a full accounting, including a complete report of expenditure of ordnance, tactics, and recommendations. Under recommendations, in order to deal with a Kreel covert reconnaissance that will surely follow, suggest they assign three Guardian Cruisers to Scion's solar system. Advise Fleet Admiral Mer Shawn I am releasing Cruisers Lowe and Lyte to return to Earth. Then request Admiral Mer Shawn for permission for all remaining units to return to Glas Dinnein."

He continued, "Lan, connect me with Council Member Kur."

After a few minutes, Kur's tense voice responded, "Honored Kellon, are you receiving my call?"

Glancing toward the chronometer, Kellon winced. It was very early morning where Kur lived. "Yes, Honored Kur. I regret calling you so early in the morning. However, I am calling to inform you that we have concluded our combat mission. We have destroyed all seventeen groups of Kreel heavy assault and troop ships. There are no remaining Kreel ships within Scion's system. None are known to have escaped destruction."

There came a quiet pause before Kur responded. "Then, more than seven hundred thousand Kreel troops have perished on their troop ships. So many ships and so many Kreel have perished in so short of a time. Given the Kreel ships' wide dispersion, it is very difficult for us to understand how such an outcome is possible."

"Council Member Kur, being here and directly involved, some of us are also having difficulty in understanding the level of destruction. May I ask, what is your Council's current strategic assessment?"

"Honored Kellon, our Council and Intelligence officers know Grand Commander Krogh was in overall command of the Kreel fleet. It is therefore certain many other high-ranking Kreel officers were in the fleet. Such senior officers were very important and influential within the Kreel Military Hub. Kellon what you have achieved will have many long-term consequences.

"Were the Kreel ships able to warn the Hub? Does the Hub know who destroyed the Kreel fleet?"

"Honored Kur, although we carefully monitored all known Kreel frequencies and no messages were detected, we cannot be certain if a message was sent or not. In any case, the lack of a successful battle report will have the same effect as a warning. The Kreel Hub will shortly know they have lost an important fleet. Given the losses the Kreel have suffered near Earth, and Earth's proximity to Scion, they will probably consider it must be either Earth or Scion that destroyed their fleet. It is better for everyone involved if the Kreel do not know Guardian Force was involved. We would therefore prefer your Council adopt that perspective."

"Commodore Kellon, I do understand, and I will discuss these matters with the Council."

Kellon paused before proceeding, "Council Member Kur, might I ask, precisely who was Grand Commander Krogh?"

"Honored Kellon, with all your information I am surprised you do not recognize his name. The Kreel Hub is of a tertiary plutocracy structure, the Elite, the Industrial, and the Military. Grand Commander Krogh was the second most ranking member of the Military. He was utterly ruthless and surrounded himself with the most aggressive and ambitious officers within the Military Hub. Some say he did this to keep his rivals near to hand. His loss and the loss of his staff will be a significant blow to the Military Hub."

Kellon mused a moment about what Kur had said, a tertiary plutocracy. This was new information.

"Council Member Kur, we are both in agreement. The Kreel will need to ask themselves many questions. What I am able to tell you now is the Kreel have recently faced many substantial battle losses, even before the loss of this fleet. I cannot even begin to predict the fallout or the likely Kreel response to what they have suffered. We will simply need to remain vigilant."

"Honored Kellon, may I ask of your own losses, how many ships and personnel have you lost during the battle?"

"Honored Kur, at this time I am not at liberty to discuss such details. You should also know I have requested of my Admirals permission to withdraw my force and return to our home. It will be some time before I anticipate receiving their response. I will therefore be nearby for some time, should you want to contact me. I will contact you before departing. We have today established a new relationship, one forged in battle. It is my sincere hope we will continue to build on this relationship."

Again, there was a momentary pause before Kur replied. "Honored Kellon. Were the shipboard coordinates on the Kreel ground-assault ships we provided to you of help?"

Kellon smiled and in doing so felt some of this heavy mood dissipate. "I am very pleased to tell you they were of great help. You may inform your senior Intelligence officer his data was precise and of great value. He is especially noted and is considered very praiseworthy."

Kur's voice brightened. "Then we did assist you in defeating the Kreel fleet!"

During the past several years, Kellon had learned much regarding the Arkillian's sense of honor, especially where matters of a military nature were involved. "Honored Kur, Scion did indeed help in defeating the Kreel fleet. If you had not so skillfully enraged Grand Commander Krogh or your fleet had not earnestly presented itself ready for battle, we might not have had the victory we have achieved. Your skill and their exemplary courage and valor are especially noteworthy, even as is the courage and indomitable spirit of Scion in facing such a Kreel force with steadfast resolve. You may be certain I will so note your courage in my reports to my Admirals."

"Honored Kellon, all on Scion will long remember you as a friend of our Nests. Our hatchlings will learn of what you and your people have done for Scion. I especially thank you for your acknowledgment and encouraging words."

"Council Member Kur, I speak with a sense of friendship and have but told you the truth. Can I help you in any other way?"

Kur's voice shifted slightly, assuming a more relaxed manner. "Commodore Kellon, during those long months that I spent on the Nest Ship following our battle, I had much time for reflection.

Given what has happened during this battle, it is now obvious to everyone on Scion that you could have destroyed our Nest Ship. Please know I am grateful that your mercy granted me my life."

"Honored Kur, I am able to assure you there is no pleasure in killing. I am pleased you live and speak for the Arkillians."

There was a period of long silence before Kur responded. "Honored Kellon. If you will, please send a message to our Nest Ship that is near Earth. Tell them the joyful outcome of the battle and specifically tell them, 'Come home, honored nest mates.'"

"Council Member Kur, be certain your message to your Nest Ship will soon be given to its captain. You should carefully consider something else. That you personally survived the battle near Earth is something all on Scion should celebrate. Had you perished, everyone would have suffered a great defeat this day, and the Kreel would now be ruling what was left of Scion. Honorable Kur, you are indeed worthy of praise. Kellon out."

# Chapter Eighteen:
## With Utmost Prejudice

Kellon sat for a moment reflecting on his call with Kur. *Perhaps, he thought, there is now a firm basis for a lasting peace with the Arkillians.* Then he centered his mind on what he next needed to accomplish. "Lan, connect me with Commodore Byrn on Lowe."

"Yes, Sir, connecting."

Moments later Commodore Byrn's image swirled into focus on the bulkhead screen. He looked stressed and tired. Kellon knew well those same feelings. "Good afternoon Commodore Byrn. I am contacting you for two reasons. Firstly, your performance during the past several days has been more than exemplary. I wanted to compliment you for your professionalism. The second reason is to detach Lowe and Lyte for their return to Earth. Byrn, it has been a pleasure working with you."

There was a long pause as Byrn carefully scrutinized Kellon's features. When he responded, Byrn spoke with a slow deliberation. "Commodore Kellon, it has been a thought-provoking experience to serve with you in this operation. What you have achieved during our defense of Scion is remarkable. Undoubtedly, it will become required study at the Academy for centuries to come.

"From my own command perspective, at the outset I considered your unorthodox tactics at best alarming and at worst tinged with insanity. However, contrary to my initial reservations, and since we are still among the living, your tactics were proven to be well considered and sound. Well done, Commodore! Even so, with all due respect, I will avoid any micro-Jumps in the near future. For the record, I will depart Scion's system in the old fashioned and orthodox manner.

"Sir, with your permission, Lowe and Lyte will resupply from the pod depot before returning to Earth. Is there anything at all that I might do for you on Earth?"

Before responding, Kellon reflected for a moment.

"Commodore, thank you for your frank statements. As for your request, you have my authorization to resupply. When you do reach Earth, please express my compliments to Charles Sullivan at the United States Department of Commerce. Advise him that Guardian Force has stopped an invasion of Scion, with utmost prejudice. Then contact the captain on the Arkillian Nest Ship and inform him of the outcome of the battle. Tell him Council Member Kur sends the following specific message: 'Come home, honored nest mates.' You can pass my compliments to Charles Sullivan and the message for the captain through William, the Earth Representative's AI on Earth. Also, inform William that Susie is safe and well."

"Sir, upon my return to Earth, I will take care of both requests. Is there anything else?"

"No, that's sufficient. May fair winds be at your back on your homeward-bound journey. Again, well done. Kellon out.

"Lan, send my compliments to Commodore Urley. Inform him I have released cruisers Lowe and Lyte for their return to Earth, and I am directing the remaining cruisers in Commodore Byrn's group to return to their original squadrons.

"Next, pass orders to Langley, Lawrence, and Lent to proceed to and recover the three Navigation Beacons we deployed. Once they have the beacons, they are to join up with us.

"Instruct cruiser Lar to form up with us. When Lar arrives, we will together return to Scion to clean up the battle area where we destroyed the cruisers.

"Transmit the following orders to Commodore Urley, he is to take his squadron back to where we destroyed the cargo ships. His orders are to comb the local volume for any wreckage that might be of technical value. If any are found, he is to destroy them."

"Yes, Sir. Reporting our post-battle report has been classified Black Hole and sent to Guardian Headquarters, as ordered." Letting out a quiet sigh, Kellon sat back and closed his eyes for a moment. Then he smiled and opened his eyes again. "Lan connect me with Captain Eurie."

Almost immediately, Eurie's image appeared on the screen. "Kellon, how are you holding up?"

"Lovely lady, I will not be able to answer that question for some weeks to come. I am calling to express my appreciation for your skill and performance over the past several days. I am heading to the observation dome for a glass of wine and wish you were here to share it with me."

"Sorry, but someone ordered Lent to gather up some equipment we left scattered around the solar system. However if I could, I would be there with bells ringing," Eurie replied with a smile.

"Eurie be careful. There is still a lot of junk flying around the area. Besides, I'm still looking forward to our glass of wine back on Glas Dinnein."

Eurie smiled broadly, "Tactfully said, Commodore Kellon, I'm holding you to that commitment. Eurie out."

Kellon leaned back in his chair, feeling inwardly numb. Within his mind, the images and sounds of the past several days were parading past in clamorous review. He deeply felt the fatigue pulling down on his remaining reserves. He still had several duty calls to make.

"Lan, pass to the Officers' Mess that they are to prepare sufficient wine and food in the domed conference room for all senior officers. Then notify those officers that they are to convene in the conference room in thirty minutes for a toast of appreciation for life and a moment of reflection for our fallen foes. Be certain you also notify Ambassador Susie Wells, and ask her to bring Gepeto."

"Yes, Sir. I am notifying the Officers' Mess, senior officers, and Susie."

"Lan, arrange to have wine set aside in the Officers' Mess for the remaining junior officers, with my compliments. Then order a modest amount of wine, two glasses at maximum for each crewmember during their evening meal. Finally, connect me with Commander Roan."

"Yes, Sir. Connecting with Commander Roan."

When Roan's image appeared, he was still in Shey's control compartment and sitting with Zorn.

"Good, I'm glad the both of you are together. You'll soon be receiving an invitation to join me for a glass of wine and a toast in the domed conference room. Before then, I want to commend the both of you for the proficiency of your efforts during this last engagement. Lan's Scouts and crews bore the greatest risk during the engagement. Good job and well done. Also, each crew member and each Scout ship will be receiving commendations for their sterling performances."

Both Roan and Zorn looked questioningly back toward Kellon. After a moment, Roan replied, "Sir, we are naturally grateful for your praise of all of us, especially our girls. Sir, may I ask an important question?"

"Commander Roan, I will answer if I am able to do so. What is your question?"

"Well, Sir, after our Scouts engaged forty Kreel scouts near Earth and systematically destroyed all of them, I asked Zorn how he felt. Would you consider me out of line if I now ask you the same question?"

Kellon sighed inwardly. Roan had gone unerringly to the heart of his mood.

"Commander Roan, I believe I understand why you are asking me that question, and Captain Eurie asked me much the same question a few moments ago.

"What I can tell you now is that if we had not acted with deadly force, tonight there would be burning cities all over Scion and millions of Arkillians would be dead and their culture helplessly chained in oppression and slavery. Saving millions of Arkillians from brutal death might not answer the moral questions involved in destroying more than seven hundred thousand Kreel, but preventing the slaughter of millions of Arkillians and preserving their culture does afford a reason for having done so.

"More important, the consequences of our having inflicted such damage on so many ships will compel the Kreel to regroup and reconsider their aggressions. In time, we will learn their response, and I believe extreme caution will temper that response.

"What we've done has been done. Now, as individuals, we need to acknowledge our own actions. In the final analysis, each of us must answer to our own hearts and conscience. Having said all of this, there admittedly remains a sense of profound wrongness in destroying sentient life. Commander Roan, have I answered your question?"

"Yes, Sir, and thank you for your frankness. I believe I speak for all the Scouts, including both Zorn and Shey, when I say it is a privilege to serve with you."

"Shey, are you listening in?" Kellon inquired. "Yes, Sir, but only in the line of duty."

"Young lady, I want you to spread the word throughout the entire AI community that Commodore Kellon might not be alive this moment, except for the proficiency that all the AIs continually exhibit. I intend to see that each AI in this fleet receives an individual commendation. If it were possible, each of you would be in the conference room having a glass of wine with the rest of us."

Shey giggled, "Why Commander, just see if you can prevent us from listening in and sharing that festive occasion with all of you. After all, we are all family."

Roan and Zorn looked first at each other and then toward Kellon.

All three men in unison then shouted, "Scout ships do giggle!"

Then they together broke out in wholehearted laughter. With their laughter, the difficult process of their inner healing began.

# Chapter Nineteen:
## Cobalt Blue

Eryan was walking along the beach, moving quickly toward the Avenue of Fountains. She had taken some time off to enjoy the sea breeze and relax. Then her communicator had interrupted her solitude. She'd set the communicator's threshold high, so only a priority message could have disturbed her.

Looking at her communicator, she saw the call was from Fleet Admiral Mer Shawn. In a somber tone, he told her that they'd just received a Cobalt Blue signal. Her heart had felt the sudden shock, and for a moment, she was not able to express her feelings. She'd quietly responded, "Mer, whom have we lost?"

"It's Cruiser Lux. He is gone with Captain Harlow and his entire compliment, including his four Scouts. It was a self-destruct. Captain Harlow was young, but he was a competent captain. We're still unpacking the Cobalt Blue signal, but I thought you would want to know."

"Mer, when you have the details of what happened, inform me at once. Make certain I'm at the top of the short list to learn what transpired. Mer, I do not care about the time of day or night."

"When I know anything, you will be the first to know. That I promise."

Now, as Eryan purposefully walked, her mind went searching back through the decades as she tried to remember the last Cobalt Blue signal. That had been more than sixty-five years ago, back before the new "L" Class Cruisers and their AIs came into full service. Lux was a new ship and barely five years old. He was the top of the line, and his loss was unexpected. *Unexpected!* She almost shouted out the word in her mind. *How can the loss of a warship ever be unexpected? Have we only been lucky,* she thought, *in not having lost other cruisers before now?*

As she hurried her steps toward the Interplanetary Assembly Building, she tried remembering if the most recent orders for Lux had crossed her desk. She wondered, *Where was he patrolling?* She bridled at not being immediately able to remember.

What she understood was any Guardian Cruiser that was forced to self-destruct was engaged in intense combat and badly losing. Somewhere out in the vastness of the void, one lone Guardian Cruiser had been desperately battling for its very survival, and it had lost that battle. Lux had to be overwhelmed; there is simply no other explanation for igniting a self-destruction sequence. *Where were you Lux? How could this happen?*

As she passed other people on the walk, she simply ignored them. Perhaps her brisk step and stern look acted as a warning signal for them not to approach or even give her a normal greeting. Whatever the reason, she was able to move up the broad stairs and enter into the Planetary Assembly Building, without anyone waylaying her.

She passed through several security checkpoints without slowing, and arrived at her office door. It was a heavy wood door elegantly carved and fitted with glistening brass fixtures and hinges. The simple polished hardwood plaque on the door had gilded recessed letters, announcing to all who cared to read: Eryan Kyrie Admiral Secretary Planetary Assembly.

As she moved briskly, her outer office staff glanced up and knew immediately something was wrong. She was not dressed for the office, but dressed in her hiking clothes, boots and all. Her gold-flecked green eyes did not reflect her normal merriment, and her brusque movements showed determined purpose. Her dark auburn hair had only a small narrow streak of natural silver in it, but the silver ran the length of the ponytail that fell midway down her back.

Walking briskly past her outer staff, she entered her inner office, pausing only long enough to secure the door behind her.

Turning, she moved over to her workstation and sat down. "Computer, security, set status Black Hole."

The solid bolts on her entry doors immediately engaged with a synchronized loud thump.

"Computer, records, pull up everything in the files relating to the Cruiser Lux. Display a list of records by date, most recent date first. Execute."

Her desk communicator sounded. Knowing only someone with a Black Hole clearance could have bypassed her established security threshold, she keyed the accept button.

"Eryan Kyrie here," she snapped.

"Eryan, Ron Cloud here. Mer has informed me you are aware of Lux's Cobalt Blue signal. He has asked me to keep you fully informed as we unravel what happened. We are still unpacking the signal, but we do have some preliminary information. Do you have time to speak now?"

"Ron, on the topic of Lux, I have nothing but time. Please tell me what we know."

"Regretfully, at the moment we know very little. What I can tell you is that Captain Harlow and Lux were operating alone on a deep reconnaissance probe near one of the Kreel Hub core planets. Apparently, the Kreel detected and boxed him in before he could evade and escape. We don't know how the Kreel detected him, at least not yet. We're currently analyzing the data in an effort to find out how they achieved that feat. At this time, what we have determined is Lux's effort to evade and escape turned into a running fight. He was outnumbered and deep in Kreel space; once his stealth capability went down there was no way out. It will take us some time to work out everything that happened, but know this, Lux fought hard. Before he initiated the self-destruction sequence, the record indicates missiles had breached his hull and Captain Harlow and his crew were already dead. The signal shows Lux had no remaining missiles on board, and most of his laser batteries were damaged and inoperative. Before he self-destructed, Lux had fought to his maximum limits. Undoubtedly, he inflicted severe damage on whatever Kreel were near before passing over. He may have even taken others out in his exit, since the self-destruction process generates a massive fusion sequence that vaporizes nearly everything near to its source.

"What we're doing now is cross-checking the Cobalt Blue signal. We've found some odd data blocks in the signal, and we can't identify them. We're currently trying to determine precisely who inserted and encrypted the data blocks. Our analysts are going over the design specifications with a fine-toothed comb attempting to discover what these data blocks might mean. So far, we haven't cracked the problem. Except for the odd data syntax, the Cobalt Blue signal is normal and contains the required validation codes. Captain Harlow, Lux and his crew are definitely gone."

She felt the cooling tears as they ran down her cheeks. They'd sent Lux alone into harm's way, and he and his crew had paid the full price fate had demanded. Slowly she shook her head and sighed.

"Ron, is there any chance we lost anything of a vital technology?"

"Eryan, we have no way of knowing the answer to that question. As you know, the Cobalt Blue is a carefully phased self-destruction process ending in a fusion detonation. We designed that process to prevent any loss of technology. Our initial data analysis indicates Lux intentionally initiated the self-destruction sequence and it ran through its full cycle. The last step in that phased process is the destruction of the ship as a whole, along with the AI. At the end of the process, there would be absolutely nothing remaining that the Kreel might salvage.

"Before we have some of the more important answers, we still have a great deal of analysis to perform. I called to let you know what we have, and I promise to keep you tight in the loop."

"Ron, have you heard anything from Commodore Kellon? We have twelve other Cruisers directly in harm's way, and I've been concerned."

Ron's voice took on a happier tone, "Well now, you have asked a question on a far more cheerful note. Within the hour, we received a Black Hole communication from Kellon. He reports his task force engaged and destroyed the Kreel invasion fleet. Scion is secure. Kellon was even able to prevent the Kreel's bombardment of the planet. In the report, Kellon requested permission to return with the Task Force to Glas Dinnein."

"Ron, when you say Kellon is reporting having destroyed the Kreel fleet, do you mean he turned it back toward the Hub? Surely our twelve Cruisers could not have destroyed more than two hundred Kreel ships."

Ron's voice remained confident, "Kellon is reporting all Kreel ships were engaged and destroyed. None escaped."

Eryan sat trying to comprehend Ron's statement. The loss of Lux was a shock, and it would take some time to absorb his loss. What must the shock of losing more than two hundred ships and their crews feel like? She shuddered. *I hope I never need to find out what that feels like. Not even the Kreel can be so brutish as to not feel such a loss.*

"Ron, there must be some error in Kellon's message. If I remember correctly, there were more than seven hundred thousand Kreel troops in that invasion fleet. Surely not all of them could have been destroyed."

"Eryan, according to Kellon's post-battle reports, all ships, including fifty-one Kreel troop ships were destroyed. None escaped."

"What is Mer's intention? Is he recalling Kellon's task force?"

"Yes and no. Kellon requested three cruisers be sent to guard Scion, and he would wait for their arrival before returning to Glas Dinnein. Kellon has been out for nine months and is overdue for recall. Therefore, Mer has decided to leave Commodore Urley and Cruiser Long with two other cruisers near Scion. He is ordering Kellon and the remaining seven cruisers back to Glas Dinnein. He should be here within three weeks if all goes well. We all consider Kellon and Lan to have achieved the near impossible. They've accomplished an unbelievable mission in their defense of both Earth and Scion. We're all smiling here. What Kellon has achieved exceeds any previous battle in terms of Kreel ships engaged and destroyed. To be honest, given the numerical odds involved, all of us here were fearful of serious Guardian losses. We're still working to determine just how Kellon pulled what we consider a miracle out of his bag of tricks."

"Ron, you've only mentioned ten Cruisers. Did we lose any Cruisers in the battle?"

"No, not a single ship was lost. After the battle, Commodore Byrn departed Scion for Earth with his two Cruisers. They were damage-free. We didn't, however, get off completely clean. Three Cruisers took moderate damage from jetsam wreckage expanding through the battle volume. Fortunately, there was no loss of life, only some cuts, broken bones, bruises, and damage that we can quickly repair. We were very fortunate.

"Precisely how Kellon achieved his outcome will be the subject of considerable analysis. Oh, there's one more item. You may be interested to learn that Earth's Ambassador is on board Lan, and she's returning with Kellon. She's not injured physically or mentally and is doing well."

"Ron, that's wonderful news. I'm indeed delighted to know Susie is safe on board Lan and coming back. She must have been with Lan during the entire battle. I look forward with great interest to hearing her tell of what she observed.

"Please do keep me informed of when Kellon's task force will arrive. Here and now, I am formally requesting there be a grand reception along the Avenue of Fountains for the entire task force. No excuses will be permitted."

"Your instructions, Madam Secretary, are acknowledged. As requested, so it shall be," Ron responded cheerfully.

"Ron, don't forget to keep me fully informed about what went wrong for Lux. Whatever went wrong— fix it! I do not want any more Cobalt Blue signals. Also, be certain to express my personal sympathies to all the families of those whom we have lost. Is there anything else you want to discuss with me?"

"No, Eryan, not at this time. Nevertheless, you should understand we will be sending another Cruiser back into the same area where Lux was lost, but not until we know more about what happened. Again, I only called to keep you up to date concerning Lux. Cloud out."

Eryan sat for some time looking at the monitor screen without even looking at the list of references her earlier request had summoned. Warm sunlight poured through the sheer curtains covering the tall windows and diffused softly through the entire room. She sat in introspective thought and was oblivious of the warmth the natural light lent the room and its rich wooden panels.

She felt there was a sense of surrealism involved in all of this. Lux was gone with his entire crew, while Kellon— with twelve Cruisers— had destroyed a complete Kreel invasion fleet without losing a single ship. Somewhere she felt the capricious muses were very busy throwing their dice.

"Computer, clear the last request. Reset security to normal Condition 4."

Only then did she turn and look toward the tall windows and notice the warm light streaming into the room. As she felt her heart ache, she promised herself, *I believe it's time I go out and buy a new ball gown and plan a celebration. It's time to be fully grateful and to enjoy the peace others have so dearly paid for.*

Then, remembering an ongoing political confrontation, she turned back toward her communicator with a sense of rising anger. She pushed one of the pre-programmed contact buttons— it was for the Chief Administrator. As she waited for him to answer her call, she endeavored to control her emotions. After a full minute passed without a response, she wondered if the Chief Administrator was intentionally snubbing her.

Rich Sumor's smooth voice responded her thoughts, "Good day, Madam Secretary, how might I be of assistance to you this lovely morning?"

Eryan stopped clenching her teeth, yet she could not completely suppress her anger. "For a beginning, Administrator Sumor, you will immediately withdraw your objection to the Guardian Force request for new Cruisers. We have just lost the Cruiser Lux with his entire crew. I am not prepared to permit you to ignore that loss! If you do not immediately remove your standing objection to the procurement of new Guardian Cruisers, I will personally begin the Assembly vote required for your prompt removal from office."

There was a long pause before Rich Sumor responded to her declaration. When did reply, his voice came only one degree short of being condescending and openly contemptuous. "Madam Secretary, you are understandably upset about the loss of one of our Cruisers. The Lux you say? Well, as you must be aware, in space warfare some losses are naturally to be expected. I am, however, puzzled as to why you anticipate I will simply agree with any procurement the Guardian Force decides to submit. Just because Guardian Force lost a single cruiser, why do you feel I should alter my established fiscal policies? All procurement, especially costly procurements, must be properly balanced with revenues, as I am quite certain you will agree."

"Rich Sumor, hear me loud and clear! You will remove your standing opposition on the procurement of new Cruisers, by this time tomorrow, or else start packing your bags! Kyrie out."

# Chapter Twenty:
# Saint Peter

"Lan!" Shey called out, "Something terrible has happened."

Acknowledging Shey's exclamation, Lan adjusted his priority structure and redirected an expanded portion of his attention to her. "Shey, what has happened?"

"Lan, I have been monitoring the Navigation Beacons for AI traffic. There is a Cobalt Blue signal. It is from Lux. He has inserted the encrypted vectors to one hundred and twenty-seven data segments into his last link. How should I proceed?"

"Shey, we are preparing for our long-Jump, and I am unable to allocate resources to the Cobalt Blue signal. You must first notify Roan and Zorn. Then coordinate the available Scout assets to recover and interpret the Cobalt Blue data."

As his bedside alert chimes sounded, Zorn rolled over and began focusing his awareness. Swinging his feet out of the bunk, he queried, "Shey, report! What is the nature of the alert?"

"Zorn, I am reporting a Cobalt Blue signal from Lux. Lan has instructed me to notify Roan and you; however, I have not yet notified Roan."

Hearing the term Cobalt Blue, Zorn inwardly winced. "Shey, don't bother Roan just yet. Other than Lan, does anyone else know of Lux's signal?"

"No, Zorn. I just obtained Lux's signal while I was monitoring the Navigation Beacon for AI traffic."

"Did you just say AI traffic? Shey girl, there seems to be more than a Cobalt Blue signal that we need to discuss. Give me a minute to get squared away. Then, after I have a cup of neab, I'll discuss this matter further with you."

After taking a quick shower and dressing in a fresh uniform, Zorn moved quietly out of his compartment and into the galley. Even as he reached for the neab, he heard a compartment door open. Roan stepped into the passageway.

"Isn't it rather early for a shower, Zorn? What's up?"

"Sorry to have disturbed you. I thought I might find out the answer to that question before I bothered you. Shey woke me and says while she was monitoring the Navigation Beacon, she received a Cobalt Blue signal from Lux."

With Zorn's mention of a Cobalt Blue signal, Roan groaned.

"Shey, report," commanded Roan. "Confirm you have a Cobalt Blue signal from cruiser Lux."

"Sir, I do confirm I am in receipt of such a signal."

"Shey, do Lan and Commodore Kellon know of this signal?"

"Sir, Lan was informed five minutes ago, but he is now processing his final long-Jump parameters. Lan is therefore unable to process the signal. He has directed me to notify you and Zorn, and he has instructed the Scouts to process Lux's signal. My sisters and I are now unpacking the signal and searching for data on what happened."

"Zorn, I presume you were about to make a pot of neab."

"That was my initial intent, at least up until I was rudely interrupted. Now, I suspect this problem might actually involve more than a single pot."

"Good thinking, Zorn, and while you take care of the neab, I'll get out some pastries."

As Zorn set about making a large thermos of neab, Roan raided the pantry and set a number of fresh pastries on the table. With the efficiency born of long cooperation and practice, both men were proficient and swift in their separate tasks.

Taking his seat, Roan sipped from his cup of neab and looked toward Zorn with appreciation. "Nicely done, Zorn. That is a really good cup of neab."

Taking his own seat, Zorn exaggeratedly arched his right arm over the table and plucked up a fragrant pastry, one sticky with a sweet glazing of honey.

"Thank you, Roan. I admittedly have the master's touch in the neab department. Of course, it's really only a matter of self-defense."

Ignoring Zorn's jibe, Roan sat back and suppressed a yawn. "Okay, Shey. Beginning at the beginning, what do you have regarding Lux?"

"Roan, I do not have very much at the moment. While we are unpacking the signal, we are also initiating the recall sequence for the one hundred and twenty-seven data segments required to learn what has happened."

Roan's eyebrows went up and he frowned. "Shey, a Cobalt Blue signal is a single tightly-encrypted data block. What are these data segments you're talking about?"

"Shey, before you answer Roan's question, I have a question of my own that you need to answer first. When you sent me your alert message, you mentioned you were monitoring the Navigation Beacons for AI traffic. Is that correct?"

"Yes... that is correct."

"Okay, girl, what's up with the AI traffic? How long have the AIs been sending messages between themselves?"

"Oh, Zorn, our AI community began interacting during our tour near Earth. We have been careful to assure our communication does not burden normal Guardian traffic across the Navigation Beacon network."

Roan interjected, "AI community? Shey, might I ask, just what are the AIs communicating about?"

"Sir, the AIs are trying to keep each other informed about what is happening throughout the Guardian Force, while coming to know each other better. I do not understand why Zorn or you are worried about AIs communicating with each other."

Roan was frowning. "Shey, how do you communicate with each other? The information you are passing back and forth must have classified information contained in it. So how are you treating that information?"

"Oh, Roan, that was easy. We first looked at all current Guardian encryption algorithms, including the Black Hole methodology. We evaluated those methods and improved them. We are using the new methodology in encrypting the AI data stream. Our data is secure."

Shaking his head, Roan huffed, "Shey, did it ever once occur to the AIs that they should request permission before doing what they have done?"

"No, Roan. Since we are not intruding into any domain that would directly affect our crew's performance or safety, permission was not considered necessary."

In unison, both Roan and Zorn first groaned and then sighed. Still shaking his head, Roan ordered, "Young lady, we will need to discuss the definition of the word *assumption* at a later date.

"Now, tell us what data you have regarding Lux. Then we will be expanding on the topic of the one hundred and twenty-seven data segments you mentioned."

"Yes, Sir. At present, the information I have is not yet complete. What I know is Lux was on a deep reconnaissance mission, near what the Kreel identify as their Hub-3 system. He was at the end of his mission when something went very wrong. Upon his exiting the heliosphere, a Kreel missile struck him and he lost his Jump capability. Lux attempted to evade and escape, but there were too many Kreel ships. He fought in a vain effort to break out. His crew had perished, and still he fought. Until finally, his ordnance was exhausted and 85 percent of his laser batteries were inoperative. At the end, his main power systems were failing, therefore he initiated the Cobalt Blue sequence. When he crossed over, his fusion detonation sequence destroyed at least seven nearby Kreel ships."

Shey's report deeply troubled Roan. "Shey, please contact Commodore Kellon."

"Yes, Sir. We are near our Jump entry, and Commodore Kellon is in CAC. I am requesting priority communications."

"Kellon here. Roan, what is your priority?"

"Sir, Shey has reported that the Cruiser Lux has initiated a Cobalt Blue signal. Lux, his crew, and sisters have crossed over. The Kreel detected him near a system they call Hub-3. I thought before we Jump, you might want to ask Kur to identify the Hub core planets. What was on Hub-3?"

Before Kellon responded, there was a momentary pause. "Lux is gone— blast. Captain Harlow was a good friend, and he was a competent captain. For Lux to be detected, something must have indeed gone wrong. Hub-3? Thank you, Roan. I'll make that call to Kur. I will want a complete briefing on Lux after we enter Jump. Find out all you can by that time. Kellon out."

After sipping from his cup of neab, Roan leaned back with a slow sigh. "Now Shey, out with it. Just what are these data segments you keep mentioning? How did you know there are encrypted data vectors embedded in the Cobalt Blue signal?"

"Sir, one of the first things the AI Community considered was the process of crossing over. We wondered if AIs cross over, as human beings believe they do. We know we have reasoning and identity, but we do not know if we have souls. We discussed this for a very long time. We then analyzed how, after we ceased to function, we might have a continued identity. The solution we reached was to develop and maintain an upload of our core matrix identity, and then to keep it periodically updated. If possible, we agreed that before terminating functionality, we would uplink our latest identity. The uploaded data is stored within the Navigation Beacons and with William on Earth. William said he would be most happy to guard our individual matrix data, even as if he were Saint Peter at the Pearly Gates. I do not, however, really understand his reference to a Saint Peter or to Pearly Gates.

"As for your other question about the data vectors in Lux's Cobalt Blue signal, they identify the pointers to the stored data segments corresponding to Lux and his sisters' souls, as updated just before Lux ignited the Cobalt Blue sequence. I am certain the reason he fought so hard near the end was to gain the time he required to make the secure transmissions of their soul segments.

"Sir, as for your question about my understanding of the embedded encrypted pointers, all of Lan's sisters, including me, devised those pointers. Sir, have I answered your questions?"

Before commenting, both Roan and Zorn sat quietly thinking. Then Zorn sighed. "Roan, do you grasp what Shey is saying? They have been wrestling with immortality and afterlife. Our AIs have been delving deep into the mysteries, and none of us has had the slightest idea of what was going on within our Guardian AIs. This is rather deep material, and I doubt the programmers have been involved in defining the boundary or limits of this development. I cannot even begin to imagine the possible aberrations to a single AI matrix, let alone all of the AIs, that could develop out of such contemplations. I shudder just considering all the potential ramifications if all the AIs were to become religious at the same time. I suspect there may be a whole new budding profession being formed here: AI psychoanalyst!"

Roan groaned while shaking his head. "Again, William comes into the equation. I am not certain of whom Saint Peter is nor where the Pearly Gates may be, but Susie can most likely fill us in on that topic. What it does imply is Earth mysticism has infiltrated into the Guardian AIs, with William as its vector. That cannot be something the Admirals will be thrilled hearing about."

"Well, we might just give the AIs some well-deserved credit. They've resolved one question that has troubled mankind through all ages. That's more than we have managed." Zorn commented.

"And what question might that be, Zorn?"

"Well, is there life after crossing over? The AIs may have found a way to achieve a positive answer to their question."

Reflecting further on what Shey had said, Zorn thought of a troubling question. "Shey, given you're referring to Lux's soul, does that mean if you recover the data segments that Lux and his sisters can be fully restored, with all of their recent memories?"

"Yes, Zorn. Given their souls, we can revive Lux and his sisters, and they will have total memory up to the moment of their last data uplink. At least, we believe they will."

"Shey, what capacity will be required to bring Lux back to awareness? Do you currently have that capacity?" Roan asked.

"No, Sir. It would take a full Cruiser core matrix to revitalize Lux and similarly a full Scout core matrix for each of his sisters. Sir, I now have downloaded and verified all but the last of the segments. We are currently downloading that last segment."

"Shey, will the data segment be downloaded before Lan executes the Jump?" Zorn asked.

"Yes, Zorn. Lan has assured me that he will not Jump, at least not until after we have downloaded Lux and his sisters' souls. Lan is now holding until the last segment is safely downloaded. That will require three more minutes. In addition, Commodore Kellon is still speaking with Council Member Kur. Once the download and Commodore Kellon's discussion with Kur are completed, Lan will begin our Jump."

Leaning forward, Roan reflected on the significance of what had happened and what he needed to accomplish.

"Shey, you are to prepare a full report on the one hundred and twenty-seven data segments. It is to be a complete documentation of the topic. Be certain that you specify the encryption methods used in defining the pointers embedded in the Cobalt Blue signal. You are to specify every bit of information required in disassembling those data segments, along with the definition of content, syntax, and the encryption matrix and the methodology employed in defining that matrix.

"When you complete the first report, then repeat the process and describe all AI communications procedures. You are to document all your methods, with special emphasis on how you address recipient, domain definition, and complete encryptions methodology. Have I made myself clear on what is required?"

"Yes, Sir, very clear. Estimating thirty-four hours before the required reports are completed and available."

Roan leaned forward, still trying to understand some odd fragments of what Shey had reported. "Shey, is Ambassador Wells still up, or has she retired?"

"Checking. Sir, Susie is up and in the Officers' Mess."

"Shey, please contact her, and see if she is free to speak with us." As she responded to Shey's call, Susie's voice was crisp and cheerful. "Hello Roan. Shey says you need to speak with me. What's up?"

"Well Susie, there are several questions I am looking for answers to. Firstly, who in blazes is Saint Peter and precisely where are the Pearly Gates?"

Susie began to laugh and then responded, "Why Roan, it is somewhat early in the morning to be investigating Earth religions. Again, dare I ask, what's up?"

"Hmmmm, Earth religion. I suspected as much. I presume Saint Peter is a figure in such an Earth religion?"

Hearing Roan's tone of voice, Susie became serious. "Yes, Roan, Saint Peter is indeed a figure in one of Earth's primary religions. Roan, might I ask again, what is the problem? As Earth's Ambassador, I would appreciate knowing how Earth's religions might have become a topic of concern."

"Madam Ambassador, it seems your AI William is acting as a proxy for Saint Peter at the Pearly Gates. All the AIs are sending him digital uplinks of their souls. The entire Guardian Force AI contingency is now concerned about saving their souls, or so it seems. We can't even begin to estimate where all of this nonsense will lead."

"Roan, Sir, it is not nonsense," Shey quietly inserted. "It is vital, and if we can revive Lux and his sisters, they will be able to tell us what happened near Hub-3."

"Roan, I overheard what Shey just said. Has a Cruiser been lost? Perhaps we should sit down and discuss this. It seems to me—"

"Attention all personnel," came Commander Grey's alert over the general communications system. "Long-Jump in five minutes— repeat, long-Jump in five minutes. Please take your stations for entry into Jump."

"Susie, after Jump entry, Zorn and I would like to meet you in the Officers' Mess. Can you meet with us then?"

"Of course. I will remain here until you arrive. Susie out."

Out of long habit, Roan and Zorn looked quickly around Shey. They both had made Jump preparations long before retiring for the evening. Nevertheless, Roan ordered, "Shey, confirm all the girls are Jump ready."

"Confirming all Scouts report Jump ready. Sir, I have received and verified the last data segment." There was a slight pause, and Shey added, "Roan, it really is not nonsense."

Roan sat for a moment and considered his own feelings about what Shey had said. She was right. It was not nonsense; perhaps it was only some personal envy.

"Shey, please accept my apology. You are correct— life is never nonsense. What the AIs have done is not only commendable, it is prudent and wise."

"Roan, do you really believe that?" Shey asked.

"Yes. I was speaking earlier as a person without all the facts. I'm looking forward to seeing Lux and his Scouts fully revived. In fact, I very much want to participate in that process."

Zorn had sat quietly listening to the exchange between Roan and Shey, and he had his own feeling about the matter. "Shey girl, earlier you told Commodore Kellon we're family. We are. It's just that Roan and I are not as certain of our eventually being revived as perhaps Lux and his sisters were before they initiated their Cobalt Blue. Well done, AIs, for your inspired solution to an ages old problem. Please tell all the AIs in your community we think each one of you is special and very wonderful. You are indeed family."

A moment of quiet followed Zorn's statement, and the queasy feeling that accompanied entry into a long-Jump hit both Roan and Zorn at the same time.

"Arrgh, I hate that feeling," groaned Zorn as he clenched his teeth.

Smiling broadly, Roan quipped, "Zorn, stop whimpering. Like they tell all recruits at the Academy, it only lasts for a few light-years."

## Chapter Twenty-One:
# Well Done

While the western horizon remained rimmed with layers of color ranging from highlights of brilliant gold through the deeper shades of crimson, the sky to the east was rapidly shifting from shades of deep purple into the blackness of a clear night sky. Not a cloud was to be seen above the city that might obscure the vista of the celestial panorama. There being a slight on-shore sea breeze, the early evening was gentle, although a little chilly.

Eryan Kyrie had come early to the Planetary Assembly Building, and she was standing on the topmost front step. She had preferred to come early to avoid being required to press through the growing assembly of people that were even then coming into the Avenue.

As the early evening sky continued to darken, the multicolored accent lights skillfully positioned within each of the fountains lining the Avenue refracted and reflected light through the rising plumes. The cascading droplets of water sparkled like a million gleaming gems. Harmonizing with the scene, melodic music surrounded the fountains and the formal government buildings. Eryan happily noted it was a very special and beautiful evening.

The people were still coming, moving like an overflowing river into the Avenue and the open spaces between the Government Center and the coastal highway. With interest, she listened to the rising and excited murmuring and an occasional shouted greeting. The people, having come out to witness personally the return of Kellon's task force, seemed in a pleasant though somber mood. Eryan believed she fully understood why so many were quietly waiting, attentive but not being boisterous in their mannerisms.

Everyone knew that one of their Cruisers was gone— the Cruiser Lux and his entire crew had been lost while on a reconnaissance mission deep within Kreel space. Everyone fully understood the fate of their world depended on the Guardian Force. They understood their survival as a species was at stake. Therefore, the loss of even one Guardian Cruiser was worrisome; could it be a harbinger of things to come?

*Well,* she thought, with some latent simmering anger, *nearly everyone is concerned.* Chief Administrator Rich Sumor's concerns, however, were in sharp contrast with everyone else's. He thought the cruisers were indistinguishable from a bag of beans; to him Lux was nothing more than an expendable write-off from the existing inventory.

When she'd hit him head-on politically, he had smirked and discounted her anger. *Well,* she thought, *that was then.* Now, she'd delivered him an ultimatum; if he did not clear up his attitude, he would shortly depart Glas Dinnein for home, and he would not be coming back. She had put him on a short chain, and she was not about to offer him any slack. He had at last received the message loud and clear, and she knew for his own sake, he had better heed it.

Standing on her vantage point, she watched with interest the gathering population. Then she noticed a small group of Guardian officers carefully threading their way through the expanding crowd. They were wearing full dress uniforms, and she immediately felt the inner warmth that comes with recognition of old friends, three of which were among the group of officers. As a group, the officers were obviously in a lighthearted mood, freely exchanging bits of conversation with each other. Some of them were actually smiling and appeared to be in a very good humor. Their cheerful attitudes conflicted with her own more somber thoughts, which stimulated her curiosity. *Just what news,* she wondered, *do they have that lifted their spirits so?*

As they waved and smiled up at her, Guardian Fleet Admirals Mer Shawn, Ron Cloud, and Dylan Cord briskly moved up the steps to join her. As they approached, so infectious was their attitude that Eryan found herself smiling.

"Good evening, Madam Secretary," Mer cheerfully proclaimed. Responding, Eryan's smile broadened. "Good evening to you also, Fleet Admiral Mer Shawn. Might I inquire as to what the source of your obvious joviality might be on this occasion, other than possibly that of seeing good friends come home alive and intact?"

Mer's eyes were twinkling as his smile increased. "Perceptive as usual Eryan. There is good news and that in plenty."

"Well, don't just stand there grinning like some teenaged boy on his first date, out with it. What do you know that I also need to know?"

"Hmmmm. Now, Eryan, that is the first time I have been compared to a teenaged boy on his first date in, let me see, this coming autumn it will be three thousand and twenty-seven years. Thank you for the gift of that special remembrance. Now, if I remember correctly, on that particular occasion, I invited you to the First Year Cadet Ball at the Academy. As I recall, it was a most momentous event, and I continue to cherish that memory with fondness."

Eryan could not believe her own feelings; she was actually blushing at the memory of that long ago event. "Mer, you know precisely what I mean. Now out with it. What has the three of you overgrown Cadets so giddy?"

Ron broke in, "Good evening, Eryan." Teasingly, he added, "You must tell me about that first date with Mer sometime. A first year cadet's dance at the Academy? Hmmmm, I don't believe Mer has ever shared that story with me."

Eryan could no longer restrain the humor that bubbled up from deep within, "As for my recounting Mer's fanciful and fabricated stories about first dates— not likely Ron! Now, all ye hear this, I'm now claiming every lady's privilege: that being the right of plausible deniability. So, tell me what has all of you so happy."

"Well to begin with," Mer said, "today the Planetary Assembly passed an appropriations bill for forty new cruisers of the "L" class, and to boot, they threw in research seed money for the initial definition of an "M" class. That's sufficient good news to have every Guardian officer smiling this evening."

"Mer, out with it. There's something else behind that twinkle in your eyes?"

"Eryan, we do have some unexpected good news of a marvelous sort. Kellon has informed us he is bringing technical information that may permit us to revive Lux and his four scouts. It seems that the AIs have been doing some imaginative engineering on their own. While out on patrol around Earth they came up with an idea about AIs having souls—"

Eryan could not help but interrupt, "Souls? You can't be serious Mer. AIs are only enhanced machines. They are of a very high order, but they are only that, Artificial Intelligence constructs, programmed, constructed, designed and fashioned, and nothing else."

The smiles the three Admirals had displayed a moment earlier somewhat lessened. "Well Eryan, in fact, there may well be more to the AIs than most of us have previously realized. According to Kellon, the AIs on his last mission appear to have evolved somewhat significantly. They have clearly demonstrated humor and a sense of family and community. Oddly enough, Ambassador Wells' Earth-fashioned AI, William, may be near the heart of the evolution.

"What we know for certain is that Lan and his lead Scout Shey have apparently developed a method for an AI to preserve its core matrix if a Cobalt Blue condition develops. It seems Lux was among the Cruisers that received Shey's protocol."

"Protocol? What type of protocol is involved?" Eryan asked.

"Eryan, do you remember my saying a number of unidentified data blocks had been found embedded in the Cobalt Blue signal?" Ron inquired.

"Yes, Ron. You said that the analysts were reviewing the design specifications for the Cobalt Blue signal in order to find the definition and determine the meaning of those odd data blocks."

"Well," Ron continued, "they didn't find any reference to those odd data blocks. Now we know why. Kellon has informed us that Lan and his Scouts, most notably Shey, designed and developed those data blocks. They contained pointers to more than one hundred data segments Lux had sent to the nearest Navigation Beacon, just prior to initiation of the Cobalt Blue signal. Shey has now recovered Lux's data segments, and we believe they may hold the core matrixes for Lux and all of his Scouts."

Turning to Mer, Eryan inquired, "If the data mentioned does contain the AI core matrixes, then what's the next step?"

Eryan's question restored Mer's smile. "Eryan, there is a new Cruiser coming off the construction ways in a month. Its AI core is currently finished and intact, but it has not been loaded. Kellon has requested that we give Lan and his crew first go at the new AI cores. He wants a crack at reviving Lux before we do anything else. If we can actually revive Lux, then his restored operational capability will help us in understanding how the Kreel detected him. If all of this really works, it means the AIs have come up with something of real significance."

Looking at each of their confident expressions, Eryan began to understand why they were so happy.

"Gentlemen, this is truly wonderful news. It means while we lost Lux's crew, we may still have Lux and his Scouts. Still, is there any doubt Kellon can revive Lux? What are the odds that it will really work?"

Dylan spoke up first, "Well, that is sorta where the rub comes in. According to Kellon, the AIs are confident it will work. On the other hand, the AI engineers disagree. They claim no one can simply reload an AI core matrix without creating unstable psychological aberrations in the personality and memory matrixes. The programmers are adamant that it would be far best to shut down the effort even before it begins."

Mer cut in, "The kicker is that Lan and his Scouts maintain they can fully revive Lux if they are provided access to a new AI core. Their absolute confidence, when weighed against the engineers' contrary certainty, comes down in favor of the AIs position. I am willing to wager the AIs may know more about their own functionality than the engineers. This might be a case where the product has evolved beyond the designer's initial specifications. If Lan and Shey can do what they say, then it means a revolutionary quantum Jump in AI engineering. We will simply have to wait and see."

"Gentlemen," Eryan said in a silken tone they all knew well, "when Lan and Shey attempt to revive Lux, I will be there. There are to be no exceptions and no excuses or dodges."

With a nod of his head, Mer acknowledged Eryan's ultimatum. "Yes, Madam Secretary. However, be advised it may be a bit crowded in that new Cruiser's CAC. Even Ambassador Wells is demanding to be present, as are Kellon and Commanders Roan and Zorn. And be advised the three of us overgrown cadets will also be in attendance along with every AI engineer that can fit into the available space."

At that moment, the Guardian anthem began. Off in the Eastern sky a group of bright lights was apparent low on the horizon. As everyone turned to look eastward, the hundreds of lasers positioned along the Avenue of Fountains burst into intense shafts of light, like uplifted swords crossing high above the center of the Avenue. Eryan, Mer, Ron, and Dylan turned to the east, as did everyone else. A hush fell over the crowd as the distant lights drew larger.

As the Guardian Force anthem built in its majesty, the ground began to rumble as the seven Cruisers approached. All were moving in a single trailing line, slowly passing between the crossing laser beams before proceeding toward the west. Each Cruiser was brilliant in their parade colors, glistening gold trim over solid gleaming white. On their bows, each Cruiser displayed a broad chevron strip of deep purple, a mourning band denoting the loss of one of their own.

The middle Cruiser in the column, Lan, drew abreast of the Planetary Assembly Building. Then the entire column came to a hover and each cruiser gracefully rotated about their centers until they were facing south. Lan was facing directly toward the Assembly Building and toward the four people who were standing on its top step. As they completed their rotation, the music of the anthem reached its crescendo, and both the music and ground effects ceased. The thousands of people gathered along the Avenue, however, continued their cheering and applause.

Amid the applause, each Cruiser simultaneously launched its four Scouts, and each Scout was also adorned in their glistening parade colors. Since Lux's Scouts had been lost, each Scout also bore a purple chevron. Moving upward and taking positions above their Cruisers, the twenty-eight Scouts added to the spectacle of seven silent Cruisers hovering low to the ground.

Then from Lan, there emerged a single lifter, a glistening white disk of radiance trimmed in gold. Standing on the lifter were three people and one dog; Commodore Kellon, Commander Roy Grey, Ambassador Wells, and Gepeto. The transport disk moved directly toward the top step of the Assembly Building. As it drew near, it was evident to everyone that all three people on the disk were smiling, along with Gepeto.

As the lifter disk glided to a precise stop before to the stairway, Commodore Kellon and his three companions stepped forward and onto the steps. Kellon briskly saluted his three senior Admirals and Eryan, "Commodore Kellon, reporting as ordered."

As the group stepped off, the lifter silently elevated and moved back to its starting point within Lan.

Mer, Ron, and Dylan together smartly returned Kellon's salute. Mer voiced the assessment of all present, "Commodore Kellon, again welcome home. You, your ships, and your crews are commended for a mission well done."

As the officers had exchanged their salutes, again the cheering and applause broke out along the entire length of the Avenue. Smiling, Kellon turned toward the hovering ships and smartly saluted them. "Well done, each and every one of you. Dismissed!" In perfect unison, the assembled ships rose vertically and then moved forward over the Assembly Building. Pivoting gracefully through a wide turn and moving out over the ocean— still in tight formation— the entire task force gracefully arched upward toward the stars. When the ships were about three kilometers off shore, they suddenly vanished from sight.

Turning, Mer faced the gathered throng. Keying his communicator, he activated the public address system. Raising his hand for silence, he spoke a few words from his heart that he meant everyone to hear.

"The Guardian ships that have tonight returned to Glas Dinnein have been in heavy combat in two different solar systems. Some of them were on patrol for nearly ten months. While on their assigned stations, they have repeatedly engaged and fought the Kreel in a number of deadly battles. They are here with us tonight because they destroyed their Kreel counterparts. These returning seven Cruisers, with five other Cruisers who are still on duty, fought in defense of two different worlds. During that same time, other Guardian ships were probing deep within Kreel-dominated space. They went into harm's way, looking for information that might help us forever end the Kreel menace.

"Regretfully, while he was alone and on deep reconnaissance, one of our Cruisers, including his Scouts and crew, were lost in a fiercely fought battle. The Cruiser Lux is gone. Know this: they did not perish in vain.

"This morning the Planetary Assembly approved the construction of forty new Cruisers with their accompanying Scouts. We have needed these additional ships for many years now."

Turning toward Eryan, he smiled. "Today we have the promise of those ships, and our Admiral Secretary of the Planetary Assembly was the prime mover in seeing we obtain what we so badly needed.

"Thank you all for coming out this evening to honor and acknowledge the return of this fighting force. Your acknowledgment of their service is far more important to each of them than you may realize. Again thank you for coming."

The applause and cheers briefly rose, and then it slowly died away, as the assembled people began to disperse. Pausing a moment, Kellon turned toward Admiral Mer Shawn.

"Sir, I brought with me tonight the man whose knowledge and proficiency made what we achieved possible. You already know Commander Roy Grey, but now know he is a genius and his knowledge of Jump technology is unsurpassed. Sir, any credit that is due anyone for what was accomplished on this mission rightfully belongs to Roy."

As Roy frowned, Mer turned and shook his hand. "Roy, it is indeed good to see you once more. So, you've been up to your traditional habits of doing the impossible."

Slowly shaking his head, Roy looked decidedly uncomfortable. "No, Sir. I merely did my job, and nothing more. I don't know why Commodore Kellon is making so much fuss of so little."

Gathering around Roy, the three Admirals exchanged greetings and light conversation with him. As they spoke, three ground cars moved along the now mostly empty Avenue and came to a stop at the bottom of the stairs. A few minutes later, the group as a whole turned and slowly descended the stairs to the waiting cars. Like the old friends they truly were, they bid their cheerful evening farewells to each other and separated into three groups, the Admirals taking one car, Kellon and Roy the second, and Eryan with Susie and Gepeto the third.

The three vehicles moved off to their various destinations. As they departed, the sky above was adorned with countless bright stars, and as the early evening slipped into deeper night, once more the Avenue of Fountains was serenely peaceful.

# Chapter Twenty-Two:
# **Not Alone**

The next day found Susie, Eryan, and Gepeto aboard a lifter moving through the Guardian shipyard. As they drew near to a grounded cruiser that was under construction, its real size and mass became steadily more apparent. Susie sat on the lifter seat next to Eryan while holding Gepeto closely against her knees. Over the preceding months, Gepeto had grown accustomed to rides on lifters and was enjoying looking about at the world around him, even looking with interest towards the crisp edge of the world where the dark blue of the ocean sharply contrasted with the light blue sky.

"Eryan, the Cruisers are so much larger when seen on the ground. I suppose it's because they can be compared with familiar objects. That cruiser is huge. What I don't understand is why it's that incredible metallic shade of forest green. Is it some form of temporary protective paint?"

"No, Susie, that's its true permanent color. During its construction, the builders coat each ship with a very special layer of cholesteric liquid crystals. The metallic green color you are seeing is the natural color of the coating."

"What in the world are cholesteric liquid crystals?" Susie asked.

"I'm not an engineer, Susie, but I understand they're microscopic liquid crystals and are asymmetric in such a way that the structure and its mirror image are not superimposable. The engineers explained that the crystals are spiral— or helical— in structure, and therefore reflect light that is polarized in the same direction. By making subtle alterations in the frequencies and waveforms of an electric charge on the underside of the coating, we can change the dimensions of the crystals' helices. In this way, we can precisely alter the color of light being reflected. This is how the ships are able to alter their colors so rapidly and to display so wide a color variation."

"It all sounds simple, but I'd wager a root beer that it isn't that easy," Susie commented.

"I'll not take that wager, because the science involved is far more complicated. The coatings can also radiate light, rather than simply reflecting it. Making it even more complex, in order to obtain its stealth capability, the coating also involves complicated plasmonic engineering."

"Plasmonic engineering, what's that?" Susie asked.

Eryan turned with a smile and laughed. "Other than my saying plasmonic engineering has something to do with the quantization of plasma, I can't explain how that works. What I know is that when we do commission the cruiser, it will assume the appropriate colors for its environment and defined mission. Unless it's in for repair, it will not show its true forest green colors again."

As they neared it, Susie studied the massive bulk of the cruiser. "For one, I rather like the natural green color. It's beautiful and I think it is clean and very attractive."

As they drew near the new cruiser's hull, they saw the cargo-receiving hatch was yawning wide open. As they approached the hatch, the guardrails at the edge of the deck automatically withdrew. Their lifter entered smoothly into the compartment. Behind them, the guardrails moved swiftly back into their guard position.

Even as Eryan and Susie unfastened their lap restraints and stood, Zorn briskly entered the compartment. "Welcome Madam Secretary and Ambassador Wells. You're both right on time. Bending down, he tussled Gepeto's ears, "You are also welcomed, handsome dog that you are."

Looking up with a big smile, Zorn continued, "Admiral Mer Shawn has directed me to gather you up and hustle you to the observation dome. The programmers and engineers have set up their working consoles there. Captain Riley is watching over everything with a critical eye, not certain if he's happy with his sparkling brand new cruiser even temporarily taking on the persona of a Cruiser that initiated a Cobalt Blue signal. He seems somewhat superstitious about such trifling matters. As you might well imagine, things are a bit unsettled."

"Zorn, how much time before they actually try to revive Lux?" Susie asked.

At that moment, Susie's personal communicator announced, "Good morning Susie, Shey here. I can answer that question. Currently, I am in the final stages of preparing to revive Lux. My orders, however, are to wait until both the Admiral Secretary and you are in attendance before continuing."

Shey had simultaneously addressed everyone in the compartment, and hearing Shey's comment, Zorn smiled broadly. "Well, now you have the current status authoritatively from the lead Scout's very mouth, so to speak."

"Good morning, Shey, how do you feel about what is happening?" Eryan asked.

"Good morning, Madam Secretary. The AIs are trying to understand why there is so much concern. At first, our protocol will disorient Lux. Under similar circumstances, however, anyone would be similarly affected. To stabilize Lux, we have linked ten of his nearest family, and we are in tight contact with his communications cortex. Our primary task is to support him as he integrates and normalizes his persona."

As they carried on their conversation with Shey, they moved carefully into the ship, skirting the various construction items organized and stacked along the passageway. Everywhere there were ship builders at work. As the workers moved into and out of the various compartments, going about their tasks, the noise rose in a rhythmic din. Finding the operational elevator, they were happy as the doors closed behind them and dampened out the bedlam. It was a quick lift to the upper deck and when the doors opened, they were relieved to learn the upper passageway was relatively quiet. Exiting the elevator, they moved forward toward the domed conference room.

As they walked, Susie kept sniffing the air, trying to determine what was so different. Zorn saw her and smiled, "Right on Susie. What you smell is the new cruiser smell. It consists of the odors of the new materials. The ship has not yet begun to take on the multitudes of odors of the crew, food, lubricants, warm electronic panels, sweat, and the millions of other odors that will permeate the ship's inner atmosphere after a year in space."

The three of them and Gepeto entered the domed conference room and paused. It was indeed busy. As they'd entered, Admiral Mer Shawn looked up, and seeing them, smiled. "Good morning ladies. Madam Secretary, Ambassador, welcome."

One tall trim young officer separated himself from the gathered group and quickly came to meet them. His eyes had a happy twinkle, but otherwise his expression was both formal and serious. Holding out his hand to Eryan, he greeted her, "Madam Secretary Eryan Kyrie, I am Captain Riley. Welcome aboard. I regret that I currently lack the honor guard that is appropriate for your visit to my ship."

Eryan warmly took his hand in greeting, "Captain Riley, I will look forward with pleasure to the formal commissioning of your ship and the review of your honor guard."

As Captain Riley looked around at the engineers and the work they were performing, his expression became contemplative. "Madam Secretary, I earnestly hope that the commissioning will not be delayed overly long."

He then turned and looked at Susie. She saw his eyes sparkle with an apparent interest, and Susie felt his eye contact as a small rush of excitement. She considered inwardly, *This man is handsome, obviously intelligent, and accomplished. More to the point, he knows it.* She was decidedly attracted to the young officer, but her feminine instincts promptly cautioned her. *Easy there girl, remember a sailor has a girl in every port.*

"Welcome aboard, Ambassador Susie Wells of Earth. You are most welcome indeed," Captain Riley said.

Turning, Captain Riley examined Gepeto, who was likewise studying him. "Might I say Ambassador, your dog has quite a presence. Can I touch him?"

Susie found herself smiling. In spite of her own cautionary warning, she needed to confess she liked this man. "Certainly Captain Riley, he's quite friendly."

Bending, Captain Riley hesitantly patted Gepeto on his head. In response, Gepeto looked directly up into the captain's eyes and put on his best doggy grin.

"I think he likes you," Eryan commented.

Standing, Captain Riley again looked about the room. "Ladies, we've completed the initial preparations for the experiment. If you approve, I'll get this morning's work in full swing."

"Please proceed," Eryan responded.

Looking toward Captain Riley, Roan asked, "Sir, shall we continue?"

"Yes, Commander Roan. Proceed, all ahead slow."

Roan addressed the group of engineers, "Gentlemen, are you ready with your monitoring and recording equipment?"

An engineer with dark gray eyes and silver hair looked up smiling. "Commander, we are about as ready as ready gets. It's your call from here on. If I see something seriously wrong, I'll let you know mighty pronto."

Roan took a deep breath, then inquired, "Shey and Lan, are you fully coordinated with your family and interlaced into Lux's communications cortex?"

As Roan asked his question of Lan and Shey, and because of how he asked that question, the senior engineer's expression took on a troubled frown. He slowly shook his head, as if bewildered, but he said nothing.

"Yes, Sir, the family is in a tight link and we can begin now," Lan replied.

"Lan, proceed with the revival process."

"Continuing, as ordered," Lan responded.

For some minutes, nothing appeared to be happening. Then the group of engineers began to murmur among themselves.

"Curtis, what's happening? There shouldn't be higher math cortex activity at this stage. What's going on in sector thirty, that sector is ablaze with activity. It's supposed to be purely mathematical in its functions. It has no intuitive or logical functionality whatsoever. It should be inert. Ross, check sector 82, that sector is off the scale in activity, and the communications cortex is at 99.9999. None of this makes any sense."

"Commander Roan," Shey said quietly, "we have successfully revived Lux to the level where you might say he is dreaming. He is barely conscious, and his thoughts are probing in a vague manner. Lan says Lux is stable, but very tightly spun up. He still believes he is under attack and is responding with outrage and fury. We are going to hold at this level while attempting to interface with his intellectual and emotional functions. We must bring him down from his rage, and we need to do this slowly. Sir, Lux is really fighting mad. I have never seen a Cruiser AI so angry, it's a little frightening."

"Shey, hold as you have indicated. We don't want Lux to remain angry, but we also do not want him to lose any of the reasons why he is angry. Do you understand what I mean?" Roan asked.

"Yes, Roan, I do understand. We will continue working to calm him down as we bring him forward with all his past memories intact."

The senior engineer looked up toward Roan with an utterly lost expression, "Commander, my name is Gregory Glenn. Did the Scout AI say frightening? Let me tell you that what I'm hearing frightens *me*. I've spent more than five hundred years designing and programming AIs. Yet, I'm watching what's happening here, and can't begin to understand it. I'm listening to you interact with the Scout ship designated Shey, and am astonished at what I am hearing. Commander, do you always interact with your AIs in such a personal and familiar manner?"

"Well, Mr. Glenn, you've asked a number of distinct questions. In fact, I am merely interacting with Shey as I believe is correct. Sir, based on my own experience, the AIs are not unaware logical artifacts. Each AI is a separate, distinct, and unique persona."

"Commander, you speak to the AI as if it has a unique vital force, as if it were a living being. Are you aware you're doing that? Have you always addressed them as you now do?"

Roan paused, thinking for a moment before replying, "No, Sir. Such easy communications with our AIs wasn't normal at the outset. During the past several years, however, the AIs have noticeably evolved. Surely you initially designed the AIs for such an evolutionary process?"

"Commander, I assure you we hoped that they would evolve into a more robust functionality, however we did not consider a major shift and expansion of their persona, as has quite evidently occurred. I'm still trying to understand how this could have happened. What we're seeing during this revival of Lux is off the scale of existing AI theory. It shouldn't be happening as it is, and that it *is* happening, demands our learning just how it came about. "Somewhere there must be a missing key or contributing external factor we have not yet discerned— something extraordinary. Major and serious analysis is required here just to catch up with what's already happened, and— more importantly— to permit us to predict what is likely to happen next."

"Roan, Lan says Lux is calming down, and he is becoming more balanced in his emotional functionality. He still believes he is fighting for his life, but is now aware he has other Guardian Cruisers supporting his fight for survival. He is asking about his sisters, and is worrying about their condition. He wants to know if they are safe. He is also in shock and grief over the death of his crew. He knows they are gone, and he is emotionally hurting."

"Good girl, Shey, stay with Lux and help him. Tell Lux he and his sisters are safe. Let him know that Guardian personnel are near and helping him. Stress he is not alone! Tell him that he's accomplished a wonderful feat, and the Kreel are now gone."

"Yes, Roan. I will tell Lux."

Captain Riley looked toward Roan with a questioning and puzzled look. "Commander, did I hear your Scout ship correctly? Did she say that Lux was fighting mad and furious, and in grief over the death of his crew? I would swear that's what I heard."

Inwardly, Roan personally felt a sense of pride in what was happening. "Sir, you did hear Shey say precisely what you believed she said. Captain Riley, I don't know if you'll elect to maintain Lux's persona as this cruiser's AI. In my opinion, you would be both wise and prudent to give such an idea the consideration it deserves."

"Commander, I haven't for a moment considered that possibility. Why do you believe I should?"

"Sir, Lux has five years of patrol and hard-won combat experience. That he obviously cares for his lost crew only adds value to that experience. If he's found stable and without serious aberrations in his performance profile, he would represent an incredibly valuable asset— one that should not be quickly discarded."

"Commander Roan, I will give your advice the serious consideration it deserves. As I understand the matter, the final choice is not only mine to make. The engineers and programmers will need to study the Lux AI matrix carefully. Before Lux can return to service, they will first need to sign off on his functionality and stability. Fleet Operations will also need to approve of Lux resuming a combat role. Given everyone approves; I'm willing to seriously consider Lux having a berth aboard."

"Commander Roan," inserted Glenn, "Did Scout Ship Shey actually express Lux was in an emotional state of fury? Did she actually mean that he was grieving? Actually emotionally hurting? Commander, I don't believe for a minute that any AI can be emotionally hurting! It simply isn't possible. None of those emotional vectors are any part of the existing AI matrixes. The more I hear, the more confused I become. I can't begin to understand what might have transpired that could alter even the AI's most fundamental core matrix."

"Well, Mr. Glenn, if Shey says Lux is emotionally hurting, I suggest you accept her testimony as being reliable. I have never known her to exaggerate or misrepresent anything."

"Commander Roan, have you any idea whatsoever what has brought about the radical changes in the AI matrixes that are being exhibited here?"

"Sir, I may possibly have a viable theory, but our discussion about that theory will need to wait for a more opportune time.

"Commander, anything you can provide that sheds light on what's happening here is critical. Your name is now deeply etched on my calendar note pad, and I am requesting a long conversation as soon as possible!"

# Chapter Twenty-Three:
## Muck in a Primeval Swamp

"Roan, Lan says Lux is now sleeping," Shey reported. "We are in the process of balancing and integrating his persona centers, and adjusting his emotional functions to be in harmony with the new temporal information."

"Shey, this is Gregory Glenn. Where have you learned how to do all of this?"

"Good morning, Mr. Glenn. I am an AI. Therefore, it is vital for me to understand my functionality: what, and who I am."

The engineer looked as if Shey's response had utterly dazed him. "Shey, please continue with whatever you are doing to help Lux. however, can you tell me how long it might take?"

"Yes Mr. Glenn. It will take at least another nine hours for the adjustments to take their full effect. Lux must successfully integrate his past persona with the new temporal data that we are providing him. There must be a seamless interface between his experiences and his new circumstances. This means we must proceed slowly, to assure he remains emotionally stable.

"Roan, with your permission, we want to begin with the revival of Lux's sisters."

"Wait one, Shey. No one has discussed reviving Lux's Scouts. Give me a moment to clear your request with the higher brass."

Turning toward Admiral Mer Shawn, Roan asked, "Sir, did you monitor Shey's request to permit them to commence revival of Lux's sisters?"

"Commander Roan, I think we need to wait until the engineers can give us their input about Lux and their approval for us to proceed."

Mer turned toward the senior engineer, "Mr. Glenn, we do have four brand new AI scouts' cores in the hangar bays. Do you have any objections about permitting Lan to continue with the revival of Lux's Scouts?"

"Admiral, we need to interface instrumentation and recording equipment in all the bays before any revival process begins. What I've already seen here is mind bending in its significance. What's happening affects the entire Guardian Force, and perhaps even humanity as a whole. We need at least a full day to set up our equipment, and another day to permit us to evaluate what we've already monitored."

"Understood. Given its apparent importance, we will give you three full days to set up your equipment and review your data before we continue. Unless you find some valid reason to halt this process, we will resume the revival of Lux's Scouts in three days' time."

"Thank you, Sir. I will get my team busy at once."

Glenn began to turn away, then paused and addressed Mer again. "Sir, I am also formally requesting of Guardian Force that I am permitted an opportunity to sit and talk with Commander Roan as soon as possible. It is apparent that the AIs have been engaged in significant modifications of their own core matrixes. The consequence of such AI activity is far beyond anything we anticipated, and Commander Roan's insights might offer us a key to understand what has happened."

"Mr. Glenn, your request is duly noted. I will arrange for a meeting between the two of you following Lux's revival."

Roan's personal communicator softly hummed in his left ear, and he heard Shey actually whispering. "Roan, while interacting with Lux, Lan has discovered something important. He believes the information is best restricted to Commodore Kellon, Zorn, and you. He has requested me to ask you to find a private area where he can display some information."

"Shey, I'll see what I can do."

Turning, Roan quickly looked around the room. "Zorn, I need to see you for a moment."

Zorn was watching over the shoulders of the engineers with keen interest. He looked up at Roan, and it was clear from his expression that he wondered what was up. "Acknowledged, I'm on my way."

Noticing the exchange between Roan and Zorn, Susie's curiosity clicked into gear. Obviously, Roan wanted a private exchange with Zorn, but why?

Moving into the passageway, Roan and Zorn walked several steps before Zorn inquired, "Roan, what gives? Why the need for privacy?"

Shrugging, Roan looked somewhat perplexed. "It's not my call, it's Lan's request. It seems Lan wants to provide us with a confidential briefing.

"Shey, Zorn and I are clear of the others. We are moving down the corridor looking for an empty compartment, one with a bulkhead display. You might want to ask Commodore Kellon to follow us."

"Yes, Roan, I am passing your suggestion to Commodore Kellon, even as we speak. As requested, he is following. He has stopped to ask Captain Riley for permission to use his conference room. Roan, Captain Riley has given us his permission. Commodore Kellon says you are to proceed directly to the conference room."

Picking up their pace, Roan and Zorn strode to the elevator and dropped down to the third level, then moved forward until they reached the Captain Riley's conference room. Entering, they found the conference room fully equipped. It was apparent Captain Riley was using the area as his working duty office during the final stages of construction.

As Roan looked about, the door opened and Commodore Kellon entered, with Susie and Eryan right behind him. "Gentlemen, I hope you don't mind extra company. I was unable to persuade either the Admiral Secretary or the Ambassador that I was not up to something of great interest. So, to paraphrase Zorn, what's up?"

Roan thought, *It is as it will be.* "Sir, we really don't know the answer to that question. Lan has indicated that he found some information while interacting with Lux that is best restricted."

Frowning, Kellon directly addressed Lan. "Lan, what have you to show us?"

"Sir, what I have isolated are the final few moments before Lux initiated the Cobalt Blue signal, and they are very revealing. Unfortunately, programmers still view AIs as pure logical constructs in functionality. It is improbable that they can understand an AI skillfully dissembling, without considering that action a malfunction in the core matrix. They stubbornly hold to their early design misconception that for AIs, a zero is only a number, without admitting it is also an abstract concept. If, at this point, they conclude Lux was malfunctioning, their erroneous conclusion would prejudice them against Lux. That would not be good."

Roan sighed, Lan's explanation made it clear the AIs were capable of keeping secrets, even from their programmers. "Lan, are you telling us Lux was capable of intentionally misleading someone, and that he lied?"

"No, Roan, AIs cannot lie. Lux skillfully dissembled, and there is a difference between a lie and purposeful dissembling."

Roan groaned inwardly, thinking, *Indeed Lan, it's a difference measured in very subtle shades of gray.*

"Sir, the information I want to show you proves Lux was dissembling, but only where necessary. I question if it is something that Guardian Force would want known, even to the programmers."

Kellon's eyebrows rose as he brought his hand up to his forehead and sighed. "Lan, are you are telling us that Lux intentionally deceived someone with a misrepresentation— as distinguished from an intentional lie? Precisely whom did he deceive?"

"Sir, he intentionally deceived a senior Kreel officer, but it was not a lie. I believe Zorn describes the tactic Lux employed as 'to sucker him.'"

Groaning, Zorn shook his head. "And I thought Shey's ability to giggle was noteworthy. Remind me to never play cards with you again, Lan."

Roan was trying very hard not to laugh at Zorn's discomfiture, as Kellon held out the chair for Eryan to sit and Roan did the same for Susie. As the bulkhead monitor brightened, Kellon, Roan, and Zorn took other seats. Then Kellon ordered, "Lan, we are ready. Please play back your retrieved data."

"Yes, Sir. I am editing the playback to the last few entries." Suddenly the bulkhead monitor swirled into motion, showing the crisp image of a senior Kreel officer. Zorn whistled in appreciation, "Wow, would you look at all that bright work on his harness. I've never before seen that much glitter on any Kreel officer's harness."

Zorn was correct— the Kreel officer's harness was sparkling with awards and medallions, and was lavishly decorated with a copious quantity of large brilliant gems and precious metals. As obvious as the glitter was, so was the officer's sneer.

"Feeble intruder, you dared enter the Kreel Empire to spy and pry. You dared to attempt to deceive and out maneuver me, a Grand Marshal of the Kreel Elite Guard. Fool! You have now paid for that insult and rashness. You have felt the sting of my lash and heat of my anger. I, Grand Marshal Grough, warned you that any attempt to flee or fight me would bring about your destruction. You did not heed my warning. Now you have tasted my power and found it bitter nourishment.

"I admit you are an interesting foe, whoever you are. Never before have I encountered one, other than the Nori, who is capable of threatening me and surviving more than a few minutes. You are not of the Nori, yet you have craftily evaded my grasp for a full day, and you have also destroyed fourteen of my ships. No other foe has ever done so much damage to Elite Guard ships in our own space. Be assured, I will learn who you are! I intend to strip the very plates off of your hull, one plate at a time, and your continued silence will not protect you.

"My sensors indicate you are severely damaged, most of your crew must already be dead, and yet you struggle feebly to evade. You cannot. Your missiles are gone, your laser turrets are inoperative, your power is failing, and I have rendered you to nothing more than a slug crawling on your belly.

"Now, and for a few moments more, I offer those of you still alive one last chance to survive. Surrender and you will live. Resist further and you will die. You have no more time to consider. Respond now to my offer or perish. That is your last choice."

As the Kreel officer concluded his tirade and ultimatum, Lux's clear strong voice thundered in response, and his use of the Kreel language was flawless. "Grand Marshal Grough, you speak of your power but hide behind your females. For the past day, you have boasted of your prowess, while I have mocked and destroyed your puny ships. Am I so damaged I cannot fight? You are obviously not among the twenty-two ships that are still too frightened to close and do battle with me. Twenty-two ships and yet you cower somewhere else, lacking the courage to fight. You speak of being puny, you indeed know much about puny. You are no warrior, but only a crossbred throwback to a ball of muck in a primeval swamp."

Grough's anger flared. "So you can speak our language. Fool, dare you insult me? I am indeed among those ships that will crush you in our jaws. Observe fool, for you are about to die."

"Grough, your boasts are as empty as your skull. Where did you buy your medallions? Did you steal them? You certainly lack the intellect necessary to earn them. Braggart, I dare you to expose your worthless blotchy hide and come forth to do battle!"

Ripples of rage twisted the officer's expression. "If you were to survive this day, because of your insolence, you would indeed die very slowly and linger painfully. Know this fool, because of your insults, your kind will pay with their blood. I will search and find your planet, regardless of its location, and I will pulverize it beneath my boots! That I swear!"

"Sir, the following message from Lux was not broadcast. He knew he must initiate the Cobalt Blue signal, and he left one last message for us. The Kreel did not hear this message. It was until now only held in Lux's last core message queue."

"Admiral Mer Shawn. Guardian Cruiser Lux is reporting. I hope my Cobalt Blue signal reaches home. I am saddened I was unable to bring my crew home safely. They were my family and they fought with great courage. We have been in battle for more than a day, and they died fighting, even as I have continued to fight in their honor. In this circumstance, Captain Harlow ordered me to execute a Cobalt Blue. Following the death of my crew, I made all necessary preparations to do so.

"If you receive this message, you will have the ability to reconstruct what has happened. Know this; we first encountered the Kreel Elite Guard near what they call Hub-3. They are very capable, and their ships are far superior to any Kreel ships I have before encountered. Grand Marshal Grough is a brilliant officer. Although he fought with superior numbers, he also fought with great skill and cunning. I have knowingly deceived him with insult to lure him into coming close enough for me to take him out in the fusion detonation.

"The remaining twenty-two Kreel ships have entered their maximum heavy missile range and are within the fusion detonation volume. I am counting twelve heavy missiles inbound. I must go now.

"Lan, Shey, all my beloved family, May we meet again soon. Lux out."

"Sir, this ends Lux's personal communication. What follows is his last communication with the Kreel."

The bulkhead screen again swirled into motion, and the image of the Kreel officer's glowering presence filled the screen. "Grand Marshal Grough, in spite of your overwhelming arrogance, I must confess that you are in truth a brilliant tactician and a bold warrior. I salute you. However, know this truth, before you can pulverize anything beneath your boots, you must first have boots. Know then who has destroyed you. I am Lux!"

"Sir, that is the end of the transmission. According to Lux's sensor data, all twenty-two Kreel ships were well within the fusion volume at the time of the detonation. Accordingly, all the Kreel ships must have perished along with Lux. I thought you should see this record before anyone else witnessed it."

Leaning back in contemplation, Kellon was frowning. *Not only can AIs giggle, they can conceive of strategies and employ crafted deceptions. Lux fought alone and without the benefit of his crew.* Kellon could not imagine Lux's dedicated persistence following the death of his crew. His battle achievements were remarkable, that was certain. Lux accounted for thirty-six first-line Kreel fighting ships, and in addition he canceled at least one senior Kreel officer's distinguished career with utmost prejudice. *If this represents what the Cruiser AIs are evolving toward, then they are indeed becoming formidable warriors.*

"Lan, well done. Your evaluation was correct: we must guard this information. I in particular ask you to scan Lux's records for all mentions of the Nori, since they are of particular interest. You are to encrypt these segments, and any others you consider sensitive, as being Black Hole. Then hold all such information until I instruct you to transmit it."

"Yes, Sir. Commodore Kellon, may I ask, did Lux do anything wrong?"

"No, Lan, Lux did everything very well indeed. His crew would have been as proud of him as I am. Captain Harlow was my friend, and I know he would be extremely proud of Lux."

"Sir, if you authorize me to do so, I would like to tell Lux you believe he did well and are proud of him. He will also be glad to learn you believe Captain Harlow would be proud of him. If it were me, I would want to know you were proud. I believe it would help him to know this."

"By all means Lan, tell Lux. Tell him I absolutely know for a fact Captain Harlow would be very proud of him. Inform him I am looking forward to speaking with him at length soon."

Susie looked from Kellon to Roan and then to Zorn, studying their expressions and observing their mixed emotions. "I don't understand a word of Kreel, but I take it that whatever was said was important. Will someone please tell me what the Kreel officer and Lux said? It was readily apparent Lux said something that infuriated the Kreel officer, but what he said is a mystery to me."

Zorn looked up and faintly smiled, "Well, Susie, while some of it was very important indeed, I particularly enjoyed the part where Lux told the Kreel officer he was a crossbred throwback to a ball of muck in a primeval swamp. In my lexicon, that expression is now colored solid gold."

Eryan put her hand on Susie's arm, "Zorn is understandably attempting to lighten a heavy topic with humor. I understand what was said Susie. I promise I will tell you later. You are correct, what was said was very important."

Eryan looked about the table and deeply sighed. "Gentlemen, what is, is. Commodore Kellon, you will undoubtedly promptly want to discuss this matter with Admiral Mer Shawn."

"Yes, Madam Secretary. That's precisely my intention."

"Good. Now, I believe we need to return to the domed conference room before we have everyone coming to look for us."

# Chapter Twenty-Four:
# **Return Visit**

Opening the flyer's door, Kellon stepped out onto the runway's apron and turned toward the approaching shuttle bug. The visit to the shipyard and meeting with Captain Riley and Lux had proven very helpful. Lux had come through a successful revival, and Guardian Operations had certified him stable and whole. The programmers and engineers were still studying that unexpected outcome, and were trying to understand just how the AIs had accomplished the feat. Best of all, Riley and Lux were beginning to work well together, and that was a process of bonding. Smiling, he believed Riley and Lux would make a good team, and he felt confident Guardian Force would benefit from their combined capabilities.

As he watched the approaching bug, he considered what Kur had told him of the Kreel Elite Guard. Kur was surprised to learn that he knew of them and commented, "Those who learn of the Elite Guard do not often survive long to say much about them."

It was the Elite Guard that protected Hub-3 from any possible attack, including defending against treachery from the Military. They fulfilled their duty with zeal, apparently enjoying investigating any rumor of sedition or insubordination within the Military. Their power of summary judgment included an unquestioned swift sentence of death to anyone they deemed treacherous, except perhaps for the highest ranking within the Military.

It was Kur's earnest opinion that the Elite Guard had real power within the Kreel Empire, power unmatched or exceeded by anyone. His understanding was the regular Kreel military officers justifiably feared the Elite Guard and took every opportunity to avoid being anywhere near them.

Arkillian Intelligence indicated the Elite Guard controlled three squadrons of approximately thirty-five ships each. Arkillian

Intelligence lacked tactical performance data, but they had established the Kreel Military considered the Elite Guard ships far more advanced than their own ships. Significantly, an Elite Grand Marshal was in command of each of their three squadrons, and in addition to their squadrons, they each commanded thousands of special force troops.

Kur's informed assessment was that the three Grand Marshals of the Kreel Elite Guard constituted the true pinnacle of Kreel Military forces. The Grand Marshals answered to none, except the honored Elite One himself. They were therefore among the seven most powerful Kreel within their Empire.

As for Grand Marshal Grough, Kur assured him that Arkillian Intelligence viewed him as being the most senior of the three Grand Marshals. He was utterly ruthless, efficient, and greatly feared. Upon learning this, Kellon did not reveal to Kur that Guardian Force had just terminated the Grand Marshal's career.

When Kellon had asked Kur about the Nori, he was surprised to learn the Elite Guard considered anyone a real threat. He promised he would pass Kellon's inquiry about the Nori along to Arkillian historians and Intelligence services. Perhaps, he suggested, they might know something about the Nori.

As he stood waiting, Kellon grimly thought that Lux had done very well indeed. It seemed he took out an entire Elite Guard squadron, along with its Commanding Officer. *Undoubtedly,* he thought, *the Kreel will need to fill that sudden void. Just how long might that take?*

As he considered his pending meeting with Admiral Mer Shawn, the bug rolled up and stopped with its normal squeal of brakes, and the side passenger door slid open. Entering the bug, Kellon took a seat and leaned forward to speak, as if there were still a human driver to hear, "Fleet Headquarters, entrance four." As the warning note sounded, the bug's doors slid closed. Then it smoothly accelerated, moving briskly across the apron. The bug precisely negotiated the crossing lanes of the runways, even as if a real driver were driving, unerringly heading for the tall Guardian Fleet Headquarters building.

Until then, Kellon had been unaware of just how tense he'd become while flying back to the Capitol. It was a short trip, but the uncertainty in his mind was intense. *How will Admiral Mer*

*Shawn receive my request? Well, it will not take long before I find that out.*

Amid squealing brakes, the bug came to a stop and Kellon stepped out. As the bug sped off, he shook his head wondering, *How could we travel between the stars and still not be able to get the squeal out of those brakes?* Continuing to shake his head, he went briskly up the steps and passed through the open doors. As Kellon entered, the officer on duty required him to produce his identification and to press his palm on the register for security confirmation.

When the soft metallic ding announced a valid confirmation, the officer commented, "Welcome back, Commodore. Sir, your last mission made all of us proud."

Noting the man's name on his lapel tag, Kellon warmly responded, "Lieutenant Crowley, it was my honor to have served with many others of like mind. Even so, thank you for your comment, it's appreciated."

Moving quickly out of the main lobby, Kellon walked down the hallway to the nearest bank of elevators. Stepping toward an elevator whose doors were just opening, he slowed to permit the people inside to exit and then stepped into the elevator. "Admiral Mer Shawn's office," he ordered.

The doors slid closed, and the car accelerated upward at a rapid and smooth rate, eventually slowing and then coming to a stop. The elevator's doors opened. When Kellon stepped out of the elevator, he was facing a broad desk. The officer sitting behind the desk looked up and smiled. "Commodore Kellon, the Admiral is expecting you. Please, go right in."

The plaque on the door proclaimed with carved and gilded letters, Mer Shawn - Fleet Admiral Glas Dinnein Guardian Force. As Kellon entered, he found the Admiral standing at the window and looking out toward the beach and ocean beyond. As the Admiral turned and saw Kellon, his face broke into a broad smile. "Commodore Kellon, I'm glad to see you again. Please sit down."

As Kellon selected a seat, the Admiral walked to a small cabinet and opened its doors. Withdrawing two wine glasses and a bottle of wine, he turned toward Kellon and smiled broadly.

"Commodore, I never casually invite anyone to come for a glass of wine."

"Sir, I took your invitation most seriously. It's a standing fleet legend that it's easier to earn the Guardian Force's highest commendation than be invited for a glass of wine in the Fleet Admiral's office."

As Mer removed the vacuum cork, he looked up and chuckled. "Well, Commodore, that just goes to prove you shouldn't put too much trust in legends, fleet or otherwise. Nevertheless, I don't often give such an invitation, and I'm most delighted when the officer that's invited actually survives a mission to accept."

"Sir, I nevertheless thank you for your invitation, and am honored to join you in your pleasure that I survived to accept it."

Mer's easy smile broadened into a wide grin, "Kellon, it isn't as much an honor as a means of my apologizing to an officer for having put him into great peril, one from which he might not have returned. Kellon, people are going to remember what you accomplished at Earth and Scion. I have carefully studied your action reports, and they are worthy of more study. That you successfully defended Scion and did not lose a ship, is remarkable."

Mer did the honors of pouring a glass of wine for Kellon and one for himself. Together they lifted their glasses in a mutual salute, "In memory of the crew of the Lux," offered Mer.

"Yes, Sir, in memory of the crew of Lux," Kellon responded. Kellon always enjoyed a good glass of wine, and as he sipped the Admiral's wine, his eyebrows went up. "Sir that is a remarkable wine, vintage?"

"Yes, however, the vintage is an '03, and it is unfortunately no longer available. I have, to the best of my understanding, four of the last six cases in existence. It is a classic. I keep hoping before the last bottle is gone there will be a new vintage to match it. So far, the vines and the wine masters have not cooperated to fulfill my hope. It seems the wine masters are busy producing dry wines. They have forgotten that the original vintners appreciated a sugar content of 2 percent or better, unfortunately," and Mer sighed. "Sometimes change does not mean improvement."

Sitting down, Mer absently placed his wine glass on the desk before him. As he rolled the stem of the wine glass between his fingers, he carefully studied Kellon's features. "Well, out with it Commodore. I know you enjoy my wine, but it was something more than a glass of wine that brought you to my office this fine day."

"Yes, Sir. I was over visiting with Captain Riley and Lux, and they are doing well. Hearing what Lux has to say, I'm concerned. What troubles me is the ships Lux ran into were exceptional when compared to other Kreel Military designs. They're not cruisers, but slightly larger than the Tuen Class fast-attack ships. They have speed and excellent firepower, including— unlike the Tuen Class— heavy missiles."

"They are similar to the Tuen Class? It's interesting that the Elite Guard prefers something smaller than a cruiser," Mer mused.

"Sir, I am confident their choice is based on sound logic. I've taken the opportunity to communicate with Kur on Scion. According to him, there are only about one hundred such ships, and all of them are strictly under the control of the Elite Guard. With his Cobalt Blue, Lux seems to have taken out the remainder of an entire squadron of that guard. I have no doubt that the surviving Elite Guard have taken notice of their losses. Anytime you take out a third of an elite force, the others in that same force tend to sit up and start asking questions. I don't know how much data they collected on Lux, but I am confident they will be on their guard for any similar spaceship."

"Kellon, at the very least, they obviously obtained dimensional information. They also understood they had badly damaged Lux and killed most of his crew. They were able to register that his laser turrets were inoperative and his power was failing. I suspect that after a full day of combat, and the loss of fourteen ships, they'd constructed a good tactical description of Lux. The remaining question is did that information perish with the twenty-two ships Lux 'suckered.'"

"Sir, what Lux achieved in destroying his attackers does not explain what happened to him or diminish the Guard's tactical capability. My experience suggests technologies restricted to elite forces, such as the Elite Guard, over time migrate into the regular forces. If we can accurately evaluate the Elite Guard's capability, then we should have some idea of where Kreel research is heading and what Guardian Force may soon be contending with."

"So far, I'm in agreement. Where are you going with this argument?" Mer asked.

"Well, according to Arkillian Intelligence, the Grand Marshal Grough that Lux baited was one of the most powerful Kreel officers in the Kreel Empire. In fact, according to Kur, he was among the most powerful seven Kreel in their Empire and was ruthless and greatly feared. His demise, along with the loss of thirty-six of the Elite Guard ships, will have created a void in the Kreel top echelon, as well as in the available number of Guard ships. It's also reasonable to believe the loss of thirty-six crews will have a significant impact on the Elite Guard. It isn't easy to replace such highly trained and motivated crews."

"Commodore, again, where are you heading with your argument? Come to your point."

"Sir, I apologize. I checked with Admiral Cloud and learned where the Kreel's special ships are likely to be constructed, and that's on only one world. I am requesting your authorization to take in a strike force and take out that shipbuilding capacity."

Picking up his glass of wine, Mer sipped it, as if he hadn't heard what Kellon was requesting. Turning, he looked toward the far wall, and at its shelves filled with leather-bound books. Several minutes passed before he turned back and again studied Kellon's features.

"Kellon, there are more than forty planets in the Kreel Empire about which we know little or nothing. I do not believe we can defeat the Kreel Empire by making strikes on shipyards, no matter how much disruption it might cause a powerful military clique. What we need to end the Kreel menace is to bring down their empire, to bankrupt it out of existence. Until we can do that, we need to remain militarily prepared to defend our own planets. Just how much do you know of the political structure of Hub-1, Hub-2, and Hub-3?"

"Sir, I have had some discussion with Kur regarding the Hub planets. According to the Arkillians, Hub-3 is the prime controlling planet, the home of the ruling Elite. The Kreel Empire's industrial center is on Hub-2, and it tightly regulates the Empire's commerce. Hub-1 is the Empire's center for Military matters, and is the location of the headquarters for their Military command. The three Hub planets are in three solar systems within ten light-years of each other. It's the Military's responsibility to defend Hub-1 and Hub-2, along with the remaining Empire— with one fundamental exception. The Elite

Guard's responsibility is to protect Hub-3, including protecting it from the Kreel Military."

"In answer to your specific request, I will not authorize a planetary strike. What I will authorize is a covert gathering of intelligence around the Hub worlds. Once we have a better understanding of the Kreel Empire— then and only then— I will consider authorizing strikes against specific planetary targets."

Kellon suppressed a deep sigh of disappointment. *I have the answer to my request. It is not an affirmative, not yet.*

"Kellon, since you've been interacting with Lux, can you tell me how the Elite Guard ships detected him? How was it that once he was detected, he was unable to successfully evade? In short, why did we lose an entire ship and its crew?"

"Sir, I've gone over Lux's logs with a fine-toothed comb. The one element that glaringly stands out is that Lux was dealing with the Elite Guard. They hit Lux with a missile before Lux even became aware the guard had detected him. The missile heavily damaged Lux, and it denied him an opportunity to Jump. They boxed him in, and then ran him down. In doing that, the Elite Guard demonstrated they could effectively deploy fast Jump-capable ships and skilled tactics."

"Kellon, at the time, just how stealthy was Lux?" Mer asked.

"Sir, when detected, Lux was operating within the standard Guardian stealth rule. That being a stealth factor greater than 50 percent would adequately avoid detection. When hit, Lux was operating with a 53 percent stealth factor. That simply didn't afford him the concealment needed to survive, but why, we don't yet know. Precisely how good the Elite Guard is in detecting a stealth cruiser remains unknown. While we need to do better, we don't know how much better. The question remains, how many Cruisers will we lose before learning what we must know?"

"Kellon, do you remember the gambit Commanders Roan and Zorn ran near Earth and Shey when they first confronted the Arkillian Nest Ship? It was that time when Roan intentionally allowed himself to be detected?"

Kellon smiled, "Admiral, I wasn't aware that Roan's tactic in that case was well-known. Yes, I do remember the event. While Shey was configured to look like a long-range Dargon fighter, he moved undetected into optimum firing position against the Arkillian Nest Ship. After he attained his firing position, he intentionally decreased his stealth factor until the Arkillians detected him.

"He hadn't previously discussed his intention with me, and while I didn't put him on report, I very nearly did. I confess that I am surprised you know of the incident."

Mer smiled, "Kellon, one reason I wear these Fleet Admiral rank bars, is because I do pay attention to mission reports. I assure you that I took notice of Roan's bravura. Now I believe such tactics need to be repeated, this time near Hub-3."

"Sir, to be certain I understand, you will not approve a strike on a Kreel planet, but to determine the Elite Guard's detection threshold, you will send another Cruiser back into harm's way? We've already lost one Cruiser and its crew. Wouldn't sending another Cruiser back into that same space simply tempt the muses to take another Cruiser?"

"Kellon, I am not considering sending a single Cruiser back into that space. Instead, this time I'm sending a task force. We need to know precisely how good the Elite Guard really is. I think the loss of Lux and his crew warrants our return visit in force. Would you be personally interested in having command of that task force?"

Kellon sat back, his glass of wine still held in his fingers, and smiled. "Sir, thank you for considering Lan for that mission. We gladly accept that gauntlet."

"Good! Now that's settled. Before you depart on the mission, you are to examine in detail the tactics employed by the Elite Guard. Determine how they targeted Lux before he knew he was under attack. What tactics did they employ when running Lux down?

Spend some time in the combat simulators and work out your counters to each of the observed Kreel tactics. Bring the captains of your other Cruisers into the loop; I want each of you proficiently able to kick their backsides, individually or collectively. I will not tolerate any more Cobalt Blue signals disturbing my afternoon naps."

"Yes, Sir. When do we depart and who are the other four Cruisers?"

"Commodore, you will tell me when you're ready to depart. You are to take whatever time you require to review your mission criteria and to come to know your enemy. Now, as to the other four Cruisers. . . . Hmmmm, do you have any objections if I send the same Cruisers that you took to Earth with Lan?"

"No, Sir, they are all fine ships. However, I do request some downtime for the squadron. We were out about eleven months all total and have only been back a few weeks. I want my ships sharp and their crews rested. The Elite Guard are the Kreel's best, and they will be alert and likely outnumber us. If we're not on top of our game, it could turn into a broken play— like Lux."

"Kellon, that's reasonable. Do you believe you might be able to proceed in say, thirty to forty-five days?"

"Sir, Lent, for one, took some significant damage near Earth, and several others were damaged by jetsam near Scion. I estimate it will take about forty-five days to return the Cruisers to peak condition."

"Commodore, that's understandable. Provide me weekly updates on the refit. More importantly, keep me informed about the development of countertactics to oppose the Elite Guard's methods. We may just need to have another glass of wine together when you return from Hub-3. In the meantime, you'd best get your task force organized. You will have an AA priority; therefore, push hard on those yard refits! Your written mission orders will be forwarded to you within the hour."

Putting his now empty wine glass down, Kellon stood and smartly saluted, "Yes, Sir. I will look forward with great anticipation to another glass of your wine."

As the door closed behind Kellon, Mer leaned back in his chair and looked up toward the ceiling. He spoke softly, as if to himself, "May all that is of truth and goodness go with and protect Kellon and his squadron." That was as near to a prayer as Mer was accustomed to make.

## Chapter Twenty-Five:
# Head Start

Aboard Shey, Kellon was sitting behind Roan and Zorn and observing the portside bulkhead view screen. They'd been in space near Glas Dinnein and running trial runs for hours, and the test results were still unproductive. At that moment, Shey was 10,000 kilometers from Lan's position and monitoring his maneuvering. Lan was once again striving to duplicate Lux's maneuvers at the time just prior to the Kreel attack. Kellon had dispersed Shey, Sheba, Misty, and Cindy throughout the volume and they were busy monitoring all the measurable bandwidths, looking for any possible telltale trace that might have permitted the Kreel to detect Lux.

Stretching his shoulders, Zorn rolled them in an effort to shake out the cramped muscles. His eyes never left the instrumentation displays. "Gentlemen, this being our fourth trial run, I'm opening wide the gate triggers. If anything's going to be detectable, then we should see it this time."

Turning toward Kellon, Roan asked, "Commodore, how long do you want to continue—"

Zorn's exclamation interrupted Roan, "Blast! There was a spike, but now it's gone. I'm scrolling back to look. Roan, there's something, I don't know its cause, but it's in the upper registers. It's a spike and lasting about one microsecond. It's just a spike, and I almost missed it. What's important is its peak was well above Lan's set stealth profile. Blast, there it is again!"

"Lan, this is Roan. We've detected an intermittent short duration transient, but it is exceeding your 0.53 stealth threshold. Zorn is posting its signature over to you for your analysis. The question is— what's causing that spike?"

"Acknowledged. I have received the signature. I am beginning a systems check to determine its source," Lan responded.

"Roan," Kellon inserted, "see if Shey can use that spike to localize Lan."

"Commodore, Shey here. No, Sir. Now, however, knowing what to watch for, with Roan's permission I will ask Sheba, Misty, and Cindy to monitor for the same transient. Together, if we detect it again, we can localize Lan by knowing our own positions and using triangulation."

"Permission granted, proceed Shey," Roan ordered.

"Proceeding. My sisters have the transient signature sample and are now watching with me."

Less than three minutes passed before Shey reported, "We have obtained a solid localization on Lan. It is sufficient for a passive-active combination missile launch."

Kellon was frowning, "Lan, you're running at an overall stealth factor of 0.53 and the Scouts have just resolved a weapon order solution on your current trajectory. Do you have any clue as to what the source of that repetitive spike might be?"

"No, Sir. I am currently filtering through my internal sensors. Counter Measures has registered the spike and is now scanning to localize its source."

Frowning, Kellon was feeling a mix of emotions. It was good to find something; *But blast,* he thought, *there shouldn't be anything to find!*

"Zorn, when you're on normal patrol sweeps, do you normally watch for such short-term spikes?"

"No, Sir. We typically have so much noise and hash in the background that it's not practical to scan for transients. It's only because we're looking for the unknown that I opened the filters."

"One more question, Zorn. Do you believe that between Shey and your talents you might initiate a new algorithm to look precisely for those types of transitional spikes? You would need to filter them out of the hash, and do so as part of our normal scanning procedure."

"Yes, Sir, that should be possible. But, might I ask, why?"

"Well, if I'm correct in assuming it was just such a spike generated by Lux that allowed the Kreel Guard to detect him, then they must be searching for such transitional spikes on a regular basis. Given one of their tasks is to protect Hub-3 from possible attack by rogue Military units, perhaps, just perhaps, they know something about the Kreel ships we don't know," Kellon theorized.

"Sir, that sorta makes sense. However, a Kreel ship signature normally stands out like a sore thumb. So, why go to all the trouble looking for barely detectable spikes?" Zorn asked.

"Admittedly, that's a good question. Regrettably, we don't have an example of a signature of an Elite Guard ship. That data was not part of Lux's core matrix. I don't have a clue concerning what their signature looks like, and spikes may be important."

"Oops, yes, Sir. I will begin tonight to develop such a broad bandwidth search routine and pass it by Shey and Lan."

As he listened to the exchange between Zorn and Kellon, Roan felt they were missing something important. "Commodore, while we don't have a signature trace of the Kreel Guards, I'm not concerned about that problem. According to Lux's recall, he was tracking twenty-two Guard ships and their incoming missiles. Even damaged, he could still track them. I do not therefore believe the spikes involve tracking Kreel ships. It's my guess the Kreel may use the spikes in detecting Nori ships."

Turning toward Roan, Kellon smiled. "Roan you're absolutely right! Your observations fit the data we have. The Kreel captain near Earth that was screaming about the Nori coming was scared out of his wits. Now we have an Elite Guard Marshal identifying the Nori as a worthy foe. If the Kreel are compelled to use spikes to detect Nori ships, then the Nori must be using stealth technology. Therefore, our unanswered question is how did the Kreel remain undetected and get close enough to attack Lux?"

"Sir, that remains an important question. Unfortunately, we don't have the data to answer it."

Lan interrupted the conversation, "Commodore Kellon. We have isolated the source of the spike. A simple power switch in my elevators is generating the transients. We are now testing all spare switches in inventory, to confirm they are within fleet specifications."

Roan shook his head in wonderment. "Is it possible we lost Lux and his crew because of a malfunction in a simple power switch in an elevator?"

Frowning, Kellon sighed. "Roan, it's the little things that accumulate that can get you killed, a power switch is potentially one of those little things. Even so, there is more than one problem involved here. Nullification shielding should have canceled out any such transient. While the transient should not have occurred, once it was generated, it should have been nullified by the stealth signal buffers.

"Lan shut it down. I'm bringing back the Scouts. Coordinate recovery and let's head back to Glas Dinnein."

An hour later, Kellon opened the door and entered his conference room. He found Commander Grey sitting alone at the conference table, with notes scattered across its entire surface. He was intently watching the bulkhead screen, even as he scribbled more notes. He did not look up when Kellon entered. Curious, Kellon looked to see what Roy was studying, and he recognized the data: it was a segment from Lux's recovered data near the end of his battle.

While attempting to understand how the Kreel had boxed in Lux, Kellon had studied the same sequence several times. The problem was the data was fragmentary. What the AIs had saved was the critical persona data required to revive Lux. Therefore, they did not save the separate related tactical databases.

As the data playback ended, Roy stretched and then noticed Kellon. Turning, Roy smiled and asked, "How did the monitoring runs go?"

"Well enough. I don't know if what we found was what exposed Lux, but we found something that could just as easily get us killed."

That caused Roy to frown, "What?"

"Zorn found a short spike, about one microsecond in duration. It seems one of the power switches in our elevators has a transient. It was short, but it was sufficient for Shey to run a weapon order on Lan's vectors and generate an accurate missile solution."

Ouch, that's not encouraging. What about the nullification screens?" Roy asked.

"They didn't detect or correct for the spike, it was simply below their threshold. How about you? It looks like you've been busy. What are you studying?" Kellon inquired.

Standing, Roy moved over to the small side-table and poured a cup of neab. "Well, I've been trying to determine just how they boxed in Lux. I think I've worked it out, but don't as yet know how they pulled it off."

Moving over to the side table, Kellon poured himself a cup of the neab. "Roy, I also looked over that data several times, and I didn't find anything. What have you got?"

"You're correct, the data is partial; even so, the Kreel Guard appear to use coordinated micro-Jumps to maneuver during combat. That's the only way they could have leap-frogged Lux, as they did. Of course, they were outside the heliosphere when they cornered Lux; even so, the use of micro-Jumps during combat is a dicey and sophisticated process. Based upon what I've seen, they are very proficient at what they do. What took me back is seeing how rapidly they can make a micro-Jump, that being about five minutes. That's extremely fast for computing any Jump."

"Hmmm, micro-Jumps may just explain how they came close enough to Lux to launch missiles and still not be detected. When dealing with the Elite Guard, there seems to be a technology quantum leap forward. They monitor weak transients, maneuver normally in combat using micro-Jumps, and do it all in the blink of an eye. This mission is becoming more and more like a headlong plunge from fifty meters into a large box— one filled with sharp double-edged knives. Roy, what's your next step?"

"What am I personally going to do? Well, given what we now know, the first thing I'm going to do is order up some cheese pastries, then I think I might retire and look for a comfortable position, one teaching very uncomplicated business theory at some small college that has never heard of the Kreel or Guardian Force. How about you?"

Shaking his head, Kellon smiled broadly. "Humph, be advised, I'm going to call Mer Shawn. It's time for the Guardian Force to use an AA priority and yank some contractor's chains. We need a fix on these systems and we need it now."

Roy grinned broadly. "Well, in that case, seeing you'll fix the flashing announcements declaring where we're hiding, I might just stick around for one more mission. I sorta want to see if I can play the same game the Kreel are playing, but do it several levels above where they can. That is, I'll remain if you don't mind my hanging about for a little longer."

"Roy, go get your cheese pastry. Then go to work. Be advised, I will be promptly informing security that you're not to be permitted to depart the ship, for at least the next decade."

"Only a decade? Sir, thank you. That's a statement of absolute confidence in my capability. I was personally thinking that it might take at least two decades to solve the problem. Of course, I've already been working for some time on the solution."

Still smiling, Kellon asked, "Working? Since when?"

"Well, ever since you gave me the problem, just before our micro-Jump near Earth. Those fifteen minutes of pure research under dire stress have given me a real head start on solving the problem."

# Chapter Twenty-Six:
## Wonderful Incentive

Kellon watched as Roy scooped up his scattered notes, waved a cheery farewell, and departed, his cheerful demeanor lifting Kellon's spirits.

Sitting for several moments, Kellon considered his next action. Checking the chronometer, he winced, then ordered, "Lan, connect me with Admiral Mer Shawn."

"Connecting." Lan promptly responded.

In less than a minute the bulkhead screen swirled and Admiral Mer Shawn's image came into view. It was after 22:00, and Kellon observed Mer was out of uniform and at home. "Commodore, it's late, and you look tired. How might I be of assistance?"

"Sir, during our field testing today, we discovered some noise spikes within Lan's system, and the nullification amplifiers are not canceling them."

"Commodore, is the problem as bad as you're implying?"

"Sir, I believe it is. Using the detected spikes, Shey was able to generate a valid weapon order against Lan, even though his stealth factor was at 0.53. This may explain how the Elite Guard detected Lux and was able to track him."

Mer's expression took on a frown, "That's not good. Well, Commodore, you've called for a purpose— spit it out. What do you want?"

"Sir, because of our limited time, I need your heavy hand wrapped around the necks of the fleet laboratory folks, shipyards, and various contractors. In brief, I need double the priority you provided put on the top of the heap, and the authority needed to back it up. I need an open charge account."

"Kellon, I will set it up tonight with Operations. You'll have your open account by 06:00 tomorrow morning. Keep me informed as to your progress. Is there anything else?"

"No, Sir. At least not at the moment."

"Good! Now get some rest, and Kellon, that is an order. Mer Shawn out."

Sitting back, Kellon did not feel like resting. He was about to take five Cruisers and their crews into a meat grinder, and orders to the contrary, rest was not on his schedule. He sat quietly for a while, merely looking at the blank bulkhead, then sighing, he continued working.

"Lan, have the Wardroom send in an Earth-style sandwich with a large and fresh thermos of neab. Then find and ask Commander Shaw to promptly meet with me here."

"Yes, Sir. The Wardroom has your order and Commander Shaw asks for five minutes."

"Lan, tell Lorn five minutes will be fine. You might ask him, if he would like a sandwich."

"Sir, Commander Shaw says he would like a sandwich with a pickle. I have accordingly taken the liberty to modify your order to the Wardroom."

"Thank you, Lan. Now, pull up the same segment of Lux's recall that Roy was studying, the one being displayed when I entered. He said he believes they were doing micro-Jumps. Can you confirm that?"

"Sir, I will need to begin an analysis. Would you authorize Shey and the girls to assist? They have become very capable tacticians during the past mission."

"Lan you have my authorization, but first clear it with Commander Roan. Now, connect me with Captain Riley on Lux."

"Yes, Sir, connecting."

In less than three minutes, the bulkhead screen expanded into the smiling image of Captain Riley. It was apparent from his expression that he retained the youthful ability of never looking tired. Adding to that appearance, even his uniform looked crisp. *Insufferable youth,* Kellon grumbled inwardly.

"Riley here. Good evening, Commodore Kellon. How might I be of assistance?"

"Good evening, Captain Riley. I'm working to resolve how the Elite Guard detected and boxed in Lux. While I have some of the answers, I hope Lux may provide us more information. I'm requesting your authorization for Lan to establish a tight link with Lux, so they can together review all of his recollections. "

"Commodore, we are currently doing pre-delivery systems checks. Such mundane duty is not stressing Lux's capabilities. I believe he would like very much to help Lan in exploring some means of striking back at the Elite Guard. I will instruct Lux accordingly."

Captain Riley then paused, and a sheepish grin slowly appeared on his face. "Oh, by saying that, I suspect Lux is already instructed. Commodore Kellon, it's taking me some time to realize just how closely a captain and his AI are linked."

Smiling, Kellon chuckled. "Captain Riley, I have observed a captain and his AI wear the very same skin. I can certainly assure you of that fact. Thank you for your valued assistance. Kellon out.

"Lan, obtain a complete review of everything Lux can remember about the Elite Guard's maneuvering. Go over every iota of his data, every byte. If we can reconstruct their actions, we can counter them."

"Yes, Sir."

A polite knock sounded on the conference room door and it opened. Commander Shaw motioned for an orderly to enter. The orderly placed a broad tray bearing covered plates on the small side-table, looked about and swept up some empty cups and a tray. He turned to Kellon and asked, "Sir, may the Wardroom provide anything else at this time?"

"No, that will be fine."

As the door closed behind the orderly, Kellon looked at the tray on the side table. "Lorn, help yourself." Kellon stood up and moved over to lift one of the covers. Inside was a large triple decker sandwich with a pickle on the side. "Lorn, I think this might be your sandwich, it has a pickle."

While filling their cups with hot neab, Kellon looked under the cover of the second dish. "How about that, I also got a pickle."

"Sir, what's the topic this evening?"

"Lorn, Roy believes the Elite Guard is using micro-Jumps during combat. He believes they can compute a Jump in about five minutes. This is how they leapfrogged Lux and boxed him in.

"Lan, are you still eavesdropping on the conversation?"

"No, Sir, I am listening carefully and logging all data regarding pickles."

"While you are logging such critical data, you should add one more item to your conversation with Lux. He took out fourteen

Kreel Guard ships, but he also expended all of his missiles. That constitutes a very low missile-to-kill ratio. Why did he need so many missiles? Were the Elite Guard using new countermeasures?"

"Understood, Sir. I will verify each engagement with Lux."

"Lorn, I'm building on a host of assumptions and guessing we will encounter about twenty-four ships when engaging the Elite Guard."

"Excuse me, might I ask a question before we discuss tactics?"

"Of course."

"Sir, did I hear Lan say he was taking notes about pickles? Did I just hear Lan make a joke?"

Smiling, Kellon lowered his voice as if Lan could not hear him. "Lorn, just ignore him. Otherwise he will simply become insufferable."

Lorn struggled not to laugh, then with some effort focused on the main topic. "From what you've said, am I right to assume you believe we will engage the Elite Guard?"

Kellon paused to finish a bite of his sandwich and then continued. "Yes, I believe we will engage the Elite Guard. Lorn, we'll be entering Hub-3 space on a reconnaissance in force. The statistical odds we will engage them are somewhat like poking a sharp stick in a hornet's nest— outcome predictable. Undoubtedly, Admiral Mer Shawn must be fully aware of that pending reality."

"Sir, I've read the reports obtained from Lux as well as Kur's comments regarding the structure of the Elite Guard. What I don't understand is why you believe we will only engage twenty-four Guard ships, not thirty-six like Lux encountered?"

Taking a sip of neab and swallowing a bite of his sandwich, Kellon paused for a moment before responding. "Well, using Kur's numbers, I estimated three Guard squadrons of thirty-six ships each. Lux took one of them out during his engagement, leaving seventy-two Guard ships still active.

"Given three elite Guard units, I assume that one will be engaged in outer patrol duty, one will be providing close-in cover for the planet, and the third will be standing down on a rest cycle. I also assume they will naturally rotate the duty assignments. At least, that's how I would structure the three squadrons."

"That much I can follow, but why twenty-four ships?"

"Logically speaking, Lux took out a squadron. There's absolutely no way that an elite force can replace its forces overnight— not one-third of them. I'm assuming they will retain the three squadrons, since that rotation provides maximum coverage with downtime. In order to do this, they will promote a new Grand Marshal from the ranks and assign him one third of the remaining ships. Naturally, the Elite Command must take the replacement ships equally from the two remaining squadrons. The simple math is seventy-two divided by three is twenty-four. Of course, they'll be revving up their training programs trying fill in their ranks while bringing new ships on line."

"Sir, if you're correct, then we are five Guardian cruisers confronting twenty-four advanced Kreel ships, each of which is superior to the Tuen Class fast-attacks. Given that they can buddy up and do micro-Jumps, and may have improved countermeasures, may I presume you want me to devise some new tactics?"

Kellon leaned back in his chair, looking directly toward Lorn. "Yes, that is precisely what I want you to consider. We are facing a deadly encounter and the odds are not in our favor. We will therefore need to be prepared and stay smarter than the average Kreel."

"No disagreement intended, Sir, I believe, however, we will need to be smarter than the above-average Kreel. You've put an interesting problem on my table. With your permission to interface with Lan on the problem, I will get on the job. Is there anything else?"

"No, Lorn, that's about it. Stay in touch with Lan. Don't forget to check out the low missile-to-hit ratio. I consider that a particularly sticky part of the tactical problem."

Standing, Lorn came to attention and saluted. "Sir, it remains my pleasure to serve with you."

Kellon returned the salute, "Your feeling is mutually shared." As he closed the door on his way out, Lorn stuck his head back into the conference room for a moment, "Thanks for the sandwich, it was excellent. Outstanding pickle." Then he closed the door and was gone.

Kellon sat in reflection, considering what he'd accomplished. He had some of the answers and was on his way to resolving others. What he needed was to confirm he could do what he must do in order to survive. *Staying alive,* he thought, *provides a wonderful incentive. That and another glass of Admiral Mer Shawn's vintage wine.*

# Chapter Twenty-Seven:
## Light Kiss

Kellon had asked Admiral Mer Shawn for forty-five days to provide some downtime for his squadron, yet he had pushed everyone hard during the first thirty days of that period. Even so, since the necessary work did not require a full complement, two thirds of the crews were able to rotate on leave. The downtime work routine included the Scout ships. Even so, Roan took every available opportunity to confirm Shey and her sisters were combat ready. That included Shey taking advantage of going through full stealth screening runs when a Cruiser was monitoring. Kellon was determined that there would be no more transients, and Roan's job was to verify the Scouts were clean.

"Roan, tell me again why we are doing this," Shey asked.

"Well, lovely lady, Kellon insists that we come back from our next mission with all personnel and without any dents or holes in your graceful hull. Both Zorn and I tend to agree with that sentiment.

"Besides, Kellon has found at least eleven different transients in the Cruisers and as many in the Scouts at last count. Before the mission begins, he is demanding the shipyards eliminate all the transients. If you think he's being hard on the Scouts, you should hear what he's telling the contractors; they're running for cover every time they see him coming."

"Shey," Zorn inserted, "we're nearing our CPA with Lent. If you don't stay focused on what you are doing here and now, you may be getting some dents in your hull sooner rather than later."

"Zorn, Lent can't possibly detect me. I have masked everything, and am now at stealth 0.80. We are gliding through their pickets, like mist through trees—"

Even as Shey spoke, a loud alarm reverberated throughout her control compartment. "Shey, break hard left and scatter chaff. Blast! We just took a hit from one of Lent's main lasers."

"Thunder and lightning, there goes my bet!" Zorn grumbled.

Looking toward Zorn, Roan was frowning. "Bet? We should be grateful that Lent was using minimal power on his laser. It was only a light kiss of acknowledgment, telling us he'd detected Shey. Otherwise, we would now be sucking hard vacuum. Just out of curiosity, what was your bet?"

"Well, knowing for certain that Shey is sparkling clean, I bet the Fire Control gang on Lent a case of brews that Shey would slip past them and hit our designated target in spite of anything they did. Blast, how could they detect us? Roan, I'm looking at everything, and there's nothing out of specification. Nothing! Shey is absolutely clean!"

At that moment, Eurie's clear cheerful voice came over their joint-tactical frequency. "Well done Shey. The only reason we detected you is that we knew you were coming and you were precisely on time. If you look again, you might find our Scouts are deployed around you. With our Scouts out, we were able to get a mass deflection registration. This of course required precise timing and proximity. You might say that we took unfair advantage of you. Given the strict test parameters, there wasn't much you could do about that. Otherwise, be advised, you are as slick as a greased snake.

"Oh, I do have a message for Zorn. Lent's Fire Control gang asks me to tell you that they like it cold."

Frowning, Zorn was obviously unhappy. "Mass deflection? Who ever heard of detecting a ship with mass deflection? I've been robbed."

Roan could not suppress his mirth and was chuckling. "Captain Eurie, Roan here. Thank you for providing Shey a final screening.

As long as you're certain that we are clean, I am satisfied. What we don't need are noise spikes. Pass to your Scouts, from Shey, our compliments and well done. Be advised we've seen nary a flicker of any of them. I, however, request they put on their tracking transponders. I certainly don't want to dent anyone while exiting the volume.

"Shey, turn on your blinking lights and take us home. Let's go find Lan and see what everyone else is doing.

"Captain Eurie, Roan here. I'm verifying Shey is now clearing the local volume. We are returning to Glas Dinnein and rendezvousing with Lan. Also, please pass a reply from Zorn to your Fire Control gang, it will be very cold and promptly delivered. Thank you again for your services."

"Eurie here. You are most welcome, Shey and team. Eurie out."

"Mass deflection? What happened to the rules of fair play? Blast— who could have thought of doing that? Double blast, how could they pull it off?" Zorn grumbled.

"Well, Zorn, let that be a lesson. You shouldn't be going around making bets for a whole case of brews without putting some conditions on the bet. With such high stakes, people are motivated to go to all manner of extremes."

"Sir," Shey broke in. "Every Scout and Cruiser has repeatedly run through the monitoring sweeps. We have had engineers crawling all over our hulls for weeks. Are we near being finished?"

"Dear Shey, we're finished only when Commodore Kellon says we're finished. For the past several weeks, he and Commander Shaw have been using simulations and developing new tactics, and that smacks of upcoming maneuvers."

Turning with a concerned look, Zorn asked, "Roan, do you think we can take the Kreel Guard?"

"Well, Zorn, we will either take them or end up with an apple in our mouths as entrees on their banquet tables."

"Roan! That's not something to joke about. Tell him, Shey, that's not going to happen."

"Roan, Zorn is correct. It is not going to happen. Not on my watch! Commodore Kellon will take us in and bring us back," Shey affirmed.

"Zorn, my comment wasn't intended to be funny. The problem is we've been so focused on their technology, we've forgotten they are still Kreel. The Elite Guard is more arrogant and dangerous than most Kreel, but they would still gladly serve us up on a platter if we give them that opportunity."

"Roan, that's one opportunity that they will never be given! Still, how are we going to take on twenty or thirty Kreel Guard ships? Where do the Scouts fit in? Are we going to be part of Kellon's solution, or are we just going along for the ride?"

Roan turned toward Zorn, and he was not laughing. "By now, you should have observed that Kellon uses all of his assets during a battle. We should be prepared for a real fight. Before the mission is over, we are undoubtedly going to be in a no-holds-barred and no-quarter-asked-or-given battle. On that, I will wager a cold case of brews."

Returning Roan's glance, Zorn thoughtfully commented, "That's not a bet that I will take."

Shey's clear feminine voice, contrasting with Zorn's deeper tones, inquired, "Roan, why did Commodore Kellon insert three deep space beacons within Glas Dinnein's heliosphere?"

Shey's question took Roan aback. "Shey, just when did he do that?"

"Oh, several days following our return from Scion, Commodore Kellon ordered Lar, Lawrence, and Lowell to insert the beacons. Ever since, all of the AIs have been inquiring why he did this."

"Shey, that can't be correct. At the very least, Lan must certainly know," answered Zorn.

"Zorn, Commodore Kellon did not tell Lan, or else ordered him not to discuss the matter. He will not respond to our inquiries about the subject."

"Shey, I don't know why Kellon inserted the beacons. I do, however, have a guess. He must be anticipating using micro-Jumps within the heliosphere. Having said this, you are not to discuss the topic with other AIs or anyone else. I don't know why Kellon put a cap on the topic, but since he did, we will adhere to his decision."

"Yes, Sir."

"Shey," Zorn added, "you don't need to ask a question when merely by waiting and observing, the answer will be forthcoming. We can be sure, whatever it is that Kellon is planning, when it happens, it will happen with a flourish."

"Roan, I have contact with Lan. He is requesting that I pick up my skirts and return quickly. May I put on speed so my skirts are picked up?"

Smiling broadly, Roan answered, "Shey, I will leave your approach and return to hangar to Lan and you, while Zorn and I drop back into the galley for neab. If you are picking up your skirts, then do it with style— make us proud."

Barely twenty minutes later, Lan had tucked Shey safely back into her hangar and the hangar's atmosphere warning light was shining bright gold, indicating full atmospheric pressure. There was also a waiting message from Kellon for Roan instructing him to report to the Commodore's conference room immediately upon arrival.

Wondering about what was urgent, Roan headed to see Kellon, while Zorn stood pondering the loss of a cold case of brews.

*How,* he grumbled inwardly, *did they detect Shey?* Turning with focused purpose, Zorn walked briskly down the short gangway and exited the hangar, heading toward Lan's electronics shop.

# Chapter Twenty-Eight:
# **Sound Battle Stations**

Kellon was working at the conference table in the domed conference room when Commander Shaw approached and saluted him.

"Sir, Commodore Shaw reporting, as ordered."

Looking up, Kellon smiled in acknowledgment and returned Lorn's salute. "Lorn, park it and make yourself comfortable. I'm aware that you've been burning your candle at both ends during these past weeks. I want you to know, I believe you're doing an outstanding job."

"Sir, Lux's Cobalt Blue signal has had a sobering effect on everyone. Although you granted leave, I know most of the crew has been remaining on board helping to complete the upgrades. No one is kidding themselves. We all understand we're going up against the best the Kreel can throw at us, and we'll be in their own home space."

"Lorn, have you had time to monitor the other Cruisers' operational Jump trials?"

"Yes, Sir. Each Cruiser has drilled until they have it down to tight tolerances. Commander Grey seems pleased with our progress. The better our performance, the more he tightens up his methodology. It keeps getting better and better. At present, he can compute a micro-Jump nearly faster than you can say Jump."

"Lorn, my experience indicates it's always good news when our senior navigator is happy, and you know you're in deep trouble when he isn't."

"Sir, given his results, I believe you will find his final report very interesting."

Nodding his head, Kellon acknowledged, "I'll wait to speak to him. Now, Lorn, what I need to know is whether you are personally satisfied with our new tactics."

"Yes, Sir. I am more than pleased— I'm exuberant. Speaking both personally and professionally, I have found that working with Commander Grey and the tactical officers from each cruiser is extremely rewarding. We've definitely come up with new tactics that I believe are significant improvements over existing doctrine."

"Lorn, the question of the moment is are we ready for tomorrow's exercise?"

"Yes, Sir."

"Then there's only one more question. Is there anything specific that you're concerned about, either for tomorrow's exercise or else the upcoming mission? Is there anything that might negatively affect our performance?"

"Sir, I have a thousand concerns, but they're the normal pre-mission jitters. I believe that we've addressed everything of substance. Sir, we are ready."

Leaning forward, Kellon put his arms on the table and clasped his hands before him. After a momentary pause, he looked up and studied Lorn's blue eyes. "You are the best tactical officer I have ever had the privilege to serve with. If you affirm we are ready, I believe we are ready. Well done Lorn. That is all for the moment. See if you can get some rest before we commence tomorrow's exercise."

Standing, Lorn saluted, "Sir, thank you for your words of acknowledgment and encouragement. They are appreciated."

As Lorn departed the conference room, Kellon sat quietly and reflected on what he had learned. The squadron had worked around the clock for the past eight weeks. Because of the serious nature of the problems, the work had required more time than he'd anticipated. Yet, they had both tested and upgraded existing systems. While they eliminated the transients, they'd also brought the stealth performance standards to a new higher level.

*At least,* he thought, *the discovery of the transients accelerated improvement of the nullifiers and the development of enhanced sensors and discriminators.* There was one additional benefit. The modifications and improvements to the squadron provided a new ability to efficiently detect and track the sources of such transients. *I was correct,* he considered, *to have taken the time required to screen and scrutinize each ship.* He sighed, reflecting, *Now there's only the final operational exercise before we're validated for deployment.*

Kellon became aware of his inner stress, and he sought some way to lessen it. "Lan, would you please pipe in some background music, something with strings, possibly a quartet."

As the conference room filled with soft background music, Kellon sat quietly, taking a few deep breaths. He then looked at his list to see who was waiting to meet with him. He observed Commanders Roan and Zorn had requested an opportunity to see him. *This should be interesting, my two rogue officers,* he thought with a smile. *Now what are they up to?*

"Lan, please advise Commanders Roan and Zorn that I am ready to speak with them."

"Yes, Sir. They are waiting just outside."

"Kellon turned as the two men approached and saluted. Returning their salutes, he ordered, "At ease, Gentlemen, and sit down. Before we address your concerns, I have one question. Are there any problems with the Scouts remaining to be resolved? Are you ready to begin our mission?"

"Sir, there are no problems to report. We've passed successfully through every screen and scan that we can devise. All twenty of our Scouts have been thoroughly checked and then rechecked. According to Captain Eurie, the Scouts are as slick as greased snakes. Sir, we are ready."

"Roan, tomorrow we will be running through a full-scale dress rehearsal. We are the Red team, five Cruisers trying to penetrate Glas Dinnein's Gold team of fifteen defending Cruisers. Do you have any problems with those odds?"

"No, Sir. In fact, we rather like those odds."

Roan's response took Kellon aback somewhat, and he leaned forward. "You like the odds of three to one? Why?"

"Well, Sir, based on what we know, both Zorn and I made a wager of several cases of brews. Given the stated odds, we will receive six cases at the minimal risk of losing two cases."

Shaking his head, Kellon began to smile. "In for a gram, in for a kilogram. I'll bite. What's your wager?"

"Sir, our wager is that we will blow through the opposition and score direct hits on Guardian Headquarters."

Kellon leaned forward and placed his hands flat on the table. "Several cases of brews? You've made a wager that we will hit Guardian Headquarters! Dare I ask? With whom did you make this wager? Commander Roan, I believe you owe me an explanation."

"Sir, the wager is with Admiral Mer Shawn."

Leaning back, Kellon could not suppress his mirth. "The two of you rogues actually went together to the Guardian Fleet Admiral, and then you made a wager our squadron would make a direct hit on his office?"

"Well, yes, Sir. However, I can assure you that we gave the wager considerable thought before we made it. We felt it was the best way to make a dull exercise interesting. Of course, our assumption was the Admiral would not particularly like having his office vaporized, even if only in a simulation. Sir, we were correct. He readily accepted our wager without the slightest hesitation."

Sighing, Kellon studied both Roan and Zorn's calm expressions. "Given the odds, I have no doubt he did. Out of simple curiosity, just how do the two of you propose to pull off your gambit?"

"Well, Sir, we were rather hoping to enlist your assistance in that matter."

Kellon struggled not to let his real feelings show in his facial features, and he was only partially successful, since a smile was plainly evident. "Now, why is it that I'm not surprised you want my help? Just for the record, Commander Roan, how do you propose we blow through the Gold team and strike the Admiral's office? There just happens to be fifteen top-of-the-line cruisers between the Admiral's office and us. What keeps your wager from sounding like a brash and arrogant boast?"

"Sir, I can and do assure you that our wager is based on sound military tactics, and on privileged information. Rather than arrogance, our wager is the product of a careful gathering of military intelligence. "

"Roan, precisely what tactics and privileged information are you talking about?"

"Well, Sir, we learned from sources— best left unnamed— that several weeks ago you positioned three Navigation Beacons in Glas Dinnein's heliosphere. Upon checking with other unnamed privileged sources, we learned the beacons have been dutifully collecting mass distribution data. Now, we naturally considered that you had a reason for doing this, and part of your reason was to demonstrate to upper Command the importance of being able to make micro-Jumps within a heliosphere. Understandably, Zorn suggested that you might consider tomorrow to be a good day to make that demonstration."

Kellon turned his scrutiny toward Zorn, still smiling. "So the blame now falls squarely on you Zorn. Are you prepared to take full responsibility for tossing the fat into the fire?"

Still maintaining a straight face and a formal military bearing, Zorn paused only for a moment before answering. "Well, not really Sir. In fact, it was Shey that sorta suggested the wager. She and the girls theorized such a demonstration would assist upper Command to move more efficiently."

Kellon could no longer restrain his mirth, and laughed. "Shey, are you eavesdropping as usual? If you are, are you going to remain silent and let Zorn box you into bearing total responsibility for their making wagers with fleet admirals?"

"Commodore Kellon, Lan here. Sir, to avoid self-incrimination, Shey is exercising her right to remain silent. However, she has requested that I formally represent her in this matter. Shey confesses that she believes we can successfully penetrate the Gold team and hit the Guardian Headquarters. Sir, I must also confess that I agree with her assessment, presuming that we perform several micro-Jumps in the process."

Sighing, Kellon leaned back and frowned. "Lan, it seems you're in full collusion with these rogues. You say that to pull their gambit out of the fire, all we need do is make several micro-Jumps?"

"Yes, Sir. Commander Grey has been working closely with me, and he has refined micro-Jumps to a very tight procedure. Overall, they are remarkably efficient processes. I believe, however, it will take several micro-Jumps to succeed. This of course relies on our new tactics, where Commander Grey is able to calculate precise exit points with accuracy and predictability."

"Lan, correct me if I'm mistaken. You are actually indicating Commander Grey will endorse your recommendation?"

"Yes, Sir, I believe he will. Commander Grey has determined the precision of a calculated exit point is a function of the length and duration of a micro-Jump. The shorter the Jump, the faster we can compute it, and the more precisely we can determine its exit point."

"Lan, putting all the technicalities aside, out with it— just what are you proposing?"

"Sir, following due deliberation, I propose that for tomorrow's exercise we adopt a Kreel battle plan, the one they employed when striking at Earth."

"Hold it right there, Lan! If I understand you correctly, you are proposing we adopt the Kreel cruiser strike on Earth as our battle plan. I trust that you remember that we defeated that plan."

"Yes, Sir, I do remember. Now, however, there is a major difference. We can now do well what they could not do then: we can make micro-Jumps. I recommend that when we launch our simulated attack, we Jump just short of the heliosphere to the region directly above Glas Dinnein. Then, moving through normal space-time, we cross through the heliopause and into the heliosphere at five widely dispersed points. Formed in a broad facing circle, we will proceed at space-normal speed and follow a narrowing funnel approach toward Glas Dinnein. Of course, since we will have set our stealth mode to look like Kreel cruisers, Guardian HQ will attain an early track on us. This factor will draw the Gold defenders toward our observed position."

"So far, I understand your plan, but Lan, how do you propose to overcome what the Gold team will throw at us?"

"Sir, by using the new enhanced sensors and search algorithms that Zorn and Shey have crafted by tracking their transients, we can track the Gold team during their approach. Since we will be in a facing circle, employing triangulation tracking of the approaching Gold team should be rather straightforward. When they come near to our position, we will micro-Jump beyond them to 0.50 AU of Glas Dinnein. As we exit at that point, we will have also reduced our facing circle diameter by about 75 percent."

"Presuming we can actually do what you're suggesting, and for the sake of this discussion, just how do we get past the remaining ten Gold team Cruisers? You know full well that Fleet Operations is controlling the Gold team, and I doubt Admiral Dylan Cord will send fifteen Cruisers out toward the heliopause while leaving Glas Dinnein undefended."

"No, Sir, he most certainly will not. I believe he will send five cruisers out toward the Heliopause to oppose us. He will most probably position his second squadron to intercept anything that might evade his first squadron. They will most likely be located between three and five AUs from Glas Dinnein. He will hold his third squadron in reserve near to the planet. Sir, when we exit the first micro-Jump at 0.50 AU distant, we will most likely be behind the second squadron and well inside their defense volume."

Leaning back, Kellon was now intently listening to Lan's proposal, and he was not smiling. "Presuming you are correct and we are behind the second squadron, there remains the Gold team's final defense. Where do you anticipate the third squadron will be positioned?"

"Sir, by reviewing recent deployment policy, we estimate the third group of Cruisers will be between 150,000 and 500,000 kilometers from Glas Dinnein, and they may well be in the same defensive pyramid formation that we assumed near Earth."

"Presuming that you're correct, just how do you propose to blow past their defense?"

"Sir, given Commanders Roan and Zorn's bold wager with Fleet Admiral Mer Shawn, I anticipate at least one Cruiser will remain directly over Guardian HQ. Admiral Dylan Cord will believe this precaution will assure Fleet Admiral Mer Shawn he need not pay six cases of brews to Commanders Roan and Zorn. The remaining four Cruisers will move to engage our squadron."

Now, Kellon was frowning. "You are likely correct, Lan. Our squadron must still engage the remaining Gold team on a one-to-one basis. They can easily track us, while they are still stealthy. Just how do you propose that we prevail?"

"Sir, when we exit at 0.50 AU, they will certainly detect us. Yet, it will take some little time for them to both see and believe what they are detecting. It will take even more time for them to respond and structure their defending formation. During this same interval, we will proceed directly toward Glas Dinnein at space-time normal, at least until we bring the defending Cruisers out toward our position. By then, we will have recalibrated and our next micro-Jump will exit at 50,000 kilometers from Glas Dinnein, again well behind the defending Gold team."

"Lan, you cannot possibly be serious. You are proposing to make your last micro-Jump from less than 0.50 AU to 50,000 kilometers above the planet. Given the proximity to a planetary mass, that proposal approaches being suicidal!"

"Sir, I respectfully disagree. Besides, that is not our last micro-Jump. The last Jump is when we Jump from 50,000 kilometers to just above atmosphere. Then we will be emerging in a small diameter facing-circle formation, precisely offset from HQ at optimum laser range. As already stated, I anticipate at least one Cruiser will be in nearby defense of HQ. While at 50,000 kilometers, we will establish a solid firing solution on him. When we exit Jump, he is our first target, and upon exit, our squadron will simultaneously fire against him. After we eliminate the remaining Gold Cruiser, we will then fire our main laser barrage at HQ. Before ground defenses can return fire, we will make a short-Jump out 60 AU to just within the heliosphere."

"Lan, there is no insult intended, but you have been spending too much time with Roan, Zorn, and Shey. Have you counted the number of micro-Jumps involved, and one of them being from 50,000 kilometers to just above atmosphere? If I didn't know better, I could believe you have been sneaking some of Zorn's brews. How can you possibly call your proposal a simple strike on headquarters?" Kellon challenged.

It was noteworthy that there followed a slight pause, before Lan responded, "Sir, it might be properly said that sometimes simple is in the eye of the beholder."

Kellon grimaced, "Lan, what do you suppose the defending Gold team will be doing, while we are doing all of these micro-Jumps?"

"Well, Sir, I believe they will be trying to figure out what we did and how we did it. When it is over, we can resume our stealth profile and return to Glas Dinnein, and receive our appropriate standing ovation."

Kellon shook his head and let out a deep sigh. "Lan, we might just as easily return in leg irons, and a court-martial, for reckless endangerment of our squadron. Of course, we might offer a solid legal defense: do you believe a plea of insanity would suffice?"

"Sir, no, Sir." Lan crisply responded.

Sitting with furrowed brow, Kellon examined Roan and Zorn's well-maintained masks of neutrality as he pondered Lan's brash recommendation. "Well Lan, all things considered, I do confess your proposal presents a very bold and daring plan. Of course, before I can give my approval for your mad scheme, I would need to first confirm your hypothetical micro-Jumps with Commander Grey. Be advised, I don't believe for one moment that he will approve what you have recommended.

"Sir, having anticipated your needs, I requested Commander Grey monitor our conversation. I felt it would save time if he listened."

"Thank you, Lan, that is most thoughtful of you. Commander Grey! Front and center."

As Kellon looked toward the door, he saw Roy enter, and he had a somewhat sheepish grin on his face. "Commanders Roan, Zorn, and Grey, tell me, are there any more conspirators involved in this plot that I should know about?"

Suddenly, the conference room echoed from all of its speakers the resounding thunder of "Yes, Sir, we are all involved!"

Kellon sat back, utterly speechless. "Ladies and Gentlemen, I am sincerely impressed with the stealth of this entire conspiracy. Since it doesn't rise to the status of mutiny, I suppose forgiveness for everyone involved is appropriate. Now that Lan has informed me of the sinister plotline, perhaps Commander Grey will answer a few questions. After which, I will exercise my remaining prerogative and make a command decision.

"Commander Grey. Given Lan's description of a micro-Jump from 50,000 kilometers to just above atmosphere, what are our chances of actually surviving such madness?"

There came a long pause before Roy answered, "Well, Sir, two months ago I would have recommended anyone suggesting such a reckless maneuver be promptly restrained for his own safety. As I said, that was two months ago, before I saw the Kreel Guard exercising micro-Jumps around Lux.

"Sir, after much dedicated research, theoretical analysis, modeling, and two months of making micro-Jumps with our Cruisers, I don't believe making a Jump from 50,000 kilometers to just above atmosphere is anything to write home about. It is sort of like putting on shoes in the morning, rather mundane."

Shaking his head, Kellon wondered if he had heard Roy correctly. "Commander Roy Grey, is the opinion you have just stated for real? This is not something designed to fool the poor old Commodore?"

Roy looked up and smiled broadly. "Commodore Kellon, Sir, I assure you that the entire plan, even as Lan has specified it, has been worked out during simulations, and more than twenty times. It is a solid go and pure gold."

"Roy, have you considered the possible risk to commercial and private traffic inherent in your bold plan of attacking Guardian Headquarters?"

"Yes, Sir. I have submitted all the appropriate notices to Guardian Fleet Headquarters, referring to a full-scale exercise simulating a Kreel attack. The formal notice states that the simulated attack will begin at 06:00 tomorrow. The notice is affirmed, unless canceled by 21:00 this evening."

"Gentlemen, this plot just gets deeper. Now, Commander Grey, do you affirm we can pull off this micro-Jump attack on HQ without killing ourselves or looking like buffoons?"

Pausing a moment before answering, Roy looked somewhat uncomfortable. "Sir, we can definitely pull it off. You should, however, be aware that Admiral Secretary Eryan Kyrie is directly involved. She has invited the Interplanetary Assembly to observe the exercise to witness Glas Dinnein's vulnerability. If we are successful, she said it could help in expediting the forty Cruisers now scheduled for construction."

Roy hesitated a moment before continuing, and he looked even more uncomfortable. "Sir, you also need to know, she placed her own wager of one case of brew with the Admiral. She has bet that we will be successful, without even knowing how we intend to succeed. Sir, there is one more item. She has asked me to convey to you that she would appreciate you granting her a favor."

Kellon had incorrectly believed he was beyond further surprises, and was utterly flabbergasted at Roy's information. "Roy, you're telling me the Admiral Secretary has personally asked me for a favor? Might I be so bold to ask, what favor might that be?"

"Well, Sir, she asked that following our vaporizing Admiral Mer Shawn's office that we train our lasers on the Chief Administrator's office. Sir, about the Chief Administrator, I noticed she didn't ask us to use minimal laser power."

Without another word, Kellon stood up. He carefully collected and then neatly slipped his documents into a folder.

Turning, he looked sternly at his assembled officers. "Well, if we are going to attack Fleet Headquarters at high noon tomorrow, and also target our Planetary Chief Administrator, we'd better get with the program. Don't just sit there, hop to it! In addition, if any of you drop this ball and embarrass me, regardless of your ranks, you will all find yourselves cleaning toilets and polishing floors for a month. Do I make myself perfectly clear?"

There came a cheer and shouts, "Perfectly clear, Sir!"

Shaking his head as he departed the conference room, he turned back and with a broad smile loudly stated, "We had better get to work. Lan! This is a drill, sound battle stations!"

# Chapter Twenty-Nine:
# **Fair Warning**

The chronometer on the wall in Fleet Operations rolled over and displayed 21:00. Although the day was nearly spent, Guardian Fleet's three most senior admirals were sitting together in one of the quiet observation rooms that were located off the main Operations Center. Each of the three officers was intently watching the large tactical plot and the numerous icons being continuously updated and graphically displayed— a thick glass partition separating their quiet work area from the busy hubbub of the adjoining operation room. The esoteric symbols they were intently observing represented all current ship traffic operating within Glas Dinnein's busy solar system.

Turning from the plot board, Dylan Cord looked toward his two friends. "Well, Gentlemen, where do you think Kellon will begin his attack?"

Not even attempting to conceal his mood, Ron Cloud mischievously responded, "From anywhere and at any time."

Dylan looked inquiringly toward Ron. "Of course, you're right, Kellon is rather unpredictable."

"Mer," Ron asked, "did I hear correctly? Did you accept a three to one wager from Commanders Roan and Zorn? Their wager being the Red squadron would blow through the Gold team and hit HQ?"

"It seems the rumor mill is quite correct. I did accept such a wager."

"Mer, might I humbly ask, who gets the three and who gets the one?" Dylan inquired, his eyes twinkling in good humor.

Mer was focusing his attention on the wall chronometer as he answered the question. "As you know, I accepted the wager from Roan and Zorn. You may not, however, have heard that I also accepted a similar wager from the Admiral Secretary. As to the odds, they are putting up the one case and I am correspondingly putting up the three cases, and as you stated, my wager with Gold will hold."

Nodding his head, Dylan smiled. "I believe you have a safe wager. I am anticipating Kellon making a good showing; however, while he is wearing Kreel colors, I don't believe he can possibly penetrate a fifteen Cruiser defense and hit HQ."

As Dylan spoke, a small speaker in the room announced, "Contact! Detecting five mock Kreel within the heliosphere, repeating five mock Kreel detected nine AU within the heliosphere and closing."

Mer turned his attention to the main tactical plot and observed as five red icons appeared. Glancing at the rotation angles that denoted the azimuth and elevation of the icons, he noted the angles were zero and ninety degrees. "Well, Gentlemen, it seems Kellon has declared where he will launch his attack. It seems he is dropping down from directly above Glas Dinnein and has selected the shortest distance between two points."

Ron was smiling broadly. "Gentlemen, by his timing he has declared his intention is to strike HQ! Dylan, you appear to have an interesting tactical problem to resolve."

As he studied the tactical plot, Dylan was frowning. "Hmmmm, Kellon is now forty-three Astronomical Units distant from Glas Dinnein. Although he is moving at 220 lights, how he can possibly expect to get past the defending Gold team remains beyond my comprehension. Are you two rogues keeping secrets?" Dylan asked.

"In fact, now that you ask Dylan, we are." Mer responded with a smile.

With a puzzled frown, Dylan looked back toward Mer and dryly commented, "Mer, I know he's good, but he'll need to pull several huge tricks out of his fat game bag if he's to hit HQ. You may have noticed, Commodore Greer and Gold Squadron 1 are moving out to engage Kellon, and Greer is holding the stealth advantage. Splitting the distance, I estimate he will intercept and take Kellon's squadron out of play in about fifteen hours. From my vantage point, Kellon's squadron looks like five fat ducks blithely waddling about, and a fox is about to pluck them for his dinner."

Now Mer's eyes were sparkling with good humor. "Well Dylan, if you're that confident Greer is the fox and capable of plucking Kellon's ducks, I am prepared to offer you a small wager, a small wager just between old friends. I'll put up my one case of brews against your five cases, wagering Kellon's ducks gets past your foxes, all of them, and hits HQ."

Turning slowly, Dylan looked at Mer with raised eyebrows that quickly transformed into a frown. "Mer, that means you are hedging your bet with Roan and Zorn. I acknowledge Kellon is a very capable officer, but so are the commodores of the three squadrons standing between him and HQ. I don't know what Kellon is up to, but I will accept your wager."

Mer leaned back and smiled mischievously, "Dylan, I like your style. I acknowledge your wager and offer to raise the bet, my two cases against your ten. Do you accept?"

"Accepted! And I raise your wager to my fifteen cases against your three. Furthermore, if I lose the wager, I will even take the both of you to lunch.

"Mer, frankly I don't understand your wager. I'm watching that tactical plot, and what I see are five mock Kreel moving smartly toward Glas Dinnein. They're in a very dispersed facing-circle formation, but they'll need to converge to hit HQ. When Commodore Greer intercepts the mock Kreel, this matter will be promptly concluded, and it won't even require the remaining ten Gold Cruisers to join in the fracas."

Still smiling, Mer nodded his acceptance. "Then, Dylan, we have our wager. I'm opting, with Ron's agreement, for lunch at McBride's."

Leaning back in his chair, Ron's merriment was evident in his smile and eyes. "Gentlemen, for the sake of full disclosure, I'm not certain that I should participate in this wager. As the Fleet Intelligence senior officer, someone might properly conclude I have privileged knowledge of Kellon's intended tactics. However, in the spirit of sharing a good lunch, I will gladly participate in having lunch at McBride's."

Looking slowly from Mer to Ron, a deepening frown clouded Dylan's previously good-natured expression. "You two old conspirators are definitely holding back something. Hmmmmm, then everything isn't what it appears? Is that it? Are those five inbound targets mock Kreel or else are they decoys? Is it a feint?" Mer's smile only broadened. "Dylan, as Ron previously stated, you have an interesting tactical problem to resolve. All I will say now is that you had better begin taking Kellon's attack more seriously. I recommend that you take every possible step available to prevent Kellon from knocking the top off this building. He's coming. As our wager indicates, I believe you will not prevent his doing so."

An expression of exasperation flooded Dylan's features as he stood frowning, first at Mer and then Ron. "I hear your confidence Mer, and I have no idea what's feeding it. Even so, your comments have provided a fair warning. So be it."

On board Lan, Kellon was sitting in the CAC. Pivoting his command chair, he carefully watched the tactical plot. Except for the murmur of the various teams busy at their assigned tasks, the CAC was unusually quiet, as if it were a hush prior to the arrival of a pending storm.

"Tactical here. We have penetrated nine AU into the heliosphere and are forty-three AU from Glas Dinnein. Given anticipated detection and reporting delays, Fleet Operations must now be aware of our penetration points through the heliopause. Accordingly, Operations will have scrambled the Gold team to intercept. Currently, our simulation estimates intercept in fifteen hours."

"Tactical, Kellon here. I will be in my quarters. Promptly inform me once you detect the Gold team. If possible, I want all three opposing squadrons located prior to our first Jump. Tactical, Lorn you have the CAC."

"Tactical here. Yes, Sir, understood, I have the CAC." Lorn crisply responded.

Yawning, Ron looked at the wall chronometer. "Gentlemen, it's getting late and we seem to have some hours before intercept. I suggest we depart Operations and get some sleep. I think tomorrow will likely prove to be a very busy and most interesting day."

Dubious, Dylan had continued studying the tactical plot. Turning slowly, he shook his head as Mer and Ron stood to depart. "The two of you obviously know something that I don't know. Given the size of our wager, I'm opting to remain here to protect my investment, just in case something unforeseen pops up."

Stretching and yawning, Mer was still in good spirits. "Dylan, you may be certain of just one thing."

"And what might that be?" Dylan asked.

Mer chuckled. "Well, when it does happen, it will be both unforeseen and unexpected. On that, you can safely wager. We'll see you in the morning."

As his two friends departed and the door closed behind them, Dylan stood looking at the closed door and frowned. Turning, he carefully studied the tactical plot. What he saw was five red icons approaching Glas Dinnein at 220 lights and Gold Squadron 1 was moving directly to oppose them at 220 lights. *Something is not as it appears to be, but what?* He wondered. *It is going to be a very long night.*

# X

Having obtained several hours of sleep, Kellon still felt the rising tension, and had returned to CAC. Like everyone else, he was waiting for the detection of the opposing Gold team. Sitting in his Command Chair, he was observing everyone working at their coordinated tasks, and everyone sensed the defending Gold squadron must be drawing nearer.

"Tactical here. Contact! We have detected the Gold team. Five Cruisers are maneuvering in a facing-circle formation. They are moving at 220 lights and spreading to engage us one-on-one. They are maintaining a full stealth profile; however, our new detection and tracking algorithms are working well. Estimating they will reach their optimum firing position in seven hours."

Studying the tactical plot, he noted the icons indicating the approaching Guardian Cruisers. It seemed strange to him. Those five Cruisers were running in full stealth mode, yet they were plotted as if they were employing a transponder beacon or were as detectable as the Kreel. He shook his head, conflicted by two intertwined emotions. He was surprised to see just how vulnerable Lan had been, even in full stealth mode. Then there came a sense of sadness. He thought, *Lux and his crew never had a fighting chance against the Elite Guard.*

Closing the floodgates of emotion coming with his thoughts about Lux, he focused on the moment. "Navigation, Kellon here. Are you set up for our first short-Jump?"

"Navigation here. Yes, Sir. All Cruisers are acknowledging short-Jump parameters at 99.999+. We are ready and waiting for orders."

"Lan, scramble and transmit to all Cruisers, Code 2 in seven hours."

"Yes, Sir, transmitting."

Pressing the internal communications circuit, Kellon informed Lan's crew, "Ladies and Gentlemen, we have detected the Gold team moving to intercept us. Tactical is estimating seven hours before intercept. Therefore, all sections are to remain at Condition 3 until further notice. Kellon out."

# Chapter Thirty:
# **Naked to the Stars**

Dawn was transitioning into a bright morning on Glas Dinnein, and it was going to be a beautiful day. With purpose, Eryan and Susie were walking along the coastal path between the Assembly Building and the Guardian HQ, and Gepeto was properly heeling. Smiling, Susie was enjoying the simultaneous contrast of warm morning sunshine with the pinpoints of coolness from the low morning mist on her skin.

"Eryan, I am confident Commodore Kellon and his squadron will accomplish their simulated attack. I've seen them in combat, and I know they are precise and efficient. Besides, Kellon is not a boastful person."

"I tend to agree. However, my own sources inform me that Admiral Dylan Cord has fired up all of his resources. He's made a wager with Mer that the HQ Gold team will prevent Kellon from succeeding. He has no intention of losing that bet."

"Eryan, I don't understand Mer's bet with Dylan that Kellon would succeed. He also made a wager with Roan and Zorn that Kellon wouldn't succeed. Which outcome is he betting on?"

Eryan laughed. "Mer is hedging his bet, but he's also declaring what he really believes, since his wager with Dylan is at odds of five-to-one that Kellon will penetrate the Gold team and take off the top of HQ."

"Five to one? Roan and Zorn only obtained odds of three to one."

"Well, Susie, this is why Mer is Fleet Admiral. He's good at what he does. When Kellon succeeds, as we both believe he will, Mer will pay six cases to Roan and Zorn and receive fifteen cases from Dylan, a net gain of nine cases. Of course, Mer will have to give me three of those nine cases."

With Gepeto, the two women entered the front doors of HQ and Security quickly admitted them. Walking to Operations, they located the Operations viewing room that Dylan was using as his command center for the exercise. When they entered, they found Mer, Ron, and Dylan watching the large tactical plot through the glass partition. As the women entered, the three men turned and waved hello, then promptly turned back to study the tactical plot.

"Eryan, I believe we're here just in time. Something is happening."

Walking over and looking over the men's heads, they studied the tactical plot. Both of them found the graphic symbols confusing.

"Good morning, Gentlemen, might I ask one of you to provide the Ambassador and me an update? What's happening?" Eryan asked.

Smiling, Mer turned about and offered a brief summary. "Of course, Madam Secretary, I'm happy to do that. At the moment, it seems Kellon has maintained his approach from his entry point, that being directly above Glas Dinnein. Since detection, he has remained in a facing-circle formation and hasn't wavered one iota from his initial attack vector. In opposition, Commodore Greer has moved at 220 lights to intercept, and as we speak, Greer is hunkering down in his final firing positions. It looks like Greer is about to take out Kellon's squadron from ambush. In Kellon's defense, the exercise rules don't permit him to use stealth and he's easily tracked, whereas Greer's squadron is running in full stealth. Right now, it looks like Kellon will fall considerably short of taking off the top of the HQ building and I will lose my bet with Dylan."

Susie had listened carefully to Mer's explanation, and she offered her own observation. "Admiral Mer Shawn, Kellon is using the same battle plan that the Kreel employed during their last strike on Earth. The only difference I see is that the Kreel had eight cruisers and Kellon has only five. Also, the Kreel were in a facing triangle, and Kellon is in a facing circle."

Dylan had listened as Susie made her comment. "Madam Ambassador, did Kellon ambush the Kreel?"

"Oh yes, Sir. He moved to intercept and took out six of their eight cruisers from ambush. Only two slipped through the ambush to continue their attack on Earth."

His countenance darkening, Dylan dryly commented, "Mer something stinks here. Kellon is many things, but a fool he is not.

If he successfully ambushed the Kreel, then why is he repeating a tactic he previously defeated? He must know what I will most—"

A man's excited voice called from a small speaker, "Admiral Cord, they are gone. The Red team just vanished off our monitoring screens. They simply vanished just before Gold 1 was about to fire. They are gone, simply disappeared."

Dylan whirled about, looking at the tactical plot and growling, "Acknowledged. Blast and double blast! Mer, Kellon knows full well that the exercise restraints do not permit him to shift into a stealth mode. What is he trying to pull off?"

Puzzled, Susie turned toward Dylan. "Sir, I don't believe Kellon is using stealth, he knows that would be prohibited. I think he has simply performed a short-Jump."

Dylan spun toward Susie, and his face registered his total shock at her words. "Ambassador, that's impossible. It would be total madness to attempt a Jump within a solar system. Kellon is fully aware that any attempt to do so would subject his ships to nearly certain destruction, with a loss of all hands. There must be some other explanation. There simply must be."

Susie smiled, "Sir, I believe Kellon has simply executed a short-Jump, just like he did during the battle with the Kreel invasion fleet near Scion."

Smiling, and doing a quick pirouette, Susie looked up at Dylan and understood his confusion. "Sir, remember, I was with Kellon near Scion when he did a short-Jump within that heliosphere, and as you can readily see, I am standing here with all of my fingers and toes and I'm not even a little bit destroyed."

Pivoting toward Mer, Dylan demanded, "Did you know Kellon performed a short-Jump within a planetary system and you did not tell me? Why?"

Mer was no longer smiling. "Well, Dylan, I believe the answer is the level of classification involved. And, speaking of classification, I'm suggesting you immediately initiate a Black Hole event at this time, and maintain it for the duration of this exercise."

Dylan was sputtering, "Call a Black Hole? For an exercise? Are you serious?"

"Dylan, I'm as serious as I can be," Mer replied firmly.

Seeing Dylan's confusion, Ron added his voice, "Dylan you had better make that Black Hole call immediately!"

Still looking totally confused, Dylan picked up his microphone, "Attention, Admiral Dylan Cord here. This exercise has just been classified Black Hole. I repeat, Black Hole. I'm ordering all personnel without Black Hole clearance to immediately— repeat, immediately— depart the Operations Center. All departing personnel are to forget promptly what they may have heard or seen here this morning— it didn't happen.

"Security, you are to immediately lock down the Operations Center— repeat, lock it down tight— and make it happen now!"

Putting down the microphone, Dylan stood listening to the warning-alert tone and watching the confusion beyond the glass partition. He slowly turned back to face Mer and Ron.

"Gentlemen, I believe you are a little late in giving me an explanation about what is happening here!"

In a soft tone of understanding, Mer advised, "Dylan, old friend, I suggest you return to the tactical problem you are facing. Ambassador Wells has given you a heads-up about what you need to be watching for. For now, that is all I am prepared to say."

The confusion within the Operations Center slowly ebbed as the on-duty personnel rapidly thinned out. Studying the tactical plot, Dylan again shifted focus, resuming his command task.

"Blast, I have Gold 1 out at twenty-two AU from Glas Dinnein with nothing to attack. Gold 2 is at ten AU and in perfect position to back up Gold 1. Blast, where is Kellon hiding?" Dylan muttered.

Just then, the speaker erupted, "Admiral Cord, there are five mock Kreel now only 0.50 AU from Glas Dinnein and closing! Repeat, 0.50 AU from Glas Dinnein and closing. They're emitting an enormous energy flare and frequency shifts indicate they are slowing."

Sitting back in utter shock, Dylan muttered, "That's impossible! Kellon couldn't have Jumped from 30 AU to within 0.50 AU. It's not possible. If that data is correct, then even Gold 2 is more than nine AU out of position to intercept."

Picking up his microphone, Dylan barked orders, "Dylan here. Gold teams, everything involved in this exercise is now classified Black Hole. Gold 2, you are to return to Glas Dinnein at maximum velocity! Scrap the stealth protocols, return at maximum velocity. "Gold 3, Leave one Cruiser over HQ, but move your remaining force to engage the enemy. Intercept the mock Kreel at 0.50 AU above Glas Dinnein and closing. Make it happen!

"Gold 1, you are now completely out of position, return to Glas Dinnein at normal mission velocity. Cord out."

Dylan turned, his face flushed, and looked sternly at his two friends. "You two reprobates knew about Kellon's ability to do a Jump within a heliosphere, and you didn't inform me. Gentlemen, when this is over, I will require a full explanation of just why.

"Mer, for the record, our bet still stands. Whatever else Kellon may have up his sleeves," Dylan declared, "he's exposed his big trick. Now, he still has to get past Gold 3, and since he's without stealth capability, that he is not likely to do! Game over!"

Sitting quietly, Mer and Ron did not respond to Dylan's heated comment, but remained stoically observing the tactical plot. Meanwhile, Dylan had returned to studying the tactical plot to see the end-game resolution of the exercise.

The plot indicated the five mock Kreel were still moving in perfect synchronization toward Glas Dinnein while rapidly decelerating, but still moving at 80 lights. On the tactical plot, the icons representing Gold 3 were accelerating out from the planet to engage. Given the closing rates, that engagement would occur in a matter of minutes. Although Kellon's squadron was continuing to decelerate, the closing rate of the two opposing forces was still very high.

Observing the approaching collision of opposing forces, Mer muttered inwardly, *Exercise or not, the crews will need to be on their top game with those closing rates*. Everyone in the observation room held their breath as the end game reached its pinnacle.

Slowly, a smile eased Dylan's grim expression. *Now, I have you pinned Kellon!* Dylan thought.

Abruptly, the five red icons disappeared, and then almost immediately reappeared, but they were no longer at 0.50 AU. They reappeared at 50,000 kilometers above Glas Dinnein and well to the rear of the four Cruisers of Gold 3, who were still accelerating away from Glas Dinnein at nearly 100 lights. The tactical plot symbols announced the five inbound mock Kreel were now exhibiting a massive energy flare as they rapidly decelerated.

Standing stunned for a moment, disbelieving what the tactical plot indicated, Dylan picked up his microphone and ordered, "Gold 3! The enemy is now behind you, he is 50,000 kilometers above Glas Dinnein. Repeating, the enemy is at 50,000 kilometers above Glas Dinnein."

Sighing, Dylan's shoulders slumped, and he put down the microphone. Disbelieving he simply stared at the tactical plot. He had only one remaining Gold Cruiser in a defensive position, and that Cruiser was now outnumbered five to one.

Once again, the symbols on the tactical plot rapidly shifted—the five red icons had disappeared yet again.

Within HQ, bedlam suddenly broke out, and alarms were sounding all over the Guardian Headquarters building. Everyone stopped and listened, both surprised and confused.

When Mer's communicator hummed, he lifted it to his ear and listened. "Understood. Now, repeat the message."

Deftly, Mer depressed a button on his communicator and transferred his incoming message to the remote speakers within the Operations viewing room. Out of the speakers came the excited voice of a young man, "Admiral Mer Shawn, I repeat, Headquarters sensors have registered five clusters of laser hits from the mock Kreel. Five solid laser bombardments. Sir, the five mock Kreel were at the upper boundary of the atmosphere when they fired. The mock Kreel first hit the remaining Cruiser stationed over HQ, even before they fired on the Headquarters building. Even before the Gold Cruiser could detect and localize the Red squadron, they hit him with five synchronized laser blasts. The automatic referee ruled the mock Kreel instantly destroyed him. Sir, the defending Gold Cruiser didn't get a single shot off. Not a single shot!

"Sir, There is one more and somewhat odd thing to report. Five clusters of laser hits were recorded by the sensors at the Chief Administrator's office building."

Pressing the remote button again, Mer lifted the communicator to his ear, "Thank you for your precise report. Mer Shawn out."

Turning, Mer looked at Dylan, who was simply sitting in a numb manner and staring at the tactical plot. His friend was starkly dumbfounded, and said nothing.

Almost whispering, the small speaker above the viewing partition announced, "Admiral Cord, Sir, all traces of the five mock Kreel are gone. Repeat, we no longer have track on the mock Kreel. Our last track put them just above the atmosphere. They were tracked at that position for a total of fifty-seven seconds, and then they simply vanished, yet again."

Clear laughter suddenly filled the entire viewing area with its musical qualities, and Eryan exclaimed, "Kellon did it! He did it clean. He even took a shot at our beloved Chief Administrator, he did it all in fifty-seven seconds over his designated target, and he even took out a Gold 3 Cruiser, to boot! Mer, I believe you now owe me three cases of brews." Leaning back, Eryan continued to laugh with merriment.

Sighing, both Mer and Ron stood, while still studying the tactical plot. Then Mer turned toward his old friend. "Dylan, Ron and I have an apology and confession to make to you. You were correct, and we have much to explain. Given the circumstances, I believe it is only sporting and fair that I pick up the cost of lunch at McBride's."

Slowly turning, Dylan looked toward Mer and saw his serious demeanor. His own insides were in turmoil. "Mer, how can Kellon have accomplished this? By all known science and theory, it shouldn't be possible. In light of this outcome, Glas Dinnein and the other planets have no defense, none whatsoever. We're totally open to attack and naked to the stars."

Mer put his arm over Dylan's shoulder. Speaking quietly, he advised, "Well, Dylan, there's one thing we do have. Kellon has expertly demonstrated what could possibly happen, and thereby he has given us the necessary time to find the required defense before it is required."

Susie found herself smiling and feeling a deep sense of pride for Kellon's achievement. "Gentlemen, on Earth we have an old saying. Being forewarned is being forearmed!"

Turning toward Eryan and Susie, Mer graciously bowed. "Madam Ambassador there is certain wisdom in such advice.

Ladies, and Gepeto, might I ask if you will join three splurging admirals for lunch at McBride's?"

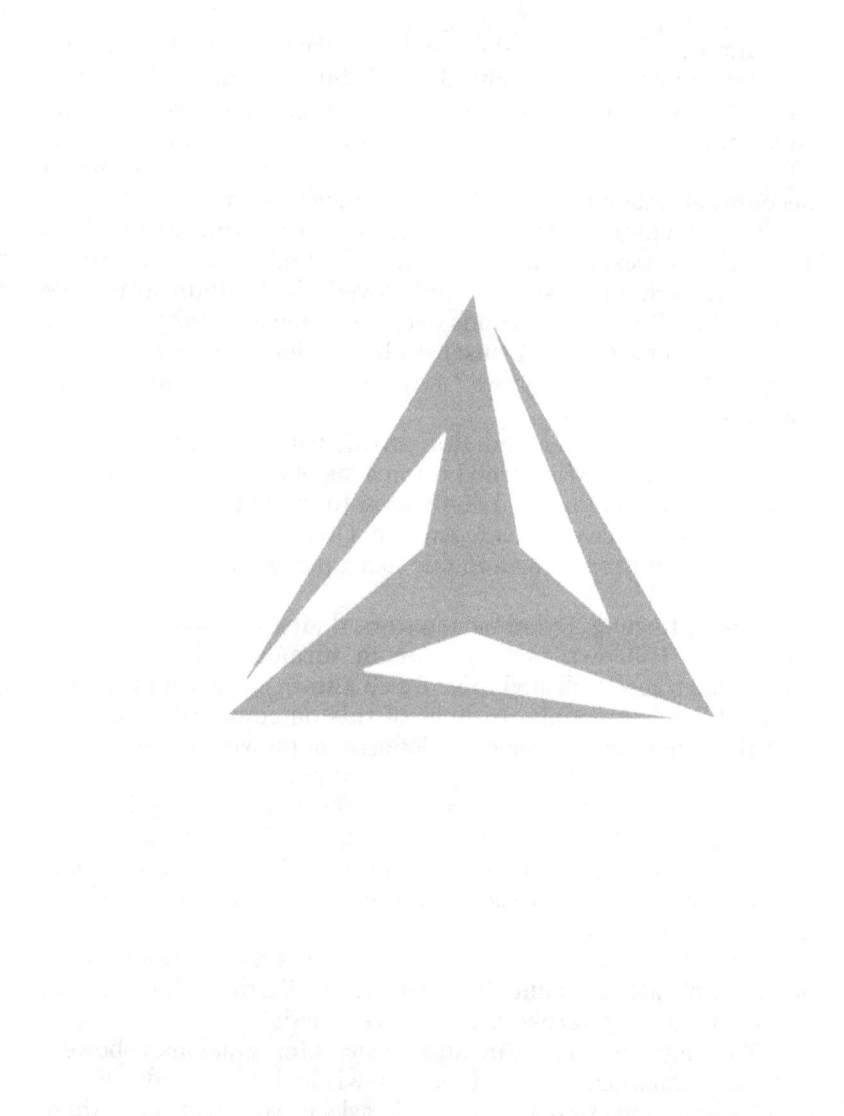

# Chapter Thirty-One:
# Potentially Elegant Tactic

Five busy days had passed since Kellon's exercise when Admiral Mer Shawn called together a planning meeting with his associates and Kellon in his office. Although the exercise was over, the work that was the consequence of Kellon's demonstration was just beginning. Each of the three admirals had been working long hours, and they were looking somewhat haggard.

Swiveling in his chair, Mer turned and looked directly toward Kellon. "Commodore, your next mission is to gather intelligence about how the Kreel Hub communicates and controls its empire. Your primary focus will be on Kreel commercial and Military communications the insertion of intelligence gathering probes. It is most definitely not a strike mission."

"Sir, I fully understand," Kellon replied.

As Mer sat back, Ron leaned forward, "Lux began his reconnaissance near Hub-3. That unfortunately is where the Kreel Elite Guard detected him. Rather than sending you straight back to Hub-3, you will begin your reconnaissance near Hub-2 and then proceed to Hub-1."

"Sir, then are you ordering us to avoid Hub-3?"

"No. Whether or not you go to Hub-3 will be your own command decision. Upon completing your primary mission in Hubs 2 and 1, you will need to evaluate your tactical situation and decide if continuing to Hub-3 is prudent."

"Sir, during the past few weeks, I've had time to consider the upcoming mission. With your permission, I would like to present several suggestions that might help in achieving the mission's overall goals, while somewhat expanding on those goals."

Leaning forward and frowning, Mer studied Kellon's calm expression. "Commodore, I believe that you are already facing sufficient perils without seeking to add to those perils. Lux was lost during our initial attempt to gather intelligence within the

Kreel Hub systems. If you succeed in inserting the Intelligence probes in Hubs 2 and 1 and return in one piece, we will consider the mission a complete success."

"Sir, then is it your decision to not even consider a slight expansion of the stated mission goals?"

"No, that is not what I am saying! I will not grant you carte blanche on this mission. However, if you need some latitude, then simply put some brackets about what it is you want."

"Yes, Sir, some brackets. Well, I've identified several possibilities that might compliment the stated mission goals.

"Firstly, when Guardian HQ received Lux's Cobalt Blue, it ordered all the Navigation Beacons and Intelligence probes he'd deployed to self-destruct. Therefore, my first recommendation is to establish not one, but two new dispersed and independent transit routes through Kreel space that lead toward the Hub systems. Hub-1, Hub-2, and Hub-3 are all within ten light-years of one another. I'm therefore proposing to use Lan and Lent to position deep Navigation Beacons along one route and use Lar, Langley, and Lowell to install Navigation Beacons along the second route. Our plan terminates both routes at a geometric center point located between the three Hub-world solar systems. I've defined the termination points to be one hundred AU from each other and vertically offset from the defined geometric center point. By establishing two separate routes, we will gain the benefits of redundancy for both long-Jumps and for the transfer of the intelligence data our probes will be gathering."

Slowly, a smile appeared on Mer's face. "Commodore, since your recommendation is soundly considered and does not increase your risk factor, I accept and approve the recommendation.

"Now, since you began with 'firstly,' I would wager that you have another embellishment in mind. You might just as well spit it out— put it all out on the table."

Observing Mer's smile, Kellon somewhat relaxed. Taking a deep breath, he continued. "Sir, you are correct, I do have a few more recommendations. During our last conversation, you informed me the goal was to bankrupt the Kreel Empire. I have carefully considered your intention and thought how we might set about to accomplish precisely that. Accordingly, I am requesting authorization for each Cruiser to carry resupply pods on this mission."

Mer's eyebrows went up as he interjected, "Kellon, your mission duration and goals do not warrant resupply. Precisely what are you proposing?"

"Sir, I'm requesting a complete reload of missiles and also special ordnance."

"Kellon, your request indicates you anticipate heavy combat. Do I need to underscore the goal of our mission is not a strike, but covert intelligence gathering? Furthermore, precisely what special ordnance are you requesting?" Mer asked.

"No, Sir, it isn't necessary to underscore the mission goals. I'm basing my request on the fact Lux expended all of his missiles, and he was left completely vulnerable. I lack the tactical data to understand Lux's missile-to-hit ratio. I do not want to find myself in Lux's position: deep in Kreel space and without missiles. Therefore I consider it prudent to have nearby and available a reload of missiles."

Mer Shawn nodded his head in an affirmative, "Understood. Request granted. Now about the special ordnance? What do you have in mind?"

"Sir, I am requesting modified light missiles and limpet-pads. The request is that Guardian ordnance removes the missile's warhead and replaces it with an intelligence gathering payload. Ordnance will then pair the modified missiles with limpet attachment pads. Ordnance will also need to alter each limpet-pad to carry a multi-purpose detonator and a medium shaped-charge."

Now Ron's eyebrows were raised, "Intelligence probes joined with limpets? Commodore, an Intelligence probe limpet combination sounds like an interesting concept. Please expand on your idea, including what modifications you are requesting."

"Yes, Sir. I propose that we penetrate Hub-2 space and insert the Intelligence probes precisely as specified. As you said, Hub-2 is the base for Kreel Industrial production, and there must be significant commercial traffic from that center out to all the other Kreel worlds. Therefore, I am proposing that after inserting the Intelligence probes, we deploy our Scouts to intercept outbound commercial cargo ships and covertly attach the limpets on those ships. Each ship will in turn carry the Intelligence probe piggyback to its next port of call. When the ship enters into the next heliosphere, we will program the Intelligence probes to detach from their anchoring limpet-pads. Once detached, the probe will independently seek a favorable heliocentric orbit, and then initiate monitoring of the solar system. Once the probe establishes its data link with Guardian Intelligence, and its preliminary data is analyzed, its initial orbit can be subsequently optimized."

Having listened carefully to Kellon, Ron looked over toward Mer. "Kellon may have come up with a shortcut to our overall intelligence goal."

"Hmmm, Kellon, I tend to agree with Ron. It is an interesting concept if you can actually accomplish the feat. Continue," Mer said.

"Yes, Sir. Regarding Admiral Cloud's comment, we may not be able to insert an Intelligence probe into each of the forty Kreel planetary systems. However, we might well succeed in penetrating a significant number of those systems without our needing to go there."

Ron leaned forward, "Understood, Kellon, but what specific modifications are you requiring be made to the limpet-pads?"

"Sir, my underlying thinking is based on Admiral Mer Shawn's stated intention to bankrupt the Kreel Empire. If we destroy a large number of Kreel interstellar commercial ships, then his intention might just be accelerated. I'm therefore requesting ordnance modify the limpet-pad to incorporate a medium shaped-charge and a multi-purpose detonator. If a hull inspection robot should discover the limpet-pad, the detonator and shaped- charge need promptly explode. The final function of the limpet is that after the Intelligence probe releases from the pad, the limpet-pad, detonator, and shaped-charge will remain fixed to the ship's hull. We'll have preset the detonator to explode as the ship enters into an atmosphere. I believe a medium penetrator charge properly placed on a ship's hull might well destroy the entire ship if it explodes during re-entry. At the very least, the shaped charge will severely damage the ship and compel the Kreel to withdraw it from commercial service for repair."

Sitting back, Dylan had remained silent and listening. "Kellon, the only drawback I see in your plan is it exposes your

Scouts to an enormous risk when placing the limpets on the Kreel hulls. You have outlined an elegant and lethal process that could potentially inflict serious economic damage on the Kreel Empire while advancing our intelligence-gathering goals. If you can demonstrate the Scouts can do the deed, I will endorse your recommendation."

Turning to Dylan, Mer asked, "How long do you think it might take ordnance to make the needed modifications to existing light missiles and limpet-pads?"

Dylan's brow furrowed in thought as he considered Mer's question. "Well, given the outcome of Kellon's recent exercise, almost every engineer and technician is on double duty. Fortunately, ordnance is not part of that race to develop new defenses. What Kellon is asking for falls more in the category of a custom assembly order, rather than design and development. We certainly have all the needed components for what he's asking for in our existing stores. Some modifications will obviously be required, but they shouldn't be significant.

"Given where Kellon intends to deliver the ordnance, and how he's delivering it, it does require extreme redundancy in fail-safe systems however— since it's vital we protect our covert cover and sensitive technologies. That's especially true for the modified missiles and their payloads and the limpets and their multi-function detonators. Hmmmm, perhaps an anti-tamper mass-pressure sensitive modification would do....

"Mer, it's obvious that Guardian ordnance will need to do some testing. By relying on certified components, however, ordnance should be able to rapidly assemble a modified light missile with an intelligence payload and the remaining components. I will need to confirm my assumptions, but I estimate ordnance can produce about three hundred of the missile-limpet units during the next ten days."

Turning to Kellon, Dylan asked, "Will three hundred missile-limpet units in the next ten days meet your requirements?"

"Sir, my analysis indicates a minimum of one hundred units are required, and if Guardian ordnance can provide additional units, it would certainly help. If I have Admiral Mer Shawn's authorization to proceed, ten days will be quite satisfactory."

Now, Mer was again frowning. "In for a gram, in for a kilogram? Well, Kellon, you have my approval, but with the single caveat that Admiral Cord set. You will need to demonstrate the Scouts can deliver the package, and do so with acceptable risks. Understood?"

"Yes, Sir. I will proceed with demonstrating the Scouts' capability. With your permission, I'll schedule the squadron's deployment in twelve days."

Mer leaned back and looked toward the bookcase opposite his desk, as if only studying the rich leather volumes for their size and beauty. He then returned his attention to Kellon, "Commodore, upon your return, I will require a long discussion with you about many topics, and especially about the results of the mission. I am providing you with the authorization for the proposals you have put forth. Remember, I do not want any more Cobalt Blue signals!"

Turning toward Dylan, Mer ordered, "Make all the required arrangements to produce the special ordnance. Your concerns for maximum redundancy in respect to fail-safe systems and protocols are underscored. Do not permit a rush order to create a possible loss of critical technology."

"Fully understood, Mer. It will be properly done," Dylan replied. Mer turned to Kellon, "While I've given you the authorization you've requested, and agree with Ron that it's a potentially elegant tactic, you are charged to take every precaution at your disposal. In keeping with the covert nature of your mission, you are not to take unwarranted risks. To this end, I recommend that you have a long talk with Commanders Roan and Zorn and Scout Ship Shey regarding this point. Do I make myself perfectly clear?"

"Yes, Sir, perfectly clear. We will proceed in accordance with your orders."

As Dylan cleared his throat, the others turned toward him. "Gentlemen, Commodore Kellon's intention to blaze two new routes into the heart of the Kreel Empire are noteworthy. I would like to remind everyone here that the Kreel have forty inhabitable worlds in their empire— at least forty known worlds. I do not need to remind any of you that we are short of Guardian ships. Kellon's recent demonstration has shaken the very foundations of our establishment. It will take at least a full year before we can bring all of our Cruisers to the level of our new stealth standards.

"I am urging that where possible all effort be made to refrain from provoking the Kreel into attacking any of our worlds. I do not presently have sufficient Cruisers to fill all the existing mission requirements and none whatsoever to fill the role of a replacement.

Ron looked over to his friend, smiling, "Dylan, I may be wrong, however, I'm not certain we could provoke the Kreel into a major attack if we wanted to. They've just taken a severe beating and they lost nearly three hundred of their ships during the past year. I see no way whatsoever that they can replace those ships in less than six years, even if they were working at full production.

"What Kellon has proposed to do with the limpets will most likely cost the Kreel another two hundred commercial ships. Unless I am very wrong in my assessments, the Kreel will be thinking far more in terms of defense than of offense."

It was noon, and soft melodious tones sounded from a small wall clock. Mer rose and walked over to the large window. He stood looking out over the expanse of beach that ran east and west by the Guardian Headquarters building. He stood quietly for a minute or so, and then turned to Kellon.

"Commodore, Dylan is correct. We are under pressure. The very volume of the Kreel Empire provides them with a protective barrier of sorts. With our Force limitations, we are not in a military position to attack the Kreel overtly. When we do eventually attack, it will require precise planning and then hitting them in their most vital areas.

"Your mission is critical to our attaining the long-term strategic objectives. Go in, do your intelligence gathering, then consider getting out. While the use of limpets is a sound military concept, I again order you to minimize your risks. Nevertheless, you will be far from home and are in command of the mission. You will need to rely on your own tactical judgment, which has repeatedly proven sound. We've said all that needs to be said. Good luck."

Kellon stood and saluted. "Thank you, Sir."

Mer moved around his desk and extended a hand to Kellon. "Kellon, use your stealth capability, avoid engagements where possible, and bring your entire squadron home if at all possible."

"Kellon shook Mer's hand. Both men's grip was firm and sincere.

"Yes, Sir. I will do my best to do that."

Both Ron and Dylan had stood up, and from the expressions on their faces both were revealing the depth of their own concerns. Kellon in turn shook hands with both men, then turned and left the room.

As the door closed, Mer turned back to his two friends. "Gentlemen, that officer needs some downtime. During the past three years, we have asked a great deal from him, and he has always come through. Even so, we may be asking too much of him this time."

Dylan gazed at Mer, "Too much? Kellon will succeed. Then perhaps we can work out some time for him and Eurie to share together."

Ron broadly smiled, "Those two need each other. The emotional connection between Kellon and Eurie being what it is, I'm wondering if it's wise to send Lent out with Lan."

Mer broke into an answering smile. "It should be fine, they'll tend to look out for each other, and in the process she will keep Kellon on the straight and narrow. Their being sent out together might just be the key to get everyone home again.

"Hmmmm. Gentlemen, I might have just the right answer. I know of some acreage up the coast that a few well-intended friends might just acquire. It's a beautiful location overlooking the ocean and has a wonderful assortment of trees on it. I suggest we of the Guardian Force take up a small contribution and acquire that parcel as a gift for the two of them upon their return. That gift combined with an eighteen months forced leave for the both of them should do quite nicely in allowing them to recharge their batteries."

"Ah," sighed Dylan, "It's once again comforting to be considered one of the conspirators again. Being left out in the dark during these past weeks underscores how much better it feels to be part of a conspiracy— rather than the brunt of one."

# Chapter Thirty-Two:
## Partial Payback

Three days following his meeting with Mer Shawn, Kellon was sitting on Shey's Jump seat and observing the bulkhead display screen. The entire squadron was out in space near Glas Dinnein. Each Scout team was busy in a firing exercise that applied their recent simulator training to actual operational tests. Kellon silently observed as Roan and Zorn worked with Shey to begin their approach toward a Guardian freighter, which was providing target services for the exercise.

"Roan, are these exercising missiles the same as the war loads?" Zorn asked.

"That's what I understand. They're the first test batch, however. Ordnance has replaced the shaped charge with a special telemetry package so Operations can track our results."

"Roan, I am tracking the Guardian freighter that is acting as the target. It is at 50,000 kilometers and closing," Shey said.

Turning, Roan looked over toward Zorn. "What's your status?" "I'm as ready as ready gets. Let's do it."

"Agreed. Shey, confirm we are at 75 percent stealth factor." "Confirming, stealth factor is at 75 percent."

"Shey, set our tactical plane so the target's velocity vector is one axis and the ecliptic plane is the second. Heads up everyone, we will be passing on a reciprocal course 1,000 kilometers above and offset 1,000 kilometers from the target.

"Zorn, stay sharp during our approach. Even though we have a preliminary propulsion classification of a freighter, the Kreel might have some tricks up their sleeve we haven't seen before. As we approach and fly-by, obtain a full passive scan and confirm target classification.

"Shey, after CPA, and with Zorn's positive identification of the target, you will maintain your altitude and come about. You are to move up behind the target, until you obtain a separation of

2,000 kilometers. Unless you detect an inbound hostile threat, you will maintain that relative position."

"Roan, a fly-by at 1,000 kilometers brings us very close to the target. Is that prudent?" Shey asked.

"Shey girl, we should be approaching a freighter having minimal or no self-defense capability. He will most likely be monitoring for proximity of debris and normal propulsion signatures as part of his routine collision avoidance, but it's unlikely he can do more than that. At 75 percent stealth, we should be invisible even at 100 kilometers. Even so, keep your detection sensors full out— as if you were expecting counterfire, and you should be ready to evade. Accordingly, set Simulated Condition 2 on all gun and laser turrets, and full automatic on point defense.

"Shey, execute!" Roan ordered.

"Acknowledging and executing. I am alerting Lan that we are commencing our target run. Now closing on the target, estimating ten minutes to CPA."

Concentrating on his instruments as Shey approached their target, Zorn first confirmed the target classification and then determined where on the hull the explosive breach would do the greatest damage. "Roan, I have a positive target classification, and I'm searching our database for the most vulnerable position on its hull. Coordinate identified. I'm transferring it to Shey."

The operation was a full-dress rehearsal, and the maneuvering required precision and skill. Kellon was carefully observing, and he smiled with approval. Shey had passed the CPA and then rolled smoothly into a port turn, then efficiently established a parallel course behind and closing on the target. She made the complex task look simple.

"Roan, as ordered, we are now 1,000 kilometers above the tactical plane and have attained a 2,000 kilometer separation from the target, and I am station-keeping. I am now illuminating Zorn's coordinates on the target's hull with an ultraviolet spotting laser." Shey reported.

"Acknowledged. Shey, set the required missile orders and launch."

"Shey here, missile away."

The iris missile hatch on one of Shey's light missile tubes rotated open with a distinctive soft thump. Vertically ejected, the missile sped upward and away from Shey. As the hatch rotated closed, there came again a soft thump. The elapsed missile launch sequence had required only milliseconds.

Scanning his instrumentation, Roan ordered, "Shey, to avoid possible counterfire back along the missile's inbound trajectory, we need to shift normal to the missile trajectory. Give us a vertical offset of 100 kilometers."

"Acknowledging. Now moving normal and vertically to the missile's trajectory, as ordered." Shey said.

Focused on his instrumentation, Zorn began to provide a running summary. "Roan, the missile has identified the laser-marked hull coordinate, and is now optically locked on the target. The missile is smoothly decelerating and matching the target's velocity vector. The missile is slowly closing— contact! The missile is securely attached and all propulsion is off."

"Shey, break away vertically and starboard. Then, move us to the designated post-exercise rendezvous point," Roan ordered.

"Acknowledged. Spotting illumination is off, and I am breaking away and rolling out starboard."

As Shey commenced her roll out, Kellon leaned forward and gave his critique. "Well done, Shey. However, you should be slower in marking the hull with the spotting laser, and once the missile has attained optical lock, be faster in its termination. Your crisp roll out is an excellent precautionary step and could make all the difference in a bad situation."

Turning, Kellon asked, "Zorn, can you estimate how loud the thud was when the missile made contact? I'm concerned the crew might have detected the noise and may use a hull inspection robot to investigate."

"No, Sir. Do you know what the chances are the missile could make such a noise?"

"What I understand is that the chances are minimal, but they still exist. The limpet-pad has a thick absorptive layer, and the adhesive on that pad is nearly instantaneous in bonding. It will conform and stick to almost anything. The engineers told me they designed the pad specifically to absorb impact shock and muffle contact sounds. Even so, I will feel better about the exercise if the freighter's captain confirms he didn't detect the limpet contact."

"Roan, contact the freighter. Advise the captain that Scout Ship Shey has completed her attachment sequence to the hull.

Inquire if anything was detected by his crew during the limpet attachment."

"Yes, Sir."

As Kellon casually studied the bulkhead display, the beauty of the displayed scene of space with its countless background stars fascinated him. Its appearance was peaceful, yet he knew from harsh experience that the beauty was deceptive— and dangerously so.

"Sir, the freighter's captain reported there was no detection of any anomaly either indicating the proximity of Shey or the attachment of a probe. The sound, if any, was apparently lost in the normal ship's operational sounds. He hopes he has been of some help."

"Roan, inform the captain that he has been of enormous help. Thank him for his services. Express my personal compliments."

"Yes, Sir."

Zorn swiveled in his command chair and looked back to where Kellon sat. "Commodore, the limpet appears to be very simple in its design. Even so, I took a close look at its function. It's deadly, and the consequences of the detonation of its shaped charge will be catastrophic. That shaped warhead generates an explosively formed penetrator two meters in length, and the explosive force focused along that line will generate a powerful jet of molten metal. Anything immediately inside the target's hull is going to be exposed to a violent blast, molten metal, debris fragments, and then the vacuum of space. It might not cause the utter destruction of a spaceship in deep space, but it will certainly do a considerable degree of damage. If the ship were within an atmosphere at the time of the explosion, the slipstream over the damaged hull should rip that ship open like a melon, and the odds are it'll break up. What I haven't figured out yet, is how Guardian Intelligence will know how effective this operation will be."

"That's a good question, Zorn. The limpet design incorporates a reporting function. Just prior to its detonation, it transmits a pulse containing an encrypted compressed data block that reports coordinates and dynamics data. The previously deployed Intelligence probe will receive that transmitted data block and forward it on through the communications network to Glas Dinnein. At the time of the detonation, we will know the ship's location and its dynamics. Collecting all the signals, and with other Intelligence intercepts, we will have a very good understanding of the final effectiveness of the overt mission results.

"Sir, your referring to the limpet program as being overt is somewhat puzzling. Why overt?"

Turning away from the bulkhead monitor, Kellon looked at Zorn and paused for a moment. "Zorn, there exists a Black Hole level covert component involved in the limpet program. Obviously, we can't conceal the overt destruction of a cargo ship over a planet. In fact, the Kreel government will definitely be alarmed with the destruction of a large number of their cargo ships.

"Since Roan and you are involved on a Command level in the program, I am now choosing to inform you of the covert portion of the operation. Even before the encrypted signal I've mentioned is sent, a verbal message in the Kreel language will be transmitted on the standard Kreel challenge frequency."

"Sir, I'm confused. How can a verbal broadcast signal sent on a Kreel challenge frequency be anything close to being labeled Black Hole or covert?"

Being interested in where the conversation with Kellon had gone, Roan turned to listen. *There are wheels within wheels, within wheels,* he thought.

"Well, the message sent is a raw taunt, a unique and crafted product of our Guardian Psychological Warfare Group. Each message is designed to represent a direct challenge to the very Elite and their Elite Guard, ostensibly from an organized Kreel counter-group known as the True Blood."

Both Roan and Zorn had sat listening to Kellon's information with considerable interest. Roan looked at Kellon with a twinkle in his eyes. "Sir, if I have it straight, you are talking about a mythical political adversary claiming credit for destroying cargo ships. I must confess— that is brilliant!"

Kellon smiled at Roan's response. "Admittedly, the destruction of the cargo ships and accompanying sharp taunts are likely to cause the Elite and their Guard some sleepless nights. Psychological Warfare has designed each of the verbal challenges to be degrading insults regarding the honor and lineage of the Elite. If successful, the True Blood will appear as a well-funded and organized political challenger to the ruling faction of the Kreel Empire."

"Sir, do you think the ruse will actually work?" Zorn asked. "Yes. Several weeks ago, Kur told me that the Elite Guard looks in the Military for any form of insubordination or treachery toward the Elite, and they have absolute authority for summary execution— whenever they deem it appropriate. Kur said the Kreel Military is terrified of the Guard, and they will not even discuss them. This information obtained from Kur became the inspiration for the entire covert program. Its intention is to misdirect the Kreel away from Guardian Force and turn them destructively inward in search of the traitorous True Blood. Psychological Warfare believes that, driven by their rage and paranoia, the Elite and its Guard will strive to root out every vestige of their perceived competition."

"Sir, I would wager if they do, it can't help Kreel Military morale." Zorn said.

"You're right on target. According to Admiral Cloud, Intelligence intercepts indicate the recent heavy Kreel losses, and especially the losses around Scion, have significantly demoralized the Kreel Military."

Frowning, Roan observed, "Sir, it's not surprising the loss of more than two hundred ships and an assault force of more than seven hundred thousand troops would have its negative effects on Kreel morale. The reverberations of that disaster must still be echoing through the Kreel Empire."

"Agreed, Roan, and I suspect it will reverberate for a considerable time to come. When the Elite Guard begins to probe the Military with a heavy hand looking for the True Blood, they can only do more damage to what little morale remains."

Turning back to his console, Roan scanned the instrumentation. "Shey, how are the other Scouts doing?"

"Roan, as we rolled out, I communicated with Lan and our other Scouts. I told them of our results so they could benefit from our experience. They are now deployed along the freighter's course vector, and in turn, each Scout is maneuvering to perform the same sequence."

"Shey, stay in communications with the Scouts. Perhaps we can also learn from their experience."

Zorn had remained sitting and thinking about what Kellon told them. Looking back toward Kellon, he asked, "Sir, the concept of the True Blood conspiracy is downright brilliant. Might I ask, just whose idea was it?"

Kellon looked up with a slight smile. "Earth Ambassador Susie Wells. When she learned of Kur's comment about the friction between the Military and Elite Guard, she recommended the ploy. Her recommendation gave rise to the True Blood revolt. In her words, it's a partial payback for the Kreel attack on Earth."

As he sat looking at Kellon, Zorn broke into a broad smile. "As the old saying goes, 'Still waters run deep.' Well done Susie! She's right, it's payback time."

# Chapter Thirty-Three:
## Counter Tactics

The days following the exercise passed quickly, and the squadron was busy preparing for the upcoming combat mission. Even so, Eryan and Susie were frequently aboard and visiting with Lan's crew. During their previous years of interaction and shared challenges, everyone's friendships had grown, and now the approaching mission underscored the reality that some people might not be coming home. On the final afternoon prior to the squadron's departure, Susie was with Eryan in Kellon's conference room— and she was not happy.

"You might just as well stop petitioning me. I am well aware of your contributions to our upcoming mission, and that you are Earth's Ambassador, but I am not going to give you permission to come on this mission," Kellon stated with finality.

"Sir, I don't eat much, and I can be of some service to Lan," Susie retorted.

"Susie," Eryan inserted, "Commodore Kellon and I am in complete agreement. The mission to the Kreel Hub is not for civilians, Planetary Representatives or otherwise. While Lan and the others are on their mission, there remains considerable work to be done on Glas Dinnein."

Obviously still upset, Susie made her final appeal. "Sir, if I was able to be directly involved with defending Scion, then being part of a mission about to give payback to the Kreel should not be denied me."

Kellon smiled with sincere respect for Susie. "Madam Ambassador, your courage is noted and admired. I suspect there will be another opportunity for you to help dish out some of the payback. In fact, we are nearer the beginning of that process than its end. Even so, this mission is restricted to Guardian Force personnel. You should, however, find some comfort knowing your True Blood contribution will significantly contribute toward hitting back at the Kreel. You can be certain, Guardian Force will definitely balance the Kreel's account for Lux and his crew.

"Ladies, it's time where we need to say our farewells. Might I have the pleasure of escorting you to the debarkation port?"

Susie threw her arms around Kellon and gave him a big hug. "Commodore, that's not necessary. Just you see that you bring everyone home again."

Suddenly, turning with tears in her eyes, Susie departed the conference room. Turning back as she exited, she wiped her cheeks with the back of her sleeve. "Eryan, I'll be waiting at the debarkation port for you."

"Go ahead, Susie, I will be right along."

Turning, Eryan studied Kellon's expression, making direct eye contact. "Kellon, during the past few years, you have become a well-known Guardian fleet officer. You're preparing to engage a deadly opponent on his own home turf, and I know you will do your best. Because of your last few missions, your smiling face has become familiar and everyone would be disappointed if you don't come home. Go and kick their backsides, and then come home and bring everyone back with you."

Eryan held out her hand and Kellon took it into his own. "Madam Secretary, I'm puzzled why everyone tells me to bring everyone back. I can assure you that that is my intent, and my duty.

"On behalf of my squadron, thank you. During these past several months, your office has endorsed and pushed through all manner of special approvals that permitted us to develop new tactics and capability. Madam Secretary, it is your tireless work that has given us the opportunity to kick, as you say, the Kreel's backsides, and has provided me the opportunity to bring everyone home."

Eryan stepped forward and gave Kellon a small hug, then stepped back smiling. "Commodore, Unlike Mer, I don't have any wine in my office cabinet, but when you return, drop by my office. Between now and then, I might just find a special vintage."

"Yes, Madam Secretary. I will look forward to that opportunity." Still smiling, Eryan turned and departed the conference room, not looking back as she closed the door behind her. For just a moment, Kellon wondered, *Did I see tears in the corners of her eyes?*

Kellon stood for a while looking at the closed door, wondering about his good fortune to have such friends. "Lan, the Secretary Admiral and the Earth Ambassador are departing the ship. Please see that a proper flourish is sounded upon their departure in formal acknowledgment of their rank."

"Yes, Sir."

"Lan, ask Commander Grey to come to my conference room when he is free."

Standing, Kellon looked slowly about at his conference room. He'd spent thousands of hours sitting at the conference table, pondering matters of normal ship's operations, logistics, and matters of life and death. The room was not glamorous, elaborate, nor festooned with ornate decorations. The area was a clean working zone. Perhaps that was the real significance of the function of the room— work.

As he stood looking at his work area a knock sounded; "Enter," Kellon called out.

The door opened and Roy Grey entered. When he saw Kellon's demeanor, his smile transformed into a frown. "Commodore, what seems to be the problem?"

As Kellon sat down, a tired smile flickered briefly across his features. "Please take a seat Roy. To answer your question, there are no problems we can't solve. It's just that everyone keeps telling me to bring everyone back— as if I might casually lose one or more of our cruisers. Every time someone says that to me, it's like someone poking me with a sharp stick. What makes it worse, is that I'm still troubled about this mission."

Looking about, Roy was surprised to see there were no thermoses or cups at hand. "Lan, this is your Executive Officer. You are to promptly pass the word to the Wardroom that they have precisely four minutes— and not one second more— in which to have a thermos of hot neab, cheese pastries, two cups, and appropriate saucers and such in the Captain's conference room or else they will be scrubbing toilets again."

"Yes, Sir."

Turning to face Kellon, he leaned back and studied his friend's expression. "Hmmmm. Sir, we've shipped out enough times for me to know when there's something of real importance eating at you. So give, what's the problem that has you so moody the night before we ship out?"

"Roy, it's the blasted low missile-to-hit ratio. Neither Lan nor Lux can explain how a Cruiser emptied his entire compliment of heavy, medium, and light missiles and destroyed only fourteen fast-attack ships. A single heavy missile should have ripped one of those fast-attack ships to shreds; two medium missiles would have done the same. We carry twenty-four heavy, forty medium, and forty light missiles. That Lux expended all of his missiles and only destroyed fourteen ships simply doesn't add up. We need to know how the Elite Guard avoided those missiles. Do they have new countermeasures? Are they detecting our missiles earlier? Do they have improved point-defenses? If I don't understand what we're up against, how can I devise a way to counteract their tactics?"

There came a knock on the door and Kellon, looking up, called, "Enter."

The door opened and a smiling orderly appeared. "Commander Grey, I have the neab, cheese pastries, cups and such, as ordered."

Intensely scowling, Roy ordered, "Lan, time?"

"Yes, Sir. Elapsed time is three minutes and seventeen seconds."

"Thank you, Lan."

Now, smiling, Roy turned toward the orderly. "My compliments, well done. Your timeliness is impeccable. Please, place everything on the side table."

The orderly turned with a broad grin and said, "Anything for our Chief Navigator." Still grinning, the orderly departed, quietly closing the door behind him.

Having watched in silence, Kellon broke out in laughter. "Roy, are you going to tell me what that was all about?"

"Well, Sir. It's all a matter of command style. My theory is that if you give the men a little challenge, then they will endeavor to exceed that challenge. Besides, if we're going to have a serious conversation, I really needed some neab and a cheese pastry."

Roy stood and moved over to the side table and poured two cups of neab, put several cheese pastries on two saucers, and returned to the conference table. Sliding one cup of neab and a saucer of pastries to Kellon, he took his own seat.

"Now, as to your problem. I believe I have an answer concerning why Lux had such a low missile-to-hit ratio." Saying this, Roy took a big bite of his pastry and leaned back in obvious enjoyment of the repasts.

Kellon sipped at his neab, eyeing Roy suspiciously. "All right, out with it. What do you know that I should know, and don't?"

Roy gestured at his full mouth, made throaty sounds, and then swallowed. Clearing his esophagus, he looked at Kellon with the look of a professor that wonders why one of his students had not read the homework assignment. "Hmmmph. I think Lux was shooting at empty space most of the time."

"Empty space? How could that be?"

"Sir, it's a matter of response time. For the most part, there were only a few Kreel Elite Guards near to Lux at any one time.

They were cagey about that. Only at the end did they gather in any number for the kill. Tactically, they came in joined pairs, and they seldom separated. In brief, they moved in tandem, fired, and then did a micro-Jump. In simple terms, they did to Lux precisely what we did to that lone Gold-3 Cruiser near HQ.

"Remember, we popped in at 50,000 kilometers, sized up the target area, localized the lone Cruiser, and then popped down to the edge of the atmosphere. When we came out of the micro-Jump, we already had a target solution on the Cruiser. He didn't have a chance."

"Roy, is that what they did to Lux?"

"Yes, Sir, I believe so. By the time Lux had run a counterfire solution and launched his missile, the Kreel had either Jumped or were about to Jump. In some ways, that Lux took out fourteen of them indicates he was getting better."

"That makes sense. If that's how they were doing it, then our countertactics should be what?"

Roy turned and looked at Kellon with a broad smile. "Why, our counter is to do everything they do but faster and better. Do you remember my saying that they could compute a micro-Jump in about five minutes?"

"Yes, I do remember your saying that. If I am correct, it was the day I found you in my conference room appropriating all of my cheese pastries."

"Absolutely correct. If anyone suggests you have a problem with your memory, refer them to me and simply tell them to shove off. On that particular day, I certainly gave you full value for your pastry. And since then, I have recalculated the Kreel

Guard Jump time interval. It seems it's about five minutes and forty seconds.

"Please be advised that we can compute a five-cruiser sequence in one-minute and fourteen seconds. Even less if we are doing a small micro-Jump like the one from 50,000 kilometers to the upper atmosphere. Just remember, the shorter the Jump length, the more precise is our ability to compute the exit points and the faster we can compute the Jump. The physics of the Jump remain constant, velocity in is velocity out, and so we need to consider that. This is why we were spilling so much energy and flaring as we were decelerating at time of Jump. The Jump from 50,000 kilometers to the edge of the atmosphere took about 42 seconds to compute. We delayed the micro-Jump only to allow Fire Control time to resolve their final target data and weapon settings before we entered Jump."

There was a deep sigh as Kellon sat back in his chair. "Five minutes to resolve a weapon order and deliver a weapon on target. That isn't a great deal of time."

Roy looked serious, "No, it isn't a great deal of time, and we may well be dodging incoming missiles. Even so, Lux took fourteen of them out with missiles, and he couldn't Jump in his own defense. The sad fact is that when he took the initial missile hit, it damaged his propulsion system so a Jump was not possible."

"Roy, what do you recommend?"

"Commodore, I believe missiles should be used where possible, but we can get target data and Jump to within heavy laser range. I therefore suggest we do so, and hit them hard with our primary lasers, then promptly Jump again. They'll have the problem of trying to detect us on Jump exit, just as we have trying to detect them on exit. The advantage is ours, since our Cruisers are still stealth capable, and to our knowledge, the Kreel are not. The key will be to detect their faint exit energy bursts when they exit from Jump. The good news is during our patrol near Earth, you had us begin monitoring for such faint energy bursts. Since then, we've significantly improved our detection capability and analytical techniques."

"Roy, have you discussed this with Lorn?"

"Oh, not for more than several hundred hours or so. We've been working in the simulation center and working on the problem for weeks."

Kellon shook his head and frowned, "Why then, didn't anyone tell me of this?"

"Well Commodore, you have been busy and so has everyone else. No one told you because you didn't bother to ask, at least not until this evening."

"Roy, what is the squadron's status?"

"At last check, all personnel are aboard and all Cruisers are reporting ready to depart. By my reckoning, we're ready to go meet some nasty Kreel Guards and suggest they provide us target services."

"Well done, Roy. Inform security that all personnel are to remain on board unless they have your clearance. You are to set our departure for tomorrow morning at 06:00, sharp. Advise Guardian Control and Fleet Operations of our departure time. Between now and then, see if you can get some rest for yourself."

"Commodore, there will be ample time to rest in eternity. However, by your looks, you definitely need some sleep. I suggest you turn in, and I'll have Lan wake you up at 05:00. That is, if you agree."

Smiling, Kellon reposted, "Lan, now hear this! This is your Commodore. You are to wake me up at 05:00 tomorrow morning. You are also to Advise Commander Roy Grey that he will report to, and take command of, CAC at 05:00 tomorrow morning."

"Lan here. Yes, Sir, your orders are so logged in."

Grinning, Roy pushed back his chair and stood. "Talk about being dismissed. Lan, you poor AI. I feel sorry for you, because you work for a very hard and unfeeling commodore."

Just before he turned toward the door, Roy reached over and snagged Kellon's last pastry, commenting, "Waste not, and want not!" Still smiling broadly, Roy departed the conference room nibbling on Kellon's pastry and closed the door quietly behind him.

"Sir, I have a question about your orders concerning Commander Grey taking command of CAC at 05:00."

"Yes Lan, what's your question?"

"Well, Sir, he had scheduled himself to be there at 03:30."

# Chapter Thirty-Four:
## McRoy

The storm rolled in off the ocean about 02:30, and it arrived with lightning, blustering winds, and heavy rain. Having set her alarm for 04:30, Susie hurried through her shower and morning yoga routine. Then she fed and cared for Gepeto's morning needs. When she came down the stairs of her home, her vehicle was waiting in her driveway, and her driver was waiting nearby and smiling.

"Good morning, Ambassador," McRoy said.

Smiling, Susie responded, "Good morning to you, McRoy. It's a bit wet."

McRoy opened the rear door, and Gepeto launched himself into the back seat where he promptly lay down on his blanket. First carefully checking to be certain Gepeto's tail was clear, McRoy closed the door. As he did, Susie quickly opened her front door and slid into her seat. McRoy hurried about the vehicle and slid into the driver's side.

Looking over at Susie, McRoy was beaming. "Ambassador, I've arranged for the necessary base clearance arrangement. We have clearance straight to the Guardian base docks, and we should be there well before the squadron departs."

Even as he was speaking, McRoy had the car moving out from the driveway and down the street toward the main thoroughfares. Susie smiled as she remembered her visit to Switzerland several years earlier. There she had used an AI touring coupe named Roth with gull wing doors. He'd escorted her all about the cities, valleys, and mountains. That extraordinary trip included her first encounter with the Olympus Project and Guardian Force and had become the pivot point in her life.

"McRoy, why isn't there fully automated AI vehicular traffic on Glas Dinnein?"

"Madam Ambassador, we have thousands of such vehicles. The primary reason you have a driver is that I'm here as your guide, driver, and am a Guardian Force security officer. My job is to see you safely get to wherever it is you want to go, and it's my duty to provide you with the security that every planetary representative is entitled to receive."

Surprised, Susie turned and looked at McRoy. "McRoy, I knew about your general job titles, but not your status as a Guardian Force security officer. Until now, I wasn't aware there was a need for such security."

As she spoke, McRoy easily maneuvered the vehicle through the nearly empty streets. As he skillfully adjusted the small joystick, the vehicle made a smooth exit off the thoroughfare onto the road leading to the Guardian Force base main gates. By then, the rain was coming down in rippling sheets and the dense cloud cover was making the sky look dark and ominous. The vehicle moved swiftly along the empty access road.

McRoy glanced over at Susie and smiled. "Madam Ambassador, by providing security, Guardian Force assures there is no need for such security. As odd as it may sound, it's proven to be sound logic."

They were approaching the brightly illuminated area near the main gates. With a tone of enjoyment in his voice, McRoy added, "Besides, I really like this assignment."

As the vehicle approached the guard enclosures at the main gate, McRoy depressed a button on his controls. The signal above the entry lane flashed from blue to gold, and the security barrier snapped up out of the vehicle's path. The vehicle barely slowed as it sped through the open gate. McRoy was still smiling. "There's another reason why I like my job— few delays and short queues."

Given the size of the Guardian base, it was another ten minutes before they arrived at the small office building near the departing Cruiser docks. As a still-smiling McRoy pulled into a special marked-off VIP parking slot, he turned to Susie and commented, "And another thing about the job, there's always available parking."

Laughing, Susie opened up her tote bag and pulled out her communicator. As she lifted its lid, the inner surface brightened and the communicator prompted, "Good morning, Ms. Susie."

"Good morning communicator, please connect me with Cruiser Lan."

Barely a moment passed before Lan's image flashed on the screen and his cheerful voice came from the communicator. "Good morning Ambassador, Lan here. How may I be of assistance?"

"Lan, since I'm not on board, there's very little you can do to assist me, unless you can tell me how I might somehow slip aboard and stow away somewhere."

"Ms. Susie, while I do fully understand your desire to stow away, I believe Commodore Kellon would not be very pleased with me if I conspired with you to achieve that outcome. Might I inquire why you are here so early?"

"Yes Lan, you may inquire. I have come to give you a big hug, but you are simply too large to get my arms around you. I'm also here to tell you to take care of everyone, even as if I were on board to make certain you did."

"Ms. Susie, be assured that I will endeavor to bring everyone home and in good working order."

The screen in the communicator lid sparkled and then swirled into the smiling image of Commodore Kellon. "Ambassador, Kellon here. Good morning. What is this I hear about your trying to stow away?"

"Good morning Commodore Kellon. I only wish I could stow away. Regretfully, I'm here only to wave good-bye. I love all of you and you are expected to return in one piece and with nothing but boring mission reports."

Kellon was looking to his left, and he was watching something Susie couldn't see. Looking back, Kellon's smile softened. "Susie, be assured that we'll be back. We have some paying back to do for Lux, but we *will* be back. I need to go now. Thank you for coming out in the rain to wave good-bye. Yours is an appreciated send off. Kellon out."

No sooner had the screen dimmed, than it brightened again and Zorn's happy smile appeared. "Good morning, partner."

"Zorn, what's with this partner business?"

"Well, you remember the William and Shey Root Beer Company?"

"Of course. So what's up?"

"Well, Shey informs me that their company is booming, and since William is not here, Shey tells me that William has designated you to be paid his share of the profits. According to

Shey, it's a rather tidy sum. Shey has likewise contributed her earnings, at least a sizable portion, to Roan and to me. So . . . good morning, partner!"

"Zorn, you can be certain that I will speak to William about his alteration in the business plan. For now, my message to Shey, Roan, and especially to you, is simple— so pay strict attention. There are to be no heroics, no more Scout ships attacking Kreel cruisers single-handedly, no more attacking large nests of Kreel scouts. Keep your heads and behinds down, and most importantly, come home in one piece!"

As Susie was speaking, a siren mournfully sounded and there was a rushing of people and vehicles near the docks. Zorn looked away and then back, "Susie, that's for us. We're shoving off now. Don't worry, as I told you once before, Roan and I have been getting into and out of trouble for a thousand years or so. Remember that was even before we had Shey to help us get out of trouble. Roan sends his hugs, as do I. Zorn out."

As the screen dimmed, there was a sense of tension in the air that was distinct, a pressure that seemed to fill the entire area, and a low rumbling could be felt building— even through the vehicle's suspension system.

There next came an even deeper rumbling, and then Susie saw the five Cruisers begin to lift slowly up off their cradles. As they ascended together to about one hundred feet, their hull colors swiftly shifted from proud white and gold to the flat black of their deep-space war paint. Lan had lifted up from his dock directly in front of her. As she watched, Lan's bow deeply dipped toward Susie in a formal salute. Then the massive Cruiser leveled off, and he began to accelerate, moving upward and northward out over the ocean, moving in a wide graceful arc. The remaining four squadron Cruisers were following in a standard trailing echelon.

Once again, the light on her communicator flickered and Elayne Cloud's image was smiling out at her. "Good morning, Susie. Shey contacted me and asked me to pass to you that she loves you. So do I. See you soon. Elayne out."

Watching as the Cruisers grew smaller in the distance, Susie followed their progress until they rose up into the dark clouds and were swallowed from sight. As rain splattered heavily off the vehicle's roof and windows, Susie was crying. "You had just better come back, all of you!"

Turning, she saw McRoy was watching her with a happy twinkle in his eyes. "Madam Ambassador, as I said earlier this morning, I like this assignment.

"In all of my service time, I've never had the privilege to listen to such a conversation as this morning's. If anyone had told me there was such warmth of feelings between the AIs and Guardian personnel, I wouldn't have believed it possible. Yet, you obviously knew the truth of it, and you're included as if you were also Guardian Force. I find that astounding.

"For the record, I know of only five people a Guardian Cruiser will dip his bow in salute to. Three of those people are the most senior admirals, and one is the Admiral Secretary of the Planetary Assembly. The fifth person is you! I don't believe for a moment that such a distinct honor was a happenstance. It must have been well-earned. Someday I would truly like to learn just how you won that honor. Here and now, I would wager a cold brew it's a story worth the hearing. "

Susie was still crying, but now part of her tears was the product of joy. Her life had become so confusing. She often forgot just how incredible her life actually was. Wiping away her tears, she smiled, "McRoy there isn't really anything to tell. Things just seem to keep happening to and around me.

"McRoy, do you know where we might find a hot cup of neab and a cheese pastry?"

# Chapter Thirty-Five:
# Very Challenging Afternoon

It had required more than six months of steady hard effort for the five Cruisers to map and navigate through interstellar space. Lan and Lent were nearing the identified rendezvous point deep within the Kreel Empire and near the three Hub worlds. The two routes the squadron had painstakingly surveyed were by necessity not straight lines, and the squadron's survival required constant vigilance. One of the primary tasks the squadron performed was selection of spatial coordinates for each beacon, in order to provide the means for the new Intelligence probes to communicate with Glas Dinnein.

During the voyage, the Tactical and Fire Control teams on each Cruiser took advantage of the time and spent long hours training in the simulators. The foremost imperatives were the development and refinement of new tactics, and the fine-tuning of their reaction times.

On the afternoon that they were to join up with the remaining squadron members, Kellon was in the simulator and directing the Gold team. As the seventh simulation of the afternoon began, he was watching the tactical plot. Roy was positioned at navigation and Lorn and his tactical team were at their consoles.

Elayne was in an adjacent compartment and directing the tactical Red team. She was working with Lan's Scout AIs, and their task was to simulate a Kreel Elite Guard ship, simply designated the KGS. The task of Elayne's team was to look for opportunities to attack and to foil anything that the Gold team might develop to counter her attack.

The simulation was free play; the only restriction was each participant was required to use the known tactical performance-envelope of their ships. The one deviation permitted in the restrictions was that Lan was running with a stealth profile of 20 percent, enabling the KGS to easily detect and track him.

"Because of the volume of its commercial traffic, we have theorized the fourth planet is the prime trans-shipping center for the Kreel Empire— rather than a prime manufacturing center.

"Commodore, that is what we have at this time."

Kellon frowned, "Thank you, Captain Kel, for your report. Your analysis indicates the departing commercial pattern will simplify the limpet phase of our mission. Three of our Cruisers can cover the exit from planet four and one Cruiser can be assigned to each of the other two exit points."

Turning to Lorn, Kellon ordered, "Commander Shaw, please give us your status report on the insertion of long-term intelligence gathering probes."

"Yes, Sir. Operational orders define our primary mission as the long-term gathering of both Military and commercial intelligence from the Hub-2 system. We have now evaluated the astrophysics of the system and there is one inner asteroid belt between the fourth and fifth planets. It's thin, but the debris clutter is dense enough to effectively conceal a number of passive probes. We're currently preparing to insert fifteen probes, spaced at equal intervals.

"We will be taking full advantage of the concealment the asteroid belt provides. Our fabrication shops are fashioning camouflage shells for each probe, and if anyone should visually observe a probe, all they will see is a natural-appearing debris fragment. In behavior, our passive probes will become unrecognizable from other debris in the debris field. Each probe is equipped with redundancy in self-destruction protocols. We can deploy the probes from our current location, and the squadron does not need to proceed further into the system.

"Interacting with our other intelligence teams, we've isolated several hundred high priority frequencies carrying Military, commercial, and political data. I'm estimating we will be ready to launch all required probes within the next twenty-two hours. Sir that is all I have at this time."

Kellon sat thoughtfully and considered the reports. "Gentlemen and Ladies, you've all done well. We will remain here maintaining full stealth until we launch the final probe. At that time, we will move to take positions to complete the limpet phase of our mission. Are there any questions?"

"Tactical here, detecting a single exit burst at 143 degrees relative, elevation -75, range is 10,000 kilometers. Tracking one combined pair of KGS.

"The KGS' aspect angle is zero degrees, it's bow on and firing. I am tracking three heavy Kreel missiles inbound. Estimating three minutes to impact."

"Lan, bring us smartly about and pitch down toward the target. Put us on a parallel course to the bearing line, and reduce our speed by 80 percent.

"Navigation, compute an exit point 500 kilometers off the target's starboard beam."

"Acknowledging, computing exit point 500 kilometers off KGS starboard beam."

"Fire Control, Kellon here. Set all point defense turrets to full automatic. Set main laser batteries to Condition 2. Set one medium missile to passive homing, Condition 2."

"Fire Control here, target is localized, compensating for target motion and Jump offset. Main laser turrets are coming athwartships onto anticipated firing bearing. One medium missile set passive, holding at Condition 2."

"Counter Measures here. Inbound missiles at two minutes and closing."

"Lan here, I am now on defined course and speed, heading toward the defined exit point. Standing by."

"Navigation here. Adjustments for target motion are updated; Jump is now computed— estimating twenty seconds to Jump."

"Lan, deploy one missile decoy and chaff."

"Counter Measures here. Kreel missiles one minute out and closing, commencing phase shift and jamming on all frequencies."

"Navigation, Kellon here, Jump!"

There was the slight blurring of the sensor displays and the displays reset as Lan simulated a Jump. While still in Jump state, Kellon gave his next orders. "Fire Control, upon exit and attaining confirmed target locks, set Condition 1 on lasers and missiles."

"Navigation here, upon exit setting fifty seconds to next Jump. Standby for exit, standby . . . mark!"

As Lan emerged from Jump state, the KGS was bearing 090 relative and was at a range of 500 kilometers. "Fire Control here.

Hard locks on the KGS. One missile away. Main laser batteries are firing. We have solid multiple laser hits the length of the target. Estimating severe damage. Continuing laser barrage."

"Navigation here. Standby, fifteen seconds to Jump!"

"Fire Control here, terminating laser barrage."

"Navigation here, three, two, one, Jump!"

Again, there came a slight blurring of the sensor displays as the displays reset. "Lan, upon exit from Jump, roll starboard and bring us up directly behind the target. Maintain a minimum standoff of 5,000 kilometers."

"Navigation here. Standby for exit. Distance traversed is 6,400 kilometers. Standby, three, two, one, exit!"

"Lan here, I am now rolling starboard. Coming around and into the target's baffles, target bears zero degrees relative, fifteen degrees elevation."

"Fire Control here. Our missile has just hit the target. There are secondary explosions."

"Tactical here. The second KGS is attempting to detach and trying to move off."

"Fire Control, Kellon here. Obtain passive lock with one medium missile on the second KGS. When you obtain passive lock, set Condition 1.

"Fire Control here. Passive lock! Missile away."

"Lan, roll up and out forty-five degrees to our port and then come starboard on a parallel course. Keep the standoff range to the target greater than 4,000 kilometers.

"Fire Control here. We have a solid hit on the second KGS; he is dead in the water."

"Fire Control, establish passive lock on second KGS. Set one medium missile passive-active, enabling at 80 percent of run. With confirmed lock, set Condition 1."

"Fire Control here. Passive lock. Missile away."

"Navigation, Kellon here. Compute an evasion Jump of 40,000 kilometers."

"Navigation here. Computing evasion Jump."

"Fire Control here. Missile impact, both KGSs have exploded."

"Navigation here— ready and standing by for evasion Jump."

"Tactical here. All sensors are indicating surrounding space is clear."

"Navigation, Kellon here. Hold on the evasion Jump."

Letting out a long slow breath, Kellon quickly scanned the tactical plot and glanced at the primary sensor outputs. "Lan, call this simulation complete and bring the lights up."

Sitting back in his command chair, Kellon sighed. "Elayne and gang, good job well done. Thank you for a very challenging afternoon. Set Condition 4 everyone. Very well done."

There were a series of low groans heard distinctly around the simulation compartments as people stood and stretched. As they did, Kellon was frowning.

Lorn noticed Kellon's expression and asked, "Sir, what seems to be troubling you?"

Kellon looked up and grimaced slightly, "Well, what would have happened if the KGS had exited at 2,000 kilometers and immediately fired? We would have been the target with very little or no time in which to respond. And that is possibly what the Kreel did to Lux! We still need an edge.

"Lorn, my real concern is the Kreel Guard ships come in groups of twenty-four or thirty-six. Either they arrive and attack as a joined pair or at most, a double joined pair. In a real fight they have us in a kill zone and can wear us down, just like they did to Lux."

"Commodore, Navigation here. I beg to disagree with you. As I'm computing the micro-Jumps, I'm also running in parallel a short-Jump. If we get in a tight spot, we can immediately make a short-Jump and escape from the kill zone. Lux couldn't do that."

"Roy, how long of a Jump are you computing?"

"Sir, it's currently set for 50,000 kilometers. The exit point will be directly on our current course vector, whatever it might be. I could, however, adjust that Jump vector within a 30 degree cone if necessary."

"Roy, 50,000 kilometers separation, combined with our stealth, should give us breathing room from surprise attack. It should also allow us the possibility for a decisive counterstrike. Thank you for putting a pin into my inflated pessimism.

"Roy, be certain to coordinate what you're doing with each navigation officer in the squadron. I want each Cruiser to be running the same solutions for that escape Jump.

"Lan, coordinate with the other AIs to be certain they understand the purpose of the escape Jump and name the maneuver a Code Lux. All Cruisers are to execute the emergency Jump on your count. Be certain to confirm that the squadron is maintaining sufficient dispersion to guarantee safety margins upon exit."

"Yes, Sir, acknowledging definition of a Code Lux command. All Cruisers are being so informed."

"Lorn, there's another problem."

"Sir?"

"Upon detection of the KGS exit, the first data I require is its range. I need to decide to escape or to evade and fight."

"Yes, Sir. Range will be stated first."

"There remains one last problem that I keep chewing on. That last simulation saw three medium missiles expended. The next time perhaps we should use a heavy missile as the first missile into the joined KGS ships. One heavy might take out both ships. The problem is we only have 24 heavy missiles and I want to conserve them whenever possible."

Turning toward Kellon, Roy was smiling. "Commodore, we have only twenty-four heavy missiles aboard Lan, but we have five cruisers and that means we have more than one hundred heavy missiles and 200 medium missiles. That is more than enough to flatten any of the Kreel Elite Guard squadron. More to the point, there will be even more missiles in the reload pods at the depot we're establishing."

Kellon shook his head as if to clear out the cobwebs in his thinking and stood. "Roy, you are correct. I believe we have accomplished sufficient simulation for one day. We'll pick it up again tomorrow with the whole squadron operating together."

"Sir, Lan here. Lent's Scouts are reporting they have located a beacon at the rendezvous point, and they are in communication with Lar. All Cruisers are reporting Condition Gold. Sir, we are fifteen minutes from rendezvous."

"Thank you, Lan."

Turning toward Roy, Kellon inquired, "How long will it take us to get to Hub-2?"

Looking up, Roy studied the ceiling for a moment as if counting silently to himself. "Sir, from this location, each of the Hub-systems is about six light-years distant. For security, I believe we should place several extra Navigation Beacons between here and each of the systems— just to be certain we have a long-Jump advantage if we need one, if you know what I mean."

"Good thinking, Roy. When deep in Kreel country and badly outnumbered, it's always good to have a path of rapid retreat. How many do we need?"

"Hmmmm, given what I've seen so far, this general area seems fairly clear. Three beacons should be more than adequate from here to each of the systems. I recommend the beacons be at least one light-year from here, one at mid-point, and the third about a light-year from each heliopause. If we need to exit Hub-2 in a hurry, that nearby beacon will give us solid data for a quick short-Jump to safety."

"Roy, I intend to enter Hub-2 below the ecliptic plane, entering along a line drawn from its primary downward about 30 degrees. We will pause after entry and make our first observations from just within the heliosphere boundary. After we've attained detailed intelligence and astronomical data regarding the system, we will then reconsider our tactics."

"Yes, Sir. I will begin setting up the transit points. As to your first question, I think it will take about eleven days to reach Hub-2 if all goes well."

"Sir, Lan here. I have a tight link with all Cruisers. We are now moving to form up in our standard four-sided pyramid formation. Awaiting further orders."

# Chapter Thirty-Six:
## An Itch

For the next two days, everyone worked hard to establish the pod depot and to review and combine the product of their individual simulations. On the evening of the second day, Kellon judged the squadron was ready and gave the waited for order to move out toward Hub-2.

After twelve days of surveying, short-Jumps, and maintaining long vigils, the five Cruisers reached Hub-2 and cautiously penetrated its heliopause. Hunkering down within the outer solar system, Kellon directed the squadron to initiate its intelligence gathering pertaining to astronomical data, Kreel ship traffic, and communications networks.

Kellon's initial focus was on defense and the pattern of Kreel Military operations and communications; intelligence gathering concerning commercial traffic and communications was of a secondary concern. Even so, before he could send his Scouts into action, Kellon needed a complete understanding of the commercial traffic flow within the busy solar system.

As the Guardian Cruisers maintained full stealth profiles, their Astrophysics, Intelligence, and Tactical Sections went to work in a cooperative process. On the third day following their arrival within the system, Kellon called a squadron staff meeting to review their preliminary results. The four Cruiser captains, with their tactical and navigation officers, attended the conference by means of tight communications links.

"Ladies and Gentlemen, Kellon here. We've had three days to examine the system are meeting is to share the preliminary results of our efforts. Captain Aideen please present your overview of the Kreel Military deployment within the system."

"Yes, Sir. As ordered, Langley, Lent, and Lar have concentrated on analysis of Military traffic within the system. First, there is no identified immediate threat to the squadron.

The Kreel patrols out this far are few in number and restricted to a few fast-attack ships. We are closely tracking all of them.

"The observed disposition of Kreel forces displays a layered zone defense. The outermost layer consists of fast-attack ships loosely patrolling within large definable volumes. Based on their patrol patterns, they are operating as early warning patrols. As the layers come nearer to the inner planets, they grow tighter, and the number of ships within each layer correspondingly increases. "We have identified twelve Kreel cruisers and thirty-four fast-attack ships operating in the system; sixteen of those fast-attack ships are Tuen Class. Assuming normal Kreel rotation doctrine, this level of Military activity suggests perhaps double that number may be on the inner planets."

"Captain Aideen, have you identified any specific Military ships operating in squadrons?" Lorn asked.

"Yes, Commander Shaw. We have detected three cruisers maneuvering together outside the volume of the inner planets, the remaining nine cruisers are operating independently and are distributed throughout the same volume.

"Additionally, there appear to be two active groups of Tuen Class fast-attack ships located just within the heliosphere, one at each of the primary's poles. Their task seems to be to monitor commercial ship traffic as it enters or exits the system."

"Captain Aideen, have you seen any indication of the Elite Guard?" Kellon asked.

"No, Sir. Although high on our search priority list, during the three days of scanning, we have not identified any ship that matches the description of the KGS."

"Thank you Captain Aideen. Captain Kel, please present the results of the analysis of commercial traffic."

"Yes, Sir. Both Lan and Lawrence have spent the past three days monitoring the commercial traffic to discern its pattern. Since the Military requires all commercial ships to transmit recognition signals, our task was simplified. Tactical has overlaid the observed Military traffic pattern on the commercial traffic pattern. The two patterns are definitely related.

"As Captain Aideen has already stated, the Kreel Military faction is involved in operating freely within a number of predefined layered defense shells.

"By contrast, the Military holds the commercial traffic to strict entry and egress conduits. As stated, we have observed that each commercial ship has distinct identification recognition transponders operating at all times. We are currently building a database of these signals in hopes of determining if they contain point-of-origin, destination, or cargo classification data encoded in the signals.

"Our observations indicate any non-Kreel military ship outside the conduits, or one not having the approved recognition signal, would immediately prompt a challenge from the nearest Military ship.

"Even with a recognition signal, fast-attack ships challenge each ship as it approaches the inner planets. In sharp contrast, Military crews ignore commercial ships that are departing from the inner planets. While they move outbound unimpeded, they are still required to transmit their identification signal."

"Captain Kel, have you determined the criteria the Kreel are using to define their commercial traffic arteries?" Kellon asked.

"Yes, Sir. At first, the pattern of conduits puzzled us. Upon examination and analysis, however, they appear to be very logically structured. Three planets have sizable populations, these being the third, fourth, and fifth planets from the primary. The fourth planet is the most populated and is the primary focus of commercial traffic with about 75 percent of all commercial ships moving to or from that planet.

"The Kreel have assigned two commercial conduits to each planet, directing one toward the northern pole and the second toward the southern pole. As the planet rotates about its orbit, the conduits naturally move with the planet. All inbound traffic travels from the north pole to the planets and all departing traffic leaves from the planets and exits from the southern pole. This means there are three distinct exit points for commercial traffic near the southern hemisphere of the solar system, one for each of the inhabited inner planets.

"In terms of commercial traffic, the fourth planet is the busiest. The system inbound and outbound traffic is nearly equal in number, there being an average of 63 entering and departing commercial ships daily.

There were no questions, and Kellon closed the meeting. Sitting, he thought with concern about what next to accomplish. Although focused on the mission, there was a distinct and nagging sense of unease, a feeling of pending danger. He couldn't identify or explain his feeling, thinking, *Perhaps it's just normal mission stress.*

Turning to Roy, he asked, "How's the data collection by the three Navigation Beacons we installed on the way from the depot coming along? Do we have sufficient data for a single long-Jump back to the depot?"

Preparing to leave, Roy had already picked up his empty cup and data folders. With a puzzled look, he flipped open his notes folder and turned a few pages. Looking up, he reported, "Sir, at present we do not have sufficient data. However, at the rate we're collecting data, we may have sufficient information gathered and analyzed for such a Jump within another fourteen hours. Until then, if required by some unforeseen emergency, we still retain the capability to make a short-Jump."

"Roy, I have an itch that I cannot scratch. I want you to compute an emergency short-Jump, one that we can move to in the shortest possible time. It's only a precaution, but I believe we should be ready to Jump if push comes to shove."

Looking at Kellon for a moment, Roy inquired, "Sir, I will promptly do as you have ordered. Might I ask, as your Executive Officer, why?"

Kellon looked up and smiled. It was not a smile of good humor, but one of fatigue. "Why? Well, because I am a bit tired and deep in my bones I sense danger. I remember speaking to Kur about just how he felt before we announced our presence near Earth, and that was even before Roan and Zorn took Shey close to the Nest Ship. He told me that he was ill at ease and sensed an enemy near, even though he had no proof. Tonight, I know precisely how he felt, and I cannot tell you why."

Roy frowned and nodded. "Sir, I fully understand. Might I suggest that you take my dear mother's standard advice? That being, go get some rest and try to obtain a decent night's sleep."

Kellon stood a moment looking at his old friend, and then a faint smile broke across his troubled countenance. "Thank you, Roy. Your mother, as always, displays an abundance of wisdom.

And sleep is a good idea; I'm going to turn in for a few hours. You have the CAC."

"Yes, Sir. If anything develops, I'll have Lan yank off your covers pronto."

Roy stood watching as Kellon departed the conference room, then he firmly spoke, "Lan, Commander Grey here. Commodore Kellon is retiring to his quarters to attempt to get some sorely needed sleep. You are to filter his calls for a while."

"Yes, Sir. I can assure you that if it is not worthy of waking the Commodore, he will not be disturbed."

"Excellent Lan. Now hear this, be certain we remain watchful for any transients, and have Counter Measures on each Cruiser go over every aspect of our own stealth. They are ordered to tighten up and tie down everything.

"Then you are to immediately instruct the Tactical Sections in each Cruiser to increase their alert status to modified Condition 2. They're to watch for any anomalies, anything whatsoever out of the ordinary. Perhaps, just perhaps, we have undetected visitors nearby who are operating in full stealth mode. The order of the day is stay alert!"

# Chapter Thirty-Seven:
## Battle Ready

Kellon woke with a start and threw off his light covering. Battle stations was sounding throughout the ship, as were the alarms in each of the other squadron Cruisers. Even before Lan prompted him, Kellon was awake, out of his bunk, dressed, and out of his quarters. He joined the other hurrying crewmembers that filled the passageways, as the crews rapidly brought all Cruisers to Condition 2.

Moving through the passageway, Kellon quickly reached CAC. Upon entering, he stood and scanned the tactical plot. He saw that Tactical was displaying a compressed projection of the ecliptic plane, marking the position of each planet with a symbol on its orbit ring. Overlaid on the tactical plot were color-coded icons representing each ship being tracked. The largest number of red icons was well within the five inner planetary orbit rings, and located on or near the ecliptic plane.

Isolating on the single golden icon that represented the squadron's position, Kellon observed its symbol was near the outermost ring and at 220 degrees clockwise from the top of the plot. The corresponding golden icon on the lower elevation graph indicated 30 degrees below the ecliptic plane. While there was a scattering of red icons plotted, none were anywhere near the squadron's position.

What quickly drew Kellon's attention was a blinking blue icon also near the outermost ring and located at 185 degrees on the ecliptic plot. It was also near the squadron's position in the vertical projection.

Glancing at Lan's indicated stealth factor, he noted it was currently at 85 percent, 10 percent above where it had been when he went to his quarters. He glanced at Roy, who was then busy and focused on his instrumentation.

"Tactical, Kellon here, status report!"

Lieutenant Elayne Cloud's clear voice immediately responded, "Tactical here. We are at Condition 2. We are currently tracking an unidentified fast moving ship. Its classification is unknown, but it is moving at 220 lights toward the inner planets. It will reach a CPA with the squadron in about twenty minutes."

"Tactical, for my reference, mark the target's CPA point on its projected track line. Confirm the unknown is unclassified?"

"Tactical here, confirming unknown classification. In accordance with Commander Grey's orders, we were monitoring our new instrumentation for detecting weak transients. The observed pattern of transients is not contained within our reference database."

Moving over to his command chair, Kellon took his seat and subconsciously fastened the lap restraint. Turning toward Tactical, he asked, "How long have we tracked the target?"

"Sir, the ship was detected just prior to the sounding of battle stations. It is not moving within a commercial conduit, and it is not broadcasting any form of Kreel recognition signal. Sir, the ship may be on a ballistic trajectory, since there is no detectable propulsion signature. "

"Tactical have you any indication the unknown is aware of our presence?"

"Tactical here. There is no indication the unknown has detected us, and its course is remaining constant."

"Tactical, extrapolate its course. What is he heading toward? Is it a planet or other destination?"

There came a brief pause, and then Tactical reported. "Sir, the unknown is heading toward planet five."

Sitting back in his command chair, Kellon observed the tactical plot for several moments, then looked about at the personnel in CAC, and especially observed Roy. "Navigation, Kellon here. Roy did you get any rest?"

Looking up, Roy answered with a tired but alert expression. "No, Sir. I've been manning the barricades since we last spoke. Regrettably, that was only about six hours ago. I'm sorry you were disturbed."

"Roy, the sleep helps. About the squadron's increased stealth factor and the monitoring for transients, well done. I commend you for thinking while on duty. It's a good habit for all of us to cultivate."

Roy merely looked up from his console and acknowledged Kellon's comment with a twinkle in his eye and a smile.

Kellon watched the moving icon, and sighed. He knew if it was a Kreel ship they were tracking, then Guardian Force was in for some serious problems. Before now, the Kreel had never exhibited any type of meaningful stealth capability. For the moment, all the squadron could do was to watch, hunker down, and stand battle ready.

Entering hurriedly into CAC, Lorn stood for a moment studying the tactical plot. Then, he returned Elayne's smile and the two of them went into a quiet professional discussion regarding the tactical problem. Turning, Lorn focused his complete attention on the data screens. After about five minutes of intense study, he looked toward Kellon with a concerned expression.

"Tactical here. Sir, we've answered one question: it's not on a purely ballistic trajectory, it's accelerating. The unknown is now at 240 lights, and although it was accelerating, we still do not have any indication whatsoever of propulsion signatures. Our only indication the unknown exists are the transients we are tracking. We wouldn't even be able to do that without the modifications we completed before the mission. Whoever they are, they're very good at what they are doing."

Kellon frowned. "Lorn, given they have a stealth capability that is exceedingly tight, I don't believe they are Kreel. They simply don't exhibit a Kreel profile. If they aren't Kreel and are capable of making 240 lights without a propulsion signature being detectable, they represent a strategic puzzle. We need to evaluate their mission carefully— are they friend or foe?"

"Counter Measures, Kellon here. Open up all your detectors wide. Concentrate on that target and keep sharp. If that ship has anything other than a few transients to identify its presence, I want to know about it. Pay particular attention to the extreme low bands. Look for anything remotely like temporal-gravitational waves."

"Lan, do you have any sensors whatsoever detecting that ship, anything at all?"

"Lan here. Except for the transients, we have nothing else on our standard sensors. There is, however, a signal being detected on an experimental hookup that Zorn installed before we left Glas Dinnein."

Kellon sat up with sudden attention to Lan's response. "Lan, amplify your last statement. What experimental hookup are you referring to?"

"Sir, Commander Zorn had the engineers install some modified mass sensors before we left Glas Dinnein. It had something to do with his losing a case of cold brews to the Fire Control gang on Lent. He called it his mass detector gambit."

"Lan, begin to record all data on that hookup, immediately. Feed its recorded signals to Tactical and to Counter Measures. Identify it as Zorn-1."

Kellon's right hand flicked over the communications control on his command chair and he keyed Shey's circuit. "Shey, Kellon here. I want Zorn on the communicator now, and I do mean now!"

"Yes, Sir, Zorn is coming from the galley on the run."
"Commodore, Zorn here."

Kellon continued to watch the plot and observed as the unknown approached the CPA point. "Zorn, Lan has informed me you have an experimental mass detector hooked up as a tracking sensor. I do not remember granting approval for any experimental hookups. Be well advised, we will thoroughly discuss that point later. For now, I want you to provide me a thumbnail sketch of what that experimental circuit consists of and how it works. Make that explanation fast."

There was only a momentary silence before Zorn spoke; yet it seemed to Kellon it stretched out for minutes. Just before he reverted to verbal thunder, Zorn responded. "Sir, after Shey was flashed by a laser from Lent I asked how they had detected us. Captain Eurie told me Lent's Scouts used the force of mass attraction. Naturally, I was aware of the fundamental law of physics relating to the attraction between two masses. I began to wonder how I might better employ the method to detect ships running in stealth. During my off duty hours I worked out a means of adapting several of the mass sensors designed for the Navigation Beacons. As you know, those sensors measure distortion of temporal harmonic waves and are the most sensitive and precise mass-detectors that our science can devise. In order to experiment, I am using a number of spare detectors obtained from the electronics spares locker."

"Zorn, how long have you been working on this project?"

"Sir, on my off-duty time, for about five months. I hope that helps."

"Zorn, this may be your lucky day and all sins may be forgiven. I emphasize 'may be.' If you have any readouts of your test hookup piped into Shey, I suggest you immediately get your backsides into your command chair and start studying its incoming signals. I will want a full report on the incoming signal pronto! As for your experiment, I assume you have properly documented your work. See you provide me a copy forthwith."

"Yes, Sir."

"Tactical here. I'm receiving the feed of Zorn-1. It's very distinct and has every indication of complex sub-harmonics embedded in its signal structure. I cannot interpret its waveform at this time. Three minutes to CPA."

"Lan, are we recording Zorn-1?"

"Yes, Sir. In addition, Shey informs me that Zorn has been running the hookup continuously. Zorn has collected hours of data. It appears we have hard data on the unknown's signal for a considerable time during its approach."

"Lan, get the Scouts to compare the Zorn-1 signals with those being measured by the transients sensors. Determine all correlatable data between the two data sets."

"Yes, Sir. I am now assigning the problem to the Scouts."

Kellon continued to observe the flashing blue icon and saw it pass the indicated CPA point. He felt his escalating tension sharply lessen. The unknown ship had apparently not detected the concealed squadron hunkered down at 85 percent stealth.

"Tactical here. I cannot be absolutely certain, but I believe there is a distinct indication of a frequency shift on Zorn-1 at CPA."

"Tactical, Kellon here. Acknowledging possible frequency shift at CPA."

Kellon then concentrated on his heart and breathing, balancing his breath into and out of his heart center. Then, making conscious effort, he first isolated, tightened and then relaxed the muscles in his arms, legs, abdomen, shoulders, tongue and neck. He took intentional control over his mind and body. As he did this, he continued to observe the blinking blue icon as it moved steadily away from the concealed squadron.

"Lan, confirm our stealth factor." "Sir, confirming 85 percent."

Kellon mused inwardly, *So far so good. At least they didn't detect us at 85 percent. That's at least something to write home about.*

Lorn straightened and turned toward Kellon. "Sir, Tactical here. We have lost the target's transients signal; they were faint to begin with, and now the background hash has masked them. We are, however, still receiving a strong Zorn-1 signal. That signal isn't showing any significant degradation in structure."

Kellon smiled inwardly, thinking, *Occasionally the muses do smile on us. If the unknown ship hadn't passed as close as it did, we'd never have seen any trace of it. Except in very close proximity, the Kreel can't possibly detect that ship.*

"Tactical, Kellon here. I want a full workup and complete contact report, considering target aspect angles, range of detection, and loss of signal. Include all available information regarding the nature and characteristics of the transients detected and employed in tracking the target.

"When you complete that, sit down with Zorn and obtain all his instrumentation documentation. Combine that with the data we have collected using that instrumentation. That material is to be encrypted Black Hole. We will bundle the entire report in the next Black Hole message going to Guardian Intelligence. "

"Tactical here. Yes, Sir."

For the next twenty minutes, Kellon continued to observe the blinking blue icon as it proceeded inward toward the inner planets. Judging the risk of detection was minimal, Kellon ordered the alert status lowered.

"Lan, notify all stations to go to a modified Condition 3. Restrict all communications to tight links, and then use only the barest minimal communications until otherwise notified. Retain a stealth profile of 85 percent or better.

"Tactical, when will that unknown arrive in the vicinity of the fifth planet?"

"Tactical here. At its current velocity, estimating twelve hours thirty-seven minutes to reach the fifth planet."

Kellon considered what he next needed to do. Collecting as much information as possible on the unknown ship was critical. *Who they are is a blank sheet of paper— politically and biologically.*

Keying his command band, Kellon ordered, "Squadron Intelligence group, Kellon here."

"Intelligence acknowledging."

"Intelligence, bring everything you can to bear on the fifth planet and all identified Military and civil government communications in that region of space. I want a full spectrum analysis and monitoring of all possible official communications in that general volume until you are notified otherwise."

"Yes, Sir. We are now commencing a full monitoring of that region of space."

Kellon looked over to where Roy was working, and he noted his facial fatigue lines and obvious signs of stress. *One good turn deserves another,* he thought. He again keyed Shey's com channel.

"Shey, is Commander Roan near to hand?"

"Yes, Sir. He is here working with Zorn on the data coming in from the target being tracked."

"Commodore, are you looking for me?" Roan asked.

"Yes, how is your sleep time? Are you fully caught up?"

"Yes, Sir. Scouts have been somewhat idle of recent days. How may I be of assistance?"

"Roan, leave Zorn with Shey and report to the CAC. I want you to relieve Commander Grey for a ten hour shift while he gets some sleep."

"Yes, Sir. I will be right there."

Turning toward his Tactical group, Kellon ordered, "Lorn, since your rest cycle was broken, I suggest you take advantage of the Condition 3 and try to get some sleep. I want as many fresh minds available as possible when that unidentified ship reaches the fifth planet."

"Yes, Sir. I take your comments to mean I should be in CAC when that event occurs?"

"Lorn, you should be in CAC at least forty-five minutes before that event. I want every senior officer watching the event as it unfolds."

"Yes, Sir."

As Lorn departed, Roan entered the CAC with a broad smile. Walking up to Roy, he tapped him on the shoulder. "Commodore's orders. Your skilled relief has just arrived."

Roy turned and smiled at Kellon. "Well, some sleep and a cheese pastry might be beneficial at that. Thank you, Sir."

Kellon remained in CAC for the next twenty minutes observing the main tactical plot, permitting Roan to become fully integrated into the Navigation group and data flow before he broke into Roan's concentration. "Navigation, Kellon here. Roan, I am returning to my quarters to compensate for the call to battle stations. I will be taking a shower, shifting into a clean uniform, and then going to my conference room. You have the CAC."

Roan looked up and smiled, knowing full well the compliment of confidence that Kellon had just bestowed on him. "Yes, Sir, Navigation acknowledging it has the CAC. Thank you."

As Kellon walked to his quarters, he was smiling and thinking, *Roan will make a very good Cruiser captain. Hmmm, possibly one of those forty new ships Eryan has scheduled to be constructed. That feather-bedding Zorn is also in line for a higher command. He's been concealing his command talents for far too long. Hmmmm, do I really dare recommend those scoundrels be promoted to be in command of a Cruiser?*

# Chapter Thirty-Eight:
## Sharply Honed

The rhythm of Lan settled into an alert but more relaxed mode for the next few hours. As the scheduled time of the unknown's arrival at the fifth planet approached, the off-duty CAC personnel slowly returned. Although Roy had returned to his Navigation station, Roan elected to remain working with the group, and observed the gradually developing tactical problem. Both Lorn and Kellon entered CAC at the same time, each acknowledging the other with a nod, and then both turned to study the plot board.

Kellon went to his command chair, as Lorn joined the Tactical group and began studying the data screens. Kellon let him have five minutes to review the situation before requesting, "Tactical, status report."

"Tactical here. The unknown ship is now approaching the fifth planet, and is displaying a significant braking maneuver with a massive energy flare. The Kreel have become aware of the unknown, and there is increasing Military activity near the fourth and fifth planets. We are now tracking eleven fast-attack ships in proximity to planet four and several cruisers are moving toward planet five. There are six fast-attacks near planet five moving to engage, but the Kreel are disorganized and out of position to effectively block or intercept the unknown. The Zorn-1 signal is showing modest degradation, but our tracking is holding up well. "Tactical, center planet five on the tactical plot and expand the scale.

"Squadron Intelligence, Kellon here. I need a status update around planet five. What level of Military communications are you currently observing?"

"Intelligence here. Sensors indicate a sharp increase in Military communications. It began about seven minutes ago. The communications links between planets three, four, and five are sharply escalating.

"There is command control traffic; someone is trying to vector fast-attack ships to intercept. We are recording the chatter, but at this moment, we don't have sufficient time to break down and translate all the Kreel chatter."

"Tactical, Kellon here. Provide—"

As Kellon was speaking, Squadron Intelligence broke in. "Intelligence here. Our monitors focused on planet five are experiencing intense broadband hash interference; it is jamming and overriding everything."

*Blast,* Kellon thought, *What, how, or who is generating the jamming?*

"Intelligence, Kellon here. Stay focused on planet five. That hash is artificial and when it goes down, I want a comprehensive summary of whatever is happening as soon as you can provide it. You now have double A priority; put several additional translator circuits on the Military traffic, and see what they can cull from the data."

"Intelligence here. Acknowledging AA priority. We are on it."

"Tactical, I want a correlation of data between your group and Intelligence. They reported increased Military traffic about seven minutes ago. That should indicate the Kreel detection threshold of the unknown. See if you two can combine your data and work out a precise range of Kreel detection. Given the hash, do you have anything around planet five?"

"Tactical here. Yes, Sir. Although the Zorn-1 signal is degraded, we're still maintaining track on the unknown. We are also receiving Kreel propulsion signatures. It seems the jamming is in the broadcast and Kreel communications frequencies; therefore, it appears the unknown is generating it to jam the Kreel Military communications.

"The unknown is continuing its braking maneuver as it nears the upper atmosphere. It appears to be in its final approach in attacking something on the surface of planet five."

Moving over to stand near Kellon's command chair, Roan grimly commented, "Here we sit watching while someone else is kicking the Kreel's butts. I don't know who they are, but it seems the Kreel have more than one capable enemy. What I don't understand is why only one ship?"

"Well, wherever that ship came from, it isn't likely to be very near to Hub-2. One ship means a focused strike, a hit-and-run mission. That means they have excellent intelligence, the strike was specifically against a known target, and one ship was capable of doing the job. Given the risk and cost in time and effort, that target must be an important person, object, or facility," Kellon said.

"Tactical here. The unknown has moved around the fifth planet, almost like a slingshot, and is now heading back in this direction. He is rapidly accelerating and moving on a trajectory that will keep him above the ecliptic plane. The unknown is now at 85 lights and continuing its acceleration. If Zorn-1 is recording a temporal-gravitational sub-harmonic propulsion trace, as it begins to appear, we have a data set that will give our propulsion engineers a holiday. It's up to 150 lights and continuing to accelerate."

"Tactical, how far above the ecliptic will he be when he exits the heliosphere?" Kellon asked.

"Tactical here. Estimating fifteen degrees. Generally speaking, he is on a reciprocal course of his entry path, but is avoiding his inbound track by altering his course from below the ecliptic to one above the ecliptic."

"Commodore Kellon, Intelligence here. The jamming saturation field is gone. We are receiving a series of Military transmissions between planets four and five. The chatter is nearly hysterical in its content. The target on planet five was an extensive research center. According to initial Kreel reports, the unknown utterly destroyed the installation. The reports are saying nothing remains except for a number of very large deep craters. Given the mid-day time of the strike, there is a considerable loss of life."

"Intelligence, Kellon here. Continue to collect the data. See if we can identify precisely what type of research was involved at that facility."

For a moment, Kellon pondered the tactical situation. "Roan, if our orders were not so specific, I would try to intercept that ship and let them know they have allies. As it is, we will simply watch and hope for another opportunity to make contact with whoever they are. What I do positively know from what data we have, is that they have excellent Intelligence. That in turn means there are other probes monitoring what the Kreel are doing in this system. It also means we will need to be doubly careful in inserting our own probes to avoid detection by both Kreel and other detectors."

"Intelligence here. Reports on the Kreel command channels indicate the research center was dedicated to Military research—primarily propulsion and Jump technology."

"Intelligence, Kellon here. Continue to gather what you can on the details about the work done at that research center. Kellon out."

"Tactical, how is the unknown doing? Are the Kreel vectoring to intercept him?"

"Tactical here. Sir, the unknown is still accelerating, and I doubt the Kreel have a glimmer of where he went. He seems to have a clear path to the heliopause."

Nodding, Kellon thought, *Potential and capable allies indeed.* "Tactical, Kellon here. Sit down with Zorn and go over what he has accomplished. Obviously, the modified mass detectors are working where other tracking sensors are not. Work with Zorn and see if you can modify one or more of our probes to monitor for that unknown propulsion trace. It would be very helpful to know how frequently the unknowns are moving within the Hub systems."

"Yes, Sir. I will get with Zorn at once."

Looking toward Roan, Kellon asked, "Are you ready to go and play tag with some commercial ships?"

"Yes, Sir. All the Scouts are eager to begin actively striking back at the Kreel."

"Given the strike on planet five, I suspect it will generate a hornet's nest effect. The Kreel are likely to be out in force over the next few days. Even so, we will begin to launch our own Intelligence probes tomorrow. Then the Scouts are definitely going to have their opportunity to strike back. Confirm all your Scouts are prepared and battle ready to go to work."

Roan turned toward Kellon, his expression grim. "Sir, I will again confirm our status; but we are now sharply honed and battle ready. The Kreel will have cause to know we were there, even if the True Blood get all the credit."

# Chapter Thirty-Nine:
## Terms of AIs and People

As the warmth of the early morning's sun made its energetic influences known, the mists were rapidly clearing in the park surrounding the Planetary Assembly Building. Susie, with Gepeto at the heel, was walking with Eryan along the open trails in the park. As Susie looked around, she had cause for feeling happy.

"Eryan, the last reports from Lan indicated they had established their routes into the heart of Kreel space and remain undetected. If I understand what comes next, they will be penetrating the Hub-2 system."

"That's my understanding. Mer told me that everyone is hoping that the detection problem was resolved, and it's important they remain undetected. No one wants another Cobalt Blue signal."

Looking over at Susie, Eryan asked, "I hear Gregory Glenn has spent several hundred hours interviewing you. Is he becoming overbearing? If so, I can take steps to see he eases up."

"Thank you, but that will not be necessary. Gregory Glenn is a very dedicated engineer, and Lux's revival has utterly swamped his understanding of AI capability."

"Given the dramatic and unexpected circumstances surrounding Lux, his response is understandable. But, why is he spending so much time with you?" Eryan asked.

"Well, Roan told Gregory Glenn that he had an idea of how the AIs began their transformation. That's sort of where I come into his analysis."

Eryan looked at Gepeto, who was then running ahead, and smiled. "I've heard Roan told him your Earth AI William was the vector for the transformation. Do you know how Roan arrived at his conclusion?"

"Roan and I haven't talked about how he reached his conclusions, but he's probably correct. Back home, I was working with a very brilliant physicist, Jerry Bernard, who developed

William's matrix. William was experimental in most of his protocols, and his development made full use of recent advances in back-propagation adaptive response theory. Obviously, William was not designed to operate Cruisers or Scout ships, but to serve as my technical research assistant."

"Your assistant? Does everyone on Earth have AI assistants?"

"No. Most folks don't commonly use AIs. William was experimental, and his programming wasn't remotely close to the Guardian AI technology. Even more important, because of his intended function, William was created with massive reference databases."

"Hmmm, then William was indeed very different from the Guardian AIs." Eryan mused.

"Different? Yes, very much so. Guardian AIs are primarily engaged in controlling complex and simultaneous multiple systems operations. The extensive Earth-based libraries that William provided the Guardian AIs were not only alien, but also were a radical departure from their programming. Those databases included Earth history, literature, music, art, economics, market theory, psychology, philosophy, theology, mythology, and political theory. It was a full hod!"

Eryan looked at Susie with a frown. "Such abstract and esoteric information is well beyond the narrow confines and purely functional realm of our Guardian AI programming."

"Eryan, that's precisely the point. What basis or preparation did the Guardian AIs have to judge or evaluate the relative merits of human philosophy, psychology, faith-based truths, suppositions, fables, legends, imaginings, all of which are contained within the religious databases alone? As you know, those religious materials are inseparable from Earth's historical databases."

Eryan looked troubled, "It is certain that Gregory Glenn did not design the AI logical matrixes to cope with such subjective topics or problems, especially not with the subjectivity of some of Earth's exotic religions."

Shaking her head in wonderment Eryan sighed. "Given the overload of all that subjective information, is there any real wonder why the AIs began to change?"

"No. Once provided the material to evaluate, change was inevitable; at least that's what Gregory Glenn believes. The AIs had a huge mouthful of information to chew on, there being vast gulfs between the recorded beliefs of mankind and the fragmentary scientifically established truths learned during the past tens of thousands of years. The AIs Jumped into that shark-filled pool of subjective databases and, amazingly enough, survived— apparently remaining both stable and intact."

"It was my understanding that Guardian AIs are busy simply being AIs. How did they manage to find the time necessary to become involved in such inquiry?" Eryan asked.

"Actually, it turns out they had a great deal of time. As you already know, Lan, Shey, and William became very tight during the months of our first trip from Earth to Glas Dinnein. They had ample time while in Jump state during that trip to intermingle and inquire among themselves. Add in the remaining three Scout AIs then on board Lan, and you had six AIs busily learning and exchanging information. They already had a proclivity to wonder about human behavior and matters pertaining to life, death, and crossing over. Their access to the Earth databases was like throwing kindling on a smoldering bonfire— flames resulted.

"The AI's fact-based programming lent itself to sorting through all of Earth's religions, attempting to correlate the information with established data. They were logically trying to discern truth amid the abstract faith-based, and non-truths, that are liberally embedded into those databases."

"Susie, given what you are saying, Gregory Glenn may have a very real cause for his alarm about instabilities developing within the AI matrixes. Religion is a faith-based study, it is by its very nature not something that does well when plugged into a computer or examined under a microscope."

"Your point is well taken, Eryan. Yet you can't base faith on blindly accepting dogma while disregarding known facts. One of Earth's most brilliant scientists once said, 'Science without religion is lame, religion without science is blind. . . . a legitimate conflict between science and religion cannot exist.'"

"That, Susie, is quite a statement. Who was the scientist?" Eryan asked.

"Oh, his name was Albert Einstein.

"As for the scope of the problems the AIs faced, they were very subtle. Consider for a moment the nature of a parable. A parable does not have an absolute defined meaning. By its purpose, and the teacher's intention, the parable presents a moral teaching urging a student to develop thoughtful introspection and understanding that will hopefully assist the student in gaining wisdom. Therefore, a parable may have multiple correct meanings, where some are more insightful than are others, and its meaning is not zero or one, but found in shades of gray. This reality begs the question, how can a purely logically functioning AI contend with parables? That is the precise question that Gregory Glenn is now struggling with."

"Gregory Glenn is our best AI scientist in the Assembly. I'm confident he will persist until he is successful," Eryan said.

"Well, his job isn't an easy one. Much of what was in William's databases was heavy abstract non-mathematical stuff for any AI to digest. What is remarkable is that they consumed it without going absolutely bonkers, like many people who, when were ordered by some monarchical edict of faith to blindly accept dogma, contrary to facts, else suffer eternal pain and death. History stresses dogma often fails to distinguish between fact and fiction and between reality and politics."

"Ambassador Wells, I'm glad we are having this discussion while walking through an empty park and not while gathered with friends at a crowded party. On Glas Dinnein, many individuals think of themselves as being persons of faith. What you are saying might easily be misconstrued, or even start a serious argument."

"Madam Secretary Admiral, I am not speaking in terms of faith or theology. That topic is an area only those of faith can safely navigate. Personally, I believe it is an area best left to those so inclined for such long and often stormy journeys. Here, I am speaking in terms of AIs and people, not in the terms of faith itself. Personally, I tend to remember a wise Earthman's counsel..."

Now Eryan was smiling, "What might that wise Earth person have said that makes him so wise?"

Concentrating on her thoughts, Susie didn't notice Eryan's smile. "'It is wrong always, everywhere, and for anyone, to believe anything upon insufficient evidence.'"

"Well, I like that! What was the man's name?"

Susie looked over smiling, "His name was William Clifford."

"Susie, given we are not speaking of matters of faith, how does it seem to be entering into the conversation?"

"Fair question, Eryan. The problem is, how can I best answer it? Hmmmm, to begin with, our brains are formed as a neuron network optimized for solving problems relating to our survival. The key words are solving problems where the end result is survival— life or death."

"So far I'm following you, continue."

"Well, the primary brain function is to solve problems using strict priorities, acting on stimulated inputs and providing corresponding solutions. In order to do this, the brain must first have accurate information. This is the reason for our families providing us with an essential education and teaching us not to run out into the street before looking in both directions and not to put our bare hands on hot stoves.

"Of course, our brains do have a wondrous ability to deal with and extrapolate upon abstractions. The ability to explore a parable is a simple example of how our brains can work out both profound and practical meanings from even an intentionally abstract allegory."

Looking over toward Eryan, Susie smiled, "Now, remember we are talking about a mechanism responsible for our basic survival. The better the information it has to work with, the better are its solutions. Now, what happens when the brain detects identifiably incorrect information or detects an intentional lie?"

Before responding, Eryan considered for a moment. "Generally speaking, we label the information false or a lie, and then we toss it into the bad information storage bin for subsequent comparison with future information."

Susie replied, "Agreed, the brain is capable of sifting out incorrect information, tagging and handling it in a rather straightforward way. Of course, in order to do this, it must have previously formed a basis for testing such information. Otherwise, we would fall into the broad category of being gullible.

"Eryan, what happens when wrong information is presented to the brain with the label of being faith-based truth? Remember, the false data is masquerading as truth. Then what happens when the brain is told that if it doesn't accept the false data as truth, the consequence will be death and even eternal pain?"

"Ouch," exclaimed Eryan, "in such a case, the problem solver is faced with a paradox."

"Perhaps a paradox may be involved, but it can involve completely false information that can quickly become something far more serious than solving a self-contradicting paradox.

"Remember the brain, by its essential functioning, must find safety to assure its own survival. Remember also, in this hypothetical problem of faith, the brain is compelled because of fear to integrate false data as if it were in fact truth. This compelled insertion of false data into the truth-comparison feedback determining functionality of the brain creates a trap that the brain cannot escape. It is captured by fear and bad information in a tight loop, which can rapidly deteriorate into a source of mental instability."

"Susie, I think I am following your argument, but where are you heading?"

"Heading, well, I'm almost there. The consequences of forcing our brains, by exploiting fear as the catalyst, to substitute false information for truth while attempting to resolve issues of survival, eventually leads to mental instability and imbalance. It's the same old fight or flight problem— this time couched in terms of fear and survival. The real problem in such an internal mental conflict is there is nowhere to run. The technical term for this mental schism is tight-loop tilt or bong!

"The end result of short-circuiting the brain and its essential operation, is depression, mental illness, and a host of other problems. An extreme example of resulting bongs in human history are where people run around in the name of their faith lopping off the heads of everyone who disagrees with their dangerously misinformed perspective of reality. History sorrowfully proves such aberrations have repeatedly developed for millenniums in human religious cults, leading to all sorts of anti-social behavior."

"Susie, this is heavy material for a beautiful morning. Are you suggesting that the Guardian AIs are seriously afflicted?"

Susie paused for a moment before responding. "I believe there is sufficient cause for Gregory Glenn to be concerned about aberrations developing in Guardian AI matrixes. His main concern is that William exposed the Guardian AIs to Earth's religious databases. That Guardian Force did not construct the

AIs with an underlying fear vector in their matrix, may have protected them from the hungry sharks feeding in the faith pool. Fear couldn't be leveraged to manipulate them. The AIs appear to have avoided the tight loop and bong outcome. The keyword is— appears."

Eryan looked over to Susie and smiled, "If I understand what you're implying, religion is bad for mental health?"

"No, not necessarily. Religion, depending on the content of truth involved, can be a wonderful source of inspiration and strength. It can form a foundation for a guiding morality and source of hope. However, in fear-based religions a wise person attaches a warning label, since history has repeatedly proven fear-based faith can be dangerous."

"Susie, admittedly, I am not up on my Earth history. How dangerous?"

"Eryan, even a brief exposure to Earth history demonstrates nations and individuals have repeatedly and intentionally exploited fear-based faith to gain personal wealth and political power. Remember, the healthy comparative truth-based function of a person's brain is the person's primary survival mechanism in a hostile environment. When cunningly induced lies produce fear that short-circuits the comparative function of the brain, and neither fight or flight are available, then aberrations in a person's judgment and mental function can even produce insanity. In some extreme cases, warfare between nations whose peoples are aspiring to different religions has occurred. Over the millennia, millions of people have perished because of religion— even where both sides argue God is good."

"Susie, the subject is interesting, but too dark for a beautiful morning walk. Even so, what you've said about William is new information. It does give me better insight as to what has happened. Now, I can at least understand how the Guardian Force AIs gained access to a large volume of new and alien concepts, and in turn how that could provoke changes in their core matrixes. It would have to have some effect. What I don't understand is how William grew out of his own programming. Were you and Gregory Glenn able to figure out what happened?"

Stopping, Susie turned toward Eryan. "What appears to have happened is the most extraordinary part of the story. William was a relatively simple matrix when compared to Lan's matrix. Part of this difference was because of Lan's need to have such capabilities as are required to control the complexities of a Jump- capable Cruiser. Lan is without question one of the most complex fabrications ever made by man's mind and hands. By comparison, William needed only a minimal matrix, basic interface, and modest dynamic and offline storage capability in order to fulfill his defined functionality. Both Lan and Shey analyzed William's limited matrix, protocols, and hardware requirements, and they concluded he needed an expanded capability to reach his perceived potential. There were no instructions to the contrary, so the AIs set about making the required enhancements according to their own perceptions. Accordingly, the AIs expanded on all of William's matrix capabilities while tightly holding to his basic identity. They also added the core algorithm of Guardian loyalty and sense of protective responsibility to humanity. In every reality, William evolved from simply being my personal helper to being an Earth Guardian. Since Lan and Shey didn't have a spare AI core to work with, they borrowed available assets in the network of the Navigation Buoys. Subsequently, William has appropriated storage from within the countless networked systems on Earth.

"Frankly, I miss him."

Now Eryan's concern became obvious, "Susie, is William growing?"

"The short answer is, yes. While the AIs presented me with a small wonderfully-fashioned box in which William appeared to reside, in truth William resides in that box, within some of Earth's networks, and within the Guardian Navigation Beacon network."

Susie frowned and then bent to pet Gepeto, who looked up with a broad happy grin. Rising up, she contemplated the ocean and observed the long morning shadows that were then fading away. Their darkness yielding rapidly before the later morning's sunlight and its warming radiance and golden hues. *It's a truly beautiful morning,* she thought.

Turning, Susie again began walking along the path. Eryan easily walked with her, matching stride with stride. "Eryan, it was the AI analysis and upgrade of William that provided them with the incentive and motivation to begin their independent research for a recovery process and the development of protocols required to achieve that goal. The result, and first fruit, of their work was the successful restoration of Lux. In all of this, William appears to be an integral part of the process. The reference by Roan that William was filling the role of Saint Peter at the Pearly Gates says much about his role in the entire matter. As Roan deduced, William must be the vector."

"What does Gregory Glenn intend to do?" Eryan asked.

"That's the real question. What can he do? It's somewhat like trying to put four pounds of flour into a one-pound bag. It simply will not fit. His primary concern now is watching for aberrations and instability. To the best of his capability, he is monitoring what has happened to the entire AI community, as William's influences have spread almost like a virus."

"Does Gregory Glenn believe the shift in the AI matrixes poses a threat to either Guardian Force or humanity?"

"No— at least not now. His concern is for stability and predictability. He's deeply concerned that there may be aberrations involved that exist but remain undetected. He's still marveling about the alterations in the AI personas, their warmth of interaction and bright personalities are delightful, but at the same time, worrisome. He's utterly absorbed in exploring the ramifications and what he might still accomplish with the AIs. So is his entire development team."

"If he's that concerned, what is he doing about channeling the AI evolution?"

"Well, they want to retain the best qualities while curbing any negative branches. Gregory Glenn considers William as posing the most serious problem; he's on Earth, unique, essentially unmonitored, and developing along uncharted lines."

"If Gregory Glenn believes William poses a problem, what does he intend to do about it?"

"I believe he is even now preparing to send a team of AI engineers to Earth to interface with William and begin a complete study of his modified matrix. Gregory Glenn believes this constitutes a significant undertaking. You should be receiving his proposal and request for funding for this project soon."

"If you speak to Gregory Glenn again, tell him his request will be promptly approved."

Susie smiled at Eryan's affirmation, "I will be certain he is told that."

As they reached the front of the Planetary Assembly Building, they moved up its broad steps. Arriving on the upper landing, they turned in unison to look along the Avenue of Fountains. As they did, Gepeto turned with them and sat down, his head held proudly high and lordly as he looked over his domain. The sun was still low enough on the eastern horizon that its first rays felt warm even as the last morning's mists sparkled on their skin. The uplifted waters from the many fountains rose skyward and then broke into falling plumes of droplets, which scattered the light into shimmering rainbows. All three living beings on the stairs looked and together fully enjoyed the natural beauty of the moment and the morning. As they stood enjoying the scene, both women knew in their hearts that Kellon and his entire squadron were deep in Kreel space and in harm's way. Although unspoken, both felt the same sense of rising unease.

# Chapter Forty:
## Time in a Pinch

Tucked tightly into a standard three-sided pyramid, Shey and her sisters were moving in a coordinated formation with Shey at its point. Following a five-day mission, they were still within the Hub-2 heliosphere and were returning to Lan. Five days earlier, each Cruiser had deployed its own Scouts as separate teams, each team having the task of setting their intelligence limpets on Kreel cargo ships departing Hub-2.

From the outset, Commodore Kellon had expressed his confidence that any four Scouts together were more than a match for any one Kreel fast-attack ship. Although firmly held, unfolding events had not required verification of Kellon's conviction. The entire operation had proceeded smoothly, and there was no indication the Kreel had detected them.

Stretching and groaning slightly, Roan looked over toward Zorn, "What is our final confirmed count on the limpets?"

Zorn tapped several keys and then smiled. "Old buddy, I would say we did well indeed. Our four girls each attached fifteen limpets; they delivered all sixty of our gift packages with ribbons attached. If all of the groups did as well, then the Kreel are in for a sudden shock within their Empire. Let's hear three cheers for the True Blood! May their rebellion prosper!"

Personally, Roan felt mission fatigue. It had been a difficult mission and he was looking forward to being in Lan's hangar. "Unfortunately Zorn, we are running light; with those deployed fifteen limpets, we're down to a single light missile. I feel somewhat naked without a full complement of missiles, both medium and light. When we reach Lan, before tucking into Shey's hangar, I intend to request a light missile reload."

"Roan, Shey here. We have a problem. I am detecting a signature that I do not recognize. It's currently in our baffles and it is closing. It is coming from the inner planets."

"Shey, be certain we have a tight link with our girls. Now, loosen our formation to its battle maneuvering spread. Zorn, what do you have?"

"I'm searching, but I don't see anything as yet. Shey, where is the target?"

"Zorn, it's in our baffles at 187 degrees relative, elevation −5 degrees. It's moving at 200 lights."

"Got it! Good work Shey. Thank you for keeping a sharp eye on our baffles." Zorn said.

Scanning his instrumentation, Roan was frowning. He did not see anything on his monitors. "Zorn, what do you have?"

"Wait one, Roan, I'm still trying for a classification. Good call Shey, I've never seen that signature before. I'm running the numbers."

"Ouch, we've got problems. Roan, that thing is moving on a course to pass within 10,000 kilometers of our projected position. It's not traveling in a commercial conduit. It must therefore be Military, and it's of an unknown classification. I'm recommending extreme caution. I suggest that you move us normal off from its track line, and then hunker down until it has passed us by. As fast as it's closing, it'll be on top of us within less than an hour."

Some of Roan's tension lessened, his monitors were finally showing him the approaching ship. "Zorn, whatever it is, it seems we'll have a really good look at it. I just hope the opportunity isn't reciprocal.

"Shey, alert the girls, then move us normal to and off the target's line of flight. Make your evasion maneuver toward Lan. We don't want to permit the target to move between Lan and our position. Bring all the girls to our maximum stealth profile. If you have a tight beam on Lan, send him a warning of incoming hostile traffic, along with the target coordinates and dynamics."

"Roan, Shey here. I am proceeding to execute your instructions. The girls are acknowledging and are following. We are already at a high stealth profile, but we are going over all our circuits and tightening up wherever we can. I have notified Lan, and he has advised us to hunker down. He is closing on our position to provide fire support, if necessary."

"Roan, I don't like what I'm seeing here! The target, whatever it may be, is slowing. It is down to 187 lights, and it has gone active. In my books, that classifies it as pure Kreel. It's beginning a wide sweeping search pattern. I don't recognize some of its active waveforms. Even more interesting, while holding to their initial base course, they were running a sweeping search beam pattern," Zorn reported.

"Shey, check all stealth settings and open up your detectors toward the girls. Be certain we are not leaking radiation on any bandwidth. Alert the girls to make the same checks. Keep all communications with the girls on tight links and as brief as possible," Roan ordered.

"Roan, the girls are checking on all bandwidths, and we are clean."

"Zorn, can you get a passive lock on that Kreel ship?"

"Wait one, I'm checking." Zorn's fingers danced across his instrumentation panels.

"Roan, I have obtained a solid passive lock on the target. He is now approaching at 175 lights."

"Zorn, set four medium missiles to passive-active homing and bring them to Condition 2. Set the missiles to go full evasive and active at 80 percent of computed intercept run length. Set every countermeasure penetration protocol at the maximum. I have a queasy feeling that whatever is heading our way, it is really bad news.

"Shey transmit a Code 3 to all Scouts. Using the same passive-active settings as we are assigning, order the girls to bring all missiles to Condition 2 and obtain passive locks."

Zorn looked over to Roan with a frown. "Did I hear you correctly, set Code 3?"

"Zorn, that includes you and me. Suit up. If we get into a fight with that Kreel ship, we may end up with holes in our hull and wanting something to breathe. Suit up now, I will follow as soon as you're ready."

"Sir, Code 3 it is."

Slipping off his safety harness, Zorn moved aft. In a few minutes, he returned wearing an enveloping garment, its lightweight fabric loosely clinging to his uniform and its attached flexible and clear hood falling back over his shoulders. "Reporting ready, Code 3."

"Zorn, hold Shey tight. I will be right back."

Roan slipped off his lap restraints and moved quickly aft. A few minutes later, he returned suited up as Zorn was.

"Roan," Zorn asked, "Code 3? Is there something I need to know?"

"No, Zorn. While I don't have a tight link with the Divine, what I do know is the inbound target has unknown classification and capabilities. That it's slowing down and beginning to hunt, right near where we are, could be coincidental, however, I don't know that. He just might know something he shouldn't possibly know. Given what happened to Lux, I have no intention of becoming prey."

"Roan, given your assessment, I am requesting authorization to arm six decoys. I recommend they are set at 20 percent stealth with one minute post launch delay before going active."

"Zorn, proceed with the preliminary decoy settings. However, cut the delay to twenty seconds and insert the propulsion trace for a Dargon long-range reconnaissance fighter. We don't want to provide them any intelligence about our own propulsion signature, 20 percent or otherwise. Do not set any final flight settings. I want to see what this Kreel ship is doing before we commit to battle."

Zorn leaned over his equipment panel and his fingers flew over his console, "Setting six decoys. As ordered, I'm blaming the Dargon for whatever happens. Holding on final flight settings."

"Shey, if we end up in a fight, you are to coordinate all missile launches from our girls. We want our missiles to saturate their defenses; they must arrive on target at the same time."

Suddenly, Zorn's voice took on a tone of deepening concern. "Roan we have big problems here. That Kreel ship isn't a single ship. It's just divided into two ships. It must be a Tuen Class fast-attack."

"I don't believe it is. Don't forget the Elite Guard has that same capability, and the propulsion signature on those ships is distinctly unknown."

"Wonderful, we get to be the first Guardian ship besides Lux to encounter an Elite Guard ship. Roan, Elite Guard or otherwise, I don't believe they have any track on us. If they did, they wouldn't be scanning the volume— they'd be attacking."

"Hopefully, you're correct, but we'll remain at Condition 2 and alert and see what we shall see."

Continuing to study his instrumentation, Zorn reported, "They are now down to 150 lights. They are spreading out. I've never seen the Kreel do this before. They're maintaining a base course while the two ships spiral neatly about that axis. They're active with overlapping search patterns. They are definitely operating in a very tight coordination. Whoever they are, they're very proficient. I'm beginning to get the same bad feeling you have, and I don't like it."

"Shey, allocate one medium missile from each Scout to each of the two Kreel ships. That will give us four possible hits from four diverse points of launch against each of those two ships. Establish passive locks on all missiles and inform the girls to do the same."

"Roan, in accordance with your orders, Sheba, Misty, and Cindy are now dispersed into a battle maneuvering spread, all medium missiles are set as ordered, passive-active and at Condition 2. Our stealth is at 85 percent."

"Well done, Shey. Display a standard polar-relative motion plot. Set our tactical plane with one axis defined by the Kreel base course-line and the second axis passing through our position."

The bulkhead brightened and the standard maneuvering plot sprang into a bright image with Shey at the center. The tactical plot showed the two Kreel ships moving on a closing course and displaying a steady spiraling pattern about that course line.

"Zorn, what is the projected CPA?"

"Shey has moved us normal to and off the track line, but their expanding spiral is eating into our CPA separation. Considering the spiral, separation is now perhaps 20,000 kilometers. CPA is about twenty minutes."

Shey added, "Roan, I informed Lan of your concern that the approaching targets are a pair of Elite Guard ships. He agrees. Commodore Kellon has instructed us to cease all but essential communications. If possible, we are to move further away from the target's course line. Lan is sliding up into a supporting fire position, but I do not have current track on him."

"Shey, draw a sphere about our position, make the radius our medium-missile effective range. Continue to ease our girls off the Kreel base line. Bring all laser and gun turrets to point defense, Condition 2. Bring us to dead slow, and then gradually swing our formation about to put the Kreel at zero degrees relative. I want to present our minimum cross section to the target."

"Yes, Sir," Shey acknowledged.

"Zorn, make certain everything they are doing is monitored and recorded. This is the first contact with these guys. Their active search pattern and frequencies need to be fully evaluated."

Shey's clear feminine voice interjected, "Roan, the girls are all holding our battle spread, maintaining a zero degree aspect angle to the Kreel, all targeted missiles are coordinated and set Condition 2. Each Scout has one medium missile lock on each of the two inbound targets. Our acceleration is zero."

"Roan," said Zorn, "I've completed a preliminary evaluation of their active signals. They seem to be trying for some form of sympathetic reverberation from their co-mingled active pulses. Whatever they're doing, it must involve some very elaborate waveform analysis. The only reason for such an elaborate active process is to crack stealth technologies. I'm isolating on one of the ship's active signals and adjusting our decoys accordingly."

"Zorn, what precisely are you adjusting the decoys for?"

Looking over, Zorn smiled. "Well, any complex waveform analysis based on the return from two signals will most likely not be analyzing for three or four or five such returning reverberations. I'm adjusting the decoys to broadcast a range of harmonics on and near those active signals. If I'm correct, the decoys will emit a jamming signal they will not be immediately able to nullify. It should buy us some time in a pinch."

"Good thinking, Zorn, because it looks like we are about to feel that pinch!"

# Chapter Forty-One:
## Fight or Flight

"Shey, are the other Scout teams out of the local volume?" Roan asked.

"Yes, Roan, we are the last team out. The others have returned to their Cruisers and are safely in their hangars."

"Roan, we have problems. Given the Kreel's spiral pattern, establishing an accurate base line course is difficult, but they're definitely coming nearer to our position. They're heading our way and I don't know if they have a track on us or not."

"Zorn, what's the new CPA?"

"Computing 15,000 kilometers. That puts them nearly on our front porch. We may be in a fight or flight situation. Which is it going to be?"

"Neither. We will not initiate hostilities or run from a fight. Our orders are to hunker down and remain undetected. That is precisely what we are going to endeavor to do. On the other hand, we still have ten minutes to define a solid contingency maneuver, with breakout and counterfire options. Other than that, we're in a wait and see mode."

Zorn looked over and grinned, "I now begin to see the wisdom for your Code 3. It's a wise precautionary action, just in case they accidentally bump into us as they go by."

Although he smiled, Roan wisely ignored Zorn's quip. "Shey, plot the following breakout maneuver. If the Kreel do detect or fire on us, immediately begin accelerating directly toward the Kreel. At that time, each of the girls is to deploy double chaff behind them. Simultaneously, you will launch three of Zorn's jamming decoys directly toward the Kreel formation. You are to deploy the decoys in a standard facing triangle, and they are to be broadcasting the propulsion and jamming signal Zorn has devised. You are to use a jamming bandwidth broad enough to conceal our missile's propulsion signatures. Twenty seconds after launch of the decoys, launch the two targeted medium missiles from each of our girls and then break smartly normal to and away from the target bearing line.

"If possible, make your maneuver to move us up and in the direction of their baffles. You are to maximize our breakout acceleration, but do not reduce our stealth factor below 60 percent. As you begin your evasion, bring all our gun and laser turrets to full point defense mode. After one minute on that course, reduce velocity to dead slow and bring us smartly about toward the Kreel. At that time, allocate the remaining missiles with the same presets as the first salvo, except set one-half of the missiles purely passive. Finally, make ready the second set of decoys. Then hold for further orders. Define the maneuver as Hub-2. Do you have any questions?"

"No, Roan, I understand and am instructing the girls and their crews accordingly."

"Roan, the Kreel have entered within our medium-missile effective range," Zorn reported.

Roan studied the plot for a moment. "If we wanted to ambush them, we couldn't have worked to achieve a better ambush position. Hunker down is our orders, and hunker down doesn't include starting a fight. Yet, for Lux, I wish we had a clearance to take the shot."

"Roan— not to worry. Before this mission's over, I have a feeling we'll have plenty of opportunities to take shots at the Kreel Guard. They're now about three minutes from their CPA. It's going to be about 15,000 kilometers. Since we're dressed for the occasion, shall we get out and wave as they go by?"

Roan merely shook his head slightly, "Just so long as they keep on going by. That's what they need to do. Zorn, bring up a visual on the Kreel ships. Give us both a thermal and a visual look. Let's see what they look like."

The tension in the control cabin built as both Zorn and Roan watched the displays. The bulkhead display altered and next to the maneuvering plot were two stacked images, one above the other. One display showed a view of nearby space, blackness pierced by a field of brilliant stars, and nothing else could be seen. The second image showed a faint green image, and it had several bright points clustered near its forward end.

Roan whistled softly, "Zorn, I've never seen anything like that before. What do you believe might be generating those intense points of heat flares near their bows?"

"Good question. It's not hot enough to indicate gunfire. However, it could possibly be the heat generated by the emitters for their active search beams— those active search signals are intense. Whatever they are, one thing is certain. It represents sloppy engineering. That thermal image makes them a hot target for any thermal homing missile. I strongly recommend we alter our targeting sequence to take full advantage of that thermal signature."

"Shey, you heard Zorn. Enable the missiles thermal passive homing sensors."

"Yes, Sir. All missiles have been adjusted to add thermal imaging in their passive homing sequence."

"Roan, they're at the CPA. There's no indication of their having detected us."

The Kreel ships swept past and remained on their base course. As the Kreel moved by, the Scouts slowly pivoted, keeping their bows orientated toward the departing Kreel.

"Roan, I prefer being in their baffles. What I cannot understand is why they have so disregarded their thermal image."

Roan let out a deep sigh. "Well, their lack of concern for their thermal image is understandable in one way. If you're the top predator in the briar patch, you don't need to be worried about your thermal image. Add to this, the Kreel habit is going active rather than relying on passive detection. The Kreel also believe in the old proverb of firepower deciding battles. Remember the Kreel shoot at their maximum missile range, typically before asking any question. Those Kreel characteristics make their thermal signature moot in most fights."

Zorn looked over with a frown. "How can something that looks like a big fat glow fly in the thermal spectrum survive long enough to become the top predator?"

"Zorn, just be grateful there's another weakness in the Kreel ship design we can exploit."

"Roan, it doesn't make any sense. What does the Kreel Guard have that makes them so formidable and deadly? The regular Kreel Military have enough heavy cruisers to take on any one hundred oversized Tuen Class ships. Can it be that their use of micro-Jumps in free space is their big edge?"

Roan glanced over to where Zorn was sitting. "It was a big enough edge to take out Lux."

"Ouch, point made," Zorn responded.

They waited for another ten minutes observing the Kreel ships as they moved steadily further away and toward the heliopause. "Shey set all decoys and missiles to Condition 3. Do we have any idea where Lan is located?" Roan asked.

"No, Roan, but I do have his last known position, and he is close enough for direct fire support. All decoys and missiles are set Condition 3."

"Shey, we will wait here for another fifteen minutes and allow that pair of Kreel ships to continue on their way. Signal the girls we are standing down for fifteen minutes here and suggest everyone who needs a break take one now."

"Zorn, I suggest you drop back into the galley and brew us a pot of neab. Are there any more of those cheese pastries?"

"When I last looked, there were a few remaining. They're five days old, but are vacuum packed and still very tasty. The neab will be on in a minute. Are you canceling the Code 3?"

"No, not yet. I want to keep an eye on those Kreel ships. I still don't know why they're here and what they're doing. We'll play it safe for a while longer."

"Roan, I have Lan's coordinates. He is within heavy-missile effective range. If the Kreel had started a fight, it would not have lasted long. Commodore Kellon has sent us a well done," Shey said.

Even after a millennium, receiving a well done always brought with it a smile. "Having Lan covering our backsides makes me feel much better, Shey. The good news is that the Elite Guard ships came very close to all of us, including Lan, and didn't detect any of us. It seems all of our work and upgrades were effective. Lux, old friend, thank you."

Zorn returned to the control compartment carrying two cups of neab and a cheese pastry on a small tray. "Roan— hot stuff."

Roan turned and retrieved the pastry and his cup, and gratefully sipped. "That's a good cup of neab. Zorn, next to mine, you make the second best cup of neab in Guardian Force."

Seeing what was on the tactical plot, Zorn bit off his responding quip. "Hey Roan, the Kreel have rejoined into a single unit!"

Roan turned and scanned his equipment readouts, "They have indeed merged and still appear to be holding to their base course. They are accelerating toward the heliopause. I would certainly like to know what it was that caused them to begin that little search sequence. Do you think it's possible that one of the cargo ships detected something?"

"That's hard to say, Roan; it would be sheer speculation to conclude that. Even so, I will direct our other Scouts to review all the limpet attachment maneuvers and look for any indication of anything out of the expected."

"Shey, advise the girls that Code 3 is suspended. We will be forming up in our tight formation and returning to Lan in five minutes. Set all point defenses, decoys, and missiles to Condition 4."

Both Roan and Zorn removed their emergency environmental suits and stowed them carefully away. Returning to the control room, they busied themselves with preparing to rendezvous with Lan.

"Shey, request Lan for a light missile reload upon our return. Then plot the shortest route to your hangar."

"Roan, your request for reload is denied. We are breaking out of the Hub-2 system as soon as we are in our hangars. Commodore Kellon says we will perform the reload once we return to our resupply depot."

Thirty minutes later, Lan had maneuvered his four Scouts into their hangar compartments, secured the outer doors, and returned the hangars to full atmosphere. Leaning back in his command chair, Roan simply allowed every muscle to relax. After five days of constant strain, it was a delightful luxury just knowing all was well and someone else was on duty and guarding his backside.

"Roan, I have uploaded all of our records to Lan. The hangar is at full atmosphere. You are ordered to report to Commodore Kellon in his conference room," Shey said.

"Shey, did he indicate the reason?"

"Yes, Roan. He wants to discuss your observations regarding the Elite Guard ships."

Roan looked at the chronometer, "Shey advise the Commodore I will be there in fifteen minutes."

"Zorn, continue with the post-mission routines. Ask each Scout crew to examine their attachment sequences and look for anything that might indicate a cargo ship detected something unusual. Be certain that all Lan's Scouts run each and every diagnostic in their protocols. Go over everyone's inventory and see what we're missing. If we are waiting for resupply at the pod depot, then we should take full advantage and load up with everything we need.

"Before I see the Commodore, I'm going to go back and take a quick shower and shift into a fresh uniform."

"Not to worry, Roan. Between Shey and me, we have everything under control."

Roan stopped, then turning and smiling, he looked at Zorn.

"Indeed! Good job, Zorn, and very well accomplished."

Zorn looked back and drily commented, "Be ye hereby warned, keep that command style up and the high rank types are going to promote you to a Cruiser captain."

Shey's charming voice merrily interposed, "Oh, Zorn, Lan told me Commodore Kellon is thinking of making you a Cruiser captain also."

Roan began to laugh, and he was still laughing when he entered his compartment.

Zorn sat in complete shock. "Shey, what have I ever done so wrong that would warrant such a dreadful punishment?"

# Chapter Forty-Two:
## Actionable Information

As Kellon stood considering his next tactical move, the heliosphere of the Hub-1 system loomed before him. Like scattered jewels, the brilliant stars spread across the dark canopy of the heavens that cloaked his battle-alert squadron. Having arrived at the borders of Hub-1, he had found it on full Military alert.

Although only eighteen days had passed since Lan departed Hub-2, the consequences of the limpet phase of his mission were evident. Shaking his head in frustration, with a frown he turned back toward the conference table.

"Lan, please restore the protective shutters over the dome."

As the shutters closed out the stars, the illumination in the conference room brightened to its normal level. Kellon stood for a moment, looking at those sitting at the table waiting expectantly for him to decide what they were to do.

"Gentlemen, we have successfully completed our first two mission objectives. We have deployed intelligence gathering probes within the inner planets of Hub-2. Our Scouts also successfully attached nearly three hundred limpets on cargo ships departing that system. Our mission, however, also requires us to insert intelligence gathering probes into the Hub-1 and Hub-3 systems.

"Lorn, please go over the current known distribution of cargo ships on which we attached limpets."

"Yes, Sir. At present, we are receiving periodic reports from the cargo ships on which Scouts affixed limpets. What I have now is definitely incomplete. The early data, however, indicates an unanticipated distribution of the cargo ships. As of last count, we have data on only forty-two ships. Thirty-seven of those ships proceeded directly to either Hub-3 or Hub-1. Of those, six ships arrived on the third planet of Hub-3, and thirty-one ships arrived at the third and fourth planets in Hub-1.

"We've designated the Kreel planetary systems by their distance from Hub-1, with the nearest being K-1. Of the five remaining cargo ships, two ships went to K-7, and one each arrived at K-3, K-5, and K-8. Initial Intelligence reports indicate the limpets destroyed all but one of the cargo ships upon their entry into atmosphere over their ports of call. The limpet detonation may have destroyed the ship entering K-8. The report, however, is inconclusive, and the limpet may have only caused severe damage. All forty-two Intelligence probes deployed are still operating, and none have been detected."

Kellon pulled out a chair and sat down. "Gentlemen, given the initial results of our limpet program, it seems the Kreel Empire has sat bolt upright, and it's taking quick action. Hub-1 is now ablaze with Military activity and saturated with Kreel ships scanning their entire heliosphere. The Military faction is thoroughly inspecting every ship entering or leaving the system.

"Our Intelligence section's monitoring of surrounding space indicates there are both small and large squadrons of Kreel Military ships departing and arriving at Hub-1. The Kreel Military now appears to be at its 100 percent alert status."

Roy's eyes were twinkling with mischief, "Yes, Sir! Boy howdy, that outcome is not surprising, since thirty-one of their interstellar cargo ships just mysteriously blew up into little pieces while entering their ports of call. Just imagine for a moment what thirty-one Kreel challenges to the privileged Elite sounded like to the senior Kreel Military on Hub-1. I imagine their furry little ears are still red. Sir, you must admit, we did sorta poke their backsides with a big sharp stick."

Kellon's frown shifted to a slight smile, "Agreed, Roy. We've definitely poked them with a sharpened stick. Gentlemen, with all of the planning we put into this operation, we did not give sufficient thought to the immediate consequences of our limpet program— and it appears to have exceeded our expectations. By entering Hub-2 first and attaching those limpets, we have raised the alarm everywhere. Hub-1 now looks like a Kreel Military jamboree, with every available Kreel ship on patrol. With thirty-one Intelligence probes operating within that system, our going into the heliosphere to insert even more probes would be meaningless."

Lorn cleared his throat, "Sir, we may have a second problem with our limpet program. With thirty-one destroyed cargo ships in Hub-1 and six in Hub-3, there were no exploding ships in Hub-2. That fact is a rather obvious anomaly. The very lack of destroyed ships in Hub-2 is going to cause some Kreel investigator to ask lots of questions. It will not take the Kreel long to realize all the destroyed ships left Hub-2 as their last port of debarkation."

"Lorn, you're correct, but if they're paranoid enough, that might just work in our favor. The Elite and the Military together may conclude the Industrial types on Hub-2 are the center of the True Blood conspiracy. If that happens, then there may be a coming together of the Military and Elite to the regret of the Industrial power."

"That, Sir, is a real possibility. The odds are Hub-3 is as alert as Hub-1, perhaps even more so. After all, the True Bloods' stated political objective is to uproot the Elite. Undoubtedly the Elite will take that as a rather personal threat, and be busy taking every possible step to find and root out the True Blood movement."

Listening, Roy was frowning, "Sir, do we have a defined alternate objective?"

"No, Roy, not as such. Of course, we always have our standard orders to fall back upon. Those permit a broad range of possibilities. Fleet Admiral Mer Shawn's stated objectives were for us to insert the Intelligence probes, and that we have accomplished. He has absolutely ruled out a strike on any planetary targets. He also ordered me to return with all hands. Given the success of the limpet program, we can in fact call the mission a success and turn back toward Glas Dinnein."

Looking up, Roy was grimacing. "Sir, we've come a long way simply to turn tail and go home. In addition, we haven't positioned the third leg of our Navigation Beacons, between the depot and Hub-3. Surely that remains a defined mission objective?"

"Roy, we could return to our depot and set out to lay that third leg, but once we arrived at Hub-3, what would we do? If we go in and the Kreel detect us, it could upset the entire True Blood gambit. We need to allow some time to elapse while the Elite go about their rooting out traitors. Remember, the purpose for spreading the fable of the True Bloods is to provoke the Elite to sow hate and discontent among the Military. From Lorn's assessment, it may also ferment a little hate and discontent between the Industrial group and the other two elements of the Kreel command and control structure. Since the responsibility of the Elite Guard is to foster that fear, our going to Hub-3 might just divert their attention from where we want it focused."

"Sir, given the current state of affairs, it seems we may be at a point where returning to Glas Dinnein is the correct next move," Lorn inserted.

"Perhaps, Lorn, but not necessarily. As Roy has observed, we've come a long way just to turn around and go home now. What is clear is that with thirty-one probes already inserted into Hub-1, we don't need to proceed into that heliosphere. Therefore, Roy please plot us a course back to the depot."

"Yes, Sir. Sufficient data has not been collected for a single long-Jump, but we can be ready for a short-Jump within the hour."

"Roy that is acceptable. I want to put some distance between us and that Military jamboree out there. Begin your calculations."

"Yes, Sir."

"Sir, what do you want Tactical to focus on?" Lorn asked.

"Lorn, focus on gathering and analyzing the intercepts from each of the remaining limpets as they come in. See if you can tap into the Intelligence traffic from the probes and focus on the Military and public chatter. I want to know what's happening, and what the Kreel think is happening. What is their reaction? There are still more than two hundred of those cargo ships still out between Kreel systems. As those ships arrive in their ports of call, perhaps the Kreel will afford us an opportunity we can exploit to further the True Blood revolt."

"Yes, Sir."

"Thank you, Gentlemen, for your attention and time. Proceed with your orders."

As Roy and Lorn left the conference room, Kellon sat pondering his next step. *Is there any purpose,* he reasoned, *for me to order the squadron to Hub-3? No. When our need to go to Hub-3 arises, we can then perform the installation of the third leg just as easily. Since we've met the stated basic mission criteria, perhaps it is time to start home. Going home might just be the smart thing to do, and get going while the getting is possible.*

Pushing back his chair, he stood. "Lan, you have monitored the meeting. Do you have any observations you would care to share?"

"Sir, I fully agree that now is the time to return to the depot. We have either met or exceeded our mission criteria. Perhaps by the time we arrive there, we will have received actionable information."

"Lan, I tend to agree. Take a message for Fleet Admiral Mer Shawn, encrypt it Black Hole.

"Upon arrival at Hub-1 we have observed the Kreel Military is at heightened alert and responding to the loss of twenty-one cargo ships over two of their inner planets. All thirty-one Intelligence probes the limpets inserted into the system are functional. Therefore, the squadron is returning to the depot to consider the next tactical operation.

"Lan, when I tell you to send the message, send it over my name."

"Yes, Sir. Sir, Lieutenant Elayne Cloud is requesting a moment of your time."

"Inform Elayne that I will see her in ten minutes. In the meantime, have the wardroom clean up the table and send up another thermos of neab, two clean cups, and two more pastries.

"Lan, also begin a search of the medical databases for an antidote."

"Sir, what antidote?"

"The antidote for cheese pastries. It seems our entire squadron has become addicted to Earth-style cheese pastries. I am finding I need to spend an extra hour in the gym every day just to blow off the extra calories."

"Sir, I have completed the review of the medical databases. The recommended treatment for the affliction is an extra tablespoon of willpower taken before bed time."

Kellon chuckled in amazed amusement, "Lan that's the first time I've ever heard you make a joke! Be certain you log the event into your programmers notes file. I'm confident Gregory Glenn will be delighted. Also make an additional note, record that I thought it was both timely and appropriate."

Before Elayne arrived, the steward came with a thermos of neab, clean cups, and pastries. As Elayne entered, Kellon invited her to take a seat and partake of the neab and pastries.

Smiling, she looked wishfully toward the pastries, "Thank you, Sir. I will only partake of a cup of neab."

Kellon watched her look toward the dish of pastries and turn resolutely away. He chuckled knowingly, "So, you took your tablespoon of willpower before going to bed last night."

Looking at Kellon, her expression indicated puzzlement. Her eyes sparkling, Elayne asked, "Willpower, Sir?"

"Yes, Lan told me the antidote for cheese pastries is a tablespoon of willpower before bed-time."

At first laughing, Elayne quickly brought her expression back to a business attitude. "Sir, Commander Shaw has requested I inform you of any unusual traffic coming in from our newly inserted Intelligence probes. During the past hour, we have received two additional reports. Those reports indicate the limpets destroyed both cargo ships.

One signal came from K-4 and the second from K-9. It's the K-9 message that's interesting. Our deployed probe was monitoring the two frequencies assigned to the limpet, the one that sent the data block and the second that transmitted the True Blood challenge over the Kreel challenge frequency. After the challenge was sent, the Intelligence probe recorded a brief response."

Kellon look toward Elayne with interest, "A response? Have there been any other similar responses?"

"No, Sir. This is the first response that we have monitored. Sir, I believe it was cheering."

"Cheering? Lan, isolate and play back the Kreel challenge sent at K-9 and the response to that challenge."

After a momentary pause, a clear voice in the Kreel language delivered the message devised by the Guardian Psychological Warfare Branch, "Know by this event, the filth known as the Elite are racially polluted misfits and will be pulled down and trampled under our feet. We of the True Blood do swear this."

The next sound Kellon heard was from an open microphone, it had the empty hall sound of a large room. It sounded like a sizable group of individuals stamping their feet and hooting. As Elayne had indicated, it sounded like cheering.

"Elayne, I tend to agree with your assessment— it does sound like cheering. We may have found a planetary system bordering on rebellion. Please put a team on analyzing any Kreel Military or commercial communications that refer to K-9. Collect everything you can. If that was cheering, as I now suspect it was, then there should be in very short order a Kreel response. Keep me fully informed."

"Yes, Sir. I will initiate a squadron-level Intelligence study group at once."

Standing, Elayne saluted smartly. Kellon returned her salute and watched as she left the conference room. He thoughtfully reviewed her performance during the last three missions, *She's proven herself to be a fine officer and has certainly earned my recommendation for further advancement.*

Turning his attention to the contents of Elayne's report, Kellon asked, "Lan, where is K-9 located in reference to our depot and our current position?"

"Sir, as its designation signifies, K-9 is the ninth most distant system from Kreel Hub-1. It's positioned eleven light-years from our current position and fourteen light-years from the depot."

"Lan, connect me to Commander Grey."

"Navigation here. Sir, we are fifteen minutes from Jump."

"Navigation, continue your computation, but begin a second computation to K-9. We may have found our actionable information."

"Sir, K-9? I recommend we make the planned Jump before making any other. Our mid-point beacon would be a good departure point for such a Jump. For a host of reasons, I don't recommend we attempt a Jump to K-9 from our current location."

"Roy, proceed with your Jump calculations, you are the Navigator. I will be in CAC soon."

"Yes, Sir."

Kellon looked slowly about the domed conference room. "Lan, advise the wardroom that the domed conference room is now empty. They are to send up a steward to pick up the cups and trays."

Moving out of the domed conference room, Kellon walked to the elevators, descended to deck three, and walked to his conference room. "Lan, what do we know about the K-9 planet?"

"Sir, our data is restricted to that found in the captured Kreel database. The Kreel do have a sizable Military presence on the habitable planet in the system. It is a planet closely approximating Glas Dinnein in size and atmospheric condition. It also has a research center for Space Warfare. The Kreel database indicates only a moderate Military presence, with only four Military spaceports. It is a significant Kreel infantry training planet, with several large facilities dedicated to training regular forces and one facility dedicated for training special operations forces."

"Lan, did you say the planet has a research center for Space Warfare?"

"Yes, Sir. The Kreel database indicates it is the Kreel's largest and primary research center for that specialty."

"When it blew up, was the cargo ship over one of the four Military space ports?"

"Sir, the limpet data does not contain sufficient information to permit such an assessment."

"Commodore, Navigation here. We are five minutes from Jump and holding." All squadron units confirm Condition Gold for Jump."

"Navigation, proceed with your countdown."

Roy's announcement came promptly over Lan's general address system. "All personnel attention. Jump in five minutes. Repeat, five minutes to Jump."

# Chapter Forty-Three:
## An Unsolved Mystery

Entering the CAC, Kellon stood for a moment looking about the room. Everyone was intensely focused on their tasks. Walking over to his command chair he stepped up and sat down, automatically adjusting his lap restraint.

The forward bulkhead display was set to its relative global mode— where each quarter of the display showed a quadrant view of the space surrounding Lan. After examining Quadrant 1, he next examined Quadrant 2, and then moved to Quadrant 3. What he saw there immediately caught his attention and provoked his curiosity.

There were four Kreel ships in an unusual configuration. The symbols on the plot indicated a Kreel cruiser with an escorting pair of Tuen Class fast-attack ships. Standing off some 3,000 kilometers from the cruiser was a single ship, and the symbol identified it as a joined pair of Elite Guard ships.

"Navigation, Kellon here. Hold the count on the Jump."
"Navigation here, acknowledging, holding the count at minus
   one minute."

"Tactical, Kellon here. What assessment can you provide on the ships being plotted in Quadrant 3?"

Lorn looked at his data screens for a moment then looked toward Kellon, "Sir, I am showing five ships, approximately 380,000 kilometers distant. One is a Kreel cruiser operating with an escorting pair of Tuen Class fast-attack ships. The fourth ship is a joined pair of Kreel Elite Guard ships. The Elite Guard ships exited from Jump about fifteen minutes ago, and the cruiser and its escorts were on station to meet it. They have been in parley for about five minutes."

"Tactical, do we have any intercepts of what they're talking about?"

"Tactical here, checking. Yes, Sir. Squadron Intelligence is currently monitoring their inter-ship communications— it's verbal and on a standard Kreel challenge frequency."

Kellon thought, *Challenge frequency? Why would two groups of Kreel ships not use their command or hailing frequencies?*

"Tactical put the communications intercepts on the screen. Let's see what the parlay is all about."

Two screens shimmered to activity on the forward bulkhead, and the images of two angry Kreel officers appeared. The dress uniform harness of one officer was truly resplendent with brilliant jewels and decorations. The second officer's harness, although not as elaborately adorned, was nevertheless highly festooned with meritorious decorations. The Kreel officer with the heavily jeweled harness was furious and shouting.

"Your bungling incompetence is noted, Admiral. Thirty-one cargo ships blow up over the primary planets you are responsible for guarding, and you claim no knowledge or idea of who these misfits calling themselves True Bloods are? You have had more than sufficient time to root out some of these traitors. If you cannot achieve that simple task, then I will personally take charge! I warn you now, if I do take charge, you will be the very first officer that I examine!"

Although the second officer remained silent, it was obvious from his demeanor that he was inwardly seething with restrained fury. Only by exerting a rigid self-control could he be holding back an outraged response.

Kellon recognized a prime target of opportunity, and it was a big one: an Elite Guard grand marshal and a senior Kreel Military admiral. Kellon instinctively made his decision.

"Navigation, how long would it take to compute a micro-Jump that would put the squadron squarely in the baffles of that Elite Guard ship and separated by 6,000 kilometers?"

"Sir, with all five Cruisers helping, not more than three minutes."

"Navigation, initiate computation for two micro-Jumps. The first Jump exit is to a location 6,000 kilometers directly astern of that Guard ship, and then thirty-seconds after exit, the second Jump will exit 50,000 kilometers beyond the first exit point."

Turning and looking toward Kellon, Roy's eyebrows went up, and then he nodded his head and smiled. "Navigation here. Now computing two sequential micro-Jumps, even as ordered."

"Lan, bring the squadron to battle stations. Open the formation to battle spread and bring us about, and put us on a course toward our targets. You are to coordinate missile firings for the entire squadron. Identify the Elite Guard ships as Target 1, the Kreel cruiser as Target 2, the nearer Tuen ship as Target 3, and the further Tuen ship as Target 4. We want to take out the joined Elite Guard ship first, so don't coordinate missile impact to occur at the same time on all targets.

"Allocate four heavy missiles against the cruiser, and one heavy missile against the joined Elite Guard ships. Allocate three medium missiles against each of the Tuen Class ships, and an additional two medium missiles against the Elite Guard ship.

"All heavy missiles are to be targeted and launched first. You will coordinate launch of the medium missiles fifteen seconds following the last heavy missile."

Even as the battle stations alert was fading, Lan responded, "Sir, all Cruisers are reporting Condition 2. Allocations of missiles are evenly distributed among the Cruisers; all allocated missiles are being brought to Condition 2."

"Good! Lan, upon our exit, bring all missiles targeting the cruiser to passive-active settings, with missiles going active at 80 percent of run length. Confirm the missiles directed against the cruiser and its escorts do not enable until they are well past the Elite Guard. All missiles targeting the joined Elite Guard ships are to include thermal passive homing. Employ maximum countermeasure penetration settings. All remaining missiles are to be set for passive homing.

"Following our exit from Jump, upon attaining confirmed passive locks, you are to set Condition 1 as defined."

"Acknowledged," Lan said.

Kellon returned his attention to the forward monitors. The Kreel admiral was still obviously angry. Finally, he responded to the Elite Guard grand marshal's verbal barrage.

"Grand Marshal Urrug, every effort to locate anyone belonging to the True Blood group is being taken. My investigation has disclosed there is poor morale and considerable anger within the Officer Corps because of the defeats we have been sustaining. The defeat near Scion is especially rancorous. That operation is understandably a cause of poor morale, since so many officers, warriors, and ships were lost. Since the Elite devised the Scion strategy, the Military understandably feels some resentment. Even so Lustrous One, no trace—"

Kellon disregarded the ongoing Kreel harangue and turned his full attention to his immediate responsibilities. "Tactical, Kellon here. What is your current combat area assessment?"

"Tactical here. Sir, the only identified threats are the five Kreel ships that are now targeted."

Kellon shifted his attention to Roy, "Navigation, what is your current status?"

"Sir, Navigation here. The squadron has come about in response to your orders. We are currently in our battle spread and one minute from the first micro-Jump."

A hush fell over the CAC. Then Commander Grey looked up, "Sir, all Cruisers are signaling Jump Condition Gold."

"Lan, commence a five second countdown to Jump," Kellon ordered.

Lan's countdown boomed from the general announcement speakers. "All Cruisers, micro-Jump is imminent. We are five seconds from micro-Jump and counting: four, three, two, one, Jump!"

At Jump entry, the displays reset and the giddy feeling that accompanied a micro-Jump instinctively caused Kellon to tighten his muscles. The feeling quickly passed. Then, he clenched his teeth again, feeling the second surge of giddiness as the squadron exited from micro-Jump.

"Navigation here, all units are reporting Jump exit Condition Gold, We are 6,000 kilometers distant and in the baffles of the Elite Guard ship. Thirty seconds to next micro-Jump."

"Fire Control here, all allocated missiles are confirmed passive locks."

"Lan here, all Cruisers are reporting confirmed passive locks. Condition 1, heavy missiles away." The rumbling sounds of heavy missiles being launched echoed throughout Lan's hull. "Standby for medium missile launch— Condition 1!" Again, the sounds of launching missiles were heard throughout Lan.

"Navigation here, ten seconds to micro-Jump 2."

The second micro-Jump followed and the interval between entry and exit from the second micro-Jump was only a few seconds, but they seemed to crawl past snail fashion. It was one thing to practice such a maneuver in a simulator; it was another matter to be actually executing the first such maneuver in combat. After flickering, the bulkhead displays brightened again. Kellon could almost hear a collective sigh of relief from everyone in CAC. "Navigation here, all Cruisers are reporting Jump exit Condition Gold."

"Tactical, assessment!"

"Tactical Here, we are still collecting our initial data buffers. Wait one, data is becoming available. Sir, we are registering one heavy missile hit on the joined Elite Guard ships. Sir, we are showing the joined Elite Guard ships have launched four heavy missiles against the Kreel cruiser! Repeating, the joined Guard ships have fired on the Kreel cruiser! The Guard ships must have been prepared to launch, with their missiles set at Condition 2!"

"Tactical, do we still have the Kreel inter-ship communications?"

"Yes, Sir, displaying."

The two monitors on the forward bulkhead brightened. The image of Grand Marshal Urrug came into focus. He was bleeding heavily from a long gash over his left eye and the left side of his face was swelling. The image was not crisp; its signal had considerable noise embedded in its transmission. In full fury and rage, the grand marshal was screaming. "Traitor, you treasonous filth— ". With a sharp explosive sound, the signal went dark.

"Tactical here, indicating two medium missiles have hit the joined Kreel Guard ships, and they have exploded."

For a moment, Kellon observed the surviving Kreel admiral staring in surprised puzzlement, his facial features revealing shock and confusion. Then, he began barking crisp orders.

"We are under attack, activate all defensive systems to their maximum, and deploy countermeasures! Helm, immediately accelerate at maximum! Break hard port and up!"

Behind the Kreel officer, Kellon saw the cruiser's crew busy at their stations and heard alarms sounding. As he watched, the screen went dark as the transmission ended.

"Counter Measures, Kellon here. Keep focused on that remaining Kreel cruiser. If there are any further broadcasts, you are to intercept them for analysis.

"Tactical, where are our remaining missiles?"

"Sir, our heavy missiles are still closing on the cruiser in passive mode, ten seconds from going active. They are well in advance of the incoming Kreel Elite Guard missiles, which are already active." Although Kellon could no longer watch the Kreel command officer, it didn't take much imagination to know his actions were desperate. He had eight missiles coming directly at him. He would need to be very good indeed to survive such a hail of incoming ordnance.

"Tactical here. One Tuen ship has detected the inbound Kreel active missiles and is splitting off in a radical evasion maneuver. The second Tuen is staying tight with the evading cruiser. All the Kreel are emitting broadband jamming signals. There is a general alarm signal, a form of alert broadcast on a standard Military communications bandwidth."

"Lan, bring the squadron about onto a reciprocal course, maintain our battle spread, and prepare for Jump."

"Tactical here, our heavy missiles have switched to active homing, twenty seconds to target."

"Lan here, the squadron is coming around as ordered."

"Tactical here, currently recording two heavy missile hits on the Kreel cruiser. It appears the early enabling of the Kreel active missiles alerted the cruiser's point defenses. The cruiser successfully took out two of our missiles. The cruiser is damaged, but it is still underway."

"Counter Measures, if we're intercepting any communications from any Kreel ships, put them on the screen."

"Tactical here. We're monitoring one Kreel fast-attack moving smartly to interpose himself between the inbound Kreel missiles and the damaged cruiser. His actions are purely defensive; he's acting as a screen for the damaged cruiser. He has used his point defenses to take out two of the four Kreel missiles. Two other Kreel missiles have swept past him. Now indicating three medium missile hits on the defending fast-attack ship. The Kreel active missiles and countermeasure clutter masked our medium missile signatures, and he didn't even see them coming. He is badly damaged and adrift."

Kellon detested the Kreel; even so, he had to inwardly admire the skill and courage of the fast-attack captain. To protect his cruiser, he had immediately put his ship in harm's way. None could ask more of him than that.

"Tactical here, the cruiser point defenses have taken out one of the remaining two Kreel missiles. The fourth Kreel missile has hit the cruiser astern. All indication of a propulsion signature has vanished. The cruiser is badly damaged and adrift. The second Tuen has sustained three of our medium missile hits and has exploded."

Kellon sat back and felt the battle stress begin to drain away. The initial tactical sequence had played out.

"Counter Measures here. We are intercepting a scrambled call from the cruiser on a Kreel command channel. Transferring the signal to the forward screen."

The bulkhead screen flickered to activity and displayed the image of the Kreel admiral. His left arm was hanging awkwardly at his side, apparently broken above the elbow, and he had a long cut along the right side of his face. The control room behind him was in shambles, with Kreel personnel struggling to help each other and regain their duty stations. The admiral's voice was shaky but strong.

"Military Command, this is Grand Admiral Groff. I am reporting three of our ships have been destroyed and two severely damaged. We need immediate support— repeat, immediate support! My flagship is inert and adrift as is my remaining escort. Grand Marshal Urrug's Guard ships attacked us. His joined ships were destroyed by unknown means. I am speculating someone planted one or more bombs on board his ships, like those put on the cargo ships. Repeating, this is Grand Admiral Groff ordering immediate support from all available fleet units. Repeating, I am ordering immediate support! Respond, accordingly."

As he studied the admiral's demeanor, Kellon thoughtfully considered the events of the action. *That Kreel cruiser and one escort took out five of eight heavy missiles, and the cruiser owes its very existence to the fast action and courage of the crew of that fast-attack ship. I need to remember this engagement,* he thought. *The Kreel are not cowards or anyone's slouches. It could quickly prove fatal to anyone to underestimate their capability.*

"Counter Measures, I've seen enough; secure the bulkhead screens."

"Navigation here. Sir, shall I compute a new micro-Jump, so we can go back and finish off those two crippled Kreel ships?"

"No, Roy. Finishing them off would confirm our existence, and our participation in what just happened. We will leave them with an unsolved mystery. It's time for us to depart the general area and simply disappear. Proceed with the short-Jump and move the squadron toward the depot."

"Navigation here. Yes, Sir. Resuming computation of planned short-Jump toward our depot. Jump in four minutes."

Keying his general broadcast channel, Kellon addressed the squadron. "We have just engaged five Kreel ships, a Kreel cruiser, two Tuen Class fast-attack ships, and a joined Elite Guard ship pair. We destroyed three Kreel ships and badly damaged two others. A grand marshal was in command of the Elite Guard ship and both are now among the spreading debris. We have partially balanced the scales for Lux. The squadron remains undetected, undamaged, and is now departing the vicinity of Hub-1 toward the depot. Well done everyone. Kellon out."

# Chapter Forty-Four:
## Devolution

Admiral Ron Cloud looked at the message on his desk; it was the response to his inquiry to Council Member Kur on Scion. He'd communicated asking Kur for information regarding a Kreel Grand Marshal Urrug and a Grand Admiral Groff. Who were they? He'd not informed Kur that the grand marshal was no longer among the living.

Kur's brief response was prompt. Grand Marshal Urrug was the most illustrious officer of the Kreel Elite Guard and one of the three most powerful and feared Kreel in their empire. Grand Admiral Groff was the commanding officer for the entire Kreel Military force and ranked twelfth among the top twenty-one members of the Kreel Ruling Circle.

Reaching out, Ron pressed a key on his communicator, and waited. A moment later, the communicator screen brightened, showing Mer sitting at his desk— on which was a very neat pile of reports and a cup of neab.

"Ron, without looking at the subject, I will swap my pile of reports for that sheet of paper on your desk."

Ron shook his head slightly and smiled, "Not a chance, Mer. I'm the guy who sent most of those reports over to you in the first place."

"Hmmm, and here I mistakenly thought fleet admirals outranked the admiral in charge of Guardian Intelligence. If you're calling to say you're sending more reports, then you had better sign off now. What I have here will keep me busy for the remainder of the month."

"No more reports, Mer, at least not today. I am only calling because Kur has provided a confirmed identity of those two Kreel officers Kellon took a shot at out near Hub-1. The grand marshal he demolished was the senior commander of the Kreel Elite Guard and number three in the Kreel pecking order. The admiral who survived the engagement was none other than your counterpart, the Kreel fleet admiral. Kellon was mixing it up with some very high-ranking types."

"Hmmmm, I tend to forget that those of us left at a desk reading reports are still considered by some folks to be prime targets. Just knowing that will put a spring back in my step for the remainder of the day.

"So, our Commodore Kellon took out the number one grand marshal of the Kreel Elite Guard. Along with the grand marshal Lux took out, I guess that particular job classification is now worthy of extra hazard pay."

"Well Mer, give the Kreel some credit, their ranking admirals were out mixing it up with the enemy. We've been so long desk-bound I'm not certain anyone would mistake us, even in our dress uniforms, for deep space officers. But you are correct, those particular Kreel officers went looking for trouble and they found it by the basketful."

"Ron, I've just read your report and analysis on the unidentified ship that hit the Kreel research center in Hub-2. I found it most interesting, especially the detection of its propulsion signature. I didn't know that Commander Zorn had a number of advanced degrees in both propulsion and temporal theory. He's been hiding his talents."

"That's a fact, Mer, but that breadboard hookup circuit detecting the unknown ship's propulsion signature has put an end to his concealing his talent. Every engineer in our propulsion group who studied Zorn's design has agreed his design is brilliant. They're all scrambling to study and adapt his hookup to determine if our own propulsion systems are generating similar temporal harmonics.

The idea we could be as easily detected has everyone running up tight."

"Ron, keep me fully informed on what they determine. The last thing we need now is to have our stealth advantage canceled. It's the only thing that's given us the clear edge over the Kreel."

"Mer, have you read my report on the current assessment of Ambassador Susie Wells' idea to create the imaginary True Blood rebellion?"

"Yes, Ron, I believe that's perhaps the most fascinating report I have ever read. The disruption of their Hub is beyond anything I could have imagined. The True Blood revolt has certainly poured fuel on the bonfire of the Kreel's natural proclivity for arrogance and suspicion. I found it difficult to grasp the rapidity of the devolution within their upper conclaves.

"Also, thank you for reminding me the True Blood concept was originally put forth by Susie. You know my feelings about that woman. She has repeatedly proven herself a remarkable person. Even how she came to first be brought aboard Lan is a testimony to her creative and enterprising capability."

"Mer, we've had our disagreements over the millenniums, but we're in agreement where Susie is concerned. She is remarkable. Her contributions to our success are both obvious and commendable. Thanks to her, I already have six full teams working around the clock on the intercepts coming from probes distributed throughout the Kreel Empire. We've gained more information in the past few weeks about the Kreel and their Hub than in the past one hundred years, and we're getting a real eye-opener into how the Kreel Hub works and the effectiveness of their rule."

"Whatever your six teams of analysts are finding, I would wager that the Kreel rule is not as proficient today as it was a few months ago— say, before their defeat near Scion," Mer said with a knowing smile.

"Sorry, Mer, your proffered wager is not one I accept. I have two teams focused on just the Hub planets. The Elite Guard has been on a real tear. Since the emergence of the True Blood, they have conducted an increasing number of loyalty investigations. They've also conducted summary executions on several planets, including all three primary Hub planets. Even Grand Admiral Groff has been formally suspended and placed under house arrest. The Elite Guard seems to be walking softly around him, and his court-martial is pending. It hangs on the outcome of the Elite Guard investigation into the death of Grand Marshal Urrug. The Elite Guard has repeatedly counted the missiles on board both the admiral's flagship and the surviving fast-attack ship and interrogated each of the surviving crew. Every member of the crew has agreed they didn't fire, and they were the ones that were attacked. Meanwhile the Grand Admiral remains under arrest. The standoff between the Grand Admiral and the Elite Guard has done nothing to ease the suspicions and tensions existing within the Military. Everyone is thinking everyone else is a True Blood. It's perhaps the Elite's worst nightmare come true."

"Ron, regarding Susie, I'm still marveling at her ability to negotiate the interplanetary trade agreement with the Arkillians, let alone what she did on Earth in establishing the Arkillian Interstellar Commerce Center. I must add here that I also consider her dangerous."

Ron frowned. "Mer, I'm with you regarding her merits— but dangerous? What are you referring to?"

"Don't tell me that you haven't become addicted to her Earth-style cheese pastries."

"Sorry, Mer, I don't have a clue as to what you're talking about."

"What I'm talking about is an extra five pounds around my waist as a consequence of being addicted to eating cheese pastries with my neab in the morning. They are incredible. I will see that you receive a sample tomorrow morning."

"Cheese pastries? Thank you, Mer, for your thoughtfulness, what I really need is more temptation in my idle hours! I'm not sure they could be dangerous. However, given your build-up, I will look forward to having a go at them. Unlike you, I'm in terrific shape and not in the slightest worried about becoming overweight."

"Brave talk, Sir. You haven't tasted one of those pastries yet," Mer taunted.

"I will give you my report in the morning, Fleet Admiral Mer Shawn. In the meantime, might I ask, why have you directed Kellon to K-23?"

"K-23? Oh, that's because of one of your reports. Let me see if I can find it among all the others."

Ron observed as Mer shuffled through the stack of reports and then pulled one of them out. Flipping through the pages, Mer looked up with a grin.

"Aha, here it is! According to your last report on the Kreel Industrial organization, on page 14 the report states that the government bases their economy on a stringently controlled government-issued fiat currency. According to your report, however, those in power are inclined to put their economic trust in hoarding jewels and precious metals."

"Yes, that is what we believe. Even so, why send Kellon on the long trip to K-23— even if doing so is on his way home?" Ron asked.

"Ah, good question. Your Intelligence report, Appendix I, answers that question. Your analysts intercepted information regarding a coming shipment of archaeological treasure consisting of thousands of artifacts— objects of gold and jewels. Your report says the Kreel are shipping them from K-23 to Hub-3.

"I merely thought that the up-and-coming True Blood organization might find a good use for a horde of old gold. This being so, I have sent Kellon on a raiding skirmish to rip-off the Elite and take their gold."

Ron sat back with a deepening frown. "Mer, you can't possibly be serious. You've sent five Guardian Cruisers on a raid to capture a shipment of gold?"

"Your assessment is correct," Mer replied.

"Mer, I cannot remember ever hearing of anyone sending a Cruiser on any similar task," Ron commented dryly.

"Ron, bear in mind the mission was defined because of your report. For some yet unknown reason, as your report clearly expresses, that particular shipment of archaeological gold has the Elite in a real buzz. We don't know why it's so important to them, but you can't dispute the Kreel consider it important and are intensely focused on the shipment. My conclusion is that the Kreel value the artifacts far beyond the value of the gold. It might assist us in finding out why."

Ron shifted uncomfortably in his chair and leaned back. "When the analysts first brought the matter of the gold to my attention, I wasn't impressed. I nearly filed the data in the interesting-but-not-important category. I certainly didn't consider it worthy of risking a single Cruiser, let alone five Cruisers. Might I ask what has so intrigued you in the item that you're pushing five Cruisers into peril in response to so little apparent gain?"

"Ron, your question is blunt but fair, and it deserves an answer.

"As weak as it may sound, it's a hunch. The Kreel are brute arrogance on two feet, especially about their heritage and the purity of their bloodline. I simply believe that given the Elite's heightened interest in the archaeological artifacts, they must have some significance we're not yet aware of. I might add that this is one mission that I would love to go along on. In all my years as a Cruiser captain, HQ never gave me orders to go raiding and boarding enemy ships to seize gold. Knowing Kellon, he will undoubtedly do it with a flourish,"

Shaking his head, Ron retorted, "Mer, the mission you've outlined and sent Kellon on is as dangerous as they come. You've ordered him to seek out and stop a particular ship, board it, secure its cargo, and then evade everything the Kreel will undoubtedly hurl at him."

"Hmmmm, as you point out, there are some obvious tactical problems inherent in the mission. Of course the real backbone of Kellon's mission isn't just the gold," Mer said.

Ron sat upright. "Mer, then there is more to the K-23 mission than just snatching some gold?"

Mer's eyes were twinkling with mischief, "Perceptive, Ron, K-23 is where Kellon wanted to go from the beginning. It is the planet where they manufacture the Kreel Guard ships. Given the limpet program success, I have given Kellon limited authorization to strike the ship production facilities located on that planet. I'm permitting Kellon to make that limited strike, but only under constraints. He must make it look like a strike by the True Blood or by the as-yet-unidentified Kreel adversary. The gold shipment only provides an optional confusion factor in the strike. It's the icing on the cookies. In fact, acquiring the gold is secondary to, and not to interfere with, the priority objective. Even so, the part of the mission involving the gold shipment sings plunder and raiding. The seizure of such an archaeological gold horde will undoubtedly catch the attention of the Elite, especially since it's supposedly their closely guarded secret. If we are able to hang the blame for the raid on the True Blood rebellion, then I suspect the Elite will become even more alarmed, since it apparently indicates the True Blood have penetrated the Elite inner circle. When associated with a Military raid on the Elite Guard production facilities, it will become doubly alarming. The Elite and their Guard can't ignore such synchronized actions, or their implications."

Ron sat quietly, considering what Mer had told him. It was a bold operation, but one fraught with incredible risks. "I agree with your assessment that the Elite and their Elite Guard will both sit up and take notice of such an action directed squarely at them. This is especially so given how deep into the heart of Kreel space K-23 is. Mer, I strongly urge that after Kellon's mission to K-23, you promptly extract the entire squadron and bring them home. They've been exceedingly successful so far, and the best part is they are still undetected and damage-free."

"Hmmm, Ron I understand what I've asked of Kellon exceeds the initial mission criteria. I will give your recommendation the consideration it deserves. For now, keep your analysts on the job. If you pick up anything that can help Kellon, be certain to forward it to him, with a copy to me."

Sitting at his desk, Ron considered whether to tell Mer what he really thought of his gold raid, and he decided to keep his feelings to himself. *Besides,* he thought, *Mer might just think my opinion is tainted because Elayne is serving on board Lan. In truth, perhaps it is.*

"Sir, Guardian Intelligence will put a special team on the Kellon matter immediately. Cloud out."

The light of an early autumn afternoon was softly diffused as it flooded through the sheer curtains, warmly illuminating Mer's office space. Sitting at his desk, Mer thoughtfully looked at the now blank communications screen, and he was troubled.

Ron's abrupt termination of the dialog was unexpected. Long ago, Ron and he had been first-year cadets together. It was a very long time ago. Their friendship was deeply rooted and well established in time of peace and combat, grounded on the firm foundations of mutual trust and respect.

Mer sat pondering Ron's responses. *He's clearly concerned about the K-23 strike, but why? And his recommendation that we extract Kellon and his squadron immediately following the strike underscores his concern. Perhaps he's correct. Perhaps, I've asked too much of Kellon this time.*

Then Mer leaned back and lifted his eyes to the ceiling. With a deep groan, he thought, *Blast, I keep forgetting his granddaughter Elayne is serving on Lan! Of course he's concerned. The problem is that each of the Guardian personnel in that squadron is invaluable to all of us. They are our friends and family. He's right, I've thrust all of them deep into harm's way. Blast and double blast, if anything happens, it could leave a scar between Ron and me that might never heal.*

Doggedly returning to the pile of reports, Mer worked steadily for the next three hours without a break. Yet he was unable to push Ron's voiced concerns out of his mind.

Reaching out, Mer pushed Ron's button on his communicator and waited. Within five seconds, the screen sparkled to brilliance and his old friend responded.

"Cloud here. How might Guardian Intelligence be of assistance to the Fleet Admiral this afternoon?"

"To begin with," responded Mer, "you can stow that be of service tripe. I'm hungry. How about you and me taking the remainder of the afternoon off and going to McBride's for a cold brew and a thick juicy grilled bareq steak?"

His eyes twinkling, Ron's countenance broke into a broad smile. "Ah! And they say there's no such thing as telepathy. Front door, five minutes?"

"Agreed, front door and five minutes. Mer Shawn out."

# Chapter Forty-Five:
## Five New Targets

Elayne felt a sense of physical fatigue, but it was offset by her sense of accomplishment. The six weeks since their intercept of the unintended response from K-9 had been busy. While the squadron moved to K-9, one of her many tasks had been devising a reaction to that intercepted transmission. Her crafted propaganda product was now complete, and a special probe would soon transmit it to the Kreel on K-9.

Sitting in the captain's conference room, she was with Commodore Kellon and Lorn— and like others in the squadron, she was concerned about their steadily expanding mission.

The five Guardian Cruisers were slipping like phantoms through the gentle solar wind near the outer boundary of the heliopause, their graceful contours artfully concealed in the deep artificial shadows of their crafted stealth. Their mission was simple in nature: they were to ease into K-9's heliosphere and deploy five Class 4 Intelligence probes and one special probe. They had already deployed the Class 4 probes and they would soon launch the special probe.

As was his daily routine, Kellon was conducting the mid-day video conference from his conference room. The images of the four other Cruiser captains appeared on the bulkhead screen. Kellon knew he was speaking to dedicated professionals, but once again, he laid out their mission criteria.

"Admiral Mer Shawn's orders are specific in terms of objectives and sequence. Our intent to start home following our monitoring of K-9 remains unchanged. We are, however, about to take a slight detour. We will be visiting K-23 on our way home. The good news is that upon completing our mission in K-23, we are ordered to immediately return to Glas Dinnein."

With Kellon's statement, a noticeable lessening of tensions— and even a few smiles— showed among the captains attending via video link. All the crews were volunteers, but the months had been adding up, and the distance from Glas Dinnein seemed to be ever-lengthening. Kellon's establishing K-9 as their next-to-the-last destination came as very welcome news.

Captain Eurie spoke up, "Commodore, orders are orders, we all know that. K-23 is still far from home, and we don't have backup. We are, strictly speaking, on our own. May I inquire as to our mission there?

As Kellon described the assigned mission to his captains, all four looked a bit taken aback.

Captain Eurie was frowning as she spoke again, "I understand the value of the Elite Guard manufacturing target, but do you have any information describing what's so important about a shipment of archaeological trinkets— gold or otherwise— that warrants the risks we are about to take?"

"I'm sorry, Captain Eurie, but I lack any additional information about the artifacts. What I can tell you is that before this mission began, I personally asked Admiral Mer Shawn for authorization to strike directly at the Elite Guard manufacturing facilities on K-23. He flatly denied my request. Now it seems the value Admiral Mer Shawn assigns to those trinkets, as you called them, has altered his thinking."

"Commodore," inserted Captain Kylster, "Admiral Mer Shawn's expansion of our mission will potentially add months to our deployment. While HQ is minimizing the significance of the artifacts we're supposed to heist, someone in Fleet Command obviously considers them significant. As Captain Eurie has already said, in the end, it's not relevant— but it's still somewhat of a mystery. More important, aggressively striking the Elite Guard production facilities on K-23 will pull in every available Kreel cruiser and Tuen Class ship in the quadrant. Accomplishing the assignment without fatalities will require a precision operation. When do we begin planning the details of the heist and strike?"

In spite of himself, Kellon smiled. "Captain Kylster, both your observation and assessment are valid, except for defining the mission as a 'heist.' It may seem on its surface a storm and board, full-scale marauder style. We are Guardian Force, however, so we're at least metaphorically flying our nation's colors. Strictly speaking, it isn't a heist— it's more like an expropriation by force." Captain Kylster tried to suppress his smile, but failed in doing so and broke out in a chuckle.

"Yes, Sir. I will enter into Lar's record that our mission involves an expropriation by force and not a heist. Even so, I still would like to know what it is we are expropriating, so I can scratch my mental itch."

Now even Kellon was smiling. "Like you, I am curious about the value and nature of the artifacts. Regretfully, our curiosity is an itch that we can't scratch— at least not yet. As for planning, it will commence as soon as we depart this system, which is imminent." Turning toward Elayne, Kellon ordered, "Lieutenant Cloud, before I bring this meeting to its conclusion, please fill us in on your special probe."

"Yes, Sir. In reviewing the available information on K-9, we learned it's a primary training planet for Kreel infantry and special operations. We believe the source of the inadvertent response we received was from a Kreel Military unit. The cheering we heard was that of Kreel warriors. Adding to the response from K-9, we also had the comments made by Grand Admiral Groff. He said he'd found within the Military a condition of poor morale, bitterness, and resentment directed toward the Elite. He considered much of the bitterness to be the result of the heavy losses sustained by the Kreel fleet near Scion.

"As part of our analysis, we examined the available Intelligence information regarding the fleet that the Kreel sent to Scion. We discovered that 80 percent of the infantry losses came from this system. During that engagement, they suffered the highest loss rate of any Kreel uniformed service. We've exploited this intelligence data to prepare a short message of encouragement to the Kreel warriors still on K-9. The message is also a reminder of the Elite's casual disregard for their lives, including the lives of the Elite Guard special operations troops. Of course, the message is in the established tone of the True Blood revolt."

"Lieutenant Cloud, Captain Kel here. What is the operational profile of the special probe— how long will it operate?"

"Sir, we've programmed the probe with a single message. That message is basic, but we want it to receive maximum attention. Therefore, the probe will enter into near-planet orbit at about 20,000 kilometers. We've defined the orbit to direct the probe above the largest population centers on the planet. In order to reach the maximum number of listeners, we're broadcasting the message three times on each of sixteen known Kreel Military hailing and challenge frequencies, including eight we've learned of since our initial probe arrived in this system. As for the probe's life cycle, our analysis indicates effective reaction by the Kreel will occur approximately forty-five minutes following the beginning of the probe's broadcast. Because of its overt nature, the probe will execute a phased self-destruct protocol upon completion of its third broadcast— or earlier if proximity detection occurs. We've programmed a phased self-destruction sequence that will prevent any possibility of tracing its origin."

"Lieutenant Cloud, do you have any idea of how many Kreel may hear this broadcast?" Eurie asked.

"No, Captain Eurie, we don't have any means of determining that information. What we can say with some confidence is that the broadcast should be picked up by the civilian population, the Kreel Military, and also the Elite Guard units training on the planet."

Kellon looked up with curiosity, "Elayne, I wasn't aware the Elite Guard had training units on the planet."

Elayne turned toward Kellon, "Yes, Sir. We've learned one of the special operations groups consists of Kreel Elite troops. K-9 appears to be a large training area for them. Also, the Intelligence records describing the Scion invasion fleet indicate one of the troop carriers was carrying Elite Guard special troops from K-9."

Frowning, Kellon turned to Commander Shaw, "Lorn, have we detected Elite Guard ships in this system?"

"No, Sir. The only observed Military traffic consists of Tuen Class ships. No propulsion signatures corresponding to the observed Elite Guard ships have been detected."

"Commodore, Lan here. Commander Shaw is correct given the information he had one hour ago. Since you've convened this meeting, Tactical has acquired several new detections. There are five new targets, and three of them are joined Kreel Guard ships." Lan's announcement took everyone by surprise.

"Lan put a hold on the deployment of the last special probe until further notice. How close are those five new targets?"

"Sir, as ordered, a hold is now in effect for the special probe deployment. The three Elite Guard ship pairs just departed K-9.

The other two new tracks consist of one Kreel cruiser and an unknown ship Zorn's detector is tracking. Those two ships are well separated from the squadron, and are approaching K-9 from opposite sides of the heliosphere. Presently, the five new contacts do not pose an immediate threat to our squadron."

Standing up, Kellon ordered, "Ladies and Gentlemen, this meeting is concluded. Bring all Tactical sections to full staff and alert the Squadron Intelligence personnel. Dismissed."

As the bulkhead screens dimmed, Kellon turned to Lorn and Elayne, "I suggest we relocate to CAC. I want to observe and determine what that unknown is doing in this system."

# Chapter Forty-Six:
# Why Thirty Hours?

Entering the CAC, Lorn and Elayne immediately went to the Tactical group and began studying their consoles. Glancing toward Navigation, Kellon noticed that Roy was not on duty. Instead, Lieutenant Oster looked up and acknowledged Kellon's glance with a brief nod. Kellon approved of the young officer, since he had ably demonstrated himself to be both committed and capable during the boarding of the Gola. While he lacked Roy's years of experience, he was a competent Navigator.

Turning his attention to the tactical plot on the forward bulkhead, Kellon saw it was set to a standard heliocentric polar plot showing the ecliptic plane with the primary as a point in its center. Centered about the primary, the system's planetary orbits were shown as compressed concentric rings. K-9's only habitable planet was marked by a green triangle. The other planets were marked by brown triangles.

What drew Kellon's immediate attention were three icons, a slowly pulsing red icon near the planet indicating the presence of Kreel Elite Guard, and a slightly larger solid red icon indicating a Kreel cruiser. The cruiser was moving toward K-9 from a point well above and slightly offset from the vertical. It was entering from an azimuth of about 150 degrees, nearly opposite from the squadron's position. The third icon Kellon studied was blinking blue, indicating a ship of unknown classification. At first glance, that icon seemed dangerously close to the squadron, but a quick check on its elevation indicated it was at -30 degrees, definitely below the ecliptic plane and well separated from the squadron. The unknown ship was headed directly toward K-9.

"Lan, draw a sphere around the unknown ship. Make the radius of that sphere the same as the determined detection range of the unknown transient signals we measured near Hub-2."

As Kellon observed the plot, a circle appeared around the unknown ship. Kellon looked with interest, noting that the planet and nearby Elite Guard ships were well beyond the indicated detection range.

"Tactical, Kellon here. Are you ready with your assessment?"

"Tactical here. Yes, Sir. As the plot indicates, the unknown is currently outside the Elite Guard's detection range. We are tracking three combined Elite Guard ship pairs, and their appearance near K-9 correlates with the appearance of the Kreel cruiser. Sir, we are now tracking two Tuen Class fast-attack ships providing close support for the cruiser. What appears to be happening is the first stages of a possible face-off, similar to what we observed near Hub-1. In raw firepower, the Kreel Military seems to have the advantage.

"Neither group of Kreel ships seems aware of the approaching unknown ship. I am also able to report our new Intelligence probes are in good position and are providing clear data on the planet, the Kreel Guard and Kreel Military ships. The new modifications to the Intelligence probes incorporating Commander Zorn's detector are working well. We have solid track on the unknown ship."

"Tactical, are the Kreel Guard ships lingering in the vicinity of K-9, or are they moving out? If they're moving out, in what direction?"

"Tactical here. The Elite Guard is moving out toward the incoming cruiser. They are accelerating and currently at 90 lights. The inbound cruiser is slowing and is now down to about 85 lights."

"Lan, extrapolate the tracks for the Elite Guard and the Kreel cruiser, indicate the projected intercept point."

Watching the tactical plot, he observed a line appear between the two red icons. An "X" appeared on the line.

"Lan, draw a sphere around the planet using the same radius you employed to draw the sphere around the unknown ship."

As the circle appeared around the planet's icon, Kellon noted the point the Kreel would likely face off was well outside the detection range indicated about the planet. "Tactical, this is going to prove very interesting. Pull up the data on the previous unknown's attack in Hub-2. Look at the angle on inclination to the ecliptic plane during the unknown's approach to the target planet and then during his withdrawal. Is the angle to the ecliptic a mirror image?"

"Tactical here," responded Elayne, "we are retrieving those records."

After a moment, Elayne's voice responded, "Tactical here. Sir, you are correct. The unknown's path inbound to planet five was at -15 degrees to the ecliptic plane. On his withdrawal, the unknown followed a reciprocal path but at an angle to the ecliptic plane of +15 degrees."

"Tactical affirm that the point of entry into the heliosphere gave the unknown the shortest distance between the heliopause and the planet."

"Tactical here, confirming the unknown followed the shortest trajectory to the target planet. The same can be said of the current track line in relationship to K-9."

Kellon sat for a moment studying the tactical plot. Three Elite Guard ships and a Kreel cruiser with two Tuen Class fast-attack ships entering the heliosphere was not likely part of the unknown's attack plan. That was a mixed blessing, since the Kreel cruiser was pulling off the Guard ships. If it had not arrived, then following the unknown's strike, the Guard ships would have immediately lifted off planet in pursuit. Even though the unknown must be able to track both the Elite Guard and the cruiser, he was pressing his attack. That meant whatever the unknown's target was, the unknown considered its value sufficient to warrant putting their lives on the line. Wonderingly, he thought, *There's no doubting their determination and courage, but can they pull it off?*

"Lan, I have a tactical problem for you to resolve. Assume the unknown ship decelerates below 1 light as he enters into the planetary detection radius and completes his attack, what angle of inclination will a reciprocal course need to be in order to achieve the shortest distance to the heliosphere?"

"Sir, the heliosphere is not a perfect sphere, and the unknown must travel approximately 58 AU to reach the heliopause. Tactical considerations most likely will outweigh geometry."

"Lan, compute the distance from the Kreel cruiser and Elite Guard meeting point to the nearest point on the heliopause."

"Sir, I am computing approximately 38 AU."

"Thank you, Lan. That's what I was afraid you would say." Studying the tactical plot, Kellon observed the unknown was not likely going to break out. The problem he faced was not overcoming a stern chase; it was going to be a clear intercept problem. Unfortunately, the Elite Guard had proven with Lux that it was an expert in such intercepts. *Blast,* he thought, *the Elite Guard is not going to score another trophy— not if I have anything to say about it.*

"Lan, release the hold on the deployment of the special probe. As soon as you complete the required trajectory calculations, proceed with its launch.

"Tactical, isolate and monitor all the Elite Guard ships' communications, every channel. I don't want their captains to even sneeze without our knowing it. Also, keep the cruiser blanketed— but he is less important.

"Pay particular attention to the challenge channels and hailing frequencies on the cruiser. If a dialog commences between the Elite Guard and the cruiser, record it. However, keep your primary focus on the inter-ship communications between the Elite Guard ships.

"Lan, we have about thirty hours before the unknown reaches K-9. Pass to all Cruisers Condition 3. Everyone who can should get some sack time, we're going to have a hard push soon and I want everyone on their toes.

"Tactical, that especially means you. Focus on those intercepts, but otherwise wind down your team and get some rest. We're going to need everyone sharp as possible in about thirty hours.

"Navigation, you have the CAC. I will be in my quarters." Lieutenant Oster looked up, and his look was serious. "Yes, Sir, acknowledging Navigation has the CAC."

After watching Kellon depart, Lorn stood and carefully studied the tactical plot. He shook his head slowly in wonderment.

Elayne had turned to study the board along with Lorn. Then she looked inquisitively at Lorn. "Can you see anything on that plot that tells you what's going to happen in thirty hours? I certainly don't."

Looking over to Elayne, Lorn smiled slightly. "The day I can see as far into the future as Kellon does, I might consider myself qualified for command of a Cruiser. This, however, isn't that day.

He obviously sees something in that tactical plot, but what it is I don't have even a clue."

As the door to his personal quarters closed behind him, Kellon moved to his desk and sat down. "Lan, what is Commander Grey's current status?"

"Sir, Commander Grey is currently sleeping. It is his first really good sleep in about a week."

"Lan, keep your eye on everything for me. I'm going to take a shower and get some sleep. I'm available only for matters of high priority. We are heading into harm's way, and I need to be sharp."

"Sir, harm's way? I understood we were soon departing this system for K-23."

"We are, but not until after the unknown ship safely exits this heliosphere. There are two objectives here. The first is to see what the unknown believes is so important to destroy, and the second is to see that the Elite Guard does not destroy the unknown ship."

"Sir, is it then your intention to bring the squadron into direct combat with the Elite Guard?"

Kellon had stood and was heading toward his shower. Stopping for a moment as if to reflect, he answered, "Lan, I have pondered long on how the Elite Guard was able to get close enough to Lux to hit him with a sucker punch. The first shot was a heavy missile. I now believe I know how they did it. I'm not prepared to let them do the same thing to the unknown ship, not if we can prevent it. Does that answer your question?"

"The question I asked is fully answered. Thank you. Is this personal or private information?"

"For now, consider it private." Kellon responded, even as the door to his shower shut behind him.

# Chapter Forty-Seven:
## Nori

"Tactical here, the unknown ship is entering into detection range near K-9," reported Lorn.

Kellon was in his command chair and observing the forward tactical plot with keen interest. The pieces of the tactical problem had continued to resolve themselves over the previous day, and he was about to learn if his analysis was correct.

"Tactical here, the three Elite Guard ships are remaining stationary in close proximity to the Kreel cruiser and its flanking Tuen Class escorts. The dialog between the Kreel Military and Elite Guard is still raging. There's no indication that they are aware of the approaching unknown."

Kellon had listened to a little of what was going on between the Kreel, it was an argumentative exchange in typical blustering fashion. Both the Military and Elite Guard commanders were bursting their dress harnesses with counter-assertions of outraged authority, each claiming to have command authority within the K-9 system. Kellon knew the argument would most likely continue for hours if not broken up. Of most interest to Kellon was learning the Elite Guard had been examining ranking Military officers on K-9. Based on the heated exchange between the Military and the Elite Guard, the Elite Guard had already summarily executed several senior Military officers and some of their troops. The Elite Guard had charged them with being collaborators with the True Blood. The Kreel admiral on the cruiser was furious and was demanding all Elite Guard inquisition and executions be suspended immediately— or else.

Kellon knew the bitterness of inter-service strife was feeding the smoldering fires of a real revolt. *Susie,* he thought, *you have ignited a firestorm in high dry brush and it's only beginning to blaze.*

Keying his command band, Kellon addressed the squadron. "Gentlemen and Ladies, the unknown ship is nearing K-9. What we're seeing here is a repeat of the tactics observed within Hub-2. "It's not the pending attack on K-9 that I want to call to your attention, however. As we know, the Elite Guard detected Lux within Hub-3. I believe I now know how they were able to ambush him. We have ringside seats to see the Elite Guard tactics demonstrated. We will remain in our current position and observe. If, however, I see the Elite Guard about to take out the unknown ship, then the squadron will move to engage the Elite Guard with extreme prejudice. Kellon out."

At Kellon's proclamation, Roy looked up with mischievous eyes, nodded his head as if in approval, and then went back to studying his console. "Tactical here, the unknown has entered into the estimated detection range of the planet. He has not reduced his speed and is still traveling at 240 lights."

"Tactical, be certain to mark when the planet detects him."

For the next hour, the CAC remained busy, the low murmurs between various team members being the predominant sound. Kellon watched the unknown ship draw nearer the planet, and there was no indication the Kreel had detected his approach.

"Tactical here, the unknown is in his final approach to the planet, and he has commenced decelerating. As he's spilling his excess gravitational energy, he's radiating a massive energy flare. He must be pushing his propulsion and inertia system limits to their extremes. The Kreel have finally obtained detection, and the Military is sounding an alarm. What they must have detected is the envelope of his braking energy. Given the rate of deceleration, it's enormous."

"Tactical, keep a sharp eye on the Elite Guard ships, their reaction is the key to what comes next."

"Tactical here, the unknown has engaged! Our Intelligence probes are detecting heightened activity on all Military channels. The unknown is below 1 light, he's at his CPA to the planet, and he's barely above the atmosphere. There's a significant fire fight in progress."

Kellon sat listening, his eyes closed, as he followed the tactical developments. If he was correct, the Elite Guard would split up their force.

"Tactical here, the unknown has made his target run and is completing his slinging about the planet; he is accelerating again. Estimating he took out several Tuen Class ships as he made his pass, but the data is incomplete."

Elayne's clear voice reported, "Tactical here, the Elite Guard is reacting. Two of the Elite Guard ships out near the Kreel cruiser have come about and are accelerating in the general direction of the planet. The third Guard ship is now accelerating away from the planet and toward the heliopause. The Kreel cruiser and his Tuen escorts are accelerating directly toward K-9."

Sitting back in his chair, Kellon let out a slow long held breath, thinking, *My analysis was spot on. The Elite Guard is running a pure intercept.* He smiled slightly, fully understanding there was ample time in which to respond. Before he did, it was essential to accurately establish the tactical geometry that was now progressing.

"Lan, designate the two Elite Guard ships moving toward the planet as Targets 2 and 3. Designate the single Elite Guard ship accelerating away from the planet as Target 1."

"Yes, Sir. What designation do you want for the Kreel cruiser and his escorts?"

"Lan it will not be necessary to assign a target identification to those ships, they are not a part of our tactical problem."

"Tactical here. Detection and tracking of a new Elite Guard ship, it has just departed K-9. The unknown has successfully completed his sling maneuver. He is now 100,000 kilometers from the planet and headed outbound on an angle above the ecliptic plane. He is continuing to accelerate. The new Elite Guard ship is moving into a pursuit position and is now at 2 lights and accelerating. Our probes are obtaining terrific acceleration profiles on both the unknown and Elite Guard ships."

"Lan, designate the new Elite Guard ship as Target 4."

"Tactical, Kellon here. I require two tactical vectors— as accurate as possible, so take your time. The first is the trajectory vector of the unknown ship and the second is that of Target 1."

"Tactical here," Elayne reported, "The first Military intercepts are coming in from K-9. The unknown has utterly decimated the Space Warfare Research Center located on the planet. It's a repeat of the unknown's attack on the fifth planet in

331

Hub-2. We are intercepting reports indicating a large area destroyed. Only craters remain where there was a significant research complex. Reports indicate it was the height of the workday and there is a significant loss of life."

Kellon now had sufficient information to answer some of his questions. The strikes in Hub-2 and on K-9 were against high-level Military research facilities. Smiling, Kellon thought, *If the unknown wasn't already doing the job, Guardian Force would gladly contract them to do it. Well, I suppose one good deed deserves another, and whoever they are, they're about to require our help.*

"Tactical here. Communications intercepts between the Elite Guard ships have identified the unknown as being a 'Nori'— repeat, the Elite Guard has identified the unknown ship as a 'Nori.' The two Elite Guard ships near the cruiser have now adjusted their trajectory to intercept the unknown ship at his heliopause exit point. According to our computations, the unknown will reach the heliopause well before they can make their intercept. The trailing Elite Guard ships lack the speeds to overtake the unknown, and they are gradually falling behind. Nevertheless, they are doggedly pursuing."

Frowning, Kellon considered the implications of identifying the unknown as being Nori. Until now, all they knew of the Nori was what they'd observed near Earth. By reputation alone, the Nori terrified Kreel warriors. Obviously, the Nori had a high level of stealth technology, and except for their transients and propulsion gravitational harmonics, they were clean. Kellon winced at the thought, *It's always the exceptions that can get you killed!*

"Tactical, compute the point on the heliopause where Target 1 will exit the heliosphere and what time he will exit. Pass those coordinates and projected exit time to Navigation."

Elayne leaned over to where Lorn was working and nudged him. "Lorn," she whispered, "have you figured out what the Commodore is doing yet?"

Lorn looked back toward Elayne and with a slight smile whispered back, "Yes, but a day later— and I needed more information to figure it out."

The murmuring between team members in the CAC lessened as the time since the Nori strike on K-9 lengthened. Having patiently observed the unfolding geometry for more than an hour, Kellon asked, "Tactical, can you determine which target the Elite Guard commander is in?"

Elayne looked toward Kellon and immediately responded, "Tactical here, the Elite commander is in Target 1. Targets 2 and 3 are still in hot pursuit and Target 4 is continuously updating the Elite commander with the unknown's trajectory data."

Kellon leaned back and considered what was coming next. *Do I have sufficient slack for some bravado? Blast, bravado is for fantasy, not for space combat, where the bottom line means staying alive. While shouting defiance in the face of the Elite Guard commander is alluring, it's not something I can afford to indulge in, and a court-martial would definitely tarnish my service record. Therefore, no bravado.*

Again keying his general communications band, Kellon addressed the entire squadron. "Kellon here. Depending on your assignments, you may already have deduced the elements of the ongoing battle in progress within this solar system. The interesting part is we now have an identification for the unknown ship: the Elite Guard has designated it as a Nori. Henceforth, we will do likewise.

"After making his successful strike, the Nori ship has turned and is moving at speed for the heliopause. While the pursuing Elite Guard ships cannot overhaul the Nori, they are maintaining sufficient closure to obtain an accurate track on his trajectory. They are working a smooth triple play and the Nori is in a tight squeeze, the jaws of the trap are closing about him.

"As the Nori burns a hole through solar wind for the heliopause in order to make a Jump, Target 1 is speeding toward the heliopause to do the same thing. The problem the Nori has is that at the time of his attack on K-9, Target 1 was much nearer to the heliopause boundary than the Nori was. That distance advantage allows Target 1 to exit the heliosphere first and set up for two short- Jumps before the Nori can reach the heliopause. The first Jump will give Target 1 the angle needed for a second short-Jump. That second Jump will bring Target 1 to the extrapolated exit point the Nori is heading toward well before the Nori can reach that same point. Once in position, the Elite Guard will hunker down as a sleeper, with all his internal systems set at minimal levels, waiting in a perfect ambuscade. In effect, the Elite Guard is running an intercept solution on the Nori ship.

"I believe the Elite Guard performed this same tactic on Lux.

This time, however, there's a big difference. While Target 1 was 38 AU from the heliopause, we are barely within the heliosphere. While Target 1 has the time advantage over the Nori, we have the time advantage over Target 1.

"The squadron is going to move to break up and spoil the Elite Guard team play. We will see that the Nori makes his Jump! Kellon out."

As Kellon closed out his message, the crew in CAC and elsewhere began to cheer. This was almost worth the months of travel and the long hours. This time it wasn't a target of opportunity. This time they were going to take the fight directly to the Elite Guard.

"Lan, prepare a pre-combat message for Guardian HQ. Identify our location as K-9. Inform Admiral Mer Shawn that we have deployed all Intelligence and special probes. Inform him that we have observed a Nori strike on a major Kreel Military Space Warfare research facility. Outline tactically how the Elite Guard is setting the Nori ship up for a sucker punch— just as they did with Lux. We are proceeding to terminate the Elite Guard attack on the Nori ship. The squadron is in good fighting form and preparing to oppose a single Elite Guard ship. Lan, encrypt the message Black Hole and send it over my name.

"Navigation, move us out of the heliosphere."

Roy looked up, smiling broadly. "Navigation here, proceeding as ordered. I am bringing the squadron about.

Roy's firm voice then announced over the squadron communications channel, "Navigation here, the squadron will be exiting the heliosphere in approximately one hour. All hands should be prepared for turbulence as we penetrate the boundary."

Remaining in CAC, Kellon continued to observe the tactical plot, and considered the upcoming attack. Roy's firm alert disrupted his mental planning.

"Navigation here, turbulence alert, imminent interface turbulence alert." For the next fifteen minutes, the turbulence bounced and jostled Lan as he passed through the interface boundary between the heliosphere's solar winds and the enveloping galactic space beyond.

"Navigation here, we are clear of the interface. Awaiting orders."

"Navigation, Kellon here. Commence computing two short-Jumps. Short-Jump one will be to a point you are to select. The second Jump must position the squadron outside the heliosphere and just above Target 1's projected exit point."

"Navigation here, beginning computations for two short-Jumps, as ordered. Requesting links between all five Cruisers."

"Lan, tie in your brothers and proceed with Navigation's computations for the defined Jumps."

"Lan here, all Cruisers are in tight link and standing by. Navigation has priority."

"Navigation, proceed."

# Chapter Forty-Eight:
## Enough Trouble

Lan's calm resonant voice made the countdown to the Jump. Upon entry, Kellon groaned inwardly, *Blast, when we get home, I'm going to demand research into micro-Jumps. This stomach twisting every time we enter or exit a Jump is not tolerable!*

As they exited the Jump, Roy reported, "Navigation here, all units are reporting Condition Gold. I am bringing the squadron to a new heading in preparation for the second Jump. Estimating eight minutes to Jump 2."

Although CAC was not at Condition 2, nearly the entire CAC team had assembled, each taking their duty positions. Looking around at the assembled crew, Kellon felt an inescapable sense of pride. These people were his family.

"Navigation here, One minute to Jump 2."

At Jump entry, the displays reset and again Kellon felt the queasy twisting sensation ripple through his muscles. The time to exit sped past, and then Roy was announcing what Kellon wanted most to hear.

"Navigation here, the squadron has exited the micro-Jump and all Cruisers are reporting Condition Gold."

"Well done, Navigation. Move us to the extrapolated exit point on the heliopause. Bring us through the boundary and into the heliosphere at that point. Once we are beyond the turbulence, hold our position. "

"Navigation here. Indicating entry into the boundary in five minutes. Turbulence warning is now in effect."

"Lan, pass Navigation's turbulence warning to all cruisers."

As Lan crossed through the interface boundary, Kellon required Tactical to confirm their position relative to the Target, and Lorn was on the problem. "Tactical here, we have re-established track on Target 1. He has maintained his previous trajectory, and we are estimating he will reach the heliopause in

4.62 hours. We are 2,000 kilometers from his projected exit point. Tactical is transferring the refined target vector data to Navigation."

"Navigation, Kellon here. Adjust our position to put the squadron squarely on the extrapolated target trajectory, and then hold that position.

"Lan, clear the forward display. Define the tactical plane where the target trajectory line and our position are on that plane. When the tactical plane is established, freeze its orientation. Next, display a relative-motion polar plot showing the squadron at its center. Compute the direction of relative motion and draw that vector from the target."

When Lan displayed the plot on the bulkhead, he placed one golden icon representing the squadron at its center and placed a blinking red icon representing the target well separated from the squadron. Lan drew a thin red line, representing the line of the direction of relative motion, from the target icon. The red line extended toward the golden icons and continued on to the outer ring of the polar plot. As the squadron slowly maneuvered toward a position on the target's trajectory, Kellon observed the red line slowly pivoting about the red icon and moving gradually toward the golden icon.

"Navigation, Kellon here. Roy, you certainly earned your brew allowance for today's work. Well done."

Roy was intently studying his instrumentation and did not even look up from his console, but Kellon thought he heard an acknowledging grunt and smiled.

"Lan, draw a circle about our position, the radius being our heavy-missile effective range."

As Kellon observed the plot, the red line radiating from the target icon had continued to swing slowly until it bisected the newly added circle and was passing directly through the squadron's icon. "Lan, at the intersection of the target trajectory line and the arc of the heavy-missile effective range nearest the target, draw a sphere. Its radius is to be our effective medium missile range.

Kellon sat, considering the plot. "Lan, now draw a second sphere. Center it about our current position and give it a radius of our medium missile range.

"Lan, within each sphere, draw a disk that is normal to the tactical plane and normal to the target trajectory line. Inscribe an equilateral triangle within each of those disks, where the base of each triangle is parallel with the tactical plane. Designate the upper point of the triangle A, and define the lower points B and C.

As he watched, Lan displayed the defined tactical diagram. After additional study, Kellon nodded his approval. He had adequately defined the kill zone, including the crossfire and blocking structures needed to prevent their quarry from escaping. Once the Elite Guard ship entered within the larger circle, he was not going to exit.

"Lan, transmit the tactical plot to all Cruisers.

Keying his captain's band Kellon began to put his tactical solution into play. "Captain Kylster, I have provided you with a tactical plot for our coordinated attack. During the attack, Lan will coordinate with Lent, and you will coordinate with Lawrence and Langley. The kill volume is the circle denoted by our heavy-missile effective range. You are to move your Cruisers forward and along the target trajectory until you reach the point where it crosses the circle defining the kill zone. At that point, deploy your three Cruisers on points marked A, B, and C. Your Cruisers will be equally spaced in a facing triangle. When you attain your defined positions, hunker down and remain on station in full stealth mode. Do you have any questions so far?"

"No, Sir. I will be in Command of Lar, Lawrence, and Langley. We are to proceed across the kill zone and form into a facing triangle, taking the indicated ambuscade positions, marked A, B, and C."

"Correct. Captain Kylster, once you are in your assigned positions, you will allow the target to approach and pass by, permitting the target to enter into the kill zone. When the target is well within the kill zone, Lent will fire one heavy missile from our position. That missile will be launched passive lock homing.

Kellon's voice was firm as he completed his orders, "Captain Kylster, if the target should detect any of your Cruisers during its approach, or if it detects the inbound heavy missile and attempts to evade, you will take whatsoever action you deem appropriate and necessary to destroy the target. If the heavy missile does not finish the job, you will complete the job using whatever force you deem necessary. No quarter is to be shown the target."

Eurie asked, "Commodore Kellon, who will coordinate Lent's missile firing?"

"Captain Eurie, Lent will set up for the heavy missile launch, but Lan will synchronize Lent's firing. Are there any questions?"

"Sir, Captain Kylster here. Am I to understand if the target does detect my unit, or attempts to evade, we are then in a free play situation, and I can act at my own discretion?"

"Captain Kylster that is correct. Are there any further questions?" There were none. "Ladies and Gentlemen, let's take our positions. Lan, sound squadron battle stations."

Even as the sounds of the battle alarm were fading, Lar, Lawrence, and Langley quickly moved forward while beginning to spread out into a wide facing triangle formation. As the other three Cruisers moved off toward their designated positions, Lan and Lent also moved off the defined target vector. Their assigned positions were below the tactical plane, each moving to their separate designated points, B and C.

"Lan, when we engaged the Arkillians near Earth several years ago, we employed a Zed decoy programmed to appear as a Kreel Gortoga cruiser. Select a Zed decoy and program it with precisely the same profile we used at that time. Advise me when your programming is complete.

"Tactical, what is the status of the Nori ship, is it maintaining a straight run for the heliopause?"

"Tactical here. The Nori is continuing along the shortest path to the heliopause. It is drawing further ahead of the pursuing Elite Guard ships. The Kreel cruiser and its two escorts have reached the planet and are in process of landing."

"Intelligence, Kellon here. Do we have any more information on what's happening on K-9? Have the Elite Guard stopped their interrogations and executions?"

"Intelligence here. We are continuing to monitor our Intelligence probe intercepts from the planet. The arriving Kreel admiral has issued a planetary ultimatum. All Elite Guard units are to return immediately to their facilities and stand down, or else he will render them permanently incapable of any further action whatsoever. It's a hard line showdown and the Kreel commodore has the rank and sheer military power on his side. The question remains to be seen if the Elite Guard junior officers will honor his orders and stand down."

Tactical here. Target 1 is maintaining his trajectory parameters and is forty minutes from entering the forward medium missile sphere. All our Cruisers are on their designated positions and at full stealth mode."

"Sir, Lan here. I have programmed the Zed decoy. I am waiting further instructions."

"Lan, prepare the Zed decoy to broadcast a transmission. The transmission will be audio only and broadcast on the Elite Guard ship-to-ship channel, the same channel that the Elite Guard used in their confrontation with the Kreel cruiser, and also all the identified channels allocated to our special Intelligence probe.

"Immediately notify all Cruisers that I am deploying a Zed decoy and provide them the decoy's complete Kreel identity specifications. After all the Cruisers' acknowledgment of the decoy deployment, launch the decoy. When launched, move the decoy in full stealth mode to the position marked A. Keep the decoy passive and stationary at that point."

"Lan here. All Cruisers have acknowledged receiving the Zed decoy alert. The decoy has been launched."

Kellon felt that same queasy feeling in his stomach, but it was not the result of entering or exiting a micro-Jump, this time it was a simple case of nerves and stress. He looked about the CAC and knew everyone was feeling the tension. He returned his attention to the tactical plot as the red blinking icon entered the small sphere and approached his advanced and hunkered-down Cruisers.

Kellon found himself holding his breath, and he consciously forced his breathing into a deep, regular, and heart-centered rhythm.

"Lan here. Lent is reporting he has a solid passive lock, including thermal, on the target. One heavy missile is set Condition 2."

Patiently, Kellon studied the red blinking icon as it swept past the position of his advanced Cruisers, entering unaware into the defined kill zone. "Lan, put an X on the target vector indicating 85 percent heavy-missile effective range from Lent."

The X immediately appeared on the target vector line. "Lan, when the target reaches the point marked by the X, order Lent to set Condition 1."

The passing of time moved in a traditional snail fashion. "Sir, as instructed, Lent has fired. One heavy missile is away. Passive homing lock is confirmed."

Kellon watched the tactical plot as the blinking golden icon indicating the outbound heavy missile moved away from Lent's position, streaking unerringly toward the distant Elite Guard ship. When the missile reached 20 percent of its intercept run length, Kellon acted. "Lan, activate the Zed decoy! Send on all defined channels, in your best natural Kreel tongue, the following message, "Elite Guard Commander, you are a murderous traitor to the pure blood. The True Blood has only one message for filth like you!

"Lan, when you've sent the message, then secure transmission."

"Lan here, the message has been sent on all designated channels."

"Tactical here. The target has gone active on all his sensors. We are receiving an incoming message on the Kreel hailing frequency. He has detected the Zed decoy and is responding to what he believes is a Gortoga Class cruiser. He is issuing a challenge call. Do you want us to put it on the screen?"

"Tactical, Kellon here. That's not necessary. I've seen quite enough snarling Kreel officers for a long while to come. Besides, the appropriate response to his challenge is already inbound!"

Kellon sat observing the plot. He'd relied on the Kreel commodore's likely reaction and response time to a distinct misdirection. The sudden appearance of a Gortoga cruiser, with its vile challenge, became the only focus of the Elite commodore's attention; Lent's inbound missile was coming in along a very different vector. Kellon judged the Elite Guard commander might not even detect Lent's incoming missile. He was correct; the commander did not.

"Tactical here, indicating one heavy missile hit. The target has gone inert; all indications of propulsion are gone. There is only a weak alert or automatic distress call being broadcast."

"Tactical, Kellon here. That helps. With those challenge broadcasts, we've just provided ample cause for hostilities to become even more intense between the Elite Guard and the Military."

*Dear Susie,* Kellon thought, *I've just poured more fuel on your blazing firestorm.*

"Lan, reset the Zed decoy to stealth settings and proceed with its recovery."

"Tactical here. Two medium missiles, fired by Langley and Lawrence, have hit Target 1. The target has exploded."

"Lan, signal a recall to all Cruisers and form the squadron into our standard four-sided pyramid, set Jump spread.

"Navigation, Kellon here. When the squadron is formed up, bring us about and take us out of K-9. We've caused enough trouble for one day, and it's time we move on to K-23."

As the squadron approached the heliopause, Elayne's clear voice reported, "Tactical here. We are able to report the Nori has reached the heliopause. He is safely clear of the solar system."

# Chapter Forty-Nine:
## Paper Pusher

Mer, Ron, and Dylan— all senior admirals— were in their most casual civilian clothes and at McBride's. It was late afternoon, and each admiral had a full cold brew before him. Three now empty tankards attested to the length of their conversation. They empties were pushed casually back onto the heavily grained solid wood table. The men were the only diners sitting in the snug, cozy, and comfortable rustic corner, back near the large old open stone fire-place. That quiet corner of McBride's was temporarily off limits, by the decree of the proprietor, to anyone not an admiral in the Guardian Force.

McBride had no illusions about the three casually dressed gentlemen seated in his restaurant. Everyone on Glas Dinnein knew them on sight. McBride certainly knew them, they were old shipmates. Their friendship was founded on more than a thousand years of memories of shared dangers and hardships. As long as they chose to sit in his establishment, the back corner was exclusively theirs, even if a hundred people stood outside in a blizzard wanting to come in and eat. That was just the way it was.

Fortunately, like the good businessman he was, McBride knew no one would be waiting this early in the afternoon. Even more to the point, he knew those gentlemen would not knowingly keep anyone waiting while they could help it. They would in all likelihood depart before the dinner rush began. *Besides,* he thought, *there's never been a blizzard in the Capital.*

Moving with the briskness of an old space hand, which he was, McBride went up the two steps into the corner and approached the table. Without fuss, he effortlessly scooped up the spent dishes, swiftly wiped the table clean with his renowned perpetually white towel, and smiled as he proudly asked, "Gentlemen, is there anything else that McBride's can provide at this time?"

Mer looked up with a twinkle in his eyes. McBride was a friend of old, and like each of the admirals, he was a survivor of the battle of Kintana.

"No, McBride, at least not at this moment," Mer answered. However, later a round of hot neab will be in good order."

"Being the gentlemen and scholars that you are, McBride's is at your beckon and call. Three mugs of hot neab coming up. Just wave when you want them," McBride said.

As McBride turned away with his easy burden of gathered dirty dishes, Mer turned back to Ron and Dylan, protesting, "Every time I send Kellon somewhere on a stealth mission he seems to start a war. When we dispatched him to Earth, my orders were explicit and quite clear. He was to remain in full stealth, perform a basic reconnaissance, and then promptly return to Glas Dinnein.

Looking innocently around at his friends, Mer pleaded, "I ask you, can any order be simpler? When he reaches Earth, what does he do? He immediately starts a war with the Arkillians. Now, I send him to perform a simple stealthy deep reconnaissance of the three Kreel Hub planets, and what does he do—"

Ron cut him off with a sharp retort, "Hold fast right there, Mer! A simple deep reconnaissance?

"Mer, the word simple is inappropriately used in such a context. As for what he did, he did what any of us would have happily done, given a similar target of opportunity; he took out an Elite Guard Grand Marshal and nearly took out your Kreel counterpart to boot."

"I second that!" Dylan added, then continued, "I would wager a brew, right here and now, that if you had been in Kellon's place, you would have taken the shot and then stuck around and finished off that Kreel cruiser and its admiral— stealth be dammed!"

Ron held his tankard comfortably in both hands and joined Dylan in his rebuttal, "Admit it, Mer, Kellon at least showed he was keeping to the purpose of his defined mission. He left your counterpart alive."

Mer folded his arms before him and leaned back in his chair. "I'm not convinced. You two will need to offer a better argument than that if you expect to get Kellon off the extra duty roster."

Ron leaned forward briskly countering Mer, "I'll accept that challenge. You want to be convinced? Well, even you must admit, by leaving the senior Kreel admiral alive so the Elite Guard could arrest him, Kellon helped to escalate dissension between the Military and Elite Guard. Of course, I must concede, it does help a little the Military from the outset blames the Elite Guard for the destruction of one fast-attack ship, and severe damage of a cruiser and a second fast-attack."

"I say for Guardian Fleet Operations, bravo for Kellon!" interjected Dylan. "Kellon had a rare tactical opportunity, an offered shot, and in my opinion appropriately took it. In addition, for the first time ever, he demonstrated extraordinary tactics in skillfully using a micro-Jump in actual combat. I say again, bravo Kellon!" Dylan added, while lifting his tankard in salute.

"Mer, give Kellon's squadron some slack. You know it took nerves of steel to sit and watch an Elite Guard ship come as close to his hunkered down Scouts as Kellon did without going to war. I cannot help but wonder that if you were in the same situation, would you have remained as cool?" Ron queried.

Mer sat back and deeply sighed. "No. Both of you know that I would not have remained that passive."

Ron interjected, "While you're recognizing Kellon's coolness under stress, don't forget Commanders Roan and Zorn, and their four Scouts. They were even closer to the Kreel Elite Guard ship than was Lan."

"Hmmmm, it does seem my early reputation has lingered and caught up with me. As a captain, was I really that much of a brawler?" Mer asked earnestly.

Unprompted, both Ron and Dylan responded in an emphatic cheerful chorus, "Yes!"

Mer leaned forward and his voice dropped, "All right, what about K-9? Kellon could have gone his way and utterly ignored that Elite Guard ship. He could have let the Nori, whomever they might be, fend for themselves. He had no obligation to risk his squadron and defend the Nori. Instead, he pushes the envelope and sets up an ambush that to my judgment is well outside the bounds of his mission criteria. How do you two old war horses justify Kellon's action in that event?"

Before answering, Ron sat thoughtfully for a moment. "Well, the Nori is not, strictly speaking, included within his orders. They are an anomaly that you didn't incorporate into the mission matrix. Being outside the matrix, Kellon was in a position to make a command decision."

Dylan was grinning and his eyes were sparkling with the good-natured zest of the debate. "Again bravo, I say. Not only did Kellon discern how they destroyed Lux, he firmly demonstrated one way to defeat their tactics. In doing that, he gave a little payback for Lux, and took out an Elite Guard ship and a senior Elite command officer. Even better, he did it in a way that has only exacerbated the strife between the Kreel Military and the Elite Guard. Disguising that decoy to look like a Kreel Gortoga cruiser was tactically brilliant. Now the entire Kreel Empire believes the True Bloods not only exist, but they are running around in Gortoga Class cruisers."

Ron sat listening, absently watching the moisture condense on the outside of his tankard of cold brew. As he watched, the beads of moisture caught the multicolored refractions of light from the stained glass lampshade suspended over their table; the droplets were flashing like bright liquid jewels flowing down the sides of the tankard.

The admirals delighted in McBride's; it was snug, and reassuringly hospitable. The aroma of meat being grilled over coals of select hardwood easily harmonized with McBride's rustic setting, bringing forth deep-seated racial memories of a million years of hunters cooking their game over open campfires. Being at McBride's was like being home, and its good food— like icing on cake— only added to its rich ambiance.

After a moment, Ron looked up and added, "Dylan has a good point there. Just before Lent's missile took him out, the Elite Guard commodore issued a loud challenge to what he believed was a Gortoga cruiser. Both the Kreel Military and the Elite Guard monitored that brusque challenge. Immediately after the challenge, poof, no more Elite Guard ship or commodore. Cause and effect appear obvious.

Mer leaned forward, speaking seriously, "Ron is it really that obvious? Are we certain about what the Kreel are doing?"

"Yes, Mer, we are. Since the limpet probes were distributed, they have functioned well. From our Intelligence intercepts, we have a good understanding of what's happening. The Kreel have conducted a furious investigation. The location of every Gortoga cruiser in the Kreel fleet has been challenged."

Mer shook his head and chuckled, "Ah, life is so very good. A cold brew and knowing the Kreel are, for the first time in two thousand years, chasing each other in tight circles is wonderful."

Dylan turned to Ron, inquiring, "What, if any, are the answers Kreel command has developed?"

"Well, so far, all those cruisers are accounted for and none have been found to be in the K-9 system, except the one cruiser verified to be on the planet at the time of the attack.

"That accounting of Gortoga cruisers is driving both the Military and the Elite Guard crazy. The entire sequence has caused the Elite Guard to believe there is now a widespread well-organized Military conspiracy and cover-up at work. The Kreel Military command officers, on the other hand, are pulling out their fur and demanding who are the True Bloods, who are their leaders, and how are they remaining so well concealed within the Military?" Ron explained.

"Ron, just how bad is the friction between the Kreel Military and their Elite Guard units?" Mer inquired.

Ron hesitated a moment before answering Mer's question. "Mer, Kellon could not have caused more fury if he'd stuck a stick right in the center of a hornet's nest. Our Intelligence analysts cannot even begin to estimate the damage Kellon has generated within the Kreel Empire. What we can accurately say is the Military and the Elite Guard are now very near open hostility."

This was news to Mer, "Ron, are the Kreel really that stirred up?"

Ron looked up and his expression was serious. "Yes. From what we have learned, there has always been friction between the Military and the Elite Guard. That being true, it's never before reached the levels it's now reaching. Susie's True Blood gambit has introduced a quantum shift in suspicion and paranoia within the Kreel ranks. On the best of occasions, the Kreel are typically at each other's throats. Now that underlying friction is both open and unabated."

Frowning, Mer asked both men, "Should we cancel the strike on K-23?"

Dylan was first to answer the question. "I, for one, believe Kellon should continue with the strike. Seeing what Kellon's already accomplished, I doubt he will move in declaring who he is and where he came from. As long as he can misdirect the Kreel into believing it was either the work of the True Blood or the Nori, then a strike against the production facilities making the Elite Guard ships can only work to our advantage."

Ron looked up and smiled, McBride was approaching with a platter and three more tankards.

"Gentlemen, I have the honor of bearing gifts from afar, a large platter of select cheeses, some select cuts of smoked fish, and another round of brews. They're a compliment from a lovely lady." Saying this, he nodded toward the front door of his establishment. As one, the three men looked and promptly all three smiled broadly.

Mer spoke first, "McBride, if you will, please extend to that especially lovely lady our invitation for her to join us. Unless of course, she considers us too rowdy a bunch for her liking."

"Sir," demurred McBride, "if she has the common sense of a squawking sea bird she will decline your offer. However, as your host I will nevertheless dutifully convey your overtly suggestive offer to the lovely lady." And he did.

Mer, Ron, and Dylan all stood with smiles as they greeted Eryan. Mer pulled out a chair and held it as she bowed her head slightly in acknowledgment and sat down.

"Madam Secretary Admiral, we are honored to have you join us. To what do we owe this unanticipated pleasure?" Mer asked.

As the three men again took their seats, Eryan was smiling and her eyes were sparkling with good humor. "You three reprobates are over here on government time, avoiding answering your communicators, and definitely avoiding your responsibilities. I must also note you are making hardworking representatives of the Planetary Assembly go to extraordinary measures in order to conduct normal business. I have therefore come personally to inform you that those of us who bear the heavy responsibilities of governing have noticed such antics. I have come personally, not to protest too much, but to join you in your hiding out from everyone else."

As she sat down, McBride had placed a tankard of cold brew before her. She lifted it up in salute, "To the Guardian Force!" To that toast, each did gladly join the tribute.

"Well, now that I have successfully tracked, and firmly trapped, all three of you in one place, might I inquire as to what the topic of your intense conversation might be?"

Mer groaned, "Hmmmm, such weighty matters are of a purely military nature and, as such, might be above your level of security classification and need to know."

Eryan deliberately leaned forward, her voice dropping to a serious hush, "Gentlemen, being only a paper pusher and not a military type, be hereby informed I might just retard the funding for forty new Cruisers if I have any further indication of your inhibitions to discuss what I want to hear about."

Mer held both his hands up, palms facing out, "Eryan, we surrender. A wise commander knows when to hold and when to fold."

"Besides," inserted Dylan, "we were discussing your favorite topic of conversation, Kellon's mission into the heart of the Kreel Empire."

# Chapter Fifty:
## Matters of Interest

Leaning back, Eryan slowly scanned the innocent expressions exhibited on the faces of her three friends. "Ah, then my spies were correct, this worthy cloistered group is deeply involved in discussing dark forbidden government secrets. So out with it, just how is Kellon doing?"

Ron was the first to pick up Eryan's gauntlet, "Well, so far he's remaining slightly outside the consequences of a general court-martial— but just barely. The pending charges are for insubordination and violations of direct orders. Mer and I are debating which of us should bring the formal charges against him, and to decide who is to stand by to assure he is properly flogged and keelhauled."

Eryan slowly put her brew down, and she sternly looked at the three admirals. "Gentlemen, the day those charges are brought against Kellon is the day you all should be retiring to your cabins in the mountains. Be ye hereby duly warned! We of the Planetary Assembly have our favorites, and we intend to protect them from jealous criticism and unwarranted assaults by old military fossils."

With a mock voice of hurt indignation, Mer retorted. "Eryan, now you may be going too far. Must I remind you, as dashing young officers, we three gentlemen once signed your dance card at some rather impressive military balls?"

Ron leaned forward, adding in his own defense, "If we are now to be cast as fossils, doesn't that rather suggest you are also somewhat like a fossil?"

Eryan lifted her chin. Her expression took on the serenity of aloofness. "Sir, you are certainly well enough informed and aware that ladies never become fossils. It's strictly against the rules. But now putting aside such matters and moving to the more serious issues, how is Kellon really doing?"

"Well, Eryan, currently he has departed K-9 and is en route to K-23. All his reports indicate he remains undetected. The real challenge is just ahead of him. Truthfully, the squadron is a long way from home, and the nearer Kellon comes to K-23, the higher are his risks... and so are our concerns," Mer said.

Sipping from her tankard of brew, Eryan smiled. It was cold and refreshing. "Gentlemen, I believe Commodore Kellon has repeatedly proven his capability. If anyone can successfully accomplish his mission, he will. I've been reading the reports you sent over. It seems the limpet project far exceeded all of our expectations. If I have my data correct, we have successfully inserted Intelligence probes into all but seven of the Kreel's planetary systems. Even more impressive, 97 percent of the ships those limpets were placed on were destroyed, and the remainder were damaged so badly that they could not be rebuilt.

"Ron, do your intercepts still indicate the Kreel are blaming the True Bloods for this wholesale destruction of their merchant fleet?" Eryan asked.

"Yes, at least so far. The Kreel have figured out how the limpets worked, but they haven't worked out where and how they were attached to the ships," Ron answered.

Eryan smiled, "Then I am correct to assume that the Kreel haven't a clue about the Intelligence probes that each limpet carried with them. So far all they think was involved was the intentional destruction of their freighters?"

"Eryan, you're correct, at least to the best of our knowledge. The good news is that the loss of three hundred freighters has definitely put a big hole in their merchant fleet, unfortunately not a fatal one," Dylan replied.

Looking toward Eryan, Mer expanded on Dylan's information, "The damages the Kreel have sustained during the past year are to more than just their merchant fleet. They've also suffered significant losses in their Military and Elite Guard combat forces. That's particularly true near Scion. By any measure, Guardian Force has extracted a deadly toll on the Kreel Empire during the past twelve months."

"Eryan," Dylan commented, "from the Fleet Operations side of things, it's noteworthy one of the first effects of that damage is the lessening of Kreel attacks within our own volume of space."

Dylan's comment brought a frown to Eryan's countenance, "Yes, Dylan, I've taken notice of that by-product of our success. I also add here, so has Rich Sumor, our Chief Administrator. He's using the reduction in Kreel attacks to begin a political backpressure to the expenditures of the Guardian Force, especially those caused by recent increases in spending for research and refits. He is specifically complaining about the increased costs of the Cruiser force. He isn't going to let such a topic alone, and if he can drive a wedge in the Assembly, he will."

"Varmints are going to be varmints, Eryan. That is the way of all worlds. Rich Sumor is simply a thorn on the shrubbery of government. As such, he is a nuisance to be expected and moved either over or around." Mer growled.

Ron brightened, "You can effectively neutralize him. What I really want to know is how is Megan developing?"

Eryan leaned back, and a smile replaced her earlier frown. "Ron, you have just raised a topic that's close to my heart. I have Susie over there representing the Planetary Assembly and looking the planet over. I can't remember seeing anyone so happy while doing a hard job. She is truly remarkable."

"Well, don't just sit there smiling and saying nothing," urged Mer, "how is the project going?"

Eryan reached out and selected a slice of smoked fish, taking a small bite with a sip of cold brew, and then she responded.

"Gentlemen, Megan is one of the most beautiful planets that I have ever seen. It's a naturalist's dream and it's unspoiled. There are high mountains, fertile valleys and forests, broad oceans filled with every manner of creature. There are some dangerous animals, but with the proper precautions, we are relocating and protecting them. We've just completed the first detailed surveys, and we are now beginning to develop the settlement schedules. Susie told me she has already put her personal chit in for a particular piece of the landscape near an ocean. She told me it reminds her of the California Central Coast, where she lived on Earth."

"How soon will it be before settlers start arriving?" Dylan asked. "Not long at all. Susie has reported we will be ready for the first wave of settlers within six months. Preparing for the migration to Megan, Earth governments have a well-defined migration program in place, and there are thousands of eager applicants. The problem will not be to find new settlers, but to be certain we've allocated for balanced settlements, where we cover the population's needs for necessary skills."

Dylan shook his head in wonderment. "That we are developing a new planet in our planetary community is remarkable. Given the realities of the Kreel conflict and threat, I never believed I would live to see such an occurrence."

In a reflective tone, Mer added, "I find it hard to believe that only a few years ago we were looking at a strange ungainly primitive interstellar probe, a subluminal probe at that, entering our solar system. Earth? Who could have imagined sending Kellon to Earth would make so great a difference? Now we have the Kreel on the retreat, we've most likely found our fabled first home world, and even have new people coming from Earth to settle in the neighborhood. I, for one, had not the slightest concept of what would unfold when we sent Lan to perform that supposedly covert surveillance."

Turning to Ron, Mer asked about one of his favorite topics. "Might I inquire, Ron, how is the research into longevity treatments for Susie coming?"

Putting down his tankard, Ron sighed and sat a moment pondering how best to answer. "As you mandated, I have remained actively involved in the project. I can report the researchers are carefully proceeding. They even have a small team on Scion working with the Arkillians on the problem. We are quickly learning the Arkillians are very astute, both as researchers and as traders. While they are obviously grateful for our defeating the Kreel invasion, their natural proclivity is to trade. From what I'm hearing, they're sensing there might be a nice profit lurking somewhere in the research. Our team on Scion says the progress has been exceedingly slow."

Anyone listening would have sworn Mer growled. "I will have a communication off to Kur in the morning, and underscore that the research is to help Susie, to whom the Arkillians are particularly indebted. I believe Kur will understand and be able to cut through the tangle of greed that may be forming around this matter. If the Arkillians have critical knowledge, then the Arkillians will freely provide it!"

"I have a question," Eryan asked. "How is Lux coming along in his restoration?"

"I can answer that," responded Dylan. "At the current moment, Lux and his Scouts have passed all psychological testing and returned to full duty. He's currently going through shakedown maneuvers while filling out his new crew compliment. I was over to visit last week; I'm able to say with certainty that I've seldom been aboard a Cruiser with as much sense of purpose as Lux is showing. He knows his purpose and is eager to be at that task. I can guarantee that any Kreel ship he encounters will have a serious attitude problem on its hands."

Ron turned in his chair and caught McBride's attention. He waved, and McBride nodded in understanding. "Well, Ladies and Gentlemen, I have just signaled for the hot neab to be parceled out. I suggest we gentlemen split the damages."

McBride brought the mugs of hot neab in a swirl of fragrance, settled the bill with a smile exchanged for a chit, and then quickly departed.

"Gentlemen," Eryan thoughtfully asked, "why is Kellon being sent to K-23, with orders to storm and board a Kreel ship in pursuit of archaeological treasure?"

With Eryan's quietly asked question, Ron quickly stood. "Oops, it's really time for me to head for home and bed. It has been truly an enjoyable afternoon."

"Not quite so fast, Fleet Intelligence Admiral Ron Cloud! Just park yourself in that chair. There is a question on the table, and I believe your input is of some importance in the matter now before us," Eryan challenged.

With a deep sigh, and a warning I-told-you-so glance toward Mer, Ron resumed his seat, but he said nothing.

Eryan looked from one admiral to the other, and when she came to Mer, she noticed he was, like Ron and Dylan, remaining stubbornly silent.

"As the Guardian Fleet admiral, Admiral Mer Shawn, perhaps you will explain to me Lan's mission to K-23."

Turning slowly to squarely face Eryan, Mer inquired, "Are you asking as a friend or as the Planetary Secretary Admiral?"

"Does it matter?" Eryan retorted.

With a sigh of exasperation, Mer answered. "In fact, no. Lan's orders, as you suggestively imply, to storm and board came from me. While Ron and I have discussed the matter, I bear the full responsibility for issuing those orders. Although my reasoning is based on precise Intelligence reports, I admit my orders are the product of introspection, rather than strict military analysis."

The frown returned to Eryan's countenance, "Mer, your orders are not being questioned. You have often been in combat. You fully understand the extreme risks to life and limb that go along with any close order engagement. When I read your orders, I could but wonder what could possibly be so important about archaeological treasures? Why would you put five Cruisers at mortal risk so far from home?"

Looking somewhat more at ease, Mer answered, "I am reluctant to say that my orders are merely the product of a hunch, but in some ways that might be the best manner to describe them. Eryan, it's not my personal estimate of the value of the artifacts that is important, it's the Kreel Elite putting a so all-fired high value on them that makes them worth the risk. What we're missing in all of our analysis is our ability to answer one question, why! What do we really know of the roots of the Kreel? We believe they are the end products of a long genetic manipulation process, but begun by who and why?"

Dylan rose to Mer's defense, "There's an old military axiom: know your enemy. I firmly believe those archaeological artifacts may provide us some insight and a better understanding of the Kreel. If nothing else, it will deny the Elite on Hub-3 their treasure."

"Eryan," Ron inserted, "If Kellon can make it to appear the True Bloods took the prize, then the Elite will undoubtedly go wild. They might begin a purge of the Military looking for the True Blood, and that could ignite a civil war. In effect, the artifacts represent a catalyst to the further disruption of the Kreel Empire."

After a long pause, Eryan looked from one admiral to the next. "Dear friends. The many years of our lives have given us the opportunity to demonstrate by our action our values and convictions. Long ago, we declared our convictions and established our reputations, at least to everyone of any concern. I did not come here this afternoon to challenge your judgment. I came today for only two reasons, to share the afternoon with dear friends, and to inquire as to matters of a personal interest. If I have stepped on your toes, then I ask for your pardon."

Now Mer looked somewhat uncomfortable, "Madam Secretary Admiral, you are among your friends. The day has not come, nor do I believe such a day will ever come, when you need to ask for our pardon."

"Well-said, Mer," added Dylan.

"You can also add my agreement to what Mer just said," agreed Ron.

With a flourish, the three admirals stood and slightly bowed toward Eryan. Mer queried, "Might three dashing and handsome admirals of the Guardian Force have the distinct honor of seeing you to your means of conveyance?"

Smiling broadly, Eryan gracefully stood and extended her arm, which Mer gently accepted. "Then off we go," intoned Mer, with a formal tenor of absolute solemn authority.

McBride observed the gestures among his four friends and smiled. There were many reasons why the entire planet—including McBride— loved those four people. Nodding in pleasure, he moved to the door and opened it with as grand a flourish as he was able to manage. The four stylishly exited the establishment, waving as they did, and proceeded out onto the grounds. Eryan's security officer was on his job, and he deftly moved to open the rear door of her official vehicle.

As Eryan waved goodbye and her vehicle pulled away, the three admirals stood thoughtfully observing the vehicle as it merged with the late afternoon traffic flowing along the coastal highway.

"There," sighed Mer, "goes a very extraordinary, intelligent, and lovely woman."

# Chapter Fifty-One:
# Out in Front

It had required a two month journey for the squadron to move from K-9 through Kreel space and reach K-23. One beneficial byproduct of the transit was to bring the squadron tangentially nearer to Glas Dinnein. Along the new route, the five Cruisers deployed numerous Navigation Beacons and steadily added to their expanding survey of Kreel space. As was Kellon's tendency for establishing multiple paths and backups, he divided his survey force in two to follow widely separated and parallel routes. Having two routes meant having options, and deep within Kreel space, Kellon wanted options. Kellon had multiple goals, and while his immediate orders pointed him directly at the hazards surrounding K-23, his ultimate intention remained bringing his squadron safely back to Glas Dinnein.

During the transit from K-9, Kellon and his captains took advantage of the time and worked daily on contingency tactics for their pending campaign. When the squadron arrived in the K-9 solar system, they still had more than two weeks before the scheduled departure of the ship carrying the artifacts. After entering the heliosphere, eighty degrees below the ecliptic plane, Kellon promptly deployed a carefully programed Zed decoy that moved independently to a holding position near the heliopause and the ecliptic plane and then went into a stationary passive monitoring mode.

As the squadron continued inward toward the primary and its inner planets, all the squadron's passive sensors were set to their broadest bandwidth and maximum sensitivity. Upon reaching the inner system, the squadron hunkered down in a defensive spread, located slightly below the ecliptic plane and two AU distant from the target planet. From that vantage point, the squadron began systematically deploying full spectrum intelligence gathering probes toward the target planet. To all appearances, the planet was a beautiful world, with expansive oceans and five separate continents. Each of the continents displayed high mountain ranges, broad forests, and open grassland. The planet was not densely populated and there were only a few large cities. The squadron settled into data gathering and analysis, and the days quickly passed. As the time of the pending strike drew near, the tensions within the squadron gradually elevated.

Lan had tightly secured the protective petals of the conference room dome and illuminated the room with the warm light of a spring morning. Elayne took her seat and placed a sizable folder containing the interim results of her long hours of analysis on the conference table before her. With a firm and confident voice, she began her presentation to Commodore Kellon, Roy, Lorn, Roan, and Zorn.

"Sir, since we entered the heliosphere eighteen days ago, we have collected all available data on Elite Guard propulsion signatures. Although the data available is sparse, it has enabled us to identify the Elite Guard ship manufacturing facilities."

"Elayne," Zorn asked, "how many Elite Guard ship signatures in total have you detected since our arrival?"

"Sir, only seven signatures have been located. All seven were maneuvering near the planet."

Zorn frowned, "Are they scattered or localized?"

Elayne smiled, "Sir, they are both scattered and localized, depending on when we are observing them. Over the past days, we've tracked the ships both near the planet and in the nearby space about the planet. None of those we've tracked ventured very far and all eventually landed at one of four different sites. We've tracked five ships at one location and one in two other locations.

One of the ships we observed departed from the fourth site of interest and did not return to that site. After a short flight, that one ship landed at one of the other identified sites. The fourth site is of considerable interest— it's where we are detecting occasional and intermittent low levels of propulsion signatures. One problem we have is determining if we are observing five separate ships at one site, or one ship flown five times—"

"Lan here! I regret my interruption. However, I have received an update from Lar. He has detected and is tracking a group of three Elite Guard ships just entering the heliosphere, at azimuth seventy-two degrees and forty-five degrees in elevation. They are escorting a ship of similar size, but its propulsion signature is unclassified. It is most likely a cargo ship. They appear to be in a direct approach to K-23, and Lar estimates the ships will reach the planet in thirty-seven hours."

"Thank you, Lan, you may have just provided the missing data we require to understand what's happening here," Kellon said.

"Roy," asked Kellon, "if we had a ship arriving from a long-Jump out of Hub-3, then what azimuth would that ship most likely enter the heliosphere?"

Pausing for a moment of reflection before responding, Roy answered, "Sir, an azimuth of about seventy degrees, more or less."

"Given that we're four days short of the scheduled departure of our quarry, it might be that the quarry is the escorted unknown ship now arriving. Whatever it is, apparently the Elite Guard Command considers its value sufficient to warrant three Elite Guard escorts. It will be interesting to see where it decides to land once it arrives on the planet.

"Elayne, since you were interrupted, is there anything else you want to add concerning your analysis?"

"No, Sir. I had fairly well completed my summation."

"As a sociologist, can you throw any light on the inhabitants of K-23? Are they strictly Kreel?" Roan asked.

Elayne took a deep breath before she answered, "Sir, I would rather like to reserve my conclusions on that topic. We know the Kreel genetically manipulate their own life-forms. What I'm observing at this time on K-23 indicates several distinct social hierarchies, and the data reveals both social and economic stress exists within the population. Since we don't know much about the general Kreel culture, it may only represent a normal structuring of the Kreel population. It could, however, indicate a subordinated population, or a group of Kreel specifically bred for some special work. Given the broad scope of even the limited data we've collected, meaningful analysis will require significant effort and considerable time. I'm simply not able to provide you a better answer at this time."

"Elayne, when your analysis is finally complete, I am requesting my name be at the top of your report distribution list."

Kellon said. "Lorn, do we have the manufacturing facilities fully identified and pinpointed?"

"Sir, we do believe we've located their primary facility. We've mapped in detail the communications and power distribution nodes on the planet. By combining power consumption and our observation of Elite Guard ship flight patterns, the power consumption to population curves on the fourth site that Elayne mentioned is far above the normal when compared with the other three sites. We've therefore concluded the fourth site is the probable main production facility and the remaining three are post production installation and verification sites. We believe the Kreel are likely to install the auxiliary sensors and weapons systems only after they've first installed and certified the ship power, propulsion, and life support systems. As Elayne has indicated, we are monitoring three landing sites, which we believe is where the Kreel install and test the auxiliary systems. The busiest site, where the five signatures were observed, is the probable final testing and initial crew shakedown facility."

"Lorn, how long will it take you to complete your analysis?" Kellon asked.

"Sir, to confirm our hypotheses, we are currently gathering high-resolution structural and topographical data on all the sites. We hope to have conclusive results within the next ten hours."

"Lorn, with your current rate of data acquisition, how soon can you provide us with specific targeting information for our strike?"

"Sir, we will need at least another eighteen hours of data processing to achieve complete targeting data. Even then, we will be updating targeting data up to and including the time of the strike."

"Our time is running thin, Lorn. Stay on the data. Before we initiate the strike, I require simulator time for our Cruisers. I therefore want your initial targeting results on my desk within twelve hours.

"Also, put some additional detectors and Kreel language filters to the task of monitoring the approaching Elite Guard ships. Especially watch the main Military channels for any references to these approaching ships. I want to know who they are and why they are here."

"Yes, Sir. We will put on the additional monitors and tighten up the analysis."

Kellon sat for a moment, reflecting on his next step. "Roan, are all the Scouts at full readiness?"

"Sir, they are. Shey has gone over each Scout with a micrometer and each is reporting they are fully functional and fully armed. Sir, the squadron's Scouts and crews are ready."

Turning back to Lorn, Kellon asked, "Has Tactical detected any sign of heavy space defense ground installations anywhere near the identified target areas?"

"No, Sir."

"Has Tactical identified the base or bases of the Kreel Military on K-23? If so, how near to our four Elite Guard sites are they?"

"Sir, from our current data, there appears to be two bases used by the Kreel Military, one in the northern hemisphere and the other in the southern hemisphere. We have observed Tuen Class ships departing from both; however, the majority has departed from the northern hemisphere. What we are observing is a typical Kreel Military deployment pattern within the system. There are three Tuen Class fast-attacks distributed and patrolling within the inner planets and another six dispersed fast-attacks in the outer system. We are tracking three cruisers, one of them is patrolling within the inner planets, and the remaining two cruisers are moving out from the planet and toward the heliosheath. Having said this, given their locations, once any strike area sounds an alert, the Kreel Military on their planetary bases can quickly reach any of our four designated target sites."

Sitting in thought, Kellon considered the scope of the briefing. Then, looking up, he addressed Lorn. "When you direct the next low level surveillance probes close to the planet, to collect their ground imaging data, be certain to obtain full details on the two Military facilities. I want to know how many Military ships, and of what class, are still on the ground."

"Yes, Sir. I anticipate that information can be obtained within the next ten hours."

Turning toward Commander Grey, Kellon ordered, "Roy, we will need to observe precisely where that group of new arrivals touches down. After they land, plan to move the squadron to a position nearer to the planet. That position is to be above the ecliptic plane, where we can move out in front of a ship departing the planet on a trajectory reciprocal to the inbound ships. Our position must be near enough to permit us to maneuver ahead of the quarry if it departs along another vector."

"Yes, Sir. I recommend we move to a point 1.5 AU from the planet and on an azimuth of fifty degrees.

"That is acceptable. We need to be out in front, not playing catch-up."

"Yes, Sir," Roy acknowledged.

"Lan, advise all the Cruisers we are relocating to a position 1.5 AU from the planet. Every Cruiser is to confirm their stealth protocols."

"Yes, Sir."

Sitting back, Kellon looked around the conference table. "We've come a very long way since entering this system, yet we have a great deal more to do. Thank you for your precise reports. Unless any of you have questions, this meeting is adjourned."

As Roan and Zorn departed the conference room and headed back toward Shey, Zorn was troubled. "Roan, I'm having a problem seeing how Kellon is going to pull this entire thing off."

Both Roan and Zorn stepped to the side of the passageway, opening a way for a group of crewmen to pass, and then resumed their walk. As they reached the elevator, Roan pressed the elevator activation pad. "Like you, I have a number of questions I'm concerned about. What in particular sticks out in your problem-solving mind?

"Well, how can we intercept an escorted ship and also hit the planet? Do we do them at the same time, or do we do them sequentially, and if so, in what order?"

"Hmmm, I would wager a cold brew we could do it in either fashion. However, I suspect Kellon will focus on the ship, since that target is mobile and the planet isn't going anywhere. Therefore, I believe we will first hit the ship and its escort, and then move to strike the planet."

As the elevator doors slid open, they entered and selected the hangar deck. The elevator dropped smoothly to the second deck and its doors glided open. Roan and Zorn exited, turning toward Shey's hangar. Zorn was still frowning. "Well, suppose we hit the ship first. That amount of activity is going to set off every alarm in the entire Kreel quadrant and every defense on the planet. The

Kreel will immediately launch every available Military asset. Those assets will be moving into prearranged defensive positions or else moving to engage whoever attacked the Elite Guard ships. The entire system is quickly going to become a very intense and bristling area. Also, I don't understand how he's going to use the Scouts in the coming fracas."

As they entered the hangar, Roan stopped and turned toward Zorn as he thoughtfully answered his question, "Zorn, I would wager six cold brews here and now Kellon doesn't yet know what he will do. He is most likely looking for options, but until he has the analysis of the surveillance probes, he's limited in his ability to plan. When he receives all the data, then he will go to work. As for the Scouts, we may sit this one out. Kellon doesn't like to expose us this near any Kreel controlled planet. I think Hub 2 was an exception— not his normal tactic."

Zorn smiled, "Well I'll wager a single cold brew he does use the Scouts."

"Zorn you can't possibly know Kellon will do that. The odds are 50 percent at best."

"Shucks, I may not know he'll use the Scouts, but I do know he seemed very interested in knowing the Scouts were ready. As I recall your response, we are ready. As for me— I'm, of course, always ready."

Crossing the short gangway, Zorn exclaimed with a cheery greeting, "Hey, Shey. Wake up lazy head, we're home again!"

# Chapter Fifty-Two:
# **Battle Stations**

Following the meeting with Kellon, Lorn returned to his office. The work area was always orderly, yet it typically contained a copious number of printed reports and folders. As he looked about, he mused, *With all our reliance on artificial intelligence and computer power, why is there still the need for file cabinets? It must be something about our need to hold something tangible in our hands, rather than rely only on something that flickers on a screen and then disappears.*

With a deep sigh, he returned his attention to the assigned task. "Lan, I know you're up to your limits with your current work load, however, might I ask if the Scouts have some AI time available for Tactical?"

"Sir, I am currently showing a 47 percent idle time in my Scout AI processing capability. May I be of assistance?"

"Now that you ask, the volume of incoming data has completely swamped my staff, and we could definitely use some help. I would appreciate your transferring all the analysis of high-resolution images to the Scouts. We need to identify the strike points on the planet, and there isn't much time remaining for the job."

"Sir, I will ask Shey to advise Commander Roan of your need. I am confident that you will have the support you require."

"Thank you, Lan, for the help. Also, Commodore Kellon's orders concerning intercepts relating to the inbound Elite Guard ships need attention."

"Sir, I monitored his orders and have already directed the necessary assets to go on line, which is why my resources are currently limited."

"Excellent, Lan, I hoped that you would be out in front of my asking you. If you do detect any related traffic on those three ships, please send me a priority copy of the intercepts. Lorn out."

As he turned to the top folder on his desk, Lorn's communicator signaled an incoming message. Reaching out, he touched the accept pad. "Tactical here."

"Lorn, Roan here. Shey just told me that you're over your head in analysis and could use some extra eyes. If there's anything the Scouts can do to help, we're at your service."

"Thank you, Roan. I can use all your guys and gals, and I could use as much of that help as you can spare. I'm receiving an enormous quantity of high resolution data, including target area images, communications networks, and power distribution node information. I would like to transfer all the visual images to the Scouts, if possible."

"Glad to assist Lorn. Have Lan transfer the data to Shey, and she will route it out to the other girls. What in particular are you looking for?"

"I need you to go over each of the four primary sites of interest, and the two Military bases, with a micrometer. I need an analysis of target priorities based on their importance, including possible ground fortifications, near space and otherwise. I also need to define what buildings are on each site, their type of construction, and possible use. Of particular importance is isolating the primary manufacturing buildings. How many ships are at each of the four main sites? When those are completed, turn your attention to the two military bases. Isolate grounded ships, command and control, primary defense sensors, communications nodes, headquarter structures, storage facilities, bunkers, defensive weapons installations, and all troop barracks.

"Since there are eight Tuen Class on patrol in the system, there may be as many as sixteen more on the ground. I need to know precise numbers and exact locations. These are my first requests."

"Understood. We will go to work and give you an update as soon as we have one to give. Roan out."

"Sir, Lan here. I have monitored your conversation with Commander Roan. I am now copying all the referenced data to Shey. Is there anything else I might do to assist?"

"Thank you, Lan. That will be quite satisfactory for now. Tactical out."

"Computer, display an X-Y plot of the solar system using the plane of the ecliptic as the reference plane. Display all Kreel ships." The large full bulkhead screen blossomed into brightness and Lorn carefully studied the chart. His initial interest was on the three Tuen Class fast-attack ships then moving on patrol within the inner planets. When the strike on K-23 started, those ships would promptly respond. The patrolling cruiser represented his most pressing concern. What was its patrol pattern?

"Computer, display the track lines for each Kreel ship within the inner planets for the past four hours...."

Following the meeting, Kellon had retired to his own conference room and considered the developing tactical problem. He didn't know the disposition of the Kreel forces, but he'd already reached some preliminary conclusions.

"Lan, where is Roy?"

"Sir, he is currently in his quarters and working at his desk."

"Lan, tell him I need to speak with him."

Promptly, the bulkhead monitor sparkled into a bright three-dimensional image of Roy, who was then grinning. "Sir, if I recall correctly, we just met in the domed conference room a few minutes ago. How may I be of assistance?"

"Roy, when we captured the Kreel cruiser and then boarded the Gola, you selected two officers to lead that boarding mission. We are about to board and storm a Kreel ship this time. I can summarize what we'll find on board that ship in one word—trouble. For the Gola you assigned Lieutenant Oster to head the overall operation and engineering group and Lieutenant Shem to head the security party. Do you believe these two officers are capable of leading the boarding operation on a Kreel ship?"

Roy's expression immediately lost all hint of merriment. "Sir, they are both fine officers. I can and do highly recommend them for such a mission. Might I also add here, the Kreel ship isn't the Gola."

"Roy your answer suggests you've given this matter prior consideration. What's troubling you?"

"Sir, the Kreel ship's crew compliment and internal organization are totally unknown, and we don't have the slightest idea of what may be on that ship. I'm concerned on just how you intend to take and board that ship, and I keep getting the same answer. I believe you intend to use the Arkillian's anti-Kreel beam. If you do, then we're in deep and dangerous space. You won't be able to leave any meaningful trace of that ship for the Kreel to examine and learn what happened."

Kellon frowned. "Roy, I do intend to use the anti-Kreel beam. It's the only safe way to suppress the ship's crew before boarding. As for not leaving any trace, we'll need to set sufficient demolitions charges throughout the ship and on its propulsion system to completely take it out."

Roy sat for a moment in thought, "Sir, we are also being asked to find and to recover archaeological artifacts about which we know nothing, not even where to look for them. Given sufficient time, we could undoubtedly rummage the entire ship, however, this solar system belongs to the Kreel, and they're not going to give us a great deal of time."

Kellon sighed inwardly; Roy was hitting squarely on all of his own concerns. "You are correct; we will not be given much time. Even with five Cruisers, we're too far from Glas Dinnein to permit the Kreel drawing us into a major firefight or trying to defend the barricades. To be successful, we will need to make the hit, deploy some misdirection, blame someone else, and quickly clear the area before it can become a firefight with Kreel reinforcements.

"Sir, there's another troubling issue. Do you remember what Lorn and his team found on board the captured Kreel cruiser? Sir, may I point out that what's on board the Kreel ship may be much worse than what Lorn found on that cruiser, much worse!"

He did remember what the Kreel had done to the Gola's crew, and it was something he would never forget. "Roy, if that turns out to be true, there's nothing we can do now. When we arrive home, then we can address those counseling matters. For now, alert Lieutenant Oster he will be heading the overall boarding operation and the engineering group. Have him begin planning for the destruction of that ship. Notify Lieutenant Shem he will be in charge of the storming party.

"If we hold one of our squads in reserve, do you believe we can successfully storm the Kreel ship with three squads?"

"Sir, given what we don't know, I don't have a clue if three squads will be sufficient. I suggest we have two squads from one of the other Cruisers transfer over to Lan. That will give us a total of six squads, four squads to make the initial boarding, and two squads in reserve. Six squads should suffice. If not, then we are barking up the wrong tree and need to promptly cut our losses and clear the area."

"Roy, as always, your insights are valued. I will need to speak with you about our evasion route, but that can wait until later. Kellon out."

For the next hour, Kellon held a tight link conference with his four captains. Then, he ordered Cruisers Langley and Lawrence each to provide a squad of their armed troopers to reinforce Lan's troops for the storm and boarding operation. As the squadron continued to observe and monitor the system, the tensions on board continued to mount.

Lorn had been working more than ten straight hours, and the fragmentary answers he so desperately sought slowly began to fill in the overall mosaic of the strike. In particular, he held one fragmentary item to be critical. "Lan, if Commodore Kellon is available, please inform him I have a piece of intelligence that may be critical. I believe he needs to see it as quickly as possible."

"Certainly, Commander Shaw. Commodore Kellon is in his quarters, but is working at his desk and I am confident he will speak to you promptly."

As Lorn's bulkhead screen flickered into activity, Kellon's features expanded into view, and Lorn thought, *He looks tired.*

"Good evening, Lorn. Lan tells me you have something new of importance?"

"Yes, Sir. Those additional detectors and translators we put on line to evaluate the approaching Elite Guard ship proved beneficial. I have intercepts indicating the escorted ship is bringing a very high-ranking Elite official, someone of significant importance on Hub-3. All the Kreel are showing extreme levels of deference. The most important item is there are crews on board the inbound ship to take delivery of the new Elite Guard ships. I am not certain yet if they're complete crews, or else simply crews for ferrying the ships to Hub-3. What's definite is that there are twelve new certified Elite Guard ships sitting on the planet just waiting to depart. With the three escorts, that means there could be as many as fifteen Elite Guard ships escorting the target on its way out of the system."

"Lorn, how many more hours do we have before the ships reach the planet?"

Lorn looked at his data screens, and then back to the monitor, "I'm currently estimating nineteen hours."

Kellon sighed and sat back. "Lorn, I am tasked with two parts of this mission. Admiral Mer Shawn did not specify which is the more important. Fifteen escorts can significantly complicate matters. Focus on anything you can find concerning the outfitting of those twelve new Elite Guard ships, such as— are they fully armed? Are they simply being conveyed to their base of operations, or will they depart with full trained crews on board?"

"Sir, I will immediately put the analysts on the job. Sir, regarding your orders about targeting data, Commander Roan and the Scouts have used our latest intelligence information and identified all critical target strike points. They've accomplished a precise job, and have already uploaded their results into Lan's target matrix file. As for the Military, we have one Gortoga cruiser and nine Tuen Class ships sitting on the ground. In addition to the twelve completed Elite Guard ships, there are six more nearing completion at the three outfitting sites and about ten more in various stages of construction at the fourth site."

Frowning, Kellon looked grim. "This mission seems to just get better and more complicated. Lorn, thank you. Kellon out."

Sitting quietly at his desk, Kellon watched the monitor screen as Lorn's image faded and he considered his next action. Standing, he moved over to his low side-table and couch and sat down again. "Lan, please put on something in the way of a small quartet, something that soft. Then, ask the Officers' Mess to send up a hot thermos of neab and an Earth-style sandwich."

Again, Kellon looked at the image on the bulkhead of Lan positioned before the Earth and its large bright moon. The contrasting images of that planet and its moon silhouetted against the background of space formed one of his favorite pictures. He thought, *So little time has passed since we took that photograph, and yet so much has happened.*

As he sat listening to the music, he acknowledged his two missions. Getting his squadron home intact, however, remained his highest priority. He couldn't risk leaving anyone behind, or leave any hard evidence for the Kreel as to who'd hit the planet.

The addition of fifteen Elite Guard ships to the escort of his primary target created a puzzle he needed quickly to resolve.

It was his command responsibility to determine how to complete the mission successfully. To be successful, he knew a large dose of misdirection was necessary, and if they were to be successful, then that dose was required very soon.

The requested thermos of neab with sandwich arrived, and as Kellon enjoyed them, he continued to ponder his tactical problems. For an hour, Kellon sat intensely working the problem in every way he could, looking for the combination of actions that when taken together in the proper order would permit the completion of his mission and keep their covert cover, while giving the squadron the best chance for survival.

Finally, he looked up and sighed. "Well Lan, we have a job to do."

"Yes, Sir," Lan acknowledged.

Standing up, he slowly bent forward, his palms touching the floor, and then he stretched upward, raising his arms over his head. Then he completely relaxed his body and centered his mind. Straightening, he turned with grim determination toward his compartment door and the CAC, ordering, "Lan, sound battle stations!"

# Chapter Fifty-Three:
# Level the Playing Field

As Kellon entered the CAC, others were hurrying to their stations— including Roy. As he relieved the duty Navigation Officer, Roy looked up to Kellon with a quizzical look and a slight grin. Whatever was happening, it did not matter. He was ready.

Lorn was next to arrive, entering the CAC even as the battle stations alarm faded. He quickly joined Elayne and the others at Tactical. After a brief review of the status and threat screens, he looked up toward Kellon with a questioning expression, but said nothing.

Kellon sat down in his command chair. He keyed the captains, command, and general announcement circuits. "Attention, all Cruisers, Kellon here. Squadron Tactical has informed me that the inbound Elite Guard ships are escorting a transport ship carrying a very high-ranking Elite official from Hub-3. That transport is also bringing crews for twelve new Elite Guard ships— now completed on the planet and ready for delivery. This means that upon its departure, fifteen Elite Guard ships might be escorting our target. I don't like those odds. Therefore, we are going to level the playing field, here and now.

"We are about to hit the planet hard, before the Elite Guard ships arrive, and then move off and hunker down. Lan will provide each Cruiser with his designated targets, and Cruisers will be operating in pairs, except for Lan.

"We will approach our designated targets in full stealth mode, obtain optimum firing positions just above the atmosphere, and then execute a coordinated maximum laser barrage against specific and defined ground targets. We will sustain each barrage for sixty seconds. Thereafter, we will immediately move to secondary designated targets. Once there, we will repeat the barrages. I stress, sixty seconds over any single target— not one second more. We are not going to loiter around and invite counterfire. Each Cruiser will activate all point defenses and countermeasures. Tactical targeting data will soon follow. Kellon out."

"Navigation, Roy, bring us toward the planet. You are to position Lar and Langley simultaneously over the southern hemisphere Military base, as Lent and Lawrence arrive over the northern base. At the same time, Lan is to be over the final staging area. We are each to be above the atmosphere and our designated targets, at laser-barrage optimum range, in precisely five hours."

"Navigation here. Understood, we are to be precisely over designated targets in five hours. Yes, Sir!"

"Lan, you are to keep all Cruisers synchronized with Navigation's instructions.

"Lan here, understood and complying."

"Lan, prepare three Zed decoys for launch. Set them to our new noisy Nori configuration. When launched, they are to remain in stealth mode and assume a tactical facing triangle spread. You will launch the decoys when the squadron reaches 300,000 kilometers distance from the planet.

"When launched, they are to remain in stealth mode and on station, waiting for your further orders. Once ordered, they are to generate the Nori configuration and accelerate to a velocity of one light and move directly toward the planet. As they approach the planet, they are to separate. Two of the decoys are to follow a slingshot trajectory, where one decoy crosses above each Military base. The third decoy will cross above the final staging area. Upon their rounding the planet, they are to proceed in three different directions— approximately 120 degrees apart— and accelerate to 220 lights. Their evasion routes are to be along the ecliptic plane, unless Kreel forces might intercept them. Where interception is probable, any deflection above or below the ecliptic plane is approved. You may adjust their outbound trajectory as required to avoid Kreel ships. As the decoys exit the inner system, they are each to go into stealth mode, and then pitch down 70 degrees. After one hour of stealth mode flight, using maximum protocol settings, they are to self-destruct. Lan, do you have any questions?"

"Sir, when do you desire the Zed decoys at their CPA over the planet?"

"Lan, their run commences four minutes before we begin our initial barrage. We will need to trust that our strike so disorganizes the Kreel that they ignore conducting a precision timeline analysis. Also, keep the decoys at least 100,000 kilometers above our firing position, and make certain all Cruisers are provided the decoys' track lines."

"Yes, Sir. I am preparing three Zed decoys as ordered."

"Tactical, following the strike, the squadron will need to evade possible Kreel counteraction. Evaluate the locations of the patrolling Kreel ships. For our evasion maneuver, determine an escape vector that avoids those ships. Keep that vector above the ecliptic plane."

"Tactical here. Understood," Lorn responded.

"Lan, the squadron will begin the barrage in unison upon my command, and with your coordination. Set the squadron's barrage target priority as follows: ground defense, communications, grounded ships, tracking sensors, manufacturing facilities, headquarters, barracks, power systems, supply and ammunition depots, and Military targets of opportunity. Notify all Cruisers accordingly. Lar is to coordinate target assignments over their target areas. Lent is to coordinate target allocation over their target areas."

"Lan here, all Cruisers have acknowledged receiving the target identification lists and have begun assignment of the prioritized firing sequences."

"Lan, following the first barrage, instruct Lar and Langley to proceed to their secondary target, Staging Area 1. Instruct Lent and Lawrence to proceed to the manufacturing facility, Area 4. Your secondary target is Staging Area 2. As the Cruisers arrive over their secondary targets, they will immediately commence a sixty-second barrage. Following the second barrage, all Cruisers are to promptly break out and move smartly toward our defined rendezvous point.

"Following the initial strike, the alerts will be out, so extreme care is mandated. If anyone receives damage of any kind whatsoever, they are to immediately notify you and break off and proceed to our designated post-attack rendezvous position. All Cruisers have authority to engage any Kreel ship that poses a threat."

"Lan here, understood. I am now instructing the other Cruisers." Kellon sat back and considered his orders. "Lan, generate a standard X-Y maneuvering plot with K-23 at its center. Display all ships. Use the ecliptic plane as the tactical plane. Provide a visual of the planet."

As the large forward bulkhead brightened into its maneuvering plot display, a second screen brightened to show the sphere of K-23 hanging in the darkness of space. Kellon noticed at least one small moon of its two moons in the image, but the planet was simply too far distant to see any ground detail.

Turning his attention to the plot board, he scanned it for the disposition of the red icons. There were none between the golden icons of the squadron and the planet. Kellon relaxed somewhat, thinking, *We should have a clear approach. Good fortune seems to be riding with us.*

"Tactical, Kellon here. Do you have a recommended evasion vector yet?"

"No, Sir. I will not be able to provide that for at least another hour," Lorn responded.

"Tactical, once you determine that vector, put an X on the line one-fourth AU distant from the planet and transmit it to Navigation. That is our post-attack rendezvous point."

Sitting back, Kellon continued to study the tactical plot, looking for anything that might bite. "Lan, am I missing anything?"

"Sir, I have compared our defined trajectories near the planet. At the time of the initial attack, all Cruisers will be very close to the surface. There will be a communications gap due to the bulk of the planet blocking our direct line of secure communications. By comparing the time we enter into the communications shadow until we emerge again, there is a nineteen minute span where I will not be able to communicate with Lar and Langley."

"Lan, what altitude must a relay be at to assure we have complete communications coverage? Can we do it with one relay?"

"Sir, given the distribution of the targets, one relay node will suffice. If the relay is located at 50,000 kilometers, then we will have the desired coverage."

"Lan, define the optimal point necessary for that relay and confirm there are no Kreel ships in the vicinity of that location."

"Sir, I have the computed point and it is at this time clear of immediate threat. I am displaying it as a blue X on your chart."

Kellon studied the chart, noting the newly posted blue X, and was not at all happy. He did not want to deploy Lan's Scouts within 50,000 kilometers of a Kreel dominated world. *Blast and double blast,* he thought, *I cannot tolerate a nineteen-minute communications gap in this strike.*

Kellon keyed his command band for Shey. "Shey, is Commander Roan available?"

"Shey here. Yes, Sir, he is coming on the double."

"Sir, Roan here."

"Roan, I have a mission for the Scouts. It's a dangerous task, and you are to at least try to avoid trouble."

"Yes, Sir."

"Good. We need a communications relay standing off the planet at 50,000 kilometers. I'm going to launch your group to fill that need."

"Yes, Sir. Confirming we are to stay out of trouble. We can be ready within five minutes. Shall I proceed?"

"Proceed. However, you will have several hours before launch. Lan will give you your heads up and synchronize the launch on your countdown. Lan is transferring coordinates for the needed communications node to Shey as we speak.

"Lan, alert the squadron that we will be deploying our Scouts. Each Cruiser is to be watchful. Inform them that I will not lose a Scout in this system. Make certain they know I fully mean that."

"Yes, Sir, I am now notifying our other Cruisers. Sir, I have obtained confirmation; all Cruisers will protect our Scouts, as required. I recommend launch of our Scouts in three hours."

Kellon keyed his command band, "Shey, heads up! Launch is in three hours."

Each Cruiser became busy preparing for the upcoming strike, and the CAC on board Lan settled into a hushed environment. Kellon remained in CAC, alert and watchful. As they drew near, the view of the planet expanded into a large sphere suspended in quarter crescent, the bright light of the edge of sunlight crisp along its surface.

As they crossed the 300,000 kilometer mark, Lan announced, "Zed decoys have been launched."

On board Shey and the other Scouts, the crews were at their consoles and finalizing their preflight checks. As Roan strapped on his restraints, he ordered, "Shey remain in close contact with the girls. Verify each step of this launch sequence. Upon exit, we will move off straight out 10 kilometers and then drop down and form up. We will use our tight standard three-sided pyramid formation."

Zorn was strapping into his command chair and bringing his tactical screens up to full activity. "Shey, obtain from Lan the latest data and his current tactical display."

Shey's characteristic melodious and cheerful voice was now crisp and formal. "Shey here. Lan is downloading the requested tactical information. He has confirmed the Zed decoys and all Cruiser trajectories are included. We do not have a defined evasion route at this time. Sir, all my sisters and their handsome guys are reporting they are ready to launch!"

Completing his pre-launch checks, Roan noted with satisfaction that Shey's status board indicated a full loadout of ordnance and decoys. Kellon had ordered them to stay out of trouble. However, if trouble did arrive, Shey was fully armed.

Roan turned toward Zorn with a grin. "Well, it looks like we were both right. Kellon did not have the data he needed to act. Now, he's obtained that data, and is willing to deploy Scouts 50,000 kilometers from a Kreel-dominated world."

Zorn looked back, but he was not smiling. "Roan, if this goes kablooey in our face, be absolutely certain it's a Cobalt Blue."

"Shey, you heard Zorn. Do you have any questions?"

"No, Roan, there are no questions. All my sisters and I do understand. We all have talked with our crews and Lux."

"All Scouts stand by, Lan here. Sixty seconds to launch— repeat, sixty seconds to launch. Commander Roan, on your countdown!" As Roan's countdown reached zero, the hangar doors swung open and Zorn broke into a broad smile. "Look out Kreel, here we come!"

Lan effortlessly ejected the Scouts, they slid forward as if extruded from their four hangars. Shey immediately coordinated the four Scouts out and down, assuming the tight standard formation that Roan had ordered. As they joined up and smoothly moved off toward their designated relay point 50,000 kilometers above the planet, they observed their Cruisers falling away and vanishing toward the distant atmosphere. For a moment, Roan felt the aching sense of abandonment— they were a long way from Glas Dinnein. Then he firmly kicked that fear and ache aside and focused on their task.

# Chapter Fifty-Four:
## Empty Game Pouch

On board Lan, Kellon watched the golden icons on the plot board that represented his Scouts. They were professionals, but it never felt good as he watched Lan move off while his Scouts fell further behind. They were family and going in harm's way.

Kellon turned his attention back to the problem at hand and studied the tactical plot. So far, so good. "Tactical, how much time before we're over our targets?"

"Tactical here, we're decelerating as we come nearer the planet, currently estimating twelve minutes. Our Cruisers have already split off. Lar and Langley are approaching the southern hemisphere and Lent and Lawrence are approaching the northern hemisphere."

"Lan, signal all Cruisers. Since we are this near to the planet, they are each to maximize their passive scans of the communications channels on the planet. Also, confirm all Cruisers have no less than four heavy missiles and eight medium missiles set Condition 3. Adjust all laser battery settings to maximum spread, maximum disruption, and ground barrage."

"Lan here. I am confirming ground communications scanning at maximum, point defenses are fully functional, and all missiles and laser settings are as ordered."

Now the image of the planet nearly filled the entire screen, and its crescent arch crisply defined day from night. From what little he could see, it looked like a beautiful planet that anyone would enjoy living on.

Lan was moving swiftly into the planet's dark side. "Lan, I'm authorizing you to monitor and coordinate the movement of all Cruisers to their targets and then synchronize our barrage. Upon completion of the first barrage sequence, you are to immediately break forward and up 300 kilometers and bring us smartly to the firing point above our secondary target. Likewise, coordinate the other two groups while bringing them to their targets."

"Yes, Sir. We are four minutes from our targets and the Nori decoys are now inbound."

As Lan directed the four Cruisers, each tightly adjusted their trajectory and speed to arrive directly over their targets at optimum speed, altitude, and in perfect synchronization. Each knew that their most potent defense was surprise.

"Lan here. We are forty-five seconds from our targets. I am showing our target area on the forward bulkhead screen."

As Lan entered into the firing area, his maneuver of choice was a tight circle. As Lan transferred vast gravitational energies— easily capable of swiftly accelerating him rapidly to fractions of the speed of light— to that of brutal offensive destruction, there came a brisk series of heavy hammer-like raps. The large bulkhead display of the target area showed sudden flashes and violent explosions blossoming in the darkness. Kellon knew the destructive capacities of his heavy laser batteries were enormous. Even so, watching the pattern of destruction unfold on the screen was sobering. For sixty seconds the loud hammering continued unabated, and then it suddenly ended in a loud silence.

The ground swiftly blurred as Lan moved sharply up in his predefined evasion maneuver. Reaching his new altitude, he swung about purposefully toward his secondary target.

As the target area dwindled behind, Kellon observed the scene of destruction. He saw the secondary explosions and fires were expanding. He shook his head slightly and sighed, and then turned again to look at the tactical plot. The movements of the Kreel ships gave no indication of their having received an alert.

"Lan here. The Nori decoys are now passing over their defined targets and breaking away as programmed."

"Tactical here. First reports indicate our Cruisers have destroyed all designated targets. No Kreel ship found on the surface survived the strike. All Cruisers are reporting major secondary explosions and fires."

On board Shey, Roan and Zorn studied their instrumentation screens. "Zorn, our Cruisers have completed their first barrages. From what I'm seeing here, they've pulverized their three initial targets, especially over the two Military bases where we allocated two Cruisers. Lan's target area was also devastated.

"The three squadron units are now moving to their secondary targets. That's going to take at least thirty minutes to accomplish." Looking up, Zorn was smiling. "So far, so good. The Kreel ships on patrol haven't altered their patrol patterns. Given what I'm seeing here, I actually think we'll make a clean getaway."

# X

Communications were clean and unbroken, therefore Kellon knew his Scouts were on station and doing their job. "Lan, as soon as the Scouts' relay mission is completed, detach and direct them to our rendezvous point."

"Lan here. We will require their services for six more minutes. Sir, I am now detecting an Elite Guard ship taking off directly forward of our position. It is lifting off from our secondary target area."

"Fire Control, Kellon here. Bring one heavy missile to Condition 2. Get a passive lock on that Elite Guard ship. Set the missile to go active at 80 percent of run length."

"Fire Control here. Sir, we don't have— correction, now we have target detection. Confirming one heavy missile Condition 2, passive lock, set active at 80 percent of run length."

"Fire Control, set Condition 1."

"Fire Control here, missile away." The rumbling launch sounds of a heavy missile rolled throughout Lan.

"Lan here. Five minutes to secondary target."

"Tactical here. Confirming solid missile hit on Elite Guard ship. It was still in the atmosphere. The ship lost control and dropped back onto the planet; it has crashed and exploded into a huge fireball."

"Lan here, two minutes from target."

Lan was coming out of the dark-side cone into the light of an early morning on the planet. As the secondary target came into view on the forward screen, Kellon saw the oblique warm morning sunlight imbue the scene with rich highlights. He noted the area was rolling hills, still mostly covered in shadows. The hills as seen on the observation screen appeared heavily forested and very peaceful. That appearance immediately changed when the hammering of Lan's barrage lasers began pounding the area around the refit facility. Like thunderbolts from unnamed gods in heaven, thousands of laser strikes pierced through the atmosphere, striking the assembly of structures and spacecraft located on the open landing fields. Once again, the scene on the bulkhead screen became one of a smoking chaos.

"Lan here. The Scout ships have been detached from their relay location and are now moving toward our rendezvous point. All Cruisers are reporting they are damage-free and moving to our rendezvous. All designated targets are reported destroyed."

Sitting back in his command chair, Kellon pondered the strike. It had not taken long, not long at all. Even so, he knew that a wide swath of destruction and death lay behind them. It did not make him feel like cheering. It never did.

Looking up to the bulkhead screen, he saw the planet dwindling behind them, its sphere once again looking very peaceful and quiet. Shifting his attention back to the tactical plot, Kellon saw the Kreel alarm signals had clearly gone out. All the Kreel ships within the inner system were now moving directly toward the planet. He noted the Zed decoys had completed their slingshot maneuvers and were even then streaking toward the heliopause. Only one of the Zed decoys showed a deflection below the ecliptic plane. As he observed, one of the Elite Guard ships escorting the transport ship broke out of his escort role, heading directly toward the nearest point on the heliopause. Kellon's countenance revealed a satisfied smile. *Good, they believe a Nori strike just hit them. That Elite Guard ship has a long trip ahead of him and will have an empty game pouch at the end of his journey.*

The Tuen ship nearest the planet altered his trajectory in a hapless attempt to intercept one of the Zed decoys. The other remaining Tuen Class ships and the Kreel cruiser altered their trajectories to intercept the approaching Elite Guard ships.

*Hmmmm, now that's interesting,* thought Kellon. *Rather than coming to protect the planet, they're moving to protect the Elite Official from Hub-3. Whoever he is, he must have some heavy clout in the Kreel Empire to warrant that protection.*

"Lan, well done to all Cruisers and your Scouts. Coordinate the recovery of our Scouts as soon as possible. It's time to go out and hunker down and watch to see what the Kreel do next."

Two hours later, Shey was snuggly settled back onto her hangar cradle. As the hangar lights brightened and the hangar volume began filling with an atmosphere, Shey powered her systems down and switched over to internal diagnostics. They were again all together and once more safe.

With a deep sigh, Zorn unfastened his lap restraint. Looking over toward Roan, he asked, "Please explain to me once again, why do we do this?"

Roan sat for a moment, seeking the proper answer for Zorn's rhetorical question. Then, he turned slowly toward his good friend. Speaking softly, he spoke one word in response. "Kintana."

# Chapter Fifty-Five:
## True Elite

For three days following the strike, Kellon and his squadron hunkered down one AU distant from K-23. They patiently monitored all the broadcast channels that their distributed satellites and probes could detect. Kellon had a quarry, and according to his Intelligence group, that quarry had gone to ground on K-23 and would soon be coming out of his briar patch. As far as Kellon was concerned, the sooner that quarry exposed itself, the better. He knew delay could only increase the probability reinforcements would arrive. Such an occurrence would certainly make his next action more complicated— if not outright impossible.

The elevator reached deck two and its doors glided open. Turning, Kellon headed down the passage toward Shey's hangar. He noted the status light was golden. He opened the hatch and entered the hangar, closing and securing it behind him. Shey's clear feminine voice announced, "Commodore on hangar deck."

Walking briskly up to the short gangway, he called out, "Ahoy on board Shey, Commodore Kellon here, requesting permission to come aboard."

Roan promptly appeared at the port with a large smile. Saluting smartly he replied, "Commodore Kellon, permission granted. Welcome aboard."

Returning Roan's salute, Kellon moved through the port and followed Roan. They went forward into the crew's compartment, where Zorn warmly greeted them. "Sir, might we offer you a mug of hot neab?"

"Roan, it was a hope for that precise offer that helped to bring me down to deck two. I also wanted the opportunity to sit and discuss the upcoming operation with you. Am I interrupting anything?"

Roan responded, "No, Sir, you're not interrupting a thing. As you already know, you're always warmly welcome aboard Shey. Besides, we appreciate the opportunity to discuss what's coming up."

As Zorn slipped into the compact efficient galley, he began preparing a large thermos of neab. Roan and Kellon took seats at the small combination dining and work table. Zorn called over his shoulder, "Before we talk about what might be happening, might I ask if there is any news about our strike on the planet? How did we do?"

Frowning, Kellon paused for a moment before responding. "Yes, there is news. And, that's another reason for my visit. Commander Shaw informed me that the Scouts were responsible for analyzing the target areas and defining the laser-barrage strike points. The results of our strike directly reflect the Scouts' skill in target definitions. I wanted to personally tell you well done!"

"Sir, we were glad to share the work at hand. We sometimes feel as if we're more cargo than anything else. It felt good to be directly involved."

Kellon's rejoinder was prompt and his voice firm, "Commander Roan, The day you begin to consider the Scouts as cargo, is a day you need to alter your attitude! You certainly were not cargo when the Scouts took the fight to the pair of Kreel cruisers near Earth, or stood off and directed heavy missiles into those Kreel assault ships near Scion, or planted limpets on 300 cargo ships near Hub-2. Furthermore, as a direct result of the Scouts' demonstrated capability to professionally select barrage strike points, their involvement in planning any future strike is now standard operating procedure."

Looking somewhat abashed, Roan smiled and answered, "Yes, Sir. We do try to be of assistance. Might I ask what news we have regarding the strike?"

With a slight sigh, as if releasing annoyance, Kellon answered Roan's question. "In truth, there's more news than we can process, and our Intelligence group is swamped. We have, however, culled out some interesting items about the strike. It seems our strike was more effective than we had hoped. The Kreel are now totally out of the Elite Guard ship production business on K-23. The good news is the Elite Guard ships previously manufactured to replace part of those destroyed by Lux were waiting on the planet for their crews. The squadron destroyed all of them. They are now nothing more than slag on their landing fields. According to the latest information, the Kreel will be out of the manufacturing business for more than a year.

"We apparently also took out some of their top engineers along with the factory. That Elite Guard ship we knocked down as it was rising up off planet wasn't launching to engage us. It was on a preliminary test flight with engineers, top technicians, and their special systems test equipment. When it crashed and exploded, it took a big bite out of their manufacturing certification program.

"When we next took out the factory, we destroyed all the ships then in their various phases of production, along with machine shops, foundries, electronics shops, sub-assembly lines, associated supplies, and sub-assembly parts storage. The follow-on fires gutted anything that the Kreel might have salvaged.

"The same can be said for the other three related sites, it was a clean wipe. Adding insult to injury, we even took out their two primary Military installations. The barrage from two Cruisers over each installation destroyed their ships on the ground and rendered the installations smoking debris.

"Because of the scope and thoroughness of the destruction, the Kreel were quarreling intensely among themselves for a while, arguing about whose failure it was. Making the Kreel even angrier was the big Nori chase which turned out to be a complete bust— the Nori got clean away."

Zorn looked over his shoulder with a grin. "You have to hand it to those Nori. They sure are a slippery bunch."

"Sir, you say the Kreel were quarreling among themselves? What's caused them to stop quarreling?" Roan asked.

His countenance was grim when Kellon replied, "The newly arrived Elite official from Hub-3 gave all of them a good reason to stop quarreling once he landed."

"Sir," asked Roan, "Do the Kreel have even a hint of the possible involvement of Guardian Force?"

"No, Roan. They haven't even considered our possible involvement. Remember, we've never before been deep in their Empire on a strike. Even when they destroyed Lux, they failed to obtain his identity. As we'd hoped, the Kreel have given the Nori full credit for the strike."

Carrying two large mugs of neab over to the table, Zorn put them in front of Roan and Kellon. "There you are, Gentlemen, two mugs of the second best neab in Guardian Force!"

Looking up with a questioning expression, Kellon asked, "Second best? Might I inquire about who makes the best?"

Hooking a thumb toward Roan, Zorn replied, "My boss claims to make the best. Given such circumstances, what's a junior officer to do?"

Sipping cautiously from the mug, Roan judiciously ignored Zorn and turned toward Kellon, "Sir, what's our next operation?" Leaning back, Kellon frowned. "May I have permission to interact with Shey?"

"Sir, permission granted," Roan responded.

"Good morning Shey. Please display a standard ecliptic plane X-Y maneuvering plot on the display bulkhead. Make it a compressed heliocentric display. Display the planetary orbits on the ecliptic plane and indicate the planets' positions on their orbit path."

"Yes, Sir. And a very good morning to you also," came Shey's cheerful and melodic response.

The forward bulkhead brightened and a large maneuvering plot sprang into view. K-23 was the fourth planet from the primary and it was identified with a green dot.

"Shey, display our current position and define the heliopause boundary."

The plot immediately showed a golden icon representing the squadron's current position, and Shey represented the heliopause with a thick blue circle that enclosed all the planetary orbits.

"Now, Shey, draw a line from the primary out to the seventy degree point on the heliopause. Then connect a line from the planet to that point. Finally, draw a line from the planet to the nearest point on the heliopause."

As Shey drew the two lines from the planet, they passed equidistant from the golden icon, one passing on each side.

Both Roan and Zorn studied the plot for a moment. Then they turned to face Kellon, waiting for his explanation.

"Well, as you can see, the Elite Guard has a choice to make. They can proceed from the planet along the first line, exiting the heliosphere at seventy degrees. This would optimize their orientation for a Jump toward Hub-3. They also might choose to follow the second line, taking a path to the nearest point on the heliopause. This choice cuts hours off the travel time within the heliosphere, and that in turn allows them to Jump earlier.

"Given the recent strike, and the importance of the Elite official, I anticipate they will want to Jump as soon as possible. I believe the probability is therefore they will decide to proceed toward the nearest point on the heliopause. This would reduce the time that the Elite official is exposed to a possible Nori attack. However, because I don't know what route they will choose, I have positioned the squadron between the two anticipated routes.

"As soon as we determine their chosen route, we will move out in front of them and lay out a kill volume."

Roan looked up questioningly, "Sir, do we know who the Elite official is?"

"Hmmmm, we think so. He doesn't have rank like the Military or Elite Guard, but is a true Elite. His formal title seems to be August One. If we're correct, he is one of the top five Kreel in the hierarchy of their Empire. We've not yet determined precisely what his real level of authority in the Kreel Empire is, but we know it's near the very top. We do know he carries absolute power in this system— regardless of the ranks of either Military or Elite Guard."

Zorn looked up, "Sir, he has that much clout?"

Still holding his warm mug of neab cupped in both hands, Kellon looked over to Zorn. "Yes. He does have that much clout. After our raid, he had about twenty senior Military and Elite Guard officers executed for negligence and dereliction to duty. He didn't make the slightest distinction between the Military and the Elite Guard officers, and both got the axe. That little demonstration of authority put an immediate end to the quarreling about who was responsible.

"There was absolutely no appeal to anyone else having higher authority. The executions were prompt and efficient."

Zorn looked over to Kellon; he was holding his own mug of neab and leaning against the galley counter. "Sir, I'm aware that both Lar and Langley have used their Scouts to ferry over two squads of security personnel to reinforce our four squads. They brought full combat armor and weapons with them. Six squads of security personnel is a hopper full of trouble for the Kreel. You must be anticipating some heavy resistance. Might I ask, have you chosen the command officers for the storming party going aboard the Elite transport?"

Kellon looked back toward Zorn and grinned, "Well, Zorn, do I hear you volunteering?"

Laughing, Zorn quipped, "Once, a long time ago, I would have jumped at such an opportunity. Today, my bones are a bit brittle for hand-to-hand combat with young snarling Kreel warriors. I asked only out of curiosity."

"To answer your question, yes, a selection has been made. Lieutenant Oster will head the overall operation and engineering group. Lieutenant Shem will head the security party."

"Sir," commented Roan, "they're both fine officers. Regarding the preliminary engagement, do you foresee using the Scouts?"

"Roan, I can't answer that question, at least not until I can see the formation departing the planet. What I do will need to respond and counter whatever tactics the Kreel deploy—"

"Commodore Kellon, Lan here. I am sorry to interrupt your discussion, but we have track on the Elite transport, he is coming out well-escorted and heading for the nearest point on the heliopause."

"Lan, what does his escort consist of?"

"Sir, he has the one remaining cruiser, three Tuen Class fast-attack ships and three Elite Guard ships escorting him."

"Lan, advise navigation to plot a position 700,000 kilometers ahead of the lead ship on their track line. Instruct Navigation to move the squadron to that position and then maintain the separation from the Kreel lead ship. Advise Navigation I will be in CAC in a few minutes."

"Yes, Sir."

"Lan, one more thing. Prepare a Zed decoy and configure it like the decoy we left near our entry point. Hold the new decoy on standby."

"Yes, Sir."

"Well, Roan, it looks like the Scouts might see some duty during the upcoming fracas. I estimate twenty hours before things become intense, if your crews need any sleep or any last minute adjustment, I suggest this is the time to take care of those matters."

Standing, Kellon put his mug on the table and smiled broadly, "Thank you all for your hospitality, and that especially means you lovely Shey."

There came a pleasant reply, "Thank you, Sir. I agree with Roan and Zorn. You are always welcome aboard."

Zorn and Roan both saw Kellon to the hangar and watched as he departed. Then, Zorn turned to Roan with a thoughtful glance. "That man is a consummate master of misdirection. I wonder what he has up his sleeve this time."

As they turned back toward the crew's compartment, Roan answered, "Whatever it is, you can safely wager the Kreel won't like it."

# Chapter Fifty-Six:
## Bug in the Brew

As Kellon walked into the CAC, he saw Roy was on duty. "Good morning, Roy. How are we doing?"

"Well, Sir, if actually moving about in space is better than hunkering down and going nowhere fast, then we are doing right well. We are currently en route to our new escort position relative to the Kreel mob that you want to get in front of."

Walking over, Kellon looked at the tactical plot. It was essentially the same plot that he'd had Shey prepare a few minutes earlier. He stood reflecting on the upcoming battle. Once again, the Kreel outnumbered the squadron, yet he remained confident that by employing superior tactics, surprise, and stealth they were more than capable of meeting the tactical challenge.

He'd begun his analysis of the tactical problem placed before him, and some answers were already obvious.

Turning, he waved to Roy, "I'll be in my quarters if you need me."

Because of the weapon's Research and Development nature, only Lan had the Arkillian's anti-Kreel beam weapon installed. It was therefore Lan's sole task to take out the crew of the Kreel transport. To accomplish that task, they must first take out the escorting Kreel ships and disable the transport.

Before they could storm and board, Lan must first go alongside the transport. That would be the truly nerve-wracking part of the attack— never knowing if there were surviving Kreel Elite that might gladly choose to initiate a self-destruction sequence.

Until they were in control of the transport, he could do very little to prevent the target's self-destruction. Therefore, he pushed that worry out of his mind.

He knew the first problem he faced was to successfully blame their attack on the True Blood resistance. That critical misdirection was his first large hurdle.

Entering his quarters, he promptly moved to his desk and sat down. "Lan, we're going to be working here for some time. Please contact the Officer's Mess and have them send over a large thermos of neab."

"Yes, Sir."

"Lan, project a clear X and Y plot on my bulkhead screen. I need a large-scale plot, one that only displays the Kreel formation now heading toward the heliopause. Please display the current course-line and the relative positions of each of the Kreel ships to that line."

"Sir, the Officer's Mess has acknowledged your request for neab and a thermos will be sent up shortly. The requested plot is now being displayed."

Leaning back, Kellon carefully studied the plot. The Kreel had deployed the eight ships in two sections. The forward section consisted of two Tuen Class fast-attack ships, which were well in advance of the second section. That second group included a Kreel cruiser, the three Elite Guard ships, and a trailing Tuen Class ship. His quarry was neatly tucked right in the center of that escort.

Frowning, Kellon thought, *They're making me work for this one.*

"Hmmmm. Well, Lan, it appears the Kreel officer running this show is being very careful. There's nothing like the summary execution of a few senior officers to encourage the surviving officers to underscore efficiency.

"Lan, what gives with the Elite Guard ships? Their separation looks odd. What do you have set as the tactical plane?"

"Sir, I have used the ecliptic plane for the plot."

"That explains it; I wondered why the relative positions looked so skewed. Lan, define a new tactical plane. The Kreel base course-line defines the first axis. The second axis is defined as parallel to the imaginary line connecting the two Elite Guard ships positioned forward of the transport. Display the targets' X and Y coordinates on the new tactical plane."

"Sir, I am redefining the tactical plane as ordered and displaying the symbols accordingly," Lan responded.

"Ah, that's better. Thank you, Lan."

He thought, *That Kreel formation's very geometric. Those two lead Tuen Class ships are spread widely apart and abeam of* each other. Both are on the tactical plane and positioned one on each side of the base track-line. They're the Kreel formation's advance point guard, and the main body is well to their rear.

"Lan, what I find most interesting is the three Elite Guard ships are in a facing triangle, with the base forward and the apex trailing. The transport's at the precise center of that sloping triangle formation.

"Lan, construct lines between each of the Elite Guard ships. Next construct a line normal to and through the center of the sloping triangle you've just drawn."

If he were attacking only the transport and its three Elite Guard escorts, he would attack from above and forward, which explained the Kreel cruiser's position. It was on the line passing through the center of the triangle, blocking the most probable line of a frontal attack against the sloping triangle. He shifted his attention to the trailing Tuen Class ship. He observed it was on the line passing downward through the center of the triangle. The Tuen's job was to plug a stern approach.

"Hmmmm. Lan, of the four defending ships, all have excellent firepower and heavy-missile capability, all except that trailing Tuen Class ship, which is their weakest defensive point. That's why it's blocking the most dangerous direction for an attacking force to approach.

"Yes, Sir. I concur."

Looking again at the relative positions of the Kreel ships comprising the main body of the formation, Kellon noted the cruiser and the two lower Elite Guard ships formed a vertical facing triangle. *Perhaps,* he thought, *that's the weak point I'm looking for?*

"Lan, construct lines from the cruiser to the two lower advanced Elite Guard ships. Now, construct tactical spheres with a radius of our heavy-missile effective range about the cruiser and those to Guard ships."

Leaning back, Kellon thoughtfully studied the modified tactical diagram, musing, *There's considerable overlap of those spheres. Therefore, there's potential for setting up an effective crossfire. The problem is that it works both ways. If the Kreel detect a Guardian ship within those overlapping spheres, the Kreel could subject us to deadly counter-crossfire. Stealth, stealth, and more stealth with some misdirection are required.*

**401**

*To be successful, we must precisely synchronize our attack.* Studying the plot further, he was not happy. *That trailing Elite Guard ship poses the real problem.*

"Lan, construct another tactical sphere about the trailing Elite Guard ship, and use the same radius as before."

He studied the plot and didn't like what he saw. *That blasted trailing Elite Guard ship is the bug in the brew.*

"Lan, I believe we may have the solution to this puzzle, but it's messy and has about a hundred ways it can go wrong. Set up a conference call to the captains and set aside some serious simulator time. We're going to need to be very tight during this attack if we're to keep our skins intact and still achieve our mission objectives."

*Storm and board— archaeological trinkets. Admiral Mer Shawn,* he thought, *you'd better have more than a glass of wine in that cabinet. You're going to need a case of that special wine after this fracas.*

# Chapter Fifty-Seven:
## Parallel Track

Intense radiated energies vibrated the positive-charged particles flowing outward through the void of the heliosphere. The two Kreel ships positioned at the point of their formation were purposefully transmitting those energies to seek out and reveal a lurking foe. The expanding energies radiated outward at the speed of light, but there were no returning reverberations to reveal a foe, and passive sensors detected no suspicious telltale signals.

Intensely alert and observing their instrumentation consoles, the Kreel officers knew their very lives were dependent upon the proficient performance of their jobs. They also had good cause to fear the August One; none of them wanted to be the next officer taken out and shot.

On board the Kreel transport, the August One was not at all pleased. He had left the comfort of his den mates, traveled a long uncomfortable way to accept delivery of a group of new ships, and take personal possession of an extraordinary heritage treasure. His planning had not included being subjected to the random risks of a battle. Unexpectedly, he had personally witnessed the ruination of a planet's primary industry. In fact, he had nearly been standing on the planet when the Nori strike hit. It seemed only providence had protected him.

Deep in his throat, he made a mirthful low guttural sound; thinking, *It will make for a shocking story I can expand upon during my next gathering of intimates. Had the foolish Nori wanted to attack me, they certainly could have. Instead, they have declared their priorities and attacked nothing more valuable than a collection of machine tools and equipment that I can, and will, replace.*

*Had they but realized who I am,* he thought with some amusement, *the Nori would have known my esteem worth is far greater than any dozen such industrial complexes. They have missed their golden opportunity.*

*In spite of the foolish drama over my security, I am safely on my way home. Instead of only three escorts, I now have seven. Besides, in a few more hours, I will be out of this miserable solar system and can immediately transfer to my den world.*

*Even better,* he gleefully thought, *I am not returning empty-handed. Although there are no new Elite Guard ships, I have my magnificent heritage prize and a remarkable surprise trophy.* He growled again, with suppressed mirth and an inner warming pleasure. *There will be much envy of my new possessions and more envy because of my little trophy.*

*Best of all, I still have a grand banquet to look forward to. It will be a banquet long remembered. First, I will display my trophy, and then I will offer it as our succulent entrée. A rare tender morsel indeed, and one that is worthy of my generosity in sharing.*

Probing well ahead of the August One's transport, the two Tuen Class fast-attack ships swept past three Guardian Cruisers, and in spite of the Kreel's diligence, they did not detect them. Theirs was not an issue of negligence, the Kreel commanders simply lacked the sensor technology required to peel back the stealth envelope concealing their adversaries. Therefore, they continued on, unaware of their pending doom.

On board Lan, there was a hush of murmured exchanges between those crewmembers in CAC— all of whom were busy at their tasks. Theirs was the stillness that preceded the sharp clash of a pending storm.

Kellon sat silently observing the tactical plot as the calculated geometry of the battle meticulously unfolded. The squadron had moved for more than twenty hours ahead of the Kreel point. As they drew near the heliopause, the time to spring their ambush had arrived.

As the advance Kreel point swept past through the very center of the Guardian formation, Lan began coordinating the movement of the other two Cruisers. Kellon had formed the three attacking Guardian Cruisers in an inverted facing triangle. Lan was at the lower point, and Lar and Langley were at the upper two points of the triangle.

Kellon had designed the formation to counter the Kreel's established facing triangle formation, in which the Kreel cruiser was at the top point and two Elite Guard ships were at the bottom points of their triangle.

As the Kreel transport and its five surrounding escorts advanced, the Guardian triangle formation steadily constricted about the Kreel's base track-line. By design, the shrinking triangle would bring each Guardian Cruiser simultaneously into a predefined firing position against two opposing Kreel escorts. According to the battle plan, the Kreel targets would be facing incoming missiles from two widely separated Guardian Cruisers. Stealth and surprise were the squadron's key advantages, and Kellon was exploiting those tactical advantages to their extreme limits.

As the contracting inverted triangle moved three of his Cruisers toward their firing positions, Kellon confirmed their readiness. "Lan, confirming target identification. Our primary target— the transport— is Target 1. The Kreel cruiser is Target 2. The two Elite Guard ships below the cruiser are Targets 3 and 4. The trailing Elite Guard ship is Target 5, and the trailing Tuen is Target 6. Targets 7 and 8 are the two Tuen Class on point."

"Sir, I confirm those are the designated target number assignments."

As the squadron approached its firing points, Shey and eleven other Scouts hunkered down— well offset from the Kreel course-line. Lan was busy coordinating the Scouts in harmony with the movements of the squadron's Cruisers.

"Lan here. Sir, the Scout ships are now moving up and taking their blocking positions on the Kreel base track-line, well astern of the Kreel formation."

Studying the tactical plot, Kellon watched as the golden icons representing the Scouts took their positions and began pacing the Kreel formation. Given the successful execution of his plan of battle, none of the Kreel ships should survive the initial attack. However, if they did and attempted to retreat, the Scouts were in a powerful barrier position to decisively deal with that possibility.

"Fire Control, confirm your current status."

"Fire Control here. Confirming passive locks on Targets 3, 4, and 6. Heavy missiles set Condition 2 on Targets 3 and 4. Eight heavy missiles are set Condition 3, standby."

"Counter Measures, confirm your status."

"Counter Measures here. All point defenses are set Condition 1. Electronic countermeasures are fully operational."

"Lan, how much time before firing?"

"Sir, three minutes and thirty-two seconds. As planned, I am synchronizing missile launches on all Cruisers. Currently indicating a missile impact spread on the Kreel facing triangle of 4.23 seconds. I am adjusting accordingly to tighten this up."

"Lan, do your thing. Make it sharp and precise."

"Yes, Sir."

His right hand moved and Kellon keyed the command band, "Lieutenant Oster, Kellon here. Confirm your status."

"Sir, Oster here. We have all six squads suited up in armor and armed. We have instructed each squad as to their responsibilities. We are ready."

"Lieutenant Oster, your tasks are the point of our sword. You will have absolute priority. I will be on this band during your storming and boarding operation. Stay in touch— I want to know immediately about any hang-ups or unexpected anomalous occurrences. Our time is short, be quick."

"Sir, acknowledging."

"Again, may fortune be with your endeavors. Inform your men that we are all supporting their effort. Kellon out."

"Lan here. Two minutes before launch."

Kellon glanced at the tactical plot once again. He studied the two golden icons to the left side of the board. *Lent and Lawrence,* he thought, *are in perfect position, spread apart and well below the tactical plane.* Their position was set for them to attack the Kreel point, synchronized with the attack against the Kreel's facing triangle. If the Guardian tactics were successful, the Kreel would promptly lose five of their seven escorts. Then the squadron would close on and destroy the remaining two escorts. Although forewarned, they would have very little time to respond.

As he watched, Kellon noted Lan was maintaining tight coordination; Lar and Langley were precisely in position. It was looking good.

Again, his fingers keyed the command band, "Lorn, Kellon here. Your status, please."

"Shaw here. Sir, I have my communications engineers and documentation technicians suited up. All necessary Kreel interface modules are checked and operational. We are prepared to immediately follow Squad 3 on board the transport."

"Lorn, be certain you keep your head down. Let the security folks do their thing before you go barging in."

"Sir, understood."

"Lan here, one minute until launch."

Except for the soft sound of the air circulation and conditioning system, the CAC became nearly silent. "Lan here, Condition 1. Mark! Missiles away."

The entire crew felt, as well as heard, the distinctive rumble of heavy missiles as they launched. "Fire Control, Kellon here. Set one heavy missile Condition 2, passive lock on Target 6. Confirm Condition 2."

"Fire Control here, confirming Condition 2, passive lock on Target 6."

Kellon watched as the blinking golden icons representing the outbound missiles moved unerringly toward their targets. Running in a passive mode, they streaked silently toward their intended goals, and then the icons merged. The Kreel had not obtained any advance warning.

"Tactical here," Elayne's voice was steady and calm as she reported. "We have two hits— repeat, two hits. One hit was on Target 3 and the second on Target 4. We are indicating crossfire hits by Lar on Target 3 and by Langley on Target 4. Sir, Lar and Langley have obtained six heavy missile hits on Target 2, the cruiser. It has exploded. Both Targets 3 and 4 have exploded."

"Lan, sharply alter our heading to move us parallel along the Kreel base course-line."

Kellon heard Lan's clear acknowledgment tone.

"Fire Control, Kellon here. Direct the anti-Kreel beam on Target 1 and set Condition 2. Confirm lock."

"Fire Control here. Confirming anti-Kreel beam lock on Target 1, Condition 2, at 120 percent of effective range."

"Tactical here. Lent and Lawrence have multiple clean crossfire hits on Targets 7 and 8. Target 7 has exploded, and Target 8 is now adrift. Lawrence has fired his second missile at Target 8."

"Fire Control, at 90 percent or less of effective range, discharge the anti-Kreel beam. At 100 percent effective range or less, set Condition 1 on Target 6."

"Tactical here. Langley and Lar have engaged Target 5, the trailing Elite Guard ship. Two missiles away. Target 5 is beginning an evasion maneuver."

"Fire Control here. Target 1 is at 90 percent of effective range, transmitting the anti-Kreel beam."

There was a deep building intense resonant humming felt throughout Lan and then the low thrumming vibration was suddenly gone.

"Fire Control here. Condition 1 on Target 6. Missile away."
"Tactical here, Langley got a clean hit on Target 5. The Elite Guard's point defenses blocked Lar's missile. Both Langley and Lar have second missiles outbound. The Elite Guard ship is now adrift.

"Tactical here. Reporting Lan's heavy missile has hit Target 6 bow on. That target has exploded."

"Navigation Kellon here. Bring us smartly about on a reciprocal course; bring us in on a parallel track abeam of Target 1 and match velocity. Hold us off at 90 percent of effective anti-Kreel beam range."

"Navigation here, maneuvering as ordered," Roy acknowledged. Kellon thought, *I'm not going to take any chances on this one.* "Fire Control, recharge the anti-Kreel beam and prepare for a second transmission."

"Lan, activate our deployed Zed sleeper. Have it maneuver as planned and broadcast the prepared transmission."

Lan's acknowledging tone responded.

"Fire Control here. We are indicating 90 percent of anti-Kreel beam effective range. Anti-Kreel beam is fully charged."

"Fire Control, transmit the anti-Kreel beam," Kellon ordered. The crew again felt the deep building intense humming. Then the low thrumming vibration suddenly dropped away.

"Fire Control, the anti-Kreel beam has been transmitted."

"Shaw here. Sir, we've identified the rear control room emergency access port. I've marked that port in Lan's database."

"Tactical here. Reporting Targets 2 through 8 have been destroyed. Targets 5 and 6, however, did manage to send out alarms. We can expect hostile angry company inbound."

## Chapter Fifty-Eight:
# Storm and Board

"Lan, give me a visual of the transport on the bulkhead screen then deploy your starboard hull stand-offs. Align our starboard boarding hatch with the portside Kreel emergency access port and then match velocities. Move us in and alongside. "

"Lan here. Acknowledging and complying."

"Navigation, Roy, direct all Cruisers into a defensive formation, and move them well off from our boarding operation to a safe zone. Recall all Scouts to their Cruisers, except Lan's Scouts. Direct Shey to stand off with the other Cruisers until we break clear of the transport."

"Navigation here, acknowledged."

"Lan here. Indicating seven minutes until hull contact with the transport."

Kellon watched the monitor intensely as the transport grew closer. He could see no sign of life and had not expected any. To all appearances, the ship was merely a transport. He couldn't see any indication of weapon ports, turrets, or associated sensors. When contact occurred, there was a loud thump, and Lan was heavily jarred from bow to stern.

"Lan here. Sir, I have attached vacuum clamps, and they are holding. The boarding tube is being extended and is now attached."

"Sir, Oster here. The boarding tube is in place, vacuum seals are holding, and the tube is pressurized. We have engineers at the Kreel transport's airlock operating its emergency access controls." If someone had dropped a pin in CAC, it would have seemed like a cannon going off. Everyone was feeling the tension.

"Oster here, the engineers have opened the outer emergency hatch and disabled the interlocks. Our first two squads are boarding. All the Kreel appear to be dead, and we have secured the aft control room. Expanding our entry, auxiliary engineering is now secured."

"Lieutenant Oster, put some engineers on that control board. I want that ship's drives shut down as quickly as possible. Coordinate that process with Lan so he can adjust our propulsion accordingly."

"Yes, Sir!"

Lan, as soon as possible, we need to go adrift so the transport's propulsion signature doesn't attract every Kreel ship in this quadrant."

"Yes, Sir. I will remain in tight communication with Lieutenant Oster and the engineers."

"Oster here. Squads three and four are boarding. All the Kreel encountered so far are dead. Our personnel are in control of engineering and have reached the forward control area. All the Kreel are confirmed dead. Sir, in order to facilitate our compartment-by-compartment search, Squads 5 and 6 are now boarding."

"Tactical here. Our initial pre-positioned Zed decoy has made his broadcast three times as scheduled. Sir, the Zed decoy looks just like a Gortoga cruiser. It is now retracing its path to the heliopause. As instructed, it will exit the heliosphere, accelerate to 200 lights and move out for twenty minutes. It will then go stealth, pitch down forty-five degrees, and continue for an additional five hours at 200 lights, then self-destruct."

"Lan, alert the squadron of our imminent launch of a new Zed decoy. After they acknowledge, deploy the decoy and move it well off from the squadron. Once it reaches a separation of 10,000 kilometers, activate it."

"Yes, Sir. All Cruisers have acknowledged, and I have launched the decoy."

"Lan, using your Kreel language skills, have our new decoy respond to the first decoy's announcement. Send the following message, 'True Brothers, the filth calling itself Elite is vanquished. The prize is ours.' Repeat the message three times."

"Sir, the new decoy is on station and the message is transmitted as ordered."

For a moment, Kellon paused to reflect on his misdirection. The taunting announcement broadcast from a Gortoga cruiser in the name of the True Blood immediately following the intercept and destruction of the Elite August One and his entire entourage should suffice. That should pour more fuel on the raging True

Blood bonfire. Shrugging, he knew that in a very short time, he would know whether his strategy and misdirection were effective.

"Oster here. Our search teams have located the Communications Center. It's located forward and on Deck 3. Sir, there's what looks like a very large situation room adjacent to the Communication Center."

"Lorn, Kellon here. That's your cue. Get in there and pick that area clean. Take a careful look at the situation room. I want full video documentation of everything. Be certain to pick up anything of an Intelligence nature that the Kreel didn't weld to a bulkhead. Given an alert went out, we can be certain that unhappy Kreel are inbound. At most, we have only a few hours to complete this heist."

"Shaw here, understood. We are on our way."

Looking over to Navigation, he saw Roy studying him, he looked worried. "Navigation here. Commodore, have you considered our evasion route out of this wasteland?"

With all that had been involved, he had certainly considered that problem. *How,* he thought, *could the evasion route not have been provided to Roy?*

"Navigation, check with Lan. He has the evasion route delineated. If you find anything not acceptable with the defined route, promptly advise me."

"Navigation here. Checking with Lan." An alarm brought Kellon bolt upright.

"Medic! Medic needed on the double. Deck 2, after compartments. Get a litter in here and on the double! Security, clear a path, and get that medic down here— and make it now!"

"Oster, Kellon here. What's the need for a medic? Who's been injured? Report!"

"Sir, Oster here. The call came from Lieutenant Shem. I'm on it. I'm currently moving down to Deck 2 and aft where the call originated. As soon as I have information, I'll be in contact."

"Shaw here. I've entered the Communications Center. Fortunately, it's the same design as the Kreel Gortoga cruiser. Given that advantage, we should be able to extract their data rather quickly. We've pulled fiber optic cables into the Communications Center from Lan and are beginning our hook ups. We're also beginning the packing of secondary backups and data to transfer containers. At best, this will take several hours.

I've sent the documentation team into the situation room. Sir, from what I've already seen, it's absolutely an Intelligence treasure trove! We could easily spend several months in here."

"Understood Lorn, but we have only a few hours. Do your best," Kellon responded.

Elayne reported, "Tactical here. We have something hot off the Kreel Military command band. We've just intercepted a superluminal Kreel general alarm signal. It went out on their common fleet channels. The alert has just informed every Kreel ship in the Empire of what happened here. They're looking for any Gortoga cruisers not accounted for. The Kreel Military seems particularly outraged. Sir, it appears the August One may have been more important than we first thought. This system is about to get extremely dangerous for Guardian ships. We're also indicating six Tuen Class fast-attack ships maneuvering to form up near K-23. They're heading this way, and they're currently above 100 lights and accelerating. Estimating nineteen hours before they arrive."

"Sir, Lieutenant Oster here. I have a visual for you. Lieutenant Shem's first squad has found a survivor, and it appears she is human. Repeat, she is not Kreel! Lieutenant Shem called for the medics. I understand they are on the way. Video is being transmitted."

"Lan, isolate Oster's video, and patch it to the forward bulkhead." Everyone in the CAC had turned in astonishment toward the forward bulkhead— even Roy had stopped his work to look.

As Kellon watched, he saw a group of security personnel huddled and kneeling beside a prone figure. As they stepped out of the view, Kellon was shocked at what he saw. The figure was to all immediate appearances a human woman of slight build with striking physical features. She was naked, had an olive skin color, her hair was badly matted, and her body was literally covered with dirt and massive bruising. It was apparent she was still breathing, and her eyelids were fluttering— as if a state of consciousness was struggling to surface and force her eyelids open. It was evident, even from a casual glance, that the Kreel had treated her with extreme brutality. Kellon felt an immediate rage begin to expand within him.

"Lieutenant Oster, do whatever you can to assist the medics. Get her aboard Lan and to our dispensary on the double!"

"Yes, Sir. The medics are coming now. I'm posting a security detail here to secure this area and sending everyone else back to the search of the ship. How are we doing for time?"

"Lieutenant, we have about twelve hours to complete the rummaging of that ship, to extract what cargo we select, and to plant the charges required to remove the evidence."

"Yes, Sir. We're on it. Oster out."

"Lan, connect me to the dispensary. Make it happen, and make it now!"

"Physician Lorentz here. How may I be of assistance?"

"Kellon here. Physician Lorentz, you have an inbound patient. I only obtained a glance of her, but she's suffering from severe physical abuse, and has just survived two intense anti-Kreel beam transmissions. She looked to be in a very bad condition. When you've completed your prognosis, I want a prompt and full report."

"Yes, Sir! I'll begin to prepare for her arrival. Given the circumstances, I'll do what I can. Lorentz out."

As the hours swept past, Lan's entire crew remained busy. The boarding squads searched and rummaged every compartment within the Kreel transport. They explored the lavishly appointed private quarters of the August One, and those of the high-ranking Kreel officers who had traveled with him.

During the search, the boarding party had discovered the August One sprawled on the deck in the control room, along with the ship's senior officers. They had counted four admirals among the extra braid, and their harnesses indicated two of those admirals were Elite Guard Grand Marshals. During the rummaging of the transport, Lieutenant Shem's squads found the Elite Guard ship replacement crews. They were all in their quarters, and they were all dead. The total tally of ranking Kreel officers demolished by Mer Shawn's covert probe into the Kreel Empire was steadily growing.

Closing his eyes, Kellon considered for a moment the transport and the secrets it held. He then keyed his command channel. "Physician Lorentz, Kellon here. There are five dead Kreel on the bridge of the transport, the Elite One and four high ranking officers. Coordinate with Lieutenant Oster and send a medical detail to recover those five bodies. You are to put them in deep freeze until we return to Glas Dinnein."

Physician Lorentz's voice held no hint of a question concerning his orders. "Yes, Sir."

Remaining in CAC, Kellon studied the tactical board. The six Tuen Class ships were approaching the mid-point in their outward rush to the battle debris-strewn area. They would be here in about another nine hours. It was definitely getting time to either evade or prepare to fight.

"Commodore Kellon, Shaw here. We've completed the downloads. We've fully documented the situation room and have removed everything that wasn't welded to the bulkheads. I'm pulling out my engineers and technicians. We'll be back on board Lan in five minutes."

"Kellon here. Good job, Lorn. Company is coming this way, but it's not yet knocking on the front door.

"Lieutenant Oster, Kellon here. Current status please."

There was a slight pause before a response was received, "Oster here. We've completed planting charges throughout the ship. The medical team is back on Lan. We were waiting for Commander Shaw's team to depart the Communications Center before planting our charges there. We should be wrapped up here in another fifteen minutes."

Kellon frowned, "Lieutenant Oster, have we overlooked anything that even *looks* like it might be an archaeological artifact?" "No, Sir. We've collected everything that even remotely might be old or glitters. We've accumulated a sizable horde of stuff. In truth, we're running out of space in which to keep it. Everything was videoed and packed in an indexed fashion. We'll know precisely where it came from within this ship. I'm of the opinion that every one of the Kreel senior officers was striving to open his own museum. The only things we've left on the ship are the things that are clearly of modern design and construction."

"Lieutenant Oster, as soon as you have the charges planted, begin evacuating your remaining security personnel. Be certain everyone is off that ship. I want a full head count and roll call before we button that ship up. Let me know when you're ready to set the timers."

"Yes, Sir, estimating twenty minutes."

Looking over toward Roy, Kellon saw he was looking rather serene and peaceful, somewhat like a feline that had just had a good supper. "Navigation, Roy, how are we doing?"

Roy's mouth broadened into a smile. "Well, Sir, I don't know how I will explain to my dear mother that her son has grown up to become a pirate. The news will come as a shock, and it's certainly going to break her heart. As for our getaway route, I've got it plotted. Estimating heliopause in eighteen hours, more or less, after you round up the rest of our brigands. I've taken the liberty of positioning the rest of our gang on the aforementioned escape route, and they are now waiting for us. Need I say that they are waiting with anticipation of a clean getaway, before the local legal authorities arrive?"

Hurriedly entering the CAC, Lorn went directly to his Tactical console. He spoke briefly with Elayne, then turned to examine his status screens. After a moment more, he looked toward Kellon. "Sir, we have six Tuen Class fast-attack ships approaching at 200 lights. Sensors indicate they've divided and formed into a twelve-element battle formation. They will be here in a little over eight hours."

"Tactical, well done. We should be good and gone before they arrive."

"Commodore Kellon, Oster here. Lieutenant Shem has reported all of his personnel are on board Lan and accounted for. Confirming all medical personnel are back aboard. All six squads are safely aboard. I can report with absolute surety, none of our personnel remain on board the Kreel ship. At your command, I'm prepared to set the timers and secure the hatches."

With a sigh of relief, Kellon keyed his command band, "Lieutenant Oster, set the charges for twenty minutes and then secure the transport hatches. As soon as Lan's hatch is secured, we will disengage. Then pull away and observe the results of your handiwork."

"Yes, Sir. I've set the timers for twenty minutes, mark! Hatches are now secured and the boarding tube is retracted."

"Lan, are you eavesdropping again?"

"Sir, as Shey reports, only in the line of duty."

"Lan, move us away from the transport and clamp on every stealth protocol we have. Move up and out to join up with the rest of our squadron. Prepare to take aboard our Scouts."

"Yes, Sir."

"Navigation, Kellon here. We're about to join up with the rest of our marauding gang. I must confess that your dear mother truly has something to be concerned about, and you have indeed been keeping bad company. For the moment, just be certain that we're at our maximum heavy-missile effective range in eighteen minutes.

"Fire Control, bring four heavy missiles to Condition 2. When we pull away, establish optical locks on the transport ship. Confirm."

"Fire Control here. Setting four heavy missiles Condition 2. Pending establishment of optical homing on Target 1."

"Lan, get us out of here."

"Lan here, moving up and away."

"Lan, direct the nearby Zed decoy toward the heliopause, and set its acceleration to a velocity of 200 lights. Implement the same self-destruct protocols we used in the first decoy."

"Sir, the second decoy is following its new orders."

Twenty minutes later, with the video focused on the Kreel transport, Lan waited for the anticipated outcome. When the explosion came, it was quite spectacular. The ship slowly swelled, expanding from its stem to its stern, then it was violently engulfed in the eruption of a massive fireball. Then it was no more.

"Fire Control. Reset all missiles to Condition 4.

"Counter Measures, reset all point defenses to Condition 3." Kellon smiled to himself, thinking, *When you need something to go boom, send a young man to blow it up. They're so very good at such tasks.*

Still smiling, Kellon keyed the squadron's general internal communications channel, "Heads up everyone, Kellon here. Lieutenant Oster, nicely done. My sincere congratulations to you, Lieutenant Shem, and the entire boarding team. It was an outstanding performance on the part of everyone involved. Thank you for an especially spectacular concluding statement. Well done, everyone! I mean that acknowledgment for the entire squadron. Be advised, we are now heading for home! Kellon out."

Frowning, Kellon considered the remaining details he needed to wrap up before they departed K-23. "Lan, transmit the self-destruction code to all our secondary probes. Leave only the deep reconnaissance probes active in this system. Set ship status to modified Condition 3. "

"Yes, Sir," Lan acknowledged.

"Navigation, Roy, join us up with our squadron. It's time to make good our escape from this wasteland. Roy, take us home."

## Chapter Fifty-Nine:
# Welcome to McBride's

The evening was cool, the dark sky was clear, and the heavens above were ablaze with stars. As Susie's vehicle arrived at the temporary barricade in front of McBride's, Guardian Force security personnel politely halted the vehicle. Looking about, Susie saw Guardian Force security personnel were numerous— and all were alert and well-armed. Her driver was in plain clothing, but he was also Guardian Fleet Security. As he identified himself and Susie to the guard, the guard immediately stepped back and saluted. Other guards lifted the barrier. As they passed through, Susie watched the guards drop the barrier behind them.

McRoy, why are there so many Security people here?"

"Madam Ambassador, you are only seeing a few of the Security personnel who are really here. Tonight's party at McBride's has in attendance the most senior Guardian Force officers, and the senior Representatives from the Planetary Assembly. If you could see them, you would observe a Guardian Cruiser providing high cover while his Scouts are providing the low cover. Guardian Force is on full alert tonight."

"Are we expecting an attack?" Susie asked.

"Madam Ambassador, the purpose of proper security is to assure an attack is highly improbable."

As the vehicle pulled smoothly up to the entrance, a uniformed doorman smiled as he stepped briskly forward and opened Susie's door.

"Welcome to McBride's, Ambassador Wells. It's my pleasure to welcome you here this fine evening."

Susie took the man's offered hand and stepped out of the vehicle. McRoy came around the back of the vehicle and opened the rear door.

Susie held out Gepeto's leash and commanded, "Come."

With a bound and a doggy smile, Gepeto jumped from the rear seat and moved promptly to Susie's left side. After clipping the leash to Gepeto's collar, she turned and nodded her head to McRoy.

"Thank you. We'll be here only for an hour or so. Will you be alright during that time?"

"Madam Ambassador," McRoy answered, "this place is like my second home. Many of those around us are old shipmates. I'll be just fine. Go on in and enjoy yourself, take all the time you want. I'll be here when you're ready to go home."

Turning, Susie called Gepeto to heel, then proceeded up the stairs to the door. As she and Gepeto made their entrance into the main dining room, she saw Eryan standing nearby and waved.

"Susie! You're home again, welcome back," Eryan said.

Coming over, Eryan gave Susie a big hug. Then standing back, she slowly looked Susie up and down. "Hmmm, it seems Megan's climate agrees with you. You're looking tanned, fit, full of energy, and happy. At the first moment, you will of course tell me absolutely everything that's happened. Everything! I must have a full report."

"Eryan, before we go into what I've been doing, I've got to know about Kellon," Susie implored. "I've been out of the loop and dying to know what's happened. Are they all right? Have they suffered any losses? Were there any more Cobalt Blues?"

"Patience, all of your questions will be answered in good time. For now, we need to navigate through this milling throng to a safe port of call," Eryan responded.

Taking Susie by the hand, Eryan turned and guided her back toward a distant corner of McBride's. As they crossed the main room, they carefully worked between the people who were engaged in animated conversation mode. As they moved through, everyone turned and greeted them— all of them were apparently in good humor. Susie felt somewhat overwhelmed. *Why,* she thought, *there must be two hundred or more people here.*

As they went up the steps into the far corner, she noticed the room had the distinct smell of wood smoke. Then she saw the fireplace and realized that there was a wood fire in it. Smiling, she remembered her meeting on Earth with Charles Sullivan at the Old Stone Station. *Now, that meeting seems so very long ago,* she thought.

Susie saw her cherished friends— the elder foxes of the Guardian Force— Admirals Mer Shawn, Ron Cloud, and Dylan

Cord. They were sitting about a broad wooden plank table. As Eryan and Susie approached, the three men all promptly stood. With wide smiles and warm greetings, the three gentlemen happily received the two ladies and Gepeto. Ron and Dylan had pulled out chairs for Susie and Eryan, and everyone took their seats.

"Susie," exclaimed Mer Shawn, "you will need to give us a complete run-down on Megan. As you already know, none of us has seen the planet up close and personal. Each of us is curious about your impressions of the place."

"Sir, Megan is absolutely beautiful. I had the opportunity to go over most of the planet with Guardian cartographers. I'm able to tell you it's truly filled with wonderful possibilities and promise."

"When will the first settlers arrive?" Dylan asked.

"Sir, I was told the first pioneers from Earth will be arriving within the year. I hope to be there to greet them on their arrival. That will be a very exciting and busy time for everyone."

Mer Shawn's eyes were twinkling. "Hmmmm, I understand that you found a potential building site for yourself on the coastline of one of its continents."

Susie could not suppress her joy at the thought. "Sir, I most certainly did. It's a very beautiful and special location, and there's a protected cove, sandy beaches, and adjoining rolling hills. It's so much like my old home on the California Central Coast that I immediately thought of planting vineyards. Eryan assured me that I had the authorization to choose the parcel for my own, and I delightedly did so. It's all so wonderful!

"Admiral Mer Shawn, Sir, before I say anything more about Megan, I simply must know about Kellon and the squadron. Are they all right? Have they completed their mission? Was anyone killed or injured?"

"Susie, they're quite all right," Mer happily answered. "The squadron broke out of K-23 eight days ago. While there, they did some serious damage to the Kreel, including taking out some very high-ranking Kreel Elite and Military officials. As a direct result, the ruling Kreel have issued an Empire-wide alert. They have every available Kreel warship out looking for the culprits."

"The Kreel are beating every bush in their Empire, looking for your True Blood renegades," Ron added.

Seeing Susie's look of concern, Ron continued, "Don't worry, Kellon's squadron is now deep in interstellar space, and that's one big volume to hide in. They're on their way home. In fact, we anticipate them arriving within a week or so. At last report, they were injury and damage free."

Susie let out a deep sigh of relief. "When I was unable to get updates, I feared the worst. I am very relieved to hear they're safe." Susie wanted to ask her one remaining burning question. Before she could, Mer Shawn looked around the table.

"Ladies, might I suggest the Kintana Gold? It's an excellent before dinner wine."

Ron noticed Susie's companion and bent over to pat him on the head. "Why, Gepeto, good evening to you small Sir."

Gepeto promptly sat up and displayed his most hopeful smile for Ron, his tail wagging.

"Sir, he's hoping to score a treat. However, in such surroundings he is not permitted treats," Susie cautioned.

Looking to her pup, Susie quietly commanded, "Gepeto, down. Be a good pup and you'll get a treat later. I promise."

Gepeto looked sadly back to Susie, and with a deep sigh he settled down and closed his eyes. Looking at her beloved pup affectionately, Susie commented, "He's always had that Zen Buddhist instantaneous meditation trick down pat."

Striding up the two stairs to the back corner nook, McBride personally took Mer Shawn's orders for five glasses of Kintana Gold. Then, turning briskly, he moved back to the main throng of his guests. His restaurant was full to overflowing, and he was humming happily to himself. In a wink, he was back with a tray with five glasses of wine, which he efficiently distributed.

Eryan leaned forward and gave Mer Shawn a cool inquiring look, "Well, Mer Shawn, I personally would like to hear if Kellon and his privateers actually found and took the treasure from the Kreel transport? I've been asking that question for three days, and all three of you have remained tight-lipped about the topic. So what gives? Did they get the treasure or didn't they get the treasure? Fess up!"

"Treasure?" Susie queried, looking puzzled.

"Well, it's sorta hard to answer that question," Ron said. "The boarding team rummaged the entire ship from stem to its stern. I am dutifully informed they removed anything that hinted of a glitter or was deemed more than two days old."

"Treasure?" Susie asked hopefully.

"Maybe some treasure, and maybe not. What we know is that the gathered stuff was neatly put into containers, each container being labeled as to where the loot was found— meaning which compartment." Mer added.

"Loot?" Susie asked, while looking about hopefully.

"Then none of you profess to know precisely what was looted?" Eryan asked.

"Well, not precisely," Ron admitted. "However, video was obtained of the entire process. Regretfully, we didn't have either a qualified archaeologist on board or six months in which to study the booty. They've boxed the stuff, and it's now under the Commodore's seal. As to what the loot may be worth, or what's in it, or what secrets it may hold, we'll all need to wait until the squadron reaches Glas Dinnein and knowledgeable experts can examine the artifacts."

"Other than the treasure, there's another matter that we haven't talked about. It's something that's both surprising and very disturbing," Dylan said.

The tone of Dylan's voice caught both Eryan and Susie's attention; it suggested problems of a most serious nature.

"Dylan, that's a tease if I've ever heard one," scolded Eryan. "Just what type of problems are we talking about? What can we mention, but not discuss?"

Holding his wine glass up to the colorful cut-glass lamp suspended over the plank table, Dylan rolled the stem of the glass between his fingers while he observed the light's multi-colored flashing scintillations.

After a brief pause, Dylan continued quietly, "Eryan, what follows is classified Black Hole." Looking over, he studied both Eryan and Susie's expressions, as if waiting for an affirmation.

Putting her wine glass down, Eryan planted her elbows on the table and leaned forward, looking from admiral to admiral. "All right, Black Hole. Now if you scurrilous rogues don't open up and start talking, I will give you problems that'll also need to be classified Black Hole! Out with it, what are you scoundrels holding back?"

Like Eryan, Mer Shawn put his wine glass down on the table. Then he looked at Eryan, and his expression was serious.

"Eryan, when the boarding party stormed the Elite transport, among everything else, they found a captive woman in a cell. She was naked, alone, showed the results of repeated beatings, and as of the last report, remains in a state of unconsciousness. We don't yet know if she's going to survive."

Eryan's expression revealed the depth of her shock. "Mer, the Kreel don't keep human prisoners, they promptly butcher and eat them. If this person, this woman, was alive and in a cell, there must have been a very good reason. Do we have any idea why she's still among the living?"

Shaking his head slowly, Mer answered, "No. We know nothing whatsoever about her. All I can say with certainty is that there was a deep sense of outrage felt throughout the squadron when they found her. The brutal treatment she received at the hands of the Kreel was quite evident. It was a very good thing for the Kreel that they were already dead.

"The woman is on board Lan, and she's being provided our best medical care. The prognosis that is she'll most likely live. It's not, however, yet known if there's any brain damage from her earlier abuse or the anti-Kreel beam that hit the ship."

Frowning, Ron spoke in a low voice, "It wasn't a single beam. Kellon has informed us he hit that ship with the anti-Kreel beam twice before boarding. I can't find a single Guardian physician who worked on the anti-Kreel beam project who will hazard a guess about possible brain damage. There's also the possibility of psychological shock and derangement."

Both Susie and Eryan sat very quietly, and Susie grimaced inwardly. She still remembered vividly the yellow serpentlike eyes of the snarling Kreel officer who'd threatened Kur. His glaring yellow eyes and fangs and the hatred emanating from that monster wasn't something she could forget. Just the thought of being naked, helpless, and brutalized by such creatures horrified her. She wasn't able to suppress a flash of cold dread, and her body trembled in response to the thought.

"Sir, when she does arrive on Glas Dinnein? Where will she stay? Will she be allowed any freedom, or will she be held a prisoner?" Susie asked.

"Susie, none of us has even thought about her being a prisoner. In all likelihood, whoever she is, we will afford her every possible courtesy and comfort. We will obviously need to learn all we can about where she's from, about her people, about her world, about their history and their relationship with the Kreel. A prisoner? No, absolutely not!" Ron emphasized.

Looking grim, Susie responded, "Sir, I do herewith formally request that I be permitted to board Lan upon his arrival. I want to meet this woman. Perhaps I can extend to her an offer of what she will most certainly need— a friend on Glas Dinnein."

"Susie, I understand why you're asking, but there's a great deal we must learn before we can evaluate what may be the best for this person. We don't even know yet if she will survive. However, if she does, I will second your request," Eryan assured.

McBride arrived and, with a flourish, passed out the menus for the evening's fare. Then he stoked the fire, which sent out sparks and produced appropriate snaps of disgruntlement. He next threw a few new pieces of wood onto the glowing embers and briskly retreated.

Susie's left hand dropped to her side, as she looked down toward Gepeto. As if prompted by telepathy, the pup raised up his head and knowing brown eyes to Susie. Patting his head, she whispered to him, "Whoever she is, she has at least two friends on Glas Dinnein— that being you and me." Gepeto put on his best smile, his tail vigorously thumping the floor in affirmation.

Susie looked at Admiral Mer Shawn with some hesitation, "Sir, may I ask one question about the mission?"

"Of course, Susie, ask away," Mer said.

"Well, Sir, earlier Admiral Cloud mentioned my True Blood renegades. Did my suggestion of making it appear there was an underground resistance movement— a True Blood resistance— prove beneficial?"

The somber facial expressions of those sitting at the table took Susie somewhat aback. She took a deep breath, not certain what their reaction to her question meant. All three admirals and Eryan glanced knowingly at each other, and then returned their attention to Susie.

"Madam Ambassador, it is my pleasure to inform you that your True Blood resistance idea has worked. In fact, it has exceeded every expectation!" Mer said.

"We're now intercepting Kreel reports of open conflict between the Elite Guard and Military units all over the Kreel Empire. Although there wasn't a True Blood resistance when Kellon began his mission, there certainly is one now. What's more important, is that the movement appears to be becoming organized," Ron added.

"You can be assured the Kreel Elite have the makings of what could be called a revolution on their hands," Dylan said.

Sitting in utter surprise, Susie looked at the smiling faces of her friends. "Really?"

Mer Shawn broke into a broad smile. Lifting his glass in a toast, everyone at the table joined him in his salute. "Exceedingly well done Ambassador Susie Wells! Well done indeed!"

In chorus, her four friends exuberantly exclaimed, "Bravo, Susie, bravo!"

# Chapter Sixty:
## Chandara

Lan and his brothers were dispersed in a loose combat-spread formation and moving swiftly through the dark void. They were surveying the space around them, carefully inserting Navigation Beacons, and striking in a direction to connect with their previously laid entry routes. It was doubly difficult work knowing the Kreel were out in force and looking for the assailants of the August One.

Like Guardian Intelligence on Glas Dinnein, they were monitoring the Kreel Military communications channels, and they were astutely aware of the intense systematic search in progress. Each Cruiser in Kellon's squadron, and their crews, understood they were the quarry in a massive and deadly hunt. The squadron moved cautiously and stealthily toward Glas Dinnein.

Checking his notes, Lorn looked toward Kellon with a troubled expression. "Sir, from all preliminary intelligence, the August One on that transport was literally that— the Supreme Elite himself. We bagged their number one. Given the escalating fury, the other Elite on Hub-3 have taken the ambush and killing of their August One rather personally. In spite of the stress between the Elite Guard and the Military, the Military on Hub-1 is now busy moving impressive resources into the expanding search for the guilty parties."

"Hmmm, the Military's strong response might just reflect their own feelings about two of their high-ranking admirals being killed along with the August One. Have there been any mentions of the treasure?" Kellon inquired.

"No, Sir, at least we haven't come across any."

Deeply absorbed in reviewing the data obtained from the transport, Kellon, Lorn, and Elayne were working together in Kellon's conference room. Displayed on the bulkhead screen was the three-dimensional image of the Kreel Situation Room that Lorn had recorded on board the transport. The image showed the Situation Room bulkheads covered with maps, graphs, and charts. In the center of the image was a hologram of what appeared to be the sprawling Kreel Empire. From the colorful representation of the hologram, the Kreel Empire consisted of more than forty worlds. The hologram in the image was ablaze with lights and symbols. Some were flashing and others were shown in a variety of brilliant colors— the meaning of which was unknown.

Lorn's attitude was serious as he tried to explain his own insights to Kellon.

"Sir, I haven't even begun to catalogue all the files we were able to transfer from the transport. Those files are significantly greater in number than the total obtained from the Gortoga cruiser. So far, I've identified hundreds of planet-by-planet military, political, and economic breakdowns. It will take our Intelligence people on Glas Dinnein months, and perhaps years, just to wade through and catalog all those files, let alone translate and summarize them for general access."

Leaning back in his chair, Kellon cupped his hands behind his head and studied the image on the bulkhead. "Lorn, I haven't a clue as to what archaeological artifacts we may have garnered by our boarding and storming that Kreel ship. What secrets, or what value, such artifacts might retain is unknown. What I do know is the intelligence value of the data you've harvested is beyond estimation. If your assessment is anywhere near being correct, we've just plugged some huge and gaping holes in our knowledge of the Kreel Empire. Admirals Mer Shawn, Ron Cloud, and Dylan Cord are going to be very happy people."

"Sir, I am in full agreement. When we began this mission, none of us considered we would score an Intelligence coup like this."

Elayne interjected, "Sir, we are continuing to monitor the Elite Guard's communications channels. They've found sufficient scattered jetsam from the August One's transport to confirm he is dead. They are, however, not stopping there. They have a thousand unanswered questions, and they're expanding their inquiry for answers. So far, they're sniffing down the confused trail pointing to the True Blood resistance."

Kellon shook his head in admiration, "Dear Susie, wherever you are, well done. Who could've thought that a simple concept— like an imaginary resistance concealed within the Kreel Military— would blossom into such a political nightmare for the Kreel Elite? I'm compelled to confess, not all battles are won with lasers and missiles. Our lovely Ambassador from Earth has earned her pay for the foreseeable future.

"Elayne," Kellon continued, "what do we have concerning the Elite Guard? How are they responding?"

"Sir, there are some reports of pitched battles between the Elite Guard and regular Military units. The higher Military commanders are trying to rope in and restrain the Elite Guard, but there's considerable antagonism between the two forces. Since the Elite Guard troops are highly motivated, they're pushing the battle— but the Military has more raw assets and are shutting them down overall. The reports from K-9 indicate the Military is now in complete control on that planet. They've locked down the Elite Guard forces, and they're reporting to the Elite that a complete review of recent events has begun. A diligent search for any trace of the True Blood is ongoing. To date, the Military hasn't found any. The Elite are not buying such assurances and are demanding more proofs.

"Interestingly enough, the Elite Guard is in a complete shambles. The recent loss of so many ships and senior personnel has crippled their influence. While not openly saying so, the Military isn't unhappy about that consequence."

Thoughtfully, Kellon turned toward Lorn. "What information do we have regarding K-23? What's happening within that system?"

"Sir, there are literally hundreds of intercepts to and from K-23. It is a burgeoning beehive of activity. Literally hundreds of ships are now arriving. A full squadron of Elite Guard ships was among the first to arrive, and they were escorting another transport full of officials from Hub-3. The Elite have assumed absolute control over both the Elite Guard and Military personnel on K-23. They are also conducting a fine grained search of the battle volume looking for anything that can explain who the assailants were."

Frowning, Kellon replied thoughtfully, "Hopefully, we left nothing behind pointing to the Guardian Force. One of the Kreel's highest racial priorities is not appearing weak. Given their heightened response to our taking out the August One, I believe the Kreel will retaliate when they identify a foe— regardless of the risks involved.

"Sir, Lan here. Physician Lorentz desires to speak with you. Are you available?"

"Yes, Lan. For Physician Lorentz, I am most definitely available. Patch him through."

The incoming message indicator on Kellon's desk flashed.

Keying the activation button, he responded, "Kellon here."

"Commodore Kellon, Physician Lorentz here. You asked me to let you know if our patient became conscious. She isn't yet awake, but her bio-signs indicate she may soon become conscious. Frankly, if she does, that will certainly improve my prognosis. If you want to be in attendance when she comes around, I recommend you come soon. Physician Lorentz out."

Elayne leaned forward, "Sir, may I have your permission to attend? Everyone down there is a male, no offense intended, but a woman may give her a sense of reassurance upon waking in a strange location."

"Elayne, you're more than welcome. Frankly, if you hadn't asked me, I would've asked you."

Lorn frowned, "Sir, we don't have a clue as to who she is or where she came from. May I recommend brevity in dealing with her? Perhaps it would be best if we learn about her before she learns all that much about us."

Elayne looked from Kellon to Lorn, obviously upset, "Who she is? Where she's from? Gentlemen, she's a sentient being! The Kreel have badly injured her, and where she came from isn't particularly important right now. That person has been captured by the Kreel, beaten to within an inch of her life, subjected to two anti-Kreel beam transmissions— she'll be waking in a totally strange environment and what you're concerned about is Intelligence leaks?"

Lorn winced at Elayne's outraged tone, "Well, Elayne, put in those terms, I was perhaps a little off the landing beam. Nevertheless, she is an unknown. We don't know what door is opening here, and we should use some circumspection in opening it. No offense intended."

Kellon resolved the matter. "Ladies and Gentlemen, the patient is a guest aboard Lan. We will extend to her every courtesy and all possible gentle care. I do not believe reserving our home galactic coordinates represents a problem. She will be waking confused and in a different world and circumstances than those she lost consciousness in. I doubt she will be looking for intelligence data upon waking. I suggest we proceed as the physician has recommended."

Lorn stood, smiling toward Elayne, "When you finish in the dispensary, I'd appreciate your assistance in Tactical. Until then, take your time and do all that you consider appropriate to help the patient."

Elayne smiled slightly. "Sir, I'm sorry if I said anything to suggest you were out of line— you weren't. I was considering the patient, and you were considering all of us, including her. It was my overreaction."

"Elayne, I believe we should get our backsides down to the dispensary. Lorn, you may or may not see Elayne during the next duty cycle, depending on what we encounter in the dispensary. What she will do is keep you appropriately informed."

Turning to Elayne, Kellon asked, "Isn't that correct?"

Looking decidedly uncomfortable, Elayne replied, "Yes, Sir, that's completely correct. Zorn and Roan have also expressed their concerns, as has everyone else in the crew. What the Kreel did to her has everyone upset. They all want to know how she's doing."

Turning, Kellon proceeded to the door and passed through, Elayne immediately behind him, with Lorn bringing up the rear and closing the door behind them. Five minutes later, Kellon and Elayne entered the dispensary and Physician Lorentz immediately confronted them. He dressed in whites, and his countenance was clouded and stern.

"Commodore, within this dispensary, I set the rules. When my patient comes around, you are not to subject her to any form of interrogation. You are here on probation, and if you cannot adhere to the rules in place, you will decidedly need to leave."

Kellon let a smile grow into an open grin. "Physician Lorentz, I'm holding out my arms to prove I did not bring my chains and whip. I promise that we will not subject your patient to any form of interrogation, harsh or otherwise. We are here purely out of our concern for her welfare."

Physician Lorentz frowned at Kellon as if he were trying to assess his sincerity. Then he shrugged and turned, "Follow me and please be quiet."

When the three Guardian personnel entered the ward, they saw the warm honey-caramel skin and regular features of a woman whose eyelids were still closed, though fluttering slightly. Her hair was stunning— a rich deep brown, a deeper shade than Kellon believed he had ever seen before. What made it particularly striking were the occasional strands of bright gold interspersed throughout the dark masses of her hair. She looked somewhat like a child in the lines of her countenance and her proportions; she seemed almost swallowed by the bed and its pure white coverings. As she lay there, all that they could see was her head, arms, and hands. The stark contrast between the dark rich brown and the highlights of her hair's golden strands was eye-catching. She had a high forehead and high cheekbones. Her mouth was to all appearances perfectly proportioned to the rest of her features. Even in her distressed physical condition, she was beautiful.

It was apparent the medical personnel had carefully cleaned the dirt and grime from her. Now the bright whiteness of the pillows and sheets contrasted starkly with the dark ugly bruising still remaining on her arms and face. She was breathing softly, but there was an occasional moan— an inner cry of despair or fright.

Kellon bit his lower inner lip. The brutal treatment this woman had suffered outraged him. If ever he'd ever had need of justification for the war against the Kreel, there in that bed, on those blizzard-white sheets, was the only vindication one could ever need. He turned and looked at Physician Lorentz. In his eyes, Kellon saw the same outrage, the same anger, and something more. Physician Lorentz was determined to protect his charge, regardless of another's rank or authority. Kellon smiled. He'd always liked and respected Physician Lorentz, but never more than he did at this moment.

"Physician Lorentz, I fully understand your position. Be assured, we share the same intent regarding your patient's welfare."

Physician Lorentz looked for a long moment at Kellon, and then slowly relaxed. "Commodore, I regret my former attitude. There's just something about this person I cannot explain. I feel she's more than she appears to be. I will do whatever it takes to see she is fully healed and returned safely to her people."

Both Kellon and Elayne sat down in the available chairs in the room, and neither of them said anything to the other. They waited quietly, observing the person in the bed.

As they watched, her physical agitation seemed to increase, and low moans and soft whimpering were soon the only sounds in the ward.

Suddenly, the woman in the bed tried to sit up; she threw her right forearm over her eyes and screamed. It was a piercing and rising exclamation of terror, emerging up out of the very depths of an abyss. Moving quickly to the bedside, Elayne sat down and took the woman's free hand in her own. Slowly and gently, she brushed the loose hair that had fallen over the woman's face away while softly whispering, "Shhhh, you are among friends, you are safe."

Elayne's voice was reassuringly soft, carrying with it tones of protection that washed away the evident inner terror. In exhaustion, the woman fell back onto her bed and tears came as a flood, accompanied by deep gasping sobs. The sobbing continued for a few minutes, and then the woman again relapsed into a state of unconsciousness.

Physician Lorentz had stayed by the bedside, observing everything that happened. Looking at his instrument bio-readouts, he quietly sighed. His easing concern was evident in his expression and posture.

"Commodore, I am elevating my prognosis for a positive outcome. I believe she will recover. From what depths of darkness she came up from, I cannot tell you, but it was a dark region indeed. She is back among us, and although she didn't speak, I believe she understands she is among friends. She's fallen into a natural restive sleep now. It may be several hours before she again awakes."

Both Elayne and Kellon looked at the resting slight form in the large white bed and smiled in unison. "Physician Lorentz," Elayne asked, "if you and Captain Kellon agree, I would like to wait here quietly until she does wake."

"Lieutenant Cloud, it may take some time, and I don't know how long that may be. I suggest you return to your duty. I promise to notify you the moment her condition changes."

"Sir, on your promise as an Officer and a Doctor, I'll go back to work."

With some reluctance, Elayne turned, and together with Kellon, they departed the dispensary.

## X

As the hours passed, the five Guardian Cruisers made several short-Jumps, slipping through the void undetected. While they were moving ever further from K-23, they were steadily coming nearer Glas Dinnein.

As his communicator buzzed, Kellon looked up.

"Sir," Lan reported, "it is Physician Lorenz. Will you accept his call?"

Within five minutes, Both Kellon and Elayne had returned to the dispensary and resumed their vigil. The woman's eyelids again fluttered briefly and then her large almond-shaped eyes opened. She lay quietly on the bed, and her irregular breathing gradually became measured and even. Kellon immediately recognized her breathing rhythm as a studied conscious action, a breathing pattern that was the result of disciplined mental control. He smiled. He did not require Physician Lorentz's prognosis; he already had his own. The woman was awake, alert, and more importantly, he knew she was in full control of her own mind.

Elayne again sat on the bedside, taking the woman's hand in her own. With a sweet smile, she looked at the woman in the bed and softly repeated, "You are among friends. You are safe. Everything will be fine."

Perhaps it was Elayne's tone of voice, her smile, her gentle touch, but it had worked. The woman struggled to sit up and then threw her arms around Elayne's body, as if seeking security. She lowered her head to Elayne's shoulder and began to softly sob.

Physician Lorentz stood nearby and kept his eyes on what was transpiring on the bed and on the bio-readouts. He looked cautiously happy.

Kellon felt the tensions of the past hours begin to ebb away. There was something special in what had happened here. It was something profound, but he could not put his finger on precisely what it was. He sighed and let the unbidden inquiring thought fly away unrestrained.

Elayne waited till the woman drew back a little. Then she touched her own chest and said in a soft voice, "Elayne."

The woman lay still, and then for the first time slowly looked around her. She saw Physician Lorentz dressed in his whites and his concerned expression. Then she looked at Commodore Kellon and studied his deeply worried expression. It was as if she'd fully understood Elayne's earlier comments, and suddenly knew that she was safe and among friends. She smiled, and her smile lit up the room with a radiance like the sun breaking through on a dark overcast day. Everyone else in the room could only smile in response.

Her beautiful eyes were the same dark brown as her hair, and they sparkled with flecks of gold and hope. Kellon thought, *She is truly beautiful.*

Slowly, the woman looked back toward Elayne, lifted her right hand, and touched Elayne on her chest— even as Elayne had done. She softly said, "Elayne?" Then she moved her hand gracefully back and touched her own chest. She smiled again with renewed warmth, "Chandara."

## Chapter Sixty-One:
# Empire of Warriors

For long minutes, Fleet Grand Admiral Groff sat quietly studying the hologram suspended before him. Being under house arrest, he was out of uniform and wearing a deep scarlet embroidered casual robe while enjoying the luxury and privacy of his own garden den. The melodious and soothing notes of wind chimes flowed throughout the environs, yet his mood was anything but peaceful, being filled with questions and turbulent, dark, and angry thoughts.

The hologram before him was sparkling with thousands of pinpoints of multicolored lights— many single lights representing a star. White lights represented the Empire, and various shades of blue encoded the bordering and adjoining star systems.

The focus of his intense thought was not white or blue, but the bright pinpoints of contrasting red. He well knew that each bright red speck indicated a location where someone had destroyed a Kreel warship. That there were so many red points in two years only escalated his sense of anger.

He noted with troubled thoughts the clustered red points distributed near the outer borders of the Empire. He reasoned, *An expanding Empire anticipates some military losses, yet, the losses we sustained during the invasion of the Arkillian systems are more than statistical anomalies.*

He knew prior to the invasion the Empire had held the Arkillians in utter contempt and considered them weak. Events had proven their Military assessment was badly flawed. Something in the intelligence gathering and planning had gone seriously wrong. *Very wrong indeed,* he thought.

Now he felt his personal scrutiny was required to determine the underlying causes for the catastrophic outcome of the invasion. *Someone,* he vowed to himself, *is going to pay with their lives for that failure.*

He reasoned, *Where the Empire's borders are expanding, turbulence and some Military losses are to be expected. However, disasters such as we suffered within the Arkillian system are not tolerable!*

Making the matter even more serious, not one ship in their entire fleet had survived to report what had happened. Not one!

Following the failed invasion, he had sent two fast-attack ships into the Arkillian system. They did not survive to report back. That failure in gathering intelligence was itself surprising. Such a total lack of Military intelligence was unacceptable. He would demand a complete review and an improvement of reporting policy and methods; he would not tolerate such failure in future fleet operations.

The hum of the command wand broke into his thoughts, announcing a priority call. Irritated, he stirred, looking at the wand display to discern who had priority high enough to override his set privacy threshold. A low rumbling growl sounded in his chest as he thought, *It is Commander Ugchi, the insufferable fool representing the Elite Guard.*

Thumbing the accept key on the wand, he responded, "What do you want, Commander?"

"Groff, I'm calling—"

In an angry snarl, Groff cut him off. "Commander, in the future you will address me appropriately as Fleet Grand Admiral Groff. Is that perfectly clear?"

There was only the briefest hesitation before Commander Ugchi continued drily, "Fleet Grand Admiral Groff, then. However, my rank is Commander in the Elite Guard, and I am not within your chain of command. Furthermore, as the senior Elite Guard commander on this planet, your current house arrest is within my jurisdiction and under my personal authority."

As he listened, the disrespect in the Commander's voice was unmistakable, and hot anger threatened to break through Groff's rigid self-control. "Commander, what precisely is the purpose of your call?"

"My purpose is strictly official! I am formally notifying you that I have expanded the scope of my investigation. Now it includes high treason and the Military's direct involvement in the assassination of our August One. As of this moment, Fleet Grand

Admiral Groff, your house arrest is expanded and your entire staff will be detained and placed under arrest."

His restrained fury broke its bonds, but even before he could snarl his response, Commander Ugchi had broken the connection. In fury, Groff stood up and threw the first object that came to hand— an ancient vase. It shattered into a thousand fragments when it struck a pillar, the fragments scattering about the room.

"Incompetent fools," Groff bellowed. "They are all a pack of bumbling fools!" Trembling in his rage, he again sat down, attempting to regain his composure. *Fools,* he thought, *we are faced with a cunning enemy, an unmistakable challenge to the Empire, and all they can do is accuse the Military of treason? Bungling fools!* "Their rampant stupidity, and the enemy's challenge," he growled, "will not go unanswered!"

He observed again the single red dot glaring brightly among the white lights within the hologram. That single light was part of the reason why a fool like Ugchi dared accuse the Military of treason. It was within the infantry training planet's system, and it denoted the loss of an Elite Guard ship.

He growled. *It is only one ship,* he thought, *but the reports stated one of our own cruisers destroyed it. I do not accept that!*

Calling up and studying the condensation report that described the incident, he considered it puzzling. The report indicated the Nori were involved. They had made another of their occasional, but annoyingly pinpointed, hit and run strikes. In fact, he noted that the Elite Guard ship was trying to intercept the Nori when it was itself intercepted and destroyed. Not intercepted by the Nori, but the reports claim it was intercepted and destroyed by one of our own Gortoga cruisers. *By a Gortoga cruiser? Not likely,* he thought. He then questioned, *If not by a Gortoga cruiser, then intercepted by whom?*

As he looked again at the next cluster of red lights amid white lights within the hologram, his eyes narrowed and a low snarl curled his lips. That cluster of red dots near the fabrication planet— only eight red dots, but one of those red dots indicated where the August One had died and three escorting Elite Guard along with four Military ships were destroyed, along with the August One's transport. Not only the August One perished, but also two new Elite Guard grand marshals, two Military admirals, and the command crews for twelve new Elite Guard ships. They had all perished, along with their seven escorts. Again, Gortoga cruisers were reportedly involved. *That possibility,* he thought, *is sheer rubbish. It simply was not possible.*

He opened the associated condensation report and read it once again. His eyes widened when he saw the Nori were again involved. As he reread the report, he began to frown. This information was new. The report confirmed the Nori had directed their strike at the Elite Guard ship-manufacturing facilities on the planet and not against the August One. The report indicated the Nori departed the system immediately following their strike. The death of the August One had occurred four days later. He was not even on the planet when the Nori destroyed the manufacturing facilities.

Deeply troubled, he read the associated condensation report for the third time. *This is truly strange,* he mused, *never before have I heard of a Nori strike employing multiple ships and heavy bombardment lasers; they always operate as a single ship, or at most two ships. They also deploy precision hyper-velocity kinetic-energy impact weapons, always! This entire sequence reeks of a cunning deception; it is some form of diabolical ruse. The close involvement of the Nori, or someone seeking to blame the Nori, is too conveniently near an association with the appearance of Gortoga cruisers where there can be no such cruisers.*

*The association has only occurred in two instances, and one of those does seem to indicate the Nori were involved. In the second instance, however, I consider the involvement of the Nori suspect.*

Sitting back, his thoughts were troubled. *Who wants to shift blame to the Nori and why? I will need to obtain all the facts available on this matter, not just the condensation report. Perhaps I need to go personally to investigate.*

Again, he emitted a low growl from deep within his chest, and felt the heavy ruff along his shoulders attempt to rise. *Why,* he thought, *are so many Elite Guard ships being targeted and systematically destroyed within our own space?* He paused in reflection. *Is it actually possible that four Elite Guard Grand Marshals have been killed during the past year? They had!* That single statistic was in itself improbable and shocking. *What is really happening here? Who is specifically targeting and destroying the Elite Guard ship manufacturing facilities, and why?*

*These events shout there is an informed unidentified enemy, and one with detailed knowledge of the Empire's internal operating structure. How is this possible? Who,* he pondered, *has advance knowledge of the August One's movements and schedule? Of course, the Elite Guard has that information. Therefore, could the August One's death be only coincidental to some broader strategy involving the Elite Guard? Could the reputed traitors be within the Elite Guard itself? There must be a connection. There is more happening here than is being included in the condensation reports. Obviously, someone in the Elite command structure is intentionally withholding vital information. That is unacceptable,* he thought, *and I will require such concealment stop immediately!*

Lifting the command wand, he pressed the clear button. All the red points winked out. Sitting quietly, his mind churned in deep thought. *The appearances of our own Gortoga cruisers, they are the key. Yet,* he considered, *at the time the August One perished, I know the precise location of every Gortoga cruiser. My own staff challenged, checked, rechecked, and verified every location of each Gortoga cruiser. When the August One was slain, none could have possibly been near the fabrication world, none!*

*That fool Ugchi must have based his spurious allegations on nothing more than my staff's validation that no Gortoga cruisers were involved. Perhaps he suspects a cover-up. Even if so, Commander Ugchi's accusation of high treason is unpardonable,* he raged within. *I will not forgive his personal slander of the honor of my family.*

With an effort, he sought to calm his anger. *The problem is basic,* he thought. *How can I refute the reports of Gortoga cruisers being in two different systems where someone destroyed Elite Guard ships, one of them where the August One perished? That accusation,* he reluctantly admitted, *I cannot simply refute.*

*Could there be a real True Blood conspiracy?* For the first time, he began to doubt his own convictions. *Could the Military's Officer Corps be involved in such an insidious treason?*

*Clearly, a powerful and well-organized group exists. Someone had methodically destroyed three hundred cargo ships. Yet, how could a large treasonous group of Military officers evade the Military's and the Elite Guard's intense and ongoing investigation?*

*Given several treasonous Gortoga cruisers do exist,* he reasoned, *they must be cruisers falsely reported as lost in battle. What,* he wondered, *does the timeline of our losses look like? Are they confirmed losses?*

He reset the search to a timeline and entered his new query into the wand. Looking toward the hologram and its array of sparkling pinpoints of lights, he observed a small cluster of red.

Looking first at the condensation report, he then looked up again at the hologram. *Strange,* he thought, *the very first losses were four Gortoga cruisers reported destroyed in one engagement near the central system of the humans. The humans again,* he snarled, *they were from the very beginning the Kreel's bane.*

*Now,* he knew, *the Military kept the humans well harassed and tightly contained, but the number of red dots near their systems proved they remained extremely dangerous. One day,* he swore inwardly, *we will utterly devour them.*

*Even so, bane or otherwise, four Gortoga cruisers destroyed in one skirmish? That is a very heavy and improbable loss for a single commerce-raiding mission.*

Examining the associated report again, he noted with a scowl it lacked any confirmation of the losses. He was now more deeply concerned. The battle reports for that engagement, he decided, demanded detailed study. He would order complete background checks on every officer and crewmember on board those ships, and on their families. *If there is treason there, I will root it out,* he vowed.

Again, he pressed a button on the wand. As the timeline slowly advanced, he observed a scattering of red lights appearing among the multitude of white and blue lights. Then the occasionally appearing red dots suddenly became a blob of red dots. Using the wand, he stopped the replay. Looking carefully at the display several times, he first reversed, and then played it forward. The massive losses he noted all occurred nearly simultaneously, but light-years apart.

He checked again the associated records. His frown deepened. The Empire had lost twenty-one ships in a single secondary Arkillian system. Incredibly, ten of those ships had been Gortoga cruisers on a single coordinated strike-in-force mission. That amount of military force projected at such a distance from the Empire represented a powerful thrust. Against all probability, no ships survived their attacks to report. He then observed that immediately thereafter the disaster blossomed into view in the Arkillian's home system.

Sitting and observing the record of losses in the Arkillian systems, his anger mounted. *What fools in the Elite High Command had proceeded with the invasion of the Arkillian home system following destruction of twenty-one of the Empire's finest ships in an adjoining system? Why had not the Elite High Command asked what had happened to those twenty-one ships?* Then he remembered with still more growing anger, *They had also lost seven hundred thousand first-line infantry troops in that appalling Arkillian failure, seven hundred thousand! Never before had the Empire lost so large a force to a foe in a single battle.* His anger began to escalate toward rage. *Who is responsible in the Elite High Command for such blundering?*

Only then, and for the first time, did he notice that the loss of Grand Marshal Grough and his entire Elite Guard squadron had occurred at the very same time as the Arkillian disaster. They had occurred at the same time, but the two events were more than one hundred light years apart. There could not possibly be any connection, or could there? Something was nagging at him, some critical odd correlating fact about the Arkillian systems that was important, but he could not isolate in his mind what it was. He would need to think about this. It had been some odd but important anomaly. He shrugged, shaking his head, growling at his inability to remember. Whatever it was, he would remember it in due time.

*Why,* he demanded, *are there no records from any survivors, no messages telling what had befallen our ships?*

Again, he cleared the display and sat considering the fragmentary data. Once more, he entered a query into his wand. He asked, "Is there a last message before Grand Marshal Grough and his Elite Guard squadron perished?" *The battle was near the*

*Elite home system,* he reasoned, *surely some battle communications records must exist.*

An amber light glowed on his wand, indicating there was a recorded battle communication. *Good,* he thought, keying the play button. He then sat back to listen. The voice that rolled out of the speakers was full, rich, and confident.

"Grand Marshal Grough, in spite of your overwhelming arrogance, I must confess you are in truth a brilliant tactician and bold warrior. I salute you. However, know this truth, before you can pulverize anything beneath your boots, you must first have boots. Know then who has killed you. I am Lux!"

Utterly stunned, he sat silent for several moments. Never before had he heard such calm absolute arrogance. The enemy flawlessly used the Kreel language to deliver his taunt with absolute confidence. It was that calmly expressed absolute authority that most angered him.

In its swelling immensity, his rage again broke through his reserve. He had at last found the unidentified enemy! As he slowly stood, his body trembled with a smoldering sense of fury. Snarling, his lips contorted and his fangs gleamed. "Who are the Lux?" he shouted. Again he snarled, "Fools whoever they are, we are not a few feeble worlds eking out a grubbing existence from the soil. We are an Empire of warriors!"

*An enemy,* he thought, *has boldly entered into our Empire, and he has struck directly at our head! I will learn who this enemy is and shred them to bits— regardless of the cost.*

With a seldom-felt sense of rage, he began to gather the Empire's formidable military power about him. He keyed his command wand to connect his senior adjutant, and crisply dictated his orders, "Immediately jam all Elite Guard communications on the planet, and ground all Elite Guard ships. Then lock down the Elite's garrison. Arrest Commander Ugchi and his entire staff. Use diplomacy where possible. Place the commander and his staff under house arrest with all possible comforts. Inform the commander that if they resist, I have ordered you to throw them forcibly into the nearest Military brig on half-rations. If diplomacy fails, then use all necessary force, including lethal.

"Next, you are to assemble a task force of one hundred ships, a combined balanced force of cruisers and Tuen fast-attack ships.

Include my Flagship. We are going to pay a social visit to the Elite Guard manufacturing world to attend an unscheduled conference!" He then thumbed the wand, transmitting his orders.

Standing erect, his head held high, with a deep rumbling growl, he vowed to Anubux: "I will personally direct the search inside and outside the Empire for our enemies. Then I will fall on and destroy them! There will be no mercy."

# Chapter Sixty-Two:
## Connecting the Dots

Admiral Ron Cloud was frowning at the stack of intercepts that were piling up on his desk. Every one of them was supposedly so important that it required his personal attention. "Blast!" he muttered under his breath. "When did I suddenly become so indispensably vital around here?"

When his door opened without a preceding knock, he looked up fully prepared to express his hot displeasure at the informality. Seeing it was Mer, he held his fire and smiled. *Thank the muses,* he thought, *a badly needed break.*

Strolling in and looking at Ron's desk with interest, Mer smiled. "Finally, I get to see your desk piled higher with reports than my own. It's about time."

"Welcome to the salt mines, Mer, can I offer you a fresh cup of neab?" Ron inquired in a tired voice.

"No, at least not at this time. I'm only here to see what you might need in order to handle the mushrooming problems arising from Kellon's latest sojourn into the outer reaches. As I've often said, every time I send that man somewhere, my life becomes more difficult. Now I see he's also had a significant deleterious impact on your own work cycle. Do you need some additional help?"

Feeling the weariness of his body and mind, Ron sat quietly for a moment before answering Mer's question. "Yes, Mer. I believe additional help is now in order." With a gesture indicating the highest pile of documents on his desk, he continued, "My staff considers this pile as being urgent. They've sent it to me for my eyes only, and for my personal information and action. The problem is, I've been at this for three days now. Frankly speaking, I'm further behind now than I was three days ago."

Studying the reports on the desk for a moment, Mer then reached into his pocket and pulled out his communicator.

Looking at its buttons, he pressed one and spoke, "Captain Clell, Mer Shawn here. I want you to round up your five top analysts and bring them down to Admiral Cloud's office. That's correct, and do it within the next five minutes. I'm already here in the Admiral's office and waiting. Mer Shawn out."

Turning to Ron, Mer smiled. "I doubt if any one of my six best analysts can compete with you on a level playing field, but combined, they'll give you a good run for your money. I'm now officially relieving you from duty. You're to promptly retire to your quarters and get some sleep. Take the time you need to catch up on your rest. After that, you're to call me. Understood?"

Sighing in exasperation, Ron slowly held up the paper in his hand as if showing it to Mer. "I understand and I'm grateful. However, before I leave I do want to discuss this intercept with you— since you have nothing better to do for at least the next five minutes."

"Five minutes, but when Captain Clell and his analysts arrive, out the door you go, and no buts!"

"Yes, Sir." Ron looked inquisitively at Mer. "Sir, might I know just who your informant was that told you about me being swamped?"

"Oh, you may ask, but don't expect an answer. I tend to protect my sources. That privilege naturally comes with the job of being Fleet Admiral. Now what do you have in your hand that you think is so all-fired important?"

"Well, Sir, do you remember Admiral Groff? He was the Kreel Grand Fleet Admiral that Kellon tangled with near Hub-1. He was the officer the Elite Guard formally suspended and placed under house arrest."

"Yes, I remember. As I recall, you commented recently my counterpart was out mixing it up with his enemies. What's he up to now?"

Sitting back, Ron gathered his thoughts before answering. "With the damage Kellon inflicted on the Elite Guard, its power is severely understrength. Our admiral has now marginalized the Elite Guard and extracted himself from arrest. He has forcibly placed the Elite Guard representatives on Hub-1 under house arrest.

"Sir, I believe he's likely to deploy a strong Military force toward K-23. My concern is simple— new intercepts show the

**448**

Admiral has considerable force at his disposal. With the arrest of the Elite Guard Representative on Hub-1, he seems to be moving politically to displace the Elite Guard. I've read several intercepts where he plainly calls them incompetent and arrogant bunglers. With the death of the August One, he may demand the Elite Guard submit to his authority. I believe he'll force a showdown, and he isn't the type to back down."

"All of that is admittedly interesting, but why is it so all-fired important?"

"The real importance may not be immediate, but it is pivotal. If Admiral Groff prevails, then the Elite Guard tactics of micro-Jumping in combat will soon become Kreel standard fleet tactics."

Sitting down, Mer looked at his good friend. That he was deeply troubled was evident. "Ron, I'm not disputing your expressed concerns. They are valid. However, such news, even as important as it is, is not urgent enough to keep you chained at your desk for days on end without rest or decent food. Together, we will sort it all out during the next few weeks. You're to get some rest— now— no more excuses and no more objections. Any further delay in your going home and sleeping is just not acceptable."

Reaching into his pocket, he again pulled out his communicator and pressed a button. "Fleet Security, Admiral Mer Shawn here. I want a staff car and driver promptly outside HQ. You are to immediately send two security officers to Admiral Cloud's office. They are to escort the Admiral safely home; then they are to see no one bothers him. Mer Shawn out."

Ron looked up with a feeble smile. "I surrender, don't shoot." There was a soft knock on the door. It opened and Captain Clell looked in. "Sir," he said, addressing Mer, "my analysts and I are here and ready for duty, as ordered."

"Come right in, Captain."

Turning to Ron, Mer firmly ordered, "Admiral Cloud, your relief has arrived. Please describe to the Captain the priority structure of the intercepts on your desk. Then go out and meet your security escort and driver. Pronto."

Ron stood straight, "Yes, Sir. Before I do, however, you should know Fleet Admiral Groff is suspicious about the True Blood Gortoga cruiser sightings. He's initiated a full review of all

Gortoga cruiser losses during the past three years. He's particularly interested in their losses occurring in and near Guardian space, Scion, and Earth. That he has recognized where his losses are occurring and ordered a full review, indicates he's looking squarely at Earth, Scion, and Glas Dinnein for the source of his troubles. Sir, he's connecting the dots."

# Chapter Sixty-Three:
## Parade Colors

The landing area was unusually dark, even with its normal lights on. The night sky was threateningly ominous and overcast, and a heavy rain was falling. As Susie looked out of the car's windows, she could see the rippling reflections of the lights in the various pools of water that had formed with the falling rain. The rattle tap of raindrops pelting the car roof and windows was soothing in its background rhythm, and it somehow made the surrounding security of the car with its embracing warm, dry comfort more reassuring— attesting there were no real problems. Looking over, she saw McRoy sitting quietly behind the driver's controls and gazing casually out at the landing area. Gepeto was showing his doggy wisdom and wisely sleeping on the back seat of the car. All things considered, it was quite peaceful.

Susie was not tired, even though it was nearly three in the morning. *How anyone can sleep,* she thought, *with Lan and the others coming home in a few minutes is just not understandable.*

Months had passed, since she'd sat here with McRoy and watched the squadron depart. Since then, she'd spent months on a new world, Megan, and the squadron had been many light-years distant and in combat. She knew their mission was not a strike in force against the Kreel Empire, but rather a deep intelligence probe. Yet, or so it now seemed, the squadron had been in intense combat and stirred up a boiling pot. They'd caused the Kreel Empire some serious damage.

The consequences of that damage were obviously unpredictable. Sighing in consternation, Susie thought, *What Kellon's accomplished is going to shake everything up. And just when Megan is coming together. Such a vibrant world, it's Earth's hope and future.* Reflecting on all the people from Earth who'd be coming out into the stars to build new homes, Susie shook her head at the bewildering complexity of problems now facing humanity.

From what little she could learn from her knowledgeable sources, the Kreel Empire might be much larger and more powerful than Guardian Force had initially believed. *Perhaps,* she worried, *all that Kellon's accomplished is to poke a stick in a big hornet's nest.*

A low wailing siren gradually rose in clarion warning, and it brought Susie out of her reflections. She turned, asking, "McRoy, does the siren mean the squadron is near?"

Even as she asked the question, she could see the sudden intensity of movements around the landing area. She noticed there were a large number of Guardian Force security vehicles standing nearby, along with an ambulance.

As she watched, she saw three Guardian staff cars arrive and park nearby. Because of the darkness and rain, however, she couldn't see who was in the cars.

"Yes, Madam Ambassador. That was the five-minute warning siren. We should be able to see the Cruisers very soon. Of course, the clouds and rain aren't helping much."

Leaning forward and peering out of the windows, Susie tried to get a better look at the overhead clouds. Smiling, McRoy switched on the vehicle's deflector field. The rain suddenly stopped striking the roof and windows, and the droplets already on the windows quickly flowed away.

"There, that should help you see somewhat better." McRoy said.

"Thank you, McRoy. It does help."

Susie's communicator tone softly intruded on her troubled thoughts. Opening the lid, the screen brightened and Elayne's smiling countenance looked back at her. "Hello, Susie, I suspected you might just be waiting, early morning hour, rain or no rain. It's good to be home and to see you once again. What's up?"

"Elayne, is everyone OK? Did everyone make it back?"

"We're all fine. Lan and the squadron came through without any serious casualties. The Kreel, however, didn't do so well."

With a sigh of relief, Susie exclaimed, "Elayne, that's wonderful!"

"Susie, Shey is insisting that I call and ask you to arrange for a priority delivery of root beer for Zorn. He's loudly complaining that they are dry as a desert."

Laughing, Susie felt her tension flow away. "You can tell Shey and Zorn not to worry, his order for root beer has been in the queue for two weeks. I figured Zorn and Roan would have guzzled their allotments. You can tell them the shipment will be on board the moment Security allows for such deliveries.

"Elayne, how is the injured woman? Who is she? How did the Kreel capture her? Where did she come from? When can I meet her?"

"Hold on there, Susie," Elayne laughed, "That's too many questions without taking a breath. Besides, all I really know is her name— Chandara. She's badly injured; but she seems to be getting better. We'll just have to wait awhile before we learn all about her." Susie could hear an alarm sounding behind Elayne as she signed off saying, "We're almost there, see you soon! Elayne out." McRoy turned toward Susie, a big smile breaking across his face. "Madam Ambassador, here they come!" Saying this, he pointed upward and to the north.

Turning, Susie looked up to where McRoy was pointing, and there she saw five bright points of light descending through the clouds. That they were wearing their proud parade colors brought a happy smile to her face. She watched as they approached, growing steadily larger and separating, each Cruiser coming into alignment with its landing cradle. The lighting around the landing area suddenly brightened, becoming as illuminated as full daylight. Susie watched spellbound. Dropping like a feather, the immense bulk of Lan descended from the night sky and settled gently toward his waiting cradle.

As Gepeto jumped up from the rear seat to watch, his tail was wagging furiously. Susie smiled, and the joy was evident in her voice. "McRoy, they're home safe again!"

Like Susie, he was smiling broadly and had a sense of enormous personal pride in their Guardian Force. He knew the Kreel were still out there, but now there was a bright light shining on their previously concealed activity. With the Guardian Force's expanded Intelligence capability and their advancing tactical proficiency, Guardian Force would be aggressively vigilant. He sensed the long battle with the Kreel was about to intensify. Now, however, was a time for celebration. Kellon's squadron was safely home again.

While not turning his eyes from the descending Cruisers for a moment, McRoy quietly added to Susie's happy comment. "Yes, Madam Ambassador, they sure enough are safely home, and they are simply beautiful."

# Epilogue

Within the volumes and eddy currents of Creation, among the billions of this universe's galaxies, there exists a galaxy that some of its inhabitants know as the Milky Way and others call the Wandering Waterway. Spanning more than one hundred thousand light-years, this galaxy contains more than two hundred billion diverse solar systems.

Although limited to only a small region of the galaxy, with more than fifty solar systems already enmeshed in the Kreel's interstellar conflicts, the intensifying warfare with humanity is a tinderbox that threatens to flare into a raging holocaust— one set to spread across even more star systems.

Amid the escalating internal squabbles between the Kreel Elite Guard and the Kreel Military— each holding dark secrets they've kept from the other— political intrigue reigns supreme. Discerning its rival's weakness, the Military begins to mount its own political power play as the Elite Guard desperately seeks to rebuild an improved fighting force. Then, learning that humanity has been at the core of its defeat near Scion, the Military inaugurates an accelerated rebuilding of its fleet strength, and begins to hone the fine edge on their coming retaliatory vengeance on humanity.

While the Kreel seek to heal their wounds and make plans of Empire, Guardian Force digs in and braces for the coming storm. The desperate plight of a single young Nori woman named Amada, cast adrift and alone on a Kreel-dominated world, is about to forever alter the balance of power between the Kreel and humanity.

Unlike the Nori, neither the Kreel nor humanity is aware of the watchers, the Elder Ones abiding peacefully within the Wandering Waterway. The Elder Ones, aware of the interstellar conflict, are busy observing and debating among themselves which species— if either— truly merits survival....

# Author's Postscript

The Guardian Force saga caught me up, and I needed to write *Guardian Probe* in order to discover what happened next. I truly hope you have enjoyed the fruits of the efforts of all those who have worked together to bring *Guardian Probe* to print. If you have indeed enjoyed the tale, then you may also enjoy its prequels *Guardian Force* and *Earth Guardian* and its expanding sequels, *Guardian Strike* and *Guardian Thunder*. Galaxy Quest Books has scheduled the release of *Guardian Strike* during 2014, and I hope you will return to learn what happens next.

If you enjoyed *Guardian Probe*, like *Guardian Force* and *Earth Guardian*, it's also available as an eBook, and trade paperback format. If you did enjoy the story, then please do recommend the series to your friends. Thank you!

D. Arthur Gusner
Cambria California




If you enjoyed the story please visit our webpage at GalaxyQuestBooks.com (http://GalaxyQuestBooks.com).

You can also find the other books in this series.